THE
NIGHT CREW

BRIAN HAIG
THE
NIGHT CREW

THOMAS & MERCER

Published by Thomas & Mercer, Seattle

www.apub.com

Amazon, the Amazon logo, and Thomas & Mercer are trademarks of Amazon.com, Inc., or its affiliates.

ISBN-13: 9781477827482
ISBN-10: 147782748X

Cover design by Salamander Hill Design Inc.

Library of Congress Control Number: 2014952439

Printed in the United States of America

To Lisa,

Brian, Pat, Donnie, and Annie

Chapter One

"Do you mind?" the attractive lady asked as I sat at a table.

I looked up and answered,somewhat emphatically, "Yes, I do."

"But you're alone."

"No . . . that seat's taken."

She either did not hear or chose to ignore me, and slipped comfortably into the chair across from mine. She sipped quietly from her beer.

"Go away," I told her.

She *was* ignoring me.

"My date's powdering her nose," I said, which was true, and, after a moment, I added, less truthfully, "She has a gun permit and psychopathic tendencies."

My interloper laughed.

We were in the officers' club at Fort Myer, Virginia, in the basement bar—to be exact, a replica of an old English pub in a stingy, minimalist sort of way. My intruder was dressed in a clingy red pantsuit that went nicely with her long black hair, emerald-green eyes, pale complexion, and lithe, ballerina-like body; I happened to be dressed in natty civilian attire—blue wool suit, red-and-blue striped club tie, starched white shirt—that did not fit in well with our current surroundings.

Around us everybody wore uniforms—a mixture of mostly senior army officers, a few generals, more than a few colonels and majors. All were men, mostly gray or graying, talking quietly about serious topics and nursing their drinks. But at the next table, drinking more ambitiously, and rambunctiously, were several younger officers: lieutenants and captains with shoulder patches from the Third Infantry—aka, the Old Guard.

The younger officers now were carefully observing my guest. I suggested to her, "They look horny and interested." I started to stand. "Here, I'll introduce—"

She grabbed my arm and inquired, not quietly, "Wait, didn't I give you my phone number?" More loudly, she answered her own question. "Yes, I'm sure . . . I definitely did."

"Did you?"

"I'm certain I left it on your bedside table the last time I saw you."

"I don't remember."

"You don't remember?"

Officers at nearby tables now were also staring in our direction. Katherine Carlson, incidentally, was a civilian attorney, formerly a classmate of yours truly at Georgetown Law, and as indicated by our present circumstance, at times she can be a king-size pain in the ass.

She and I had worked together on a court martial a few years before, in Korea. It was a legal and emotional tar pit, a public relations tinderbox, and, if that weren't bad enough, people had tried to kill me.

But Katherine is a crackerjack lawyer—smart, ruthless, compulsively ambitious—and when she chooses to be, which is most of the time, pushy and dangerously manipulative. Also, she's a left-wing menace and the aforementioned last time I saw her I was lying in a hospital bed with a bullet in my stomach. Katherine didn't put the bullet there herself; it wouldn't have gotten there without her, though.

I got up and moved to the bar carrying my Scotch on the rocks. The bartender, who had the rugged face and stringent butch cut of a moonlighting sergeant, observed, "Looks like you got lady trouble, fella."

"What was your first clue?"

"Two broads at once." He wiped a rag across the bar. "Ask me, that's trouble."

To which I replied, man to man, "Nothing I can't handle."

He laughed. He then nodded in Katherine's direction. "Well . . . ask me, she's purtier'n that other one."

In the right light, in fact, Katherine looked not merely pretty, but beautiful in a way that is often described as angelic. I suppose this is why people are so surprised when she kneecaps them. "She's the Antichrist," I informed him. He laughed. Why doesn't anybody take me seriously?

I sipped my Scotch and, through the bar mirror, kept one eye on Katherine at the table and the other on the ladies' room door.

The lady in the latrine, Julie DuBois, and I were on our first date after three weeks of shameless flirting. I'm about forty, Julie's about thirty—a PhD in English lit, a professor at American University, learned, tenured, brilliant, blonde, blue-eyed—and, not that it matters, also quite attractive.

I had been looking forward to this date for a week; I really wanted to get Julie's take on Marcel Proust's persistent use of subordinate clauses, a literary mystery I can never seem to get out of my mind—and yes, Julie was having trouble believing that, too. But men who date women for their looks alone are pigs.

But to be sure I mentioned it, Julie hds remarkable legs.

The bartender broke the silence and, with a nod of his chin, informed me, "Course that other one's a looker, too. That blonde, I mean."

"She's smart, also," I assured him.

"Uh-huh. Well . . . cain't underrate that. Sure got nice legs." Another liberated male.

I was about to ask for a refill before he wandered off, apparently to the jukebox, because a moment later Steven Stills was belting out "Love the One You're With." This song is in every officers' club bar I've ever been in, for some reason, and a pair of baby-faced lieutenants at the next table got into the spirit and began a slurred, off-kilter sing-along before a grumpy senior officer snapped at them and they shut up. Were we having fun, or what?

When I was a younger officer, officers' club bars were different: in some ways, better; in other ways, I suppose not. Strippers did the bump-and-grind on small stages and enough cheap rotgut was guzzled to float the fleet, accompanied by enough cigarette and cigar smoke to fuel an artillery duel. Friday nights were command performances, wild bacchanalias with drunken lieutenants launching carrier landings on beer-drenched tables, and tipsy colonels gyrating on stages beside ladies wearing loincloths, nipple pasties, and come-hither smiles.

Upstairs, in the dining rooms, officers acting every inch the gentlemen shared sedate meals and polite conversation with their families; downstairs, in the darkened bars, the barbarians ruled.

No sign over the entrance read "Eat, drink, and make merry, for tomorrow you may die"; clearly, though, this was the animating spirit and the army's upper ranks, who were too old to share in the festivities, or too stodgy to want to, were surprisingly indifferent, or I suppose, indulgent.

But warrior tribes need their manhood rituals. The Greeks sacrificed animals to their gods. The Mayans tore out human hearts for their gods. The Indians took scalps for their squaws.

All things considered, genuflecting before the porcelain gods in officers' club latrines was no big deal.

And in a deadly serious profession where young men were forced to shoulder outsized responsibilities, officers' clubs were the last asylum where boys could be boys and more arthritic warriors could revert back to boys, no questions asked.

The order to sexually integrate the force put an end to all that, of course. Female officers were not amused by drooling senior officers stuffing soggy dollar bills into G-strings, or, I suppose, by randy, besotted peers trying to stuff bills into *their* undies.

Times change.

Today, officers' club bars are monuments to gentility where your priggish grandmother would feel right at home—or a slightly liberal academic with nice gams, as was my case that evening. And today's army has become a sexually homogenized, happily integrated force, half a million brothers- and sisters-in-arms who live, eat, work, train, and fight wars together—all for one, one for all, e pluribus unum, Army Strong—and if you don't peer hard enough beneath the surface, you could almost believe it.

For that, at least, was the party line—though unknown to me at that moment, not a five-minute walk from where I stood sipping my Scotch at that bar, sat a young lady in a small room, accused of crimes that threatened to upend that Utopian myth, facing charges that endangered the very fabric of military order and discipline, even as they shattered the nobility of a war in a faraway land. On a more pertinent note, the bartender returned and graciously topped off my Scotch.

He motioned with his jaw. "Guess you didn't see what happened 'hind yer back 'fore you came up here, fella."

5

When I failed to respond to that surreptitious observation, he informed me, "That purty blonde, she left."

"Yes, I did miss that."

"Uh-huh, thought so. Tore outta that latrine like her panties was biting her ass."

I took my drink and wandered back to the table, and to Katherine.

She smiled at me; I smiled back. I stopped smiling. "What did you do, or say, to Julie in the ladies' room?"

"I have no idea what you're talking about."

"Tell me, Katherine."

"There's nothing to tell. I merely introduced myself."

"No, really."

"We shared a brief, entirely mundane conversation."

Katherine is a lawyer, as I said, and she doesn't lie; the truth, however, after it passes through her lips can be unrecognizable. "Introduced yourself as who?"

"I don't remember . . . exactly."

"Settle for inexactly."

"I think . . . All right, I may have said I was Katherine Drummond."

She coolly turned her attention back to her beer and I turned my attention to the soccer match on the big-screen TV, which was my way of not strangling her in front of so many witnesses.

We stayed silent awhile, she and I, as I contemplated our history, our present, and maybe our future together, which possibly included a murder. It definitely didn't include the title Mrs. Drummond.

Though I was dressed in mufti, I'm a lieutenant colonel by rank, Sean Drummond by name, formerly an infantry officer—Airborne, Ranger, Pathfinder, Special Forces, and all that—before I failed to dodge a few bullets and involuntarily sacrificed my spleen for my country. I didn't complain then and I'm not complaining now; those who've experienced a close brush with death, and live to complain, don't.

In fact, had one of those bullets struck an inch or two lower, Sean Drummond wouldn't need zippers on his trousers. It was that close. Remarking on my good fortune, the doc at Walter Reed actually informed me, "Medically speaking, both are optional organs. You can still live a long, happy life without a spleen. Without a dick, life just seems much longer. God loves you, son."

Amen, Doc.

So these days, I'm an army attorney and a happy urinal user, though at that moment, I was seconded, or loaned—or perhaps banished—to a cell in the Central Intelligence Agency. This cell is called the Office of Special Projects, and though its purpose sounds somewhat innocuous, what it actually does is cover the ass of the CIA director. What the pride of the US Army JAG corps was doing in that job was a more interesting question I was still trying to figure out. This, however, explained my civilian attire and my civilian attitude.

The only thing missing was my license to kill—a good thing for you-know-who.

But with the Global War on Terrorism going full-bore, including wars in Afghanistan and Iraq, the work is fairly interesting and at times even exciting, though being in the CIA there's a real chance of dying of boredom from all the PowerPoint briefings and meetings.

To be truthful, I was experiencing a little cultural dislocation. I mean, the spooks are okay people, and they treat me well enough; we just don't *think* alike. When I see a nail, I reach for a hammer. They study the nail and obsess over whether it might actually be, or could possibly be turned into, a bolt or a screw, and then they try playing mind games. As often as not, the nail screws them.

My musings were interrupted by my unwelcome guest. "Do you want to kill me?"

"We're beyond that, Katherine. I'm deciding where to hide your corpse."

"She had to go, Sean. We need to talk." She looked me in the eye and stipulated, "Alone."

"I'd rather drink." I met her stare and stipulated back, "Alone."

"I see you haven't changed."

"Neither have you, Katherine. You should work on that."

She smiled. "Is that any way to speak to your adoring wife?"

"If you were my wife, I'd put poison in my morning coffee."

"No," she told me. "I would happily do it for you."

"Touché."

Back to me. During most of my military legal career, I have been a prosecutor and a defense attorney, specializing in cases where the victim or accused was assigned to classified units. Usually this means Special Ops types and, in those cases, the clandestine nature of their work needs to be protected through legal proceedings that never see the light of day. These are not Star Chambers or anything draconian like that; they are normal military courts, except you won't see the verdict in the morning papers.

Katherine had her hand up for another beer. "It's late," I observed. "Isn't it past your bedtime?"

"Didn't you miss me?"

"How can I miss you if you won't go away?"

"Isn't that the title of a country song?"

"Here's a better one. If the phone don't ring, you'll know it's me."

She laughed.

To tell the truth, I missed The Work, as we called it. Special Ops types tend to be older, bolder, clever, and certainly colorful. In fact, many are trained to be master criminals, and sometimes the professional bleeds over into the personal, and when that happens, their offenses tend to be far more flamboyant and cunning than your typical GI, who usually commits mundane crimes and leaves behind a treasure trove of clues, fingerprints, fibers, DNA traces, and so forth. I mean, a lot of these people, they knot their own nooses in triplicate. But you can't believe some of the stuff the Special Ops types do, how sneaky, how ballsy, how wily.

Katherine's legal specialty is, or perhaps was, military gay cases. More than a job, that was her calling; at least, it was the last time I saw her. "Don't ask, don't tell," was shorthand for the existing policy and Katherine was an attack dog, devoted to using the courts to amend that to "Ask away, sailor; I'm dying to tell."

The lefties and tree-huggers and whale-savers hung her photos above their beds.

But when the laws are written against you, losing is par for the course, even though she made sure the army victories were pyhrric. Her bills and expenses were paid by a public interest group and for a lady who graduated number one in her class from Georgetown Law, the pay sucked and there were no benefits.

A little more about me. Army brat, son of a career army officer, ROTC at Georgetown undergrad, seventeen years in uniform, and as you might expect, I'm very much a product of my environment and my upbringing—politically, culturally, socially, and otherwise.

Katherine, on the other hand, was born in the mountains of Colorado, bred on a commune, had unrepentant hippies for parents, wears Indian jewelry and large bangles, probably has Joni Mitchell's face tattooed above her left breast, and . . . why belabor the point?

It wasn't surprising that she ended up a public interest attorney, nor was it surprising that she chose a carbonized institution such as the army as her target: like most of her legal ilk, her every waking hour is spent thinking up ways to stick it to The Man.

In more ways than I care to think about, I am The Man.

I took a long sip from my Scotch. It was a little after nine; Katherine, by my calculation, must have arrived on post at least thirty minutes earlier. I inquired of her, "Don't you have better things to do with your Friday night than bother me?"

"Like what?"

"A boyfriend? Husband? Children?" I then asked, "Am I being too conventional for you?"

"Is this your clumsy but indirect way of asking if I'm married, or currently involved?"

"Why would I care?"

"Good point. Why would you?"

I should mention here that, perhaps cynically, I had always assumed that Katherine's attraction to her peculiar cause opened interesting questions about her AC/DC connections. A modern, sensitive male would never ask such questions of a lady, of course. Nobody has ever accused me of being modern or sensitive, but even I don't have those size balls.

Yet, when a lady *that* attractive and smart and successful is never once observed in the company of a male date, well, one does wonder. I'm not judgmental about this; nobody who has prosecuted twenty rape cases and other variations of sexual hijinks and kinkery walks away all that convinced that heterosexuals deserve a revered place on the pedestal of sexual intolerance.

But as I learned to my surprise in Korea, Katherine's calling was philosophical, not biological.

But, if you're interested, our relationship had always been platonic, owing mainly to her testy nature, our different lifestyles, different temperaments, different outlooks, and, of course, the aforementioned biological compatibility issues. That, however, was the old, misunderstood Katherine. You might say she and I were now reinterpreting our relationship on all new grounds.

I wouldn't say we were getting off on the best foot.

Apropos of that last thought, she mused, "Why do men assume that all women dream of a white picket fence, two-point-three kids, and a dumb mutt named Rover to fetch the morning paper?"

"I don't think that. Besides, Rover's a stupid name for a dog."

"Dog?" Katherine informed me, "He's the husband."

Katherine does not tell many jokes so, to be polite, I laughed.

I returned to watching the soccer match on TV, and Katherine went back to nursing her beer. As long as we've known each other, I've never been good at reading her thoughts. Partly because, like most men, I don't understand women; they have only one brain. Also, I tend to be fairly blunt and transparent, which works well in the army where the badge on your collar defines everything you need to know about human interaction. Katherine is rarely emotional, and while she is professionally manipulative, on a personal level, she is not a schemer. She does play things close to her vest, however, and with her, it can be hard to distinguish the personal from the professional.

And here we had a case in point: despite our social setting, she was here with an agenda and was taking her sweet time, and mine, to get to it.

"What do you want?" I asked her.

"I want you to cool down," she replied. "I'd rather not have this discussion while you're angry."

"What makes you think I'm angry?"

"Your face is red, your knuckles are white, and you snort when you talk." She further notified me, "Actually, I did you a big favor. You'll thank me later."

"There won't be a later."

"Look, Sean, it was bound to end unhappily."

"I think I'm capable of chasing off my own dates. Really, Katherine."

She laughed and said, "True enough," then added, "She wasn't your type."

"And what's my type?"

"Well . . . whatever your ideal beau is, I'm sure it has lots of body hair, cloven hooves, and eats with its hands."

Apparently this also was funny, because again, she laughed.

Also, the two captains seated at the next table apparently were into eavesdropping because they too chuckled. I think one of the things I don't miss about officers' club bars are the bottom-feeders looking for scraps.

But Katherine apparently changed her mind about waiting for my mood to improve, because she set her briefcase on the table and announced, "I'm not going to beat around the bush. I need a military cocounsel."

"Then call the civilian reps at JAG Branch and ask them to hook you up. You know the process, Katherine. I shouldn't have to explain it."

"I want you."

I knew she was going to say that. "No."

"Don't you at least want to hear about the case?"

"No. And in case you're not getting the message, no."

"It's not another gay case, Sean," she continued, as if I hadn't spoken. "It's a criminal case, a very complex one. An important one."

I sipped my Scotch and ignored her.

"Aren't you the least bit curious?"

"Curiosity killed the cat."

"I thought you were a tough guy, not a pussy."

She smiled. I ignored her.

"Come on, listen to the case."

"How did you know where to find me?"

The more things change, the more they stay the same. Rather than respond to my query, she adhered to her own agenda and continued, "Any JAG officer won't do. I need someone who knows combat, who understands the pressures of living on the edge of reason. What makes people fall over that edge, what makes them snap."

"So you thought of me. How nice."

"Look, you're a fine lawyer. Your legal advice would be helpful . . ."

"And . . . ?"

"And . . . an Airborne Ranger with a Combat Infantry Badge and a chestful of combat decorations at the defense table would be invaluable for my team."

It did not escape my notice that, for whatever reason, Katherine had disclosed neither the name of her client, nor the nature of the charges. She was tipping her hand, though, and it wasn't all that hard to figure out. So I paused to make a few lazy deductions and casual inferences.

Deduction One: the alleged crime occurred in a combat zone; perhaps Afghanistan, more likely Iraq, where most of the action was.

Deduction Two: physical violence was involved; and Deduction Three: the charges were serious, usually a redundant thought.

And then, Inference One: the Court Martial Board was going to be composed mostly of combat veterans, men and women who had experienced enemy fire.

As in civil law, the accused in the military is entitled to a jury of his or her peers, and ordinarily, a soldier is a soldier, a part of the green machine, interchangeable with any other. There are, however, occasions when such is not the case. When the case involves fratricide or violations of the Geneva Convention, charges that are unique to the battlefield, a peer then becomes someone who has been there, done that, with a combat unit patch stitched to his or her right shoulder to prove it. A soldier who hasn't seen combat might look at it too abstractly, too ephemerally, compared to one who shares with the accused a firsthand familiarity with the smell of roasting flesh, the peculiar fear, and unique judgment—or more often, lack of rational judgment—made when friends are dying around you and somebody is trying to kill you. Any defense lawyers worth their salt would use the voir dire process to winnow the board down to as many combat vets as possible.

But Katherine Carlson, as I mentioned, is a fine lawyer. She understood this and, no doubt, she was factoring it into her preparations. In no other court in the land is a jury so monochromatic—so bound by common beliefs, common attitudes, common lifestyles.

Civilian attorneys trigger engrained prejudices and subliminal distrusts under the best of circumstances—they may belong in a courtroom, but they are clearly dressed in the wrong attire, often with the wrong mindset.

And if I was right about the war crime or fratricide angle, then no, I would not want to be Katherine Carlson—female, civilian, iconic antimilitary poster girl—trying to sell an uphill case to seven steely eyed, battle-tested soldiers.

And, too, she was right about another thing—just any vanilla JAG officer wouldn't rebalance the scales of justice.

And then there was what she didn't say but clearly implied: she wanted a mannequin, a decorated dummy to look impressive, to sway the ecumenical balance, and keep his mouth shut.

She should've known better—about me, that is.

And last though not least, Inference Two: she wouldn't be in the Fort Myer Officers' Club at this late hour on a Friday night, lamely backdooring her way into an explanation, were the evidence against her client not overwhelming.

I looked her in the eye. "Find someone else. Hundreds of army lawyers have been crawling around Afghanistan and Iraq." I glanced around the bar. "I'll bet I can find you one here."

She grabbed my arm. "I need one who's killed, who's tasted blood, who took prisoners, who's lost friends, who understands battlefield rage."

I made no reply.

This tack wasn't working. She knew it, and after a long pause, she suggested, "I thought we worked well together in Korea."

I laughed. Back to that case. The accused in the military has the option of free military representation or, in those instances in which they are willing to foot the fare, they may engage a civilian attorney of their own choosing. In those cases, a JAG officer is normally assigned as cocounsel because the military is a unique culture, and military law has some parochial twists and provisions outsiders might not comprehend. Civilian law, for instance, is based on the overriding proposition that individual rights are sacrosanct and elevated above all other considerations, such as justice; military law answers a different calling, the mission always comes first, and when necessary, the needs of the institution and the demands of the mission trump the rights of the individual. Or, in the words of my first drill sergeant: "You have whatever fucking rights I say you have." Which means, very few.

Bottom line here: the army does not want convicted felons appealing on the grounds that their hired civilian guns didn't know the difference between a latrine pit and a dining facility—though perhaps that's not such a good example.

So for reasons I still don't comprehend, Katherine requested me, by name, to serve as her cocounsel, on an all-gay defense team, which proved, well . . . interesting.

Katherine observed, "Our client was well satisfied with our work."

"You never trusted me, you ignored my legal advice, and you kept secrets."

"And I hated doing that to you."

"Really? You made it look so fun."

"We won."

"And I got shot."

"But you survived." She added, sounding not all that happy. "You're here, aren't you?"

"I lost three inches of my intestine, spent two months on a Jell-O diet, the nurses were mean and ugly, and the enemas were cold."

"You mean you're no longer full of sh—"

"Enough, Katherine."

"Sorry. Bad joke." She crossed her heart and said, "You won't get shot this time. Promise."

"You're right. I won't. No."

So that was it. Case closed. End of discussion, end of Katherine.

I should've stood up and left, but Katherine was the interloper here, and a man has to stand his ground so, in fact, I did not.

That was my first big mistake.

Chapter Two

She pointed at my nearly empty glass and observed, "You need another Scotch," then promised, "It's on me."

As usual with Katherine, business preceded pleasure, and now it was time to catch up, exchange pleasantries and whatever. She leaned back into her faux-leather chair and folded her hands in front of her lips. "So how are you doing?"

"Don't you have somewhere you need to be?"

Maybe this was too subtle, because she looked at her watch. "Later, yes, I do. But I've got twenty minutes to kill."

This was an obvious invitation for me to inquire about what was on her schedule, so to piss her off, I did not.

"I'm fine," I informed her.

She stuck up a finger in the direction of the bartender, who was keeping a close watch on our table, probably worrying about a homicide in his club. Katherine observed, "I see you made lieutenant colonel. Congratulations."

"The gold card rank," I replied. "I'm good to go for retirement, unless I do something stupid."

"Well, let's bet against the odds and hope you make it. We should toast that."

She raised her beer bottle, and I hoisted my glass. In fact, I had only pinned on the silver leaf of a lieutenant colonel a few months before, and I found it interesting that Katherine would know that since I was dressed in mufti—undercover, so to speak.

"Where are you living these days?" I asked her.

"Nearby. Same old apartment from law school, a few blocks off Dupont Circle. Mostly, though, out of suitcases. Gypsy law—I go where the cases carry me."

"Are you still working for—"

"No, I'm . . . I . . ." Whatever she intended to say, she apparently changed her mind. "I hate to lose. I think you know this. It became depressing and I needed . . . something different." She toyed with the clasp on her briefcase and asked, "What about you?"

I didn't really want to tell her about my current job in the CIA, so I instead answered her question with a question. "Who's paying your bills these days?"

"Another public interest group."

"Different kind of work?"

"Same work. Different kinds of cases, different challenges, different types of clients."

The bartender arrived with fresh drinks, Scotch for me, beer for her. Katherine, I recalled, is pretty much a teetotaler and usually limits herself to two Coors Lights—aka, fizzled Kool-Aid—and does not really enjoy idle chitchat. In fact, it seemed she had exhausted her limit, or her repertoire, because she asked, in a superficially offhanded way, "Have you been following the Al Basari prison scandal?"

"Is that your case?"

"So you're familiar with it," she noted. In fact, for the past month, the Al Basari scandal, or Basarigate, as the imagination-deprived media were vapidly calling it, had saturated the news almost every day.

"I know what everybody knows."

"Good. Tell me what everybody knows."

"Five American National Guard soldiers, two males and three females, got carried away at a military prison in Iraq, had a little late-night fun, got frisky and slapped around some prisoners, then got a little kinky, took a few disgusting pictures, a prisoner died, and now they're all facing general court martial. Am I missing anything?"

"A few intriguing details. A lot of open questions. But you have the general gist of it. What do you think about that?"

"I believe it was criminal behavior. They brought enormous shame on the army, humiliation on the country, and did grievous harm to our war effort. Any other stupid questions?"

"The logical one. Do you believe they're guilty?"

"They're definitely guilty of something."

"Because of the pictures?"

This reference was to the aforementioned photographs, taken, apparently, by the soldiers themselves, perhaps as trophies or as souvenirs, or perhaps out of some perverse fascination with their own behavior. Somehow, a number of these pictures found their way to a member of the press, then, predictably, got sensationalized across nearly every newspaper, magazine cover, and television screen in the world.

The few I had seen in the news were fairly upsetting: a bloated corpse wrapped in a blood-stained sleeping bag, nude prisoners stacked on top of one another, prisoners being forced to perform sexually humiliating gestures and actions, and so forth.

Also, the instant the story broke, the Islamic world went predictably nuts, roasted two American embassies, and assassinated three US diplomats in Pakistan.

This was not the first prisoner abuse scandal of the wars in Afghanistan and Iraq. Nor, barring some mysterious change in human nature, would it be anywhere near the last. War is an ugly business, and battling insurgencies is uglier still; for the participants it is emotionally unsettling and, for some, it is emotionally unhinging, so occasionally soldiers slip over the line, and occasionally, they get caught.

This, though, by any mark or measure, was the most stupefying and inflammatory scandal. Also, where the other scandals were based on oral accounts, here there was visual imagery, a pictorial montage of carnal behavior the Marquis de Sade might have pinned on his bathroom walls.

As if that weren't enough, the graphic sexual degradation of helpless Arab males amplified every Moslem superstition and indictment about the moral inferiority and depravity of the West.

As I said, the typical GI does stupid crimes and leaves behind enough clues, leads, and evidence to end up in a suite at Leavenworth or earn a reservation on the hotseat, whichever applies. This, however, went way beyond leaving a few fingerprints or errant hair samples— and way beyond stupidity. In an act of surreal self-incrimination, they included themselves in the pictures, and downloaded those photos onto computers, and ultimately, burned their own faces into the consciousness of the entire planet.

Katherine was watching my face. "Let me rephrase that. Do you believe they can get a fair trial?"

"Yes, of course."

"Really? You already said *you're* convinced they're guilty."

"I said they're guilty of something. But with five different soldiers, that means five different levels of guilt, of most likely different crimes, and five different sets of extenuating and mitigating circumstances." I added, "Guilt is a relative term, as are fairness, justice, and punishment. You know this, Katherine."

She opened her briefcase and reached inside, fishing around for something. I remained silent as she withdrew a blown-up, nine-by-twelve color photograph that she slid across the table; I picked it up and studied it.

I did not need to be told that this was another of the Al Basari photos. But I was sure this was the first time I had seen it, and I was sure, as well, that the American public had never laid eyes on it.

A female soldier, whose face I vaguely recognized, was squatting, naked, and peeing on the head of a prostrate Arab gentleman. It was a frontal shot, looking down from a higher angle; though not blurry, it was slightly off-centered and definitely off-angled, suggesting that the photographer was an amateur, with questionable artistic skills at that.

As I mentioned, the poor guy being used as a toilet looked Arabic, probably Iraqi, and was skinny and bony to the point of emaciation. People in that region tend to age prematurely and, though he looked seventy, he could easily have been closer to fifty. And, though his eyes and mouth were squeezed tightly shut, his reactive expression could not have been more emphatically evocative—a combination of terror, helplessness, disgust, and shame.

I could see why this particular photo had not been shown by the press, who normally will exploit anything that shocks or appalls. I'm old enough to be called worldly, and young enough to be part of the generation that has been bombarded with pornographic imagery by Hollywood, by Madison Avenue, and by every magazine rack in every roadside convenience store. And while I'm not squeamish or prudish, I was instinctively offended, reviled, and yes, shocked—and I don't mean merely by the monumental vulgarity of her act, but because the squatting soldier, otherwise completely nude, wore her black army beret perched awkwardly on her head.

This was definitely not a soldier being all she could be; or, in fact, should be.

Despite her evident effort to be erotic, the effect was not titillating or alluring; it was, in fact, repulsive. I found myself looking around to be sure nobody was observing me observing this.

Katherine sensed my discomfort and asked, "Intriguing picture, don't you think?"

"That's not the adjective I'd choose."

"Okay. How would you describe it?"

"I'm at a loss for words," I answered, truthfully. I turned the picture face down. "Are there more like this?"

She recognized what I was asking and casually flipped the picture back over. "Many hundreds, in fact, and some are worse. Think about this picture and let your imagination do the rest." She allowed me to process that, then asked, "How do you think a Court Martial Board will react?"

"I wouldn't give them the opportunity. I'd move heaven and earth to get these photos suppressed."

"That's an interesting suggestion. On what grounds?"

"Irrelevancy, of course. And they're poisonously prejudicial to a fair trial."

"Do you think that will work?"

"The first point might be a stretch, but a generous judge might buy the second."

She seemed to think about this, then asked, "Do you recognize her?"

I nodded. Her name escaped me though I knew it had been all over the news—but definitely I recalled her face from a few of the more radioactive photos. For reasons of both modesty and good taste, certain strategic sections of those photos had been doctored or blurred for public consumption, but what she was doing was far from ambiguous—I recalled one shot where she was on her knees, smiling and pointing at the groins of some disgruntled nude prisoners; in another, she was dragging one unhappy soul around by a string tied to his puddly.

I glanced again at the picture that lay face up on the table between Katherine and me. Cops always focus on the perp first, lawyers on the victim. I turned my attention to the lady in question.

The soldier was short, I estimated 5'2" or so, and young, nineteen or possibly twenty. Though not fat, nor even chubby, she had a low, squat build, and was thick-limbed, with a round face and plump cheeks. Her hairstyle, probably intended to appear seductively tomboyish or, I suppose, bawdily pixyish, actually looked monkish and ridiculous. She was not ugly, but neither was she attractive or in any way alluring or particularly sexy.

In fact, she looked stupid—not ditzy or spacey—but simpleminded; or, considering the very graphic evidence, the better adjective might be empty-minded. A half-smoked cigarette dangled lazily from her lips at the moment the photo was taken, and she was smiling, not into the camera, per se, though she seemed not to be unaware of its presence.

Her smile had this weird, bothersome, lazy afterglow I couldn't quite put my finger on—not forced, not hesitant, nor embarrassed or even sadistic—any or all of which seemed to be the predictable adjectives, given her activity at that moment.

To the contrary, I thought her smile looked unbridled, uninhibited, maybe frivolous. The proper adjective seemed, for some reason, important, and it struck me that the right word was narcissistic, but in the same way a small child performing her first clumsy ballet recital smiles at an audience.

I was suddenly overjoyed that I hadn't taken Katherine's offer. I'd been away from the army long enough that I was no longer in touch with current politics or barracks scuttlebutt. But from the news reports about what happened inside Al Basari prison, clearly

23

this was about more than a few misbehaving jailors molesting and humiliating their prisoners: it was a shocking breakdown in military discipline; it was a failure of leadership that possibly included more than a few general officers and quite possibly some senior officials at the Pentagon and White House; it was a crime that was possibly allowed, abetted, or even encouraged by political dictates and pressure to make the prisoners talk.

When you add all that together, typically the institutional response is some form of cover-up, or ass cover, or monumental spin project. Then again, this was total conjecture on my part: I had no idea any such thing was afoot. I also had no idea it wasn't.

And last, though not least selfish, it was an opportunity for some overeager military lawyer to throw his career down the toilet. No, I did not need this.

Turning the photo facedown again, I asked Katherine, "This is your client?"

She nodded as she slid a few pieces of stapled papers across the bar table, at me. "I also think you might want to take a look at these."

The papers looked amazingly like a set of military orders.

Upon closer examination they *were* orders, signed by Major General Harold Fister, Chief of the US Army JAG Corps, effective 10 February, assigning some poor schmuck whose name sounded remarkably like mine as Military Cocounsel for the defense of Private First Class Lydia Eddelston.

"Forget it." I slid the orders back in her direction. "I am *not* currently assigned to the JAG branch. General Fister has neither the authority nor the jurisdiction to give me orders."

She slid the orders back at me. "General Fister called your current employer . . ." She hesitated then asked, I think insincerely, "Ms. Phyllis Carney, right?"

The orders sat right where they were.

Katherine continued, a bit smugly, "She was enormously helpful. She generously agreed to release you, TDY, back to the JAG branch for up to sixty days, or until the trial ends, whichever applies."

"Then I'll call her."

"Feel free."

"I don't need your permission, Katherine."

"No . . . but you should know that she didn't sound unhappy to lose you." In case I wasn't getting the message, Katherine confided, "She sounded delighted, I thought."

The lady under discussion, Phyllis Carney, was my presumptive boss at the CIA, an older lady, between eighty and ninety, very ladylike, and pleasant and charming in a quaint, old-fashioned manner; all of which is an illusion, of course, except her age. Maybe.

Phyllis does not suffer fools gladly, which I approve of, and she often encourages her subordinates to "be bold, to think outside the box," to exercise "initiative" and other new wave management aphorisms—which I might push a little too far.

So we're not exactly salt and pepper: more like vinegar and SweeTARTS, to continue the bad food metaphors.

That aside, I actually like Phyllis, and at times, I think she likes me, too, so I was a little surprised that she released me so readily.

Anyway, an uncomfortable silence had settled over our table, which Katherine broke, stating, "I'm sorry. I should probably have told you about this at the beginning."

"Yes, you probably should have."

"I had a good reason for my little charade."

"You always do, Katherine. That's your problem. You play games. You *withhold*."

"I just wanted to—"

"I really don't care why—"

"Would you shut up, Sean? Let me finish . . . please."

Just like old times.

She gazed into her beer, collecting her thoughts, or constructing her alibi. "I wanted to . . . to gauge your reaction before you knew she was your client. You're a lawyer, but you're an army officer, first, last, and always. I needed to see how someone like you reacted to that picture."

I leaned across the table until our noses nearly touched. "No, you wanted to prove you're smarter and more clever than I am. Okay, you've proven it. Great. Whoopee, Katherine. And now you have a head start on this case, and I'm coming into it blind, which gives you a big advantage. And though I'm your cocounsel you intend to keep your knee on my chest and keep me second fiddle. So you need me for credibility with the jury, but maybe I know more about war than you do, and maybe I can cut through the roadblocks and red tape the army will construct, and maybe my Top Secret clearance will allow me to see things you can't, and maybe I'll understand a few things you don't. So our client will be better served if we use our ammunition on the prosecutor instead of each other, so save the empty apologies and cut the bullshit, Katherine."

I'll mention again here that Katherine was first in her class at Georgetown Law—and Sean Drummond, by an almost infinitesimal margin, was number two. Given her bohemian breeding, disposition, and outlook, I don't think she bought into the whole law review, dog-eat-dog, be-number-one-at-any-cost thing that seems to permeate every law school in the country.

I seem to bring out something in Katherine that only Freud could explain.

And now, here she was unexpectedly reappearing in my life again. And no, I did not for a minute believe she was seeking my legal talents, my military credentials, or my charming company.

I'm not that charming, for one thing.

Anyway, she was laughing, as though this was a big joke. I said, "It's not funny."

"Well . . . I'm sorry if . . . if I maybe mishandled you."

"No ifs about it, sister."

"I really do want to work with you." She stuck out her hand. "Come on, shake."

We sat for a moment staring at each other.

With her hand still out, Katherine glanced at the watch on her other wrist. "Our client's waiting, so let's get this over with. Come on, shake."

We shook, and she stood up and excused herself to go to the ladies' room. Instead she headed straight for the stairs and stuck me with the bar bill.

Chapter Three

We walked out of the officers' club main entrance and in the direction of the military police station at Fort Myer, which, conveniently, is only a five-minute walk from the officers' club, via a short connecting sidewalk.

The night was cold and dark, but army posts tend to be over-organized and anal about everything, including lighting. To our right was a fenced-in, outdoor tennis court and just beyond that, the stately quarters of the military's most senior officers, the army Chief of Staff, and the Chairman of the Joint Chiefs, and to our rear, homes for enough two- and three-star generals to lead another invasion of Europe.

Quartered in one of those houses was Major General Fister, the JAG chief who assigned me this gig. I made a mental note to myself to leave a sack of burning dog poop on his doorstep.

I should grow up and rise above such puerile gestures; then again, he started it.

In case you're interested, Fort Myer is one of the older army bases, established in the early years of the Civil War on a hill with a commanding view of the capital across the river, from which large batteries of artillery could rain death and destruction on any rebels attempting to snatch the northern capital. That war is long over, its dead and survivors alike long since buried, and the once imposing rows of batteries have dwindled to a few lonely cannons, rusted evidence of the noble mission this post once served. None of our recent wars have required defenses for our national capital, though September 11th came pretty close.

So, these days, Fort Myer's purpose is mostly pomp and ceremonies; it has a spit-and-polish parade-ground unit appropriate to that mission, a large parade ground for them to march around, a lovely chapel, and is adjoined to the military's most hallowed ground, Arlington National Cemetery.

Though I've been stationed in Washington for years, I don't come here often, and when I do, it always brings back memories, some warm, some otherwise. As a kid, when Pop was stationed at the Pentagon, like most military families in DC, we rented a small bungalow on the economy—a term that betrays everything about how military people view the civilian world. During Washington's long, torrid summers, Mom used to pack big brother Johnny and little Sean into our Country Squire wagon, and we'd race here, frolic in the o-club pool, get our weekly army butch cuts, load up the back of the wagon with inexpensive commissary groceries, top off with cheap gas, and then return to the land of the taxpayers who made all this largesse possible.

The Vietnam War was in its final throes then, and Pop already had orders for his second and ultimately, his final tour in Vietnam, and, as it turned out, in the army. While we frolicked and eyed the good-looking general's daughters in their skimpy bikinis, in the distance you could hear the frequent drone of the bugle and rifle pops from funeral details rendering the final salute to another fallen soldier—somebody's dad, son, or husband. When your own dad is a month from deployment, every little pop puts a lump in your throat.

Unfortunately, with two wars raging, those echoes are again rampant—and for the senior generals who live here, the sounds of death are omnipresent, inescapable, sobering. This might not be exactly what the army intended when it placed its premier cemetery next to this base, but neither is it a bad idea.

Katherine and I walked in silence for a while before I inquired of her, "How long has Lydia Eddelston been your client?"

"A little over two weeks."

"But it's been, what, three months since her arrest. Right?"

"Two, to be precise. She had a military attorney, initially. Captain Bradley Howser. Do you know him?"

I shook my head.

"A good lawyer from what I gather. He was pressuring her to plead out. He told her he had arranged a good deal."

"Charges?" I asked.

"Conspiracy to commit murder, conspiracy to obstruct, multiple counts of making a false statement, multiple counts of assault and indecent acts, maltreating detainees, dereliction of duty, conduct unbecoming . . ." She paused, then confessed, "Without the full written script, I'm afraid I can't recall all of it."

I stared at her a moment.

"I know." She gave me a knowing glance. "They're throwing the book at her."

This was a fairly common practice, especially whenever conspiracy is involved or suspected. To get one of the coconspirators to turn evidence on their colleagues, you pile up a smorgasbord of charges, from the profoundly serious to the drolly inconsequential, from those where the evidence is flimsy and guilt nearly impossible to prove, to those—such as dereliction of duty and/or conduct unbecoming—that are so broad and encompassing that a fart in a public place virtually assures a guilty verdict. The prosecutor then has a high-probability conviction, along with an arsenal of charges he or she can barter for a deal; the defense attorney has a mountain of shit piled on his lap.

As a prosecutor, I've done this myself, and, as a defense attorney, I've been on the receiving end; I'd rather play Russian roulette with five and a half rounds in the chamber. I asked Katherine, "How good a deal?"

"Five years in Leavenworth. Reduction to Private, E-1. Bad conduct discharge."

"Depending on which charges are waived, that doesn't sound like a bad bargain."

"Maybe not. She would have to admit guilt, cooperate, and give testimony against the others, of course. This wasn't what she wanted."

"I don't see the problem, Katherine. Even military lawyers don't overrule their client's wishes."

"She understood that, Sean. As did he. She didn't fire him . . . unfortunately, Captain Howser had . . . well, he experienced an unfortunate accident. About three weeks ago."

"How unfortunate?"

"He died."

"I see. What was the nature of this . . . accident?"

"Automobile. Driving in the mountains of Colorado along a narrow twisted road, he got sideswiped, and went off a cliff."

I remained silent.

"The police classified it a hit and run," she felt it necessary to explain.

"And they're *sure* it was an accident?"

She stared at me. "You know, I asked the same question."

"And . . . ?"

"Okay, so here's what I was told. Captain Howser owned a Porsche—a not particularly well-maintained old one that he bought used—was a bachelor, and for extracurricular fun he did

31

high-altitude, black slope skiing, and paragliding off mountain tops." She concluded, "A life in search of an accident."

"Don't generalize, Katherine. Those who live fast, sometimes die of old age in their beds."

She rolled her eyes at this questionable wisdom, and clarified, "From the skid marks the police estimated he was doing sixty on a bend marked for thirty."

"Got it."

She nodded.

"The normal practice, Katherine, is for the army to appoint a replacement attorney and, if necessary, to reschedule the trial date. So, why you?"

"In fact, the army was in the process of assigning a new JAG officer. Lydia met with him a few times, he didn't seem to particularly believe in her innocence, and she didn't particularly believe in his passion for her case. You know how it goes—no client is comfortable when their own lawyer doubts their innocence."

"If they *are* innocent," I stipulated.

She evaded that implied question and continued, "So, for various reasons, my employer became interested in her case. I was asked to make a stab at representing her. I did, the army candidate went away, and here we are."

"Were you given Captain Howser's files?"

She nodded. "The local JAG carted it all up, packed it in boxes, and delivered them."

"And . . . ?"

"And, here's the good news. Howser had already received the discovery materials, and there is a detailed transcription from the Article 32 hearings."

Discovery is the required legal process whereby the prosecutor must turn over to the defense all the evidence he intends to employ in court against the accused, both that which could be incriminating, and that which might prove exculpatory, which on occasion, prosecutors forget to include. And an Article 32 is the military version of a grand jury process, the first step in building the scaffold. I asked Katherine, "And had the good captain done his homework?"

"It's the usual mixture—some solid investigation, some misdirected bullshit. Although he lived risky, as I said, he was a good lawyer. Very detail-oriented. His files are well-organized." She looked away for a moment. "But he either hadn't wound up his investigation or a few critical files are missing. There are some gaps I found surprising."

Apropos of that thought, I replied, "I don't always trust the work of other lawyers."

She knew whom I was referring to, but refused to rise to the bait. "I recommend we approach this like a fresh case. Use his files as background."

"Good idea. And who is your mysterious employer?"

"Vietnam Veterans Who Oppose the War in Iraq."

"Who?"

"They're new, and not very large. Don't underestimate them, though. They're very serious, and very, very seriously funded."

Echoing her theme, I pointed out, "And they're very, very, very seriously confusing their wars."

She watched the sidewalk awhile, then asked, "Have you heard of Nelson Arnold?"

"The billionaire?" She gave me a half-nod, and I continued, "Big hedge fund guy, right? New Yorker, collects beautiful women, big yachts, and oversize mansions."

"He also collects causes he believes in. He's a Vietnam vet with no fond memories of his war. For various reasons, he's opened up his checkbook."

"What are those reasons?" I looked at Katherine and specified, "More to the point, what's his, or what's their interest in Private First Class Lydia Eddelston?"

"Not her, necessarily. They have a larger interest."

"Which would be what?"

"She and the other accused are being made into scapegoats. Meaning the lower ranks are getting railroaded and screwed, and the people who are ultimately responsible get a free pass." She added, "They saw this happen in Vietnam. They are intent on doing something about it this time."

"They should mind their own business and allow the army to do its job."

"You're so predictable."

"This is a legal case, Katherine, not a political inquisition."

"You don't know enough about this case to draw that conclusion."

"I know the army."

"So do I, Sean."

"Give it a break, Katherine. Really."

"There are different kinds of patriotism, Drummond. Hard as it might be for you to get through your thick, Orwellian mindset, dissent and criticism can be the highest form of loyalty."

I wasn't really interested in hearing her quote scripture and verse from the gospel according to Saint Henry David Thoreau, so I changed the subject. "Where will the court martial be convened?"

"West Point, New York. It has a large population of officers who have seen combat from which to create a fair board, and a secure facility for the proceedings. Lydia is being held there."

"Then what's she doing here?"

"She was flown down for a deposition concerning one of the other defendants."

I nodded again. Five soldiers had been charged with whatever happened at Al Basari, so it sounded like two or more of their defense attorneys had cooked up a cooperative witness arrangement of some sort. By inference, Private Eddelston and her attorney had agreed to testify on behalf of one or more of her codefendants, and probably that meant a quo quid pro; and, probably, prior to his untimely demise, that deal had been worked out by Captain Howser. Obviously, Katherine was going with it.

I hate walking into cases where somebody else has already decided on the trial strategy. I prefer to make my own mistakes; usually they're smart mistakes, because they're mine.

But also, if you read between the lines of what Katherine was saying, she and her financial backers intended to use this case to prosecute the army and the administration for their lenient rules on torture and interrogation, if not for the overall flawed execution of the war. This had been Katherine's modus operandi in gay cases where it was a foregone conclusion that most of her clients would lose, but she exploited the court martials to show the public the cruelty and farcicality of the laws banning openly gay soldiers from serving.

Her gay clients were sacrificial lambs to get the laws overturned, and consequently, Katherine's legal tactics and strategies were more offensive than defensive, directed less toward disproving the case against her clients and more toward proving the government's guilt. But, I thought, what worked for the gay cause would not work in this case where the court martial board would be composed of seven professional soldiers who might not take kindly to an attorney attempting to convict their own service of ineptitude and, as combat veterans, might not share Katherine's squeamishness about torture and interrogation techniques that were intended to save soldier's lives and win battles.

I could see another battle brewing between her and me over how to approach Eddelston's defense.

In that light, I asked, "And what's your impression of Private Lydia Eddelston? Guilty or innocent?"

"We'll trade opinions *after* you've met her."

Which was a good note to end on because we were standing on the stoop of the military police station.

Chapter Four

In character with the rest of the post, the building was a neat-as-a-pin, red brick, faux colonial-style affair, with close-cropped shrubbery and a precisely handpainted sign announcing its purpose. Compared with MP stations at larger military bases, this building was small and definitely looked sleepy.

But, as the residents on this post were either senior officers or handpicked soldiers from the Old Guard, a big sheriff was neither needed, wanted, nor, probably, all that good an idea. I mean, generals don't really like their kids getting busted for dope, or their wives getting pulled over for speeding tickets.

We entered and moved straight to the good-looking staff sergeant behind a desk who glanced up and asked in a polite but firm tone, "How can I help you?"

I identified myself, flashed my military ID, and introduced Katherine. He appeared to be expecting us and, glancing at his watch, informed us, "The prisoner is waiting in an interrogation room. Follow me, sir."

He led us down a narrow stairwell to the lower level and stopped beside the second door on the left. There was no guard posted, so Lydia Eddelston was apparently not regarded as a danger to herself or to others, nor was she considered a flight risk, which I guess I understood.

Given all the publicity surrounding this case, Lydia Eddelston couldn't walk two steps off this post without some kid pointing at her and saying, "Look, Mommy, there's the lady who led that man around by his ding-dong."

I thanked the sergeant and inquired, "Is this room cleared of listening and observation devices?"

"Yes, sir."

"How long do we have?"

"One hour."

"Thank you, Sergeant. We don't wish to be disturbed." I turned to Katherine, who nodded, and I pushed open the door. We entered a small, rectangular room, about eight by fifteen, furnished in the functional, minimalist manner the army prefers, with only a long wooden table and ten wooden chairs.

Private First Class Lydia Eddelston was seated, wearing a desert battle dress uniform, sans handcuffs, at the long wooden conference table. Her nose was stuffed inside a *People* magazine with Tom Cruise doing his I-get-paid-twenty-five-million-bucks-for-being-a-movie-stud smile on the cover—at the sound of the door being opened, she looked up, first at Katherine, whom she smiled at, then at me: the smile faded.

We moved to the table and sat across from her. By way of introduction, Katherine stated, "Lydia, you remember I told you that a military lawyer had to be involved as cocounsel?"

"I guess."

"This is Lieutenant Colonel Sean Drummond. We were classmates at law school and worked another case together."

Lydia stared at me, and it did not seem to compute that I was dressed in civilian attire.

I extended my hand. As a senior officer I did not need to do this, but enlisted clients tend to become stiff or timid around senior officers and informal gestures can go a long way toward breaking the ice.

Lydia Eddelston, however, was either too young, or was from a socioeconomic background where handshakes were not a common form of greeting. She stared at my hand for a few beats, then, almost hesitantly, we shook.

I said, "Despite my rank, Private Eddelston, I work for you." I continued with my standard spiel about lawyer-client relations, lawyer confidentiality, and so forth and so on, and ended, as I usually do, by asking, "Do you have any opening questions you'd like to ask me?"

She thought about this too briefly. "No, sir. Don't guess I do."

"After we've become better acquainted, maybe you will. In the meantime, I'm new to this case, and I have a few questions." Like, what in the hell were you thinking when you idiots took pictures? But I didn't say this, of course.

She looked at Katherine, who nodded, which I regarded as a revealing gesture, then nodded at me.

I started off, "Where are you from?"

"Justin, West Virginia."

"Age?"

"Twenty, sir."

"How long have you been in the National Guard?"

"'Bout two years. Ever since high school. Signed up under delayed entry six months 'fore graduation."

"Like it?"

"Sure . . . well enuff." She paused for a moment, then had a reasonable second thought. "Least-wise, 'fore all this happened."

I did not want to talk about that yet, and asked, "Why did you join?"

"Thought it would be fun. Maybe pick up a few skills fer afterward."

"Maybe earn a little college money?"

"No, sir . . . didn't really care nuthin' 'bout that."

"I see." I thought about that revelation, then continued, "Justin? I've never heard of it. Small town?"

"Guess so. Only had, like forty kids in my graduatin' class."

I smiled.

Like a lot of residents from small, irrelevant bumps in the middle of nowhere, Lydia knew how to milk this angle and quickly elaborated, "Only got like, I don't know, maybe two stoplights. Got a 7-Eleven, though."

Actually, a surprising number of the army's recruits come from these anonymous pockets in the middle of Rural Nowhere, USA. For the most part, they make great soldiers—dedicated, hardy, industrious, not cynical like their big city counterparts, imbued, instead, with the kind of red-meat patriotism that equals unquestioning obedience. I would put a gun to my head if I lived in such a place, and I suspected that Lydia's motives for enlisting in the Guard were a little more dark and complicated than she was admitting to me, if not to herself. After she tried out a few more quaint anecdotal details about Justin, I asked, "And did you have a full-time civilian job?"

"Sure did. At the post office."

This was an almost irresistible set-up for a crack about postal employees, but I asked, with an admirably straight face, "Doing what?"

"Letter sorter. Good benefits. Didn't pay much, though."

And so on. Most of this stuff could be gleaned from her personnel jacket or a standard background check, of course. But with new clients it's important to build trust and rapport, to get to know each other before you get into the ickier stuff, such as, What in the hell was on your mind when you peed on that man's face?

Anyway, as we went on, my initial impressions regarding Lydia Eddelston were largely reinforced, though she was slightly cuter in person than in the photo of her emptying her bladder. Also I thought she had packed on a few pounds since those pictures, which could be accounted for by the fact that she was in confinement with nothing better to do than eat.

Her accent was thick, country-style, and grammar and diction were definitely not her friends. Though she possessed a high school diploma, she was not well educated and, occasionally she stared at me for inappropriately long periods before responding. I couldn't tell if she was dense, confused, the victim of some weird processing disorder, or all of the above.

As brazen and uninhibited as her poses and expressions appeared in the photos, in person, she came across as shy, remote, and while not depressed, clearly she was emotionally fragile. Also, she kept glancing at Katherine: fleeting, needy glances. Presumably she came from blue-collar, or possibly, no-collar stock. Regarding family, she informed me that she was raised a strict Southern Baptist, one brother, also in the National Guard, both parents still living and still married, and hopefully they weren't first cousins or, God forbid, brother and sister.

Simple. That one adjective jumped out as I listened patiently to her responses to the perfunctory questions I occasionally had to reframe, because she became easily confused. Simple answers. Simple outlooks. Mentally simple. Indeed, I was tempted to ask her for her proof of age, because, in both her mannerisms and her coyness, she seemed to me almost childlike.

The more I listened to her, the more difficult I found it to believe this intellectually austere woman was the provocateur of so much attention, trouble, and harm. If I ever met anyone predestined for a life that would arouse little interest or attention, Lydia Eddelston was the personification of it.

For some reason, I recalled Homer's aphorism about Helen of Troy—she, of the face that launched a thousand ships, and a war—and certainly here we had a paradox or an irony, for the somewhat plain face across the table from me threatened to sink a thousand careers, not to mention capsizing an entire war.

The mystery was not whether she did it or not. She definitely did. The mystery was this: How and why had such a seemingly unremarkable young lady from bucolic small-town America become the iconic figure of a war that seemed to be going off the rails?

Strange. No other word could explain it—strange girl, strange behavior. Strange case.

For a moment I closed my eyes and listened to her speech; the image that formed, inevitably, was of Lydia on a small backcountry farm, wearing slack blue coveralls, hauling milk pails or slopping pig shit, whatever it is farm hands do these days. I reopened my eyes and was instantly transported back to the photographs showing Lydia doing things that were surely the buzz of her Baptist congregation back in Justin, West Virginia. I couldn't imagine what her preacher thought, or for that matter, her parents, of their little girl engaged in such vulgar activities. I could guess, though, that they were angry—angry that the army had turned their little girl into a monster, angry that the army had gotten her into this mess, and angriest of all that the army was now trying to put their little girl in the slammer for life.

Anyway, we continued the questioning in this perfunctory vein for about another twenty minutes. At one point, I asked about her MOS—her military occupational specialty—her military experience and training. To my surprise she informed me she was a 71 bravo—a personnel clerk—rather than a military policewoman or military intelligence specialist as I had assumed she would be. So what was a paper jockey, a fair-weather pogue in military parlance, doing in a military prison cellblock in a war zone? And why was a personnel clerk involved in prisoner interrogation?

But the extent of her military training entailed a three-month stint on active duty at Fort McClellan at the start of her enlistment, where she was taught the fundamentals of the military personnel system and a few rudimentary clerking duties, typing, correspondence, and so forth. Afterward, as per the standard National Guard contractual obligation, twice each month she reported to her local armory for her required weekend drills. Depending on the Guard unit in question, that may have entailed two fast and furious days of meaningful training or an extended weekend beer bash.

Her call-up for deployment to Iraq came at the last minute. After only one frantic week of country orientation and refresher training in basic combat skills, she found herself on a troop plane bound for war.

I should mention here that National Guard people are, in the truest and noblest sense of the term, America's citizen-soldiers. They are patriotic citizens with full-time civilian jobs, families, community responsibilities—a full and demanding life outside military service—the modern-day equivalent of revolutionary-era minutemen who, at the first bang of the claxon, rush off to the ensuing environmental apocalypse or the sound of the guns, whatever the situation dictates.

But Lydia's brief odyssey from peace to war stretched even that metaphor a bit; one Monday she was cramming letters into coded boxes in gentle, desultory Justin, trying to survive the ennui of small-time life; the next, she was holding her ass, dodging mortar rounds in Iraq.

Katherine sat patiently throughout this dialogue, still and sphinx-like. I was sure she had asked Lydia many of these same questions, and I was equally sure that my military background opened a few lines of inquiry that might have escaped Katherine's scope of prurience.

Sometimes it's the small things that break a case. You never know unless you ask.

I eventually did ask Private Eddelston, "Do you mind if we shift into a few preliminary questions about what happened at Al Basari?"

She smiled. "Guess that's what we're here to do, right?"

Good guess. She was now leaning back in her seat, hands clasped behind her neck, comfortable with herself and, if not totally comfortable with me, she at least seemed to have fit me into some nonthreatening frame of reference. Actually, I did not want her *that* relaxed, but neither did I want to intimidate her, so, to put her in the right mood, I reminded her, "We're here because you're facing a general court martial, which is the highest level of military justice with the most serious consequences. And you have been charged with a number of offenses, ranging from conspiracy to commit murder, to abusing prisoners."

Her hands came down and a frown popped onto her face.

I added, "These are serious charges, Lydia. Have you been advised of the possible punishments if you're convicted?"

She bit her lower lip. "Yes, sir. That other lawyer, Captain Howser, he tole me."

"Life in prison. Is that what he said?"

"'Ceptin' I'm innocent."

The photographs screamed otherwise, but maybe she had a plausible explanation that would easily clear everything up; maybe the girl in the photos was her evil twin. "What was your assignment at the prison?" I asked her.

"Clerk. Worked at the Personnel Administration Center for the 215th MP battalion."

"I see." I thought about this, then stated, "Obviously, though, you were occasionally placed on guard duty inside the prison."

"Oh . . . no, sir."

"Never?"

"Nope . . . never."

"But those photographs, they were taken *inside* the cellblock. Correct?"

"That's right, sir. My boyfriend . . . well, he had a job there. Danny Elton. MP."

"Then you worked inside the prison as well? Maybe as part of the administrative staff?"

"No, sir."

"Well . . . where did you work?"

"Around the prison was this big FOB—a forward operating base, it's called. An infantry unit, a battalion of MPs, some military intelligence folks, a buncha civilian contractors . . . we wuz all livin' there. Sorta stuffed together, real tight, in this huge tent city."

I smiled. "What we call a clusterfuck."

She smiled back. "You said it like that, sir. Also there was way too many prisoners to fit inside the prison. So they had this big area that was roped off with high fences and barbed wire where seven or eight thousand more prisoners wuz kept. They wuz livin' in tents, like us."

"Then you lived outside the prison?"

"Yes, sir. Most ever'body lived outside—in tents. The older officers, lot of 'em stayed in these air-conditioned trailers. The heat got to 'em somethin' awful. Even most of the guards lived outside the prison."

"Then what were you doing *inside* the cellblock?"

"Oh . . ." She stared at me for a long time before she answered, "Well . . . Danny, he invited me."

"*Invited* you?"

"That's what I said . . . sir."

"In a professional capacity? A social capacity? What?"

"No, I . . . See, Danny and the MPs, they worked round the clock, pretty much ever' day. Only way we could see each other was if I went'n visited with him."

"I see . . ." *Not.* Perhaps I've been spoiled but prison is not my idea of an ideal place for a date. But maybe I was missing something, so I asked, "Did you visit him often?"

"Plenty . . . yes, sir."

"How often? An approximation will suffice."

"Near ever' night, I guess . . . 'less I came down on the duty roster, or felt sick, or was havin' my monthly," she informed us, without any evident unease or embarrassment.

I exchanged looks with Katherine. What I could safely read into her admission was that she and Danny were . . . well, fucking.

In any regard, I was surprised and I think my face showed it, though it had nothing to do with the occasional absences caused by her monthly periods—it was her casual confession that she was in the cellblock nearly *every* night.

She looked at Katherine, then back at me. With a loose shrug, she added, "Most days, usually got my job done by four or so. Wasn't really much to do at nights. Iraq's pretty boring."

"Did you have *official* permission to be in the cellblock?"

"Like I tole you—Danny invited me."

Either she was being deliberately obtuse, or we were talking past each other. So to clarify, I stated, "This cellblock contained male prisoners. Presumably *only* males—is this correct?"

She looked confused. "I guess."

"Did this cellblock have a designating name or number?"

"Cellblock One. But they wuz all real hard cases in there. The badass wing . . . ever'body called it that."

I explained, "In military prisons, the policy is that female guards are excluded from duty inside male wings. Nor are female soldiers or guests allowed to enter, and they are certainly not permitted to wander freely. Other physical considerations aside, male prisoners are horny and easily excited. Also, male prisoners regard it as an unwelcome intrusion of their privacy." I paused, then observed, "I imagine Arab males are even more sensitive to these issues."

"Well . . . I wouldn't know nuthin' 'bout that."

Maybe she didn't, but the army officials running the prison certainly knew. "I'm saying that I'm a little surprised that you and two other female soldiers were *ever* present in that cellblock." She was giving me another of those long, empty stares, and I added, "From the news reports, Lydia, your visits often occurred late at night."

The disconnected stare continued. She didn't even blink. Hello, anybody home? I was tempted to shake her head to see if anything rattled or if it was an empty vessel. "If you're wondering, that was a question."

"Oh . . . then . . . yes, sir. They always did. Like I tole you, we wuz invited."

"Look, I just—" This was becoming very annoying. I drew a long breath, then retreated into an amiable smile. "Yes, so you did tell me." After a moment, I changed tact. "And were the other women invited as well?"

"Sure wuz. Andrea and June had friends in the same unit as Danny."

"Did your senior officers *know* you were there?"

"Cain't really speak for Andrea and June."

"Of course."

"My sergeant knew, though. Dang sure, she knew." After a moment, she added, "Often as not, I slept at the cellblock."

"You *slept* there?"

"Yup. See, one of them cells got turned into a lounge fer the guards. Had bunks, coupla fans, a hotplate fer cookin'. Much better'n the tents outside. Didn't have to worry about no mortars neither."

Katherine quickly asked, "Were you ever subjected to mortar fire during your time in Iraq?"

"A few times . . . I guess I heard some goin' off."

"Near you?"

"Nope. I mean, sometimes I heard these big thumps and blasts. Like, a ways off . . . y'know, in the distance. But since I wuz sleepin' in the prison most nights, I wuz pretty safe from that."

I now knew where Katherine was going with this. She leaned closer and asked, "Did they *ever* explode near you?"

"Nope."

"Were you ever subjected to direct enemy fire? Not necessarily at the prison . . . maybe a convoy you traveled with? A bomb going off in the road? At any point during your tour in Iraq, did you experience violence?"

She shook her head. "Since all them Iraqi prisoners wuz mixed into our FOB, them insurgents didn't really mess with us too bad."

What Katherine was probing for was the chance that Lydia Eddelston had experienced combat, which might have induced battleshock or some other form of post-combat syndrome that scrambled her ability to tell right from wrong. This has become a very popular and sometimes even effective defense strategy these days.

Had she asked me first, however, I would've saved her the trouble. Jurors in a civilian court are sometimes susceptible to that defense; they are naturally predisposed to sympathize with a combat veteran, and they have no term of reference for what the vet experienced. Not so a board of battle-hardened veterans who, accurately or not, believe they came out of it perfectly normal, whatever that means in this day and age. What it does not mean is that combat induces some form of moral bulimia.

More importantly, the chance of persuading them that a clerk—in military jargon, a pogue, a REMF, aka, a Rear Echelon Mother Fucker—was driven by the demons of war to do bad things was about as good as my chance of winning Mr. Collegiality in a beauty pageant. I'm not that beautiful, for one thing.

Besides, a totally different question, or rather contradiction, was still roiling inside my mind. A lounge inside a prison cellblock? "What rank is Danny, and what was his job title?"

"Night shift leader for the block. Sergeant." She quickly stipulated, "E-5," meaning a buck sergeant, the lowest of the noncommissioned officer ranks. Typically a buck sergeant is in charge of the smallest-size unit in the army, a fire team, two to three other soldiers. As the army likes to say, buck sergeants float somewhere between whale shit and octopus shit, and typically, as I knew from my own recurring visits to army prisons, a shift leader is usually at least an E-6, staff sergeant, or more often, an E-7, sergeant first class.

So I asked, "Were *his* officers or senior noncommissioned officers aware of your presence in Cellblock One?"

"Cain't really say."

"Try."

"Hardly ever saw any of 'em."

"Then would it be equally safe to say they never saw you?"

"Guess so."

"Don't guess. Yes, or no?"

"I don't know . . . Don't think they never did."

Ignoring that troublesome double negative, I asked her, "And did you spend the night each time?"

"Not always."

"How often?"

"Often enough. Why?"

"Was there a sign-in procedure?"

49

"Yes, sir. At the gate. I always did sign in."

I have been in and out of more military prisons and holding facilities than I care to remember, and getting in is always a hassle, even when, as was my case, you have a tangible legal justification for visitation, supported by the appropriate official documentation. The army thrives on order and control, and a penal environment is like a free-fire zone for its most anal impulses. It did not sound like Al Basari resembled the army I know and love. I asked, "Were you sleeping with Sergeant Elton?"

Blank stare.

"Having sexual relations?" She still looked confused. "Were you doin' him?" I clarified. As I was picking up, with this young client you had to connect on her level.

"Yes, sir. Sure was." In response to my raised eyebrows, she added, without any visible embarrassment, "Ain't nothing wrong 'bout that. We wuz in different units and not married. I'm divorced. So's he."

Given her youth this surprised me, and I asked, "You've been married?"

"Jus' once," she said, sounding quite proud about that. "Guy I went to high school with. Didn't last longer'n jus' a few months."

"Okay." I cleared my throat. "Let's move to the night the pictures were taken."

Private Eddelston again turned her eyes toward Katherine, a sort of doesn't-this-guy-know-anything glance.

"Did I say something wrong?" I asked her.

"Well . . ." After another long pause, she informed me, "Them pictures wusn't taken in no one night, sir."

It was now my turn to stare at Katherine, whose attention had become curiously riveted to a spot on the wall.

I cleared my throat again. "Maybe you should tell me what happened. Start from the beginning."

"Ain't much to tell. Danny was tole by them intel people that we should . . . uh, they said we should soften up the prisoners."

"Soften up? Were those their exact words?"

"Uh . . . no, sir." Another of those weird, long pauses, then, "Prep 'em for interrogation. That wuz how they put it."

"So this was like . . . an every night thing?"

"Ever' night? Oh no, sir. Jus' some nights. Certain prisoners."

"How many nights?"

She got that empty, faraway look again, and I specified, "An estimate will suffice."

She eventually said, "Maybe fifteen. Maybe twenty. Could'a been more . . . probably not less, though. Them days in Iraq, they sorta all melt together."

"So would it be accurate to state that the pictures reflect *frequent* behavior?"

"Well . . . some nights went longer'n others. Purty much depended on who the prisoners wuz, how tough, how bad the intel guys needed 'em to squeal."

"I see. Well, who selected which prisoners needed to be . . . prepped?"

"Them . . . the intel folks. But Danny and Mike wuz round them prisoners ever' day and ever' night. They knew 'em better'n anybody, so's sometimes they made suggestions. Like, maybe this guy or that guy was havin' a real sorry day, or his buddies wuzn't treatin' him too good, or he seemed sorta moody or depressed."

"All right. Who brought you and the other female soldiers into these sessions?"

"Didn't really go like that."

"Then how did it go?"

"One night, things jus' . . . well, jus' kinda happened."

This endless rephrasing of simple questions was really starting to annoy me. Usually no sane defense attorney places his own client on the witness stand, particularly if he knows or suspects the client has something to hide—guilt, for instance. But I was beginning to theorize that Lydia Eddelston was an exception. I pictured the frustrated prosecutor blowing his own brains out in front of the court. "What kind of things happened?"

"Well . . . one night Danny wuz bringin' this prisoner back to his cell from interrogation. I wuz there'n so was June. Anyways, this prisoner, ever'body wuz sure he was some kinda bigwig, hotshot insurgent. Them intel folks had interrogated him like ten times and got nowhere—they was pretty worked-up'n all."

She paused and turned suddenly thoughtful. This was getting interesting and I leaned across the table toward her. "And what happened?"

"I'm . . . well, I'm tryin' to recall 'xactly how it went down. I remember, he . . . this pris'ner, he saw me'n June, and he got real uptight. Y'know, all tense-like and squirmy. So June, she's pretty forward'n all, she moved up real close to this guy and she rubbed up agin him. Y'know, jus' sorta rubbed her titties agin him. Guess the idea jus' sprung into her head . . . and he started blabberin' somethin' . . . and then, next thing you know, she started unbuttonin' her shirt, and doin' this bump'n grind. And this guy . . . well he looked like he just got a cattle prod stuffed up his rump. Got all talky and nervous. Real sudden-like."

"And what happened next?"

"Well, then June, she took her shirt and drawers off, and started doin' this dance. She was down to her undies, but Danny 'n Mike started singin' this song, and like a stripper would do, June took off her bra and started movin' her hips real slow-like, and pinchin' her boobs and all. And that prisoner, he kept shuttin' his eyes. But if you looked real close-like, you could tell he was a'peekin'. So June, she says to Danny, 'Hey, pull down his drawers. Let's see what he's got.'"

"And did Danny pull down his drawers?"

"No . . . Danny sorta had to think about that for a bit. Then, well . . . then, he said I should maybe do it . . . and . . ."

"And . . . ?"

"I figured it made sense, you know? And . . . really, it wuzn't no big deal. So I did, and this guy . . . he was . . . well, much as he acted like he wuzn't payin' June no mind, that wuz a lie, cuz he had this real huge boner. And he got real embarrassed, and started wailin' all this stuff, in Iraqi . . . jus' losin' it."

"And then?"

"June took off her underdrawers, and kept dancin', only now, she was like . . . totally stripped. That Iraqi guy, he jus' went to pieces, cryin' and howlin, throwin' a real tizzy. So Danny, he took the guy outta there, and brought 'im right back to them interrogators. He tole us later, Danny did, that the guy gave up ever'thing. Names of other Hadjis, where some big arsenal was hid . . . like, whatever they asked, he jus' couldn't spill fast enough."

I looked at Katherine, but she was preoccupied with giving our client a supportive look and ignored me. I turned back to Lydia. "And did the intel people understand the nature of the treatment that made him open up?"

"Nature of the treatment?"

"That June had disrobed and sexually taunted the prisoner. That he was psychosexually . . ." I thought about my word choice, then stated in language that would be more understandable to Lydia, "That the prisoner was sexually aroused and that this treatment induced his sudden willingness to talk."

"Oh . . . yes, sir. Danny, he tole 'em all 'bout that." She nodded at Katherine. "'They was real thankful'n all."

"They thanked you? In person?"

"Well . . . not . . . I mean, they tole Danny, then Danny let us know how 'preciative they all wuz." After a brief pause she added as though it were an afterthought, "'Fore you could say boo, we wuz handlin' all the real hard cases."

"Why the pictures?"

"Danny said them intel people wanted 'em. They gave him one of them fancy cameras that load into a computer . . . y'know, so's he could start recordin' ever'thing. Danny said then they knew who got the treatment, how bad, and how good it worked."

"And you regarded these instructions as orders?"

Her lips stiffened. "They *wuz* orders, sir."

"From the intelligence people?"

"Well, yeah."

"How did that work?"

Long stare. No answer.

"Did they give you these instructions individually?"

The stare turned blanker.

"Did they brief your group collectively? In writing? E-mail?"

"Not like that . . . no, sir."

"Then like *what*?" I snapped

Lydia instantly recoiled back into her chair with a hurt expression. Katherine quickly intervened, bent forward, and in a soothing tone, informed her client, "Colonel Drummond's not angry with you." She paused to look at me. "He sometimes experiences impulse control issues."

Lydia was looking at her, apparently unsure of the definition of impulse control yet sensing it must be bad. Katherine said to me, "You should apologize."

In case I wasn't getting the message, somebody kicked my shin under the table.

Me? Apologize? I had just transcended the urge to strangle our client, but I stated with as little enthusiasm as possible, "I'm sorry."

Lydia stared at me.

Katherine placed a hand on her arm. "Don't let him bother you, Lydia. Please continue."

There is a time and place for good cop/bad cop; I often use it myself, even on my own clients. This, though, was something else; the relationship between Katherine and Lydia seemed to verge on big sister/little sister, or a more fitting expression might be doctor-client.

Anyway, Lydia swallowed a few times, then looked at me. "What wuz yer question agin?"

Well . . . what was my question?

After a moment, I smiled at Lydia and inquired, "Exactly how did you receive your instructions on how to handle the prisoners?"

"Well . . . let me think a minute." She thought a minute—I mean, an interminably full sixty seconds passed before she said, "Them intel people, they would meet with Danny. It wuz during the day, I guess. They'd name who we wuz supposed to . . . you know . . . who we wuz supposed to soften up. Then Danny and Mike, they'd put their heads together and figure it all out . . . exactly how it'd go down. Then, after Andrea and June and me got there, Danny, he would tell us what we wuz supposed to do."

"Like a script?"

"Guess you could put it like that," she said, looking impressed by that description. "Like, Danny would say, you do this, you do that."

I took a moment and described the photo of Lydia tugging the poor Iraqi around by a string tied to his Mr. Johnson, then asked, "Did Danny order you to perform that exact treatment?"

"Not 'xactly like that, no, sir." "Then how?"

"He would jus' say sorta somethin' like, prisoner two needs a little ST today."

"ST?"

"Yep. Special treatment—ST, that's how we started callin' it, for short. Lotsa times he left it to me or June or Andrea to figure a way to do that." She smiled. "Danny's a good leader that way. Real respectful of his subordinates."

This seemed like a good lead-in to my next question, and I asked, "Was there any alcohol involved? Drugs?"

"Oh no, sir. Drinkin' ain't allowed inside the war zone," she replied, sounding very righteous about that, oblivious to the fact that neither is the torture or sexual humiliation of prisoners. "We wuz all upright soldiers. No boozers, no dopers."

"Did you ever think it was a little weird?"

"What . . . What was weird?"

I swallowed another urge to strangle her and specified, "The ST, the special treatments, prepping the prisoners for interrogation that way. Danny employing you all to break down the prisoners." Could I be any clearer?

"I . . . well . . . maybe." She hesitated a moment, then elaborated, "'Specially at first. But Danny, he said them intel guys tole 'em the best way to break an Arab was through sexual stuff. Said them Arabs had real strict . . ." She paused, searching for the right phrase: her search appeared to have no end.

"Taboos," I eventually suggested.

Blank stare.

"The Moslem faith," I explained, "enforces very strict rules about physical modesty and separation of the sexes."

Still blank.

Katherine broke the code, saying, "Arabic men are easily shocked and humiliated by nudity and sex."

"Yeah . . . guess that's so. Purty much, that's how Danny said it." Looking at me, she blushed slightly, which was interesting. "Way Danny put it wuz, flash 'em a naked pussy or make 'em pull down their drawers, and they jus' turn into crybabies. Course, them's his words, not mine."

"Of course," I dutifully replied.

"Took a while to git used to. But orders is orders."

"Who *exactly* was giving these . . . orders?"

"Like I said, Danny."

"I meant, who was giving Danny his orders?"

She looked a little resentful. "Then you should'a put it like that."

I resisted the urge to kick *her* under the table. "Yes, I probably should have."

"That captain and that warrant officer."

"What captain? What warrant officer?"

"They wuz part of that intel unit stationed at the FOB. They had a bunch'a office trailers, all surrounded by barbed wire and guards. Real standoffish folks. Usually, they only came inside for their sessions . . . you know, when they wuz interrogatin' prisoners." She thought about it, then said, "Daylight."

"What about daylight?"

"That wuz when they did most of their work. They took to callin' us the night crew."

"Do you recall their names?"

"That captain, he was named Willborn. The warrant officer was Ashad, maybe Assad . . . something like that. He was an Arab, I guess," she said, as some southern people will, overelongating their *A*s. "Spoke real good Iraqi."

"Were Willborn and Ashad present during these . . . these prep sessions?"

"No, sir."

It was important to establish how many witnesses had direct observations of these sessions and I stressed, "We need to be clear on this, Lydia. Who was? Precision is important."

"Sometimes Andrea and June, they couldn't come. Then, it was Danny, Mike'n me, jus' the three of us. Usually it was all five, though." She paused briefly to emphasize this next point. "But I always liked it better when the other girls wuz around." She diverted her eyes toward Katherine again. "Know what I'm sayin'?"

Katherine awarded her a half-nod.

Lydia continued, "But Danny . . . well, he'd always tell us how happy them intel- folks wuz. Said we wuz all big heroes."

I checked my watch and observed that our one hour was nearly up.

I asked, "Do you regret your actions in Al Basari?"

She gave me another of those chronic, disconnected stares. I was pretty sure nobody had yet asked her this, despite its obvious relevance to her present mental state, not to mention how we would approach her courtroom defense.

She eventually replied, "Nope . . . don't guess I do."

"Not mistreating the detainees?"

"I never mistreated no one."

"Not disrobing and sexually humiliating them, not to mention yourself?"

She shook her head.

"Not posing for the pictures, which are now being used as incontrovertible evidence against you?"—and shared with the entire world, including your parents, your high school friends, and your pastor, I could've added, but didn't. "You regret none of this?"

She did not miss my point, or the disapproving undertone that accompanied it, and a pout worked its way onto her lips. "Look, lotsa soldiers are gettin' killed or blown to bits over there. I wuz helpin' win the war. Why should I feel bad 'bout that stuff I did? Ain't like I killed nobody."

Actually somebody had killed somebody. But before I could venture into that line of query, without a knock, the door suddenly swung open. The good-looking staff sergeant from the desk stuck his head in, and informed me, "I know I'm not supposed to bother you, sir. But this is important."

I stood and replied—"One more minute"—then started to close the door in his face.

He was quick, however, and got his foot in the path of the door. "There's a visitor for you and Miss Carlson. Says he needs to talk to you, ASAP, about some kind of emergency."

Katherine stood also, and placed her notebook back into her briefcase. She asked our client, "Do you need anything?"

"More magazines," Lydia replied, holding up her copy of *People*, which appeared dog-eared enough to have been read a dozen times. "Some romance books would be okay. But I 'specially like to read 'bout celebrities'n all them movie folk."

What she needed to be reading were law journals, but I suppressed the urge to tell her so. We followed the sergeant and closed the door behind us, leaving Lydia Eddelston to fantasize about celebrity lifestyles.

Everybody needs to dream. I just hoped she understood the difference between rich and famous, and incarcerated and infamous.

Chapter Five

The gentleman who awaited us by the front desk wore an off-season, off-the-rack, tropical, crap-brown suit, and a pukey green necktie. Poor sartorial hygiene aside, at the moment we entered the room, he was casually looking out the window, pretending to study the night sky. He turned around and said to the sergeant, not all that politely, "This is confidential. How about finding us an empty office?"

The sergeant deferred immediately to these instructions, which I regarded as telling, and promptly led us down a short hallway to an office with a sign on the door that said "Operations Sergeant."

I took the opportunity during this brief walk to more closely examine our host who had a manners lapse and failed to introduce himself. Middle-aged, with a full head of red hair shot through with silver, and a veiny nose and face, which indicated Irish ancestors swimming around his DNA pool, and a taste for booze, so probably he was an okay guy. Also, he had a slight stomach paunch, with a tight mouth, smart, sneaky blue eyes, and bushy, skeptical eyebrows.

The face screamed cop, and considering our location and his cheap suit, odds were he was CID—Criminal Investigation

Division, the army version of a detective. By his age and his comportment, he was a senior investigator, probably a chief warrant officer four or five, which was irrelevant for conversational purposes, since all warrant officers are addressed formally as Mister, or informally, as Chief.

The sergeant showed us into the room, politely asked us not to make a mess, and disappeared.

I turned to the gentleman in the suit and asked, "Okay, Chief . . . ?"

"O'Reilly. Terry O'Reilly."

"And obviously you know our names."

"Yes, sir. Obviously I do." He regarded us a moment. "You two got the pee-chick, right?"

This was the first time I had heard that unflattering, but inevitable nickname. More interesting still, it suggested that Katherine did not possess the sole copy of the photo she had earlier revealed to me. I inquired, "What's this about?"

Before he answered, he walked over to a chair in the corner of the room. He sat, then spent a moment getting comfortable, tugging his pants out of his crotch, and whatever. As I said, he was a career cop, and he was prolonging this pause to exert control over this conversation and also, I thought, using the moment to get a better handle on us. He looked at Katherine, then at me. "You two should sit. This could take a while."

I sat on the edge of the desk, whereas Katherine chose to cross her arms and stand. I believe I already mentioned that she has some serious authority issues.

Without further ado, O'Reilly informed us, "This morning, Major Martin Weinstein was found dead in his car."

I looked at Katherine. She was staring at him with a completely impassive expression.

I said to O'Reilly, "I'm sorry to hear that, but this means what to me?"

"Well . . . by dead, I meant murdered."

I shrugged. "Once again, what does this mean to me?"

"You don't know?"

Obviously not.

"Shit . . . I thought all you defense attorneys knew one another. Weinstein was handling the defense for Sergeant Elton."

This would be Danny, the soldier, director, choreographer, and perhaps photographer of all my client's naughty deeds. Katherine had now traded her impassive expression for a pensive one, and asked, "How was he murdered?"

He looked at her a moment. Cops don't like to share information about ongoing murder investigations, especially with a pair of nosy defense attorneys.

Actually, I fully expected Chief O'Reilly to tell Katherine to screw off, though, in fact, he did not. He instead explained, "Okay, here's what we've got. Weinstein left his townhouse—part of a small complex near Quantico—slightly before six this morning. He was dressed for physical training, in sweats. Got into his car, a gray Lincoln LS, was just inserting the key into the ignition when somebody grabbed his hair, yanked his head back, and used a nonserrated blade to slash his throat."

Without losing a beat, Katherine theorized, "Indicating the killer was hiding in the backseat?"

"It does suggest that, yes. No signs of a break-in though. And the victim was obviously surprised because there are no indications of a struggle. It's a nice, peaceful community where nobody locks their cars. So probably, he—the killer—just slipped in and waited for his moment."

Katherine asked, "Do you know who the killer is? Maybe you have a preliminary list of suspects? A promising lead or two?"

"Nope."

"You said *he*."

"That is what I said, yes."

"Then how can you be confident of the gender of the killer?"

"Because the cut . . . all the way through the soft tissue, sheared the throat cavity, and actually nicked the cervical spine. One slice, and"—with his hand, as if we needed a visual, he made a quick slashing motion—"the victim was nearly decapitated. Takes a lot of strength to do that."

Katherine, thankfully, did not take offense at this unliberated view of female virility.

But since we seemed to be into conjecture and opinions, I stated, "Further suggesting that the killer knew the victim's personal habits."

"That's possible."

"No, that's likely."

Cops love know-it-all lawyers, and he smiled, wearily. "Is it?"

"Did the family have two cars?"

"Yeah, they did. A red Dodge minivan was also parked in the driveway."

"So even aside from knowing where the victim lived, the killer was aware of which car was for the wife and kids to mess up, and which car the man of the house drove. He knew the victim did physical training in the mornings, and he knew what time he left his home." O'Reilly did not disagree with any of these points, and I asked, "How was the body discovered?"

"By Mrs. Weinstein. Like many military families, he always got out of bed earlier than her. She got up about seven, woke the kids for school, went outside to get the paper, and saw his car still parked in the driveway. She went over to check, saw the blood splashed all over the windshield . . . drew closer . . . and, well . . . there he was." He felt the need to add, "Pretty awful, if you think about it."

If you think about it. I accepted his invitation, and I did think about it. The Major and his family lived in the kind of modest, quiet, peaceful, suburban townhouse community that are as mundane and commonplace around Washington as low-salaried government workers, who ordinarily are the inhabitants. I pictured twenty or thirty narrow, neat, brick-fronted, two-storied buildings, connected together and cloistered around a small courtyard or garden.

Major Weinstein, earnest officer, never imagined he was a target as he walked out the front door. At a few minutes before six on a cold February morning it was pitch dark, and probably the community had little or no public lighting.

Assuming one killer, his executioner was hunched on the floor of Weinstein's car, beneath and behind the front seats, waiting, possibly cloaked underneath a dark cloth or blanket. I never even *think* to check the rear of my car before I get in: Who would? Obviously not the good Major.

He was attired in gym gear for physical training, and probably carried an overnight or gym bag packed with toiletries and the daily uniform he would change into after his morning run and exercise. He opened the door, placed the bag on the passenger seat, got into the driver's seat, was inserting the key into the ignition, then *auggh*—a hand grabbed his forehead, and his throat was cut from ear to ear.

And here, I thought, was where it became interesting. The total absence of struggle indicated there had been no exchange of words or efforts at negotiation between killer and victim. By extrapolation, this was an execution, a cold dispatching which could indicate either a strong emotional motive, such as hatred or betrayal, or the calculated elimination of a problem. Those two aren't mutually exclusive.

Apparently Katherine had also thought about it, because she remarked, "Yes, I'm sure it was awful." She then asked him, "So it sounds like you have no idea who killed him?"

"Not a clue." He bent forward, and quickly amended that statement to, "About the killer's identity, that is. A few clues were at the scene. A big one, in fact—a note, presumably left by the killer."

I said, "Please tell us about that note."

"More a message or an announcement than a note, really. It was cut from an article—by the paper type, most likely scissored from a magazine—then pasted on a three-by-five card. The killer positioned it right on the dashboard, after he was done . . . so you couldn't miss it. It said, 'God is great.'"

Katherine and I left that one alone for a moment. I was seeing a disturbing pattern here, and noted, "So now you have two dead defense lawyers associated with the Al Basari case."

He nodded.

"Coincidence?" I asked.

He shrugged. "Maybe."

"Probably not, though."

"No . . ." he agreed, "probably not."

"And probably Captain Bradley Howser's death was not the innocent accident everybody assumed it was."

"Well . . . that case has been reopened and now is under review."

Which was bureaucrat-speak for, Yes, we fucked up and thanks for mentioning it. I wish I could have a do-over every time I screwed up; so do my clients.

But he was looking at me, and I realized it was my turn to say something. When I finally did speak, it was to query of Katherine, "What have I ever done to you?"

She decided not to address this, and instead said to O'Reilly, "You mentioned clues. Plural."

"A few hairs were vacuumed from the backseat of the car." His facial expression did not look optimistic. "Maybe the killer's, or maybe not."

I asked, "What about footprints around the car, fingerprints on or inside the car, skin under the Major's fingernails? Maybe the killer signed the note?"

Cops also love being second-guessed by pushy wiseass attorneys, and his expression turned a little agitated. But obviously the answer was none-of-the-above, because he replied, evasively, "A CID forensics team from Fort Gillem flew up this afternoon."

I should mention here that CID agents are arguably the best-trained flatfoots in the world. Unlike most civilian detective units where everybody specializes—homicide, burglary, financial crimes, and so forth—the CID initial investigating officer is a jack-of-all-vices, and ordinarily, is expected to work whatever case lands in his lap from start-to-end, from the initial forensics work-up, through tracking leads, through tying the final knots that lead to a conviction. But in those rare instances where a case is particularly complex, politically significant, or socially alarming, the army also maintains a forensics center just outside Atlanta that can dispatch a squad of specialists on short notice to assist the local team.

From what I'd just heard, this case didn't sound all that complex. The method of killing and MO, for instance, were fairly innocuous and aboveboard: a cutthroat. So by process of elimination, it was probably because this particular case assumed some great significance. I mean, as a potential target I thought the decision was brilliant; this was the most important case in the world.

Anyway, O'Reilly was looking at me. "You've worked with them before. Am I right? So you know these people. If we missed something, they'll find it."

"Assuming there's anything to find."

"They'll at least be able to tell us the type of knife the killer used."

He chuckled to show this was a joke. Aside from learning the taste in weaponry of somebody who wanted to kill me, as legal professionals we all three were aware that identifying the brand of knife was nearly always useless.

In any event, from the depth of the cut, we already knew what we were dealing with here: what technical experts call a BFB—a big fucking blade.

He commented, "Maybe we'll know more tomorrow." But from his tone it sounded more like maybe not.

I looked at Katherine again. It struck me that at no point in this discussion had Katherine flinched, or seemed upset, or surprised, or even mildly annoyed, by news that was so clearly alarming. As females go, Katherine is fairly unemotional and I certainly wouldn't expect her to flee from the room, pulling on her hair and screaming her lungs out. But to learn that she might be on a hitlist, or a shitlist, belonging to a cold-blooded killer, and remain so blasé—did I mention that Katherine was now absently studying her fingernails?—was a little cold-blooded, even for her.

And further, it struck me that Major General Fister, Chief of the JAG Corps, had to be high on the initial notification list for army lawyers that had just become corpses. Considering that CID had been notified about the body early that morning, and Katherine had met with Fister regarding my reassignment sometime that afternoon, maybe her surprising lack of surprise wasn't all that surprising after all.

This was neither the time nor place to have this conversation. But I *needed* to get on the record early, so I turned to her and said,

"I owe you." I then asked O'Reilly, "Are you part of the crime scene investigating team?"

As I suspected he might, he replied, "Nope. I visited the site but only in connection with my actual duties."

"Go on."

"I work in the Pentagon. Office of Protective Services."

"And are you now assigned to protect us?"

He gave me a terse smile. "I'm your designated guardian angel. Effective 2100 hours, all defense attorneys for the Al Basari case will be under constant surveillance and guard. We don't want another dead attorney on our hands."

No, we certainly do not—especially not this defense attorney— though if I had the killer's phone number, I might offer him a helpful tip about which throat to cut next.

The victim of my mortal ruminations asked a very pertinent question. "Exactly what does that mean?"

"It means we'll do our part to keep you safe, and you'll have to do yours." He pulled a pair of devices from his pants pocket—they looked like small amulets—and handed one to Katherine and one to me. "For starters, here are your panic buttons. Keep them on or near you at all times, even when you shower. They're waterproof. And never hesitate. If you're wrong you'll just waste a little of my time. But if you wait till a knife's already at your throat"—he ran a finger across his neck, as though we needed another graphic— "you'll be outta time. If you see something remotely suspicious, push the damn panic button."

He went on for a few minutes, offering us helpful tips and precautions we should follow. It was mostly the usual stuff a cautious person would do anyway, lock the doors and windows, close the blinds, pay attention to anybody paying you undue attention, or following you, but there was one additional precaution—always check the backseat of the car before you get in.

This is called the shutting the barn door after the cow escaped, but it wasn't a stupid suggestion.

A two-man security team would trail us at all times. All travel arrangements had to be approved through his office. He or his people were to be notified in advance of all visitors. He was aware that Katherine had already set up shop in Highland Falls, New York—the small village outside the gate of the Military Academy at West Point—and a team was already en route to scope out the place and devise a security plan.

When he finished he looked at Katherine and asked, "What are your plans now?"

"My business here is finished. I'm driving back up to New York."

He paused, then looked at me. "You understand, sir, that it would be very convenient if the two of you remained together at all times."

I looked at Katherine. "Convenient for who?"

O'Reilly was a little slow on the uptake because he felt the need to explain, "Between five defendants there are a total of nine attorneys we have to protect and—"

I interrupted him to note, "Now eight."

"Eight . . . right. But we're still spread pretty thin. For now, the service can only spare three agents for the two of you."

"Understood, Chief." What I didn't say, what I didn't need to say, was everything else I now understood. He and his unit were going through the paces, providing the appearance of security in the event the killer had not filled his quota, and the shit hit the fan. He and I both knew, though, that effective full-time protection for a single party requires a team of at least six trained agents. Three agents for two targets is what they call in the trade a deterrent force, like using a perforated Trojan rubber; maybe you'll get lucky, but maybe not.

Brian Haig

He produced a sheepish smile. "What I'm trying to suggest is, why don't you be a gentleman and drive the lady up to New York?"

I'd rather drive over the lady and drag her corpse to New York. But I nodded, then explained my need to drop by my apartment to pick up fresh uniforms, spare undergarments, shaving supplies, and one item I failed to mention—the pistol I kept hidden on the top shelf of the closet.

Chapter Six

Predictably, Katherine's car was a leased Toyota Prius, what they call a hybrid, and, though I consider myself as sensitive to the assassination of our environment as anybody, Sean Drummond was not the least bit happy with this choice.

The car didn't even require a key to get started, just this stupid button you push, then you can't even hear the engine, so after the fifth time I punched the button, Katherine said, "Stop that, Sean. The damned car is already started."

"Are you sure?"

"Unlike you, it doesn't make a lot of noise. Yes, I'm sure."

She can be very funny. We proceeded up 95 North, then the Palisades Interstate Parkway, cutting left just before the Bear Mountain Bridge. Katherine napped with her head against the window for most of the drive. Thankfully, she didn't snore and required no potty breaks, which was a treat. Men and women share an organ called a bladder, which serves roughly the same function, though theirs must be a quarter of the size and lacks an off switch.

During her few waking moments, she did share a few tidbits of relevant knowledge. She notified me, "Our court date is in one month. We'll have to work hard, and fast."

"You mean thirty days?"

"Like most months, yes, Sean. I know it's short. But I've already done a lot of the preparation."

"Have you interrogated the other accused yet?"

"No. I thought we'd do it together."

"Filed any motions, yet?"

"None have been necessary, yet. The answer's no."

"Have you met with any witnesses?"

"I have not . . . no, not yet."

"What have you done, Katherine?"

"I hired a capable staff and arranged an office. "

I shook my head. "Who's paying for all this?"

It was obvious where I was going with this line of inquiry and she chose not to answer. But I wasn't letting go and suggested, "Isn't Nelson Arnold a bit old, even for you?"

"Why do you always see the worst in other people?"

"Because the worst usually applies."

"You're underestimating him, Sean." She looked at me. "Don't."

"He's also rich, handsome, and owns half of Manhattan. Some women find that an attractive combination. Shallow, I know, but please answer the question."

"I don't think it's any of your business."

"If he's paying the bills, it's very much my business. I want to know the extent of his involvement with this case—" And with you, though I didn't say that, because obviously who Katherine sleeps with was no concern of mine. Right?

But apparently she found this topic tiresome, because Katherine put her head against the window and was instantly asleep. I think she had decided to avoid me for the rest of the trip.

Amazingly, we made it all the way to the small, sleepy village of Highland Falls on less than half a tank of gas. If they could manufacture one of these things in the size and shape of a Ford Bronco, I might even buy one.

Anyway, Highland Falls, as I mentioned, is, in the official lexicon, a village, a small, charming, but slightly depressed burg whose main purpose seems to be serving the needs of the military academy. The first foot was set here way back in 1609, according to local legend, but it wasn't until West Point was established in 1802 that any feet stopped moving. Most army bases get the garrison towns they deserve and, for the large troop bases, this means plenty of whorehouses, gin mills, pawnshops, and these days, a smattering of fast food joints and tattoo parlors. In the case of the military academy, that means a drowsy village with plenty of souvenir shops and nice churches.

I gave Katherine a poke in the arm. "We're on Main Street in Highland Falls. Where next?"

She stretched for a moment, and looked around. "Stay straight, then hang a left on Partner Lane."

Partner Lane? This sounded presumptuous, but I didn't think I could convince them to change the name just to fit my sensibilities. So I stayed straight, and, a moment after I took the left, Katherine said, "Drive to the top of the hill. A surprise is waiting for you."

I don't like surprises and anyway, Katherine had already used up her limit for the night.

I pulled up to the only house with the lights still on, and Katherine confirmed that I had made the right choice. The house was a small, two-storied clapboard affair, perhaps eighty or a hundred years old, or fifty neglectful years, green or red or yellow in color—but who cares?

Another clue that this was the right house was the man in a cheap civilian suit waiting hospitably by the curb. Presumably, O'Reilly, who was somewhere back there, following behind us, had called ahead on his cellphone to alert the troops.

"Please get your stuff quickly and follow me inside," the agent said by way of introduction and welcome.

I grabbed my duffel bag, Katherine climbed out her side, and he led us up the crumbling sidewalk to a small front porch.

The moment I stepped inside a voice from the back of the house yelled, "This here's my office, so don't you mess nothin' up. Don't you leave that damned bag on my floor, neither."

I had heard that voice before, and I had heard that order before. I replied, in my most authoritative voice, "I'm a lieutenant colonel, now. I'll put my damned bag wherever I please."

Imelda Pepperfield appeared out of a room in the back holding a pot of steaming coffee, and wearing a scowl. "Oh no you won't. I'm a civilian now, so I don't care if you got ten stars on them shoulders. You'll carry that bag up them stairs if I say so."

I thought about crossing the floor and hugging her, but Imelda would probably reward such a display of warm bonhomie with an affectionate knee in the balls.

So instead we just stood and admired each other a moment. Imelda had been a sergeant first class, and my legal assistant, years before. Katherine and I had shared her services back in Korea, and I now had a fairly good idea how Imelda was spending her retirement. A legal assistant in the army is sort of a cross between a paralegal, an office manager, and a major domo. Though she was a sergeant and I an officer, the lines of authority often became blurred. But I can be difficult as a boss, and Imelda can be difficult as a subordinate, so it worked out okay. She was single, mean, frighteningly smart, sporadically warm-hearted, as knowledgeable about the law as many attorneys, and as the current conversation indicated, she tends to be a bit on the autocratic and pushy side.

By way of compliment, she noted, "You put on a little weight. Must be gettin' lazy."

"Thank you. You look great, too."

"What're you doin' wearing that stupid suit?"

"It's Brooks Brothers," I replied with just the right whiff of a Brahmin drawl.

She shook her head. "If it belongs to them brothers, why're you wearin' it?"

I nearly explained, but of course Imelda was joking. I thought I even detected a hint of a smile.

Well, enough pleasantries and empty chitchat. Imelda pointed at a side room, apparently the dining room of this old house before it was converted into a legal office, and said, "That's your office. Already put the discovery materials and dead lawyer's files in there. Read through that first. And put it back together the way you found it. Don't leave me no mess."

"Thank you."

"Already hung curtains over all the windows, too. You leave them curtains alone. Don't want nobody shooting at us. And lock the doors whenever you leave."

"I'll also be sure to put the lid down on the toilet."

I could tell she wanted to smile but didn't want to break the mood. "Anything else you need, you see Imelda."

She placed the coffee pot on the table, where there were already four mugs, backed away, and disappeared into the kitchen.

I carried my bag upstairs with orders not to be disturbed until eight.

I would never admit this to Katherine, but I was glad to get a break from my duties in the CIA. I missed the law, I missed soldiers, and yes, I even missed the army.

Indeed, most of all, I had missed Katherine. Bickering and sexual misunderstandings aside, I had always been strongly attracted to her. But army life is murder on personal relationships, and Katherine's own causes and all-consuming dedication to her clients had left little time or opportunity for us to sort out our personal feelings for each other. She was a big unresolved issue for me; it was time to discover if I was one for her, as well.

But tomorrow I was determined to find out who had masterminded the worst scandal of the war, who had taken the pictures, and who had talked a group of fine young American ladies into such bizarre and depraved behavior. With a little luck, I would also get some idea of who had murdered the Iraqi in the sleeping bag.

But perhaps I was being overly optimistic.

In fact, had I known what lay before me, I wouldn't have slept a wink. I would've climbed back in the car and raced as far away from this place as I could get.

Chapter Seven

I was up at eight, showered, shaved and, by quarter after, I had finished my morning ablutions. I was back in uniform for the first time in months, and seated in my office with a warm cup of coffee in my hand by 8:30. All was good with the world.

I'm a fast reader, and, as with most criminal lawyers, I have a long familiarity with the forms of military justice. Though I was a little rusty, by nine it was all coming back.

Coming into a case cold, and late in the game, I have found the best place to start is with the results of the Article 32 investigation, the military equivalent of a grand jury. In this case, as I suspected, given the seriousness of the case, the commanding officer of the accused, Major General Claudia South, had appointed a JAG officer to conduct the investigation. Typically, the commanding officer appoints a field officer wearing the branch brass of the unit where the crime occurred, but General South obviously understood from the beginning that this case was special, filled with legal minefields, and any procedural mistakes would come back to bite her in the ass.

So she made the wise choice of appointing a legal professional, Lieutenant Colonel, or LTC, Dan Philcher. I knew the name and I knew, as well, that Philcher had a fine reputation as an officer and as an attorney. As it reduced the chances of a mistrial or the opportunity to disqualify important evidence, this was good news for the army and bad news for our client. A Captain Perry Winters was the prosecuting attorney.

Article 32 investigations are less formal than general court martials, though the accused retains most of the rights afforded in the civilian world. Captain Bradley Howser, now deceased, had represented Lydia, and, as per procedure, he'd been allowed to cross-examine the witnesses with wider latitude than might be permitted in court, and his client was allowed to make statements not under oath.

A court reporter had been present, and, at first glance, everything looked in order. The principal witnesses included the captain who commanded the military police company in the cellblock where the crimes occurred, the lieutenant who led the military police platoon, all five of the accused soldiers, two military intelligence officers, three Iraqi prisoners to testify firsthand about the abuse, and Lieutenant Colonel Eggers, who both commanded the military police battalion and served as commandant of the prison.

There were various other witnesses, including the two army CID warrants who performed the initial investigation into the death of the Iraqi prisoner and a few members of Lydia's chain of command, among others, but their testimony was tangential at best—what kind of soldier was she, who did she hang out with, and so forth and so on.

After thirty minutes spent surveying the case landscape and Lydia's testimony, which largely accorded with what she had already told me, I jumped ahead to the testimony of Sergeant Danny Elton, Lydia's presumptive beau, and the ranking soldier in the cellblock.

The conventional wisdom seemed to be that he was the ringleader of this sordid affair, the heavy hand, and the auteur responsible for the cinematography. But consensus, I had learned, is often just the first step into communal idiocy. Consider lemmings, for instance.

Captain Perry Winters, the prosecutor, as per tradition and procedure, had gone first and opened with the usual background questions. Full name and age—Daniel Boone Elton, 37. Marital status—divorced thrice, currently unattached. Hometown and military record—Dalton, Ohio, with fourteen years in the National Guard. Education—high school graduate, then two years in junior college, but no degree. Civilian employment—a long list of temporary, unskilled jobs from clerking in 7-Elevens, to yardwork, to being a waiter in a long list of restaurant chains. Notably lacking, it struck me, was any history at the managerial or leadership level.

I spent a moment thinking about this. Like Lydia Eddelston, Danny Elton's socioeconomic status was somewhere down there, but given his age, thirty-seven, and his clear lack of professional success in the army or in civilian life, Elton seemed doomed to remain there.

My experience has been that some people lack the social aptitude, mental skills, influential parents, or luck, to break out of the pack and improve their socioeconomic standing. Others, and I sensed that Elton might fall into this category, remain stuck in low, unchallenging jobs because they prefer it. They are, in short, fugitives from success, more or less because they choose to be. According to his personnel files he had a fairly high IQ, roughly 120, and he was in the army, which indicated no serious drug or alcohol or health issues.

Yet, at thirty-seven, he still was stuck in the rut of menial work, and after fourteen years in the National Guard had only managed to claw his way up to E-5. I briefly surveyed the efficiency ratings in his personnel file and they confirmed that Danny Elton was regarded by his superiors as less than a stellar leader of men, or even of himself. There were recurring mentions of attitude problems, authority issues, and disciplinary problems. Strong-willed was mentioned several times, not in a context that was meant to be complimentary.

I returned to my reading and was struck by this passage:

Captain Winters: "You were the shift leader of Cellblock One?"

Sergeant Elton: "Yeah, that's right. All the badasses were kept there. Jus' say, I knew how to control 'em."

Captain Winters: "How was that?"

Sergeant Elton: "How was what?"

Captain Winters: "How did you control them? Were special techniques required? Did you have unique operating instructions?"

Sergeant Elton: "Special . . . ? Look, let me clue you in about these guys. Only certain types made it to my cellblock. Career crooks, and by that I'm talking murderers, sociopaths, and . . . uh, what you might call fuckin' incorrigibles. And the bigtime terrorists. Not the gunmen or bomb throwers or street toadies. We're talkin' Hadjis who run the insurrection."

Captain Winters: "And how were these people chosen for your block?"

Sergeant Elton: Laughter. "Sometimes they came straight in. The intel types identified 'em. Maybe they had a record under Saddam, maybe they got fingered by stoolies. Lots of ways, I guess. I didn't ask. I really didn't give a shit how they got there. Sometimes, they graduated to me from other blocks. The hard cases. Their block leaders were pussies, couldn't handle 'em."

Captain Winters: "So what did you do differently to control them?"

Sergeant Elton: "Attitude."

Captain Winters: "Attitude?"

Sergeant Elton: "Ain't that what I said? You kept your boot on their chest or they'd go wild. They'd throw shit and piss in your face. They'd kick and punch and bite you. They'd cut you. They'd throw riots and mess with you in a thousand ways. You lawyers got no idea what these people are like. Ain't like nothin' back here. It's war, man. These people

don't think nothin' of blowin' up a schoolbus filled with little kiddies.
They cut off heads. It was dog eat dog in there. You hadda work hard to
be the big dog, or they'd fuckin' bury you."

I had the thought that Elton must've watched that court room
scene of Jack Nicholson and Tom Cruise verbally fencing in *A Few*
Good Men, and this sounded like his coarsened rendition of Jack
Nicholson's soliloquy, albeit replacing being "up on the wall" in the
defense of democracy with his thoughts on "being the big dog."

Just as obviously, LTC Philcher wasn't buying it, because in
reply to this oration, he said, *"Just answer the question, Sergeant. Did*
you have unique instructions or orders regarding prisoner treatment?"

Sergeant Elton: "Wasn't like that, no. Wasn't like anyone had time
to sit down and type up some neat little book of instructions. You know,
like you can do this, but just don't do that. But my officers, they knew
how I operated. And don't you let 'em act like they didn't. Hell, the whole
prison knew. Whenever any prisoners got out of line in other blocks, the
guards told 'em, quit fuckin' round or you're going to Elton's hole. And
you know what—the prisoners, they all knew what that meant."

Captain Winters: "What did they know?"

Sergeant Elton: "Come to my house, you play by my fuckin' rules."

Clearly, Sergeant Elton was a man with some serious authority
issues, and a mountain-size chip on his shoulder. A man needs to
find his role in life—father, coach, priest, bully—and Elton had
decided to be the all-knowing badass who set the rules. Power corrupts, and absolute power corrupts absolutely; and, in the dead of
night, it can create monsters.

Then, a little later:

Captain Winters: "On December 21, the death of General Yazid
Pachaci was reported in your cellblock."

Sergeant Elton: "Sounds about right."

I paused for a moment to consider this interesting exchange.
It was the first I had heard that the homicide victim was an Iraqi

general. I assumed that he had to have been one of Saddam's generals, and further, I assumed that the idiots running the cellblock had picked the wrong victim. Rank doth have its privileges and, fair or not, when you kill a general, it doth generate a crapfest.

Captain Winters: "Can you describe the circumstances that led to his death?"

Sergeant Elton. "Nope. We discovered his body in his cell and called it in."

Captain Winters: "In his cell? Did he have a cellmate?"

Sergeant Elton: "I don't recall."

Captain Winters: "Wasn't General Pachaci what the intel people called a high value target?"

Sergeant Elton: "Why don't you ask them?"

Captain Winters: "According to the records kept by the prison warden's office, General Pachaci was in an isolation cell. He lived by himself under lock and key."

Sergeant Elton: "Yeah? Well, that don't mean nothing. Hell, them records was always messed up. Any given day there was, like, eight, nine thousand prisoners. Coupla hundred comin' in, coupla hundred bein' processed out. Fuckin' clerks never kept it straight."

Captain Winters: "He was in your cellblock, Sergeant. Under your direct supervision. You have no idea how anybody got the key to his cell, entered it, and beat him to death?"

Sergeant Elton: "Do you?"

I moved on to the testimonies of the other accused soldiers: Andrea Myers, June Johnston, and Mike Tiller. I spent another hour reading their statements until I thought I had the general picture. Andrea Myers and Mike Tiller struck me as both the least informative and least knowledgeable of the night crew. I had the impression both were followers and bit players, and I placed them low on my list of interesting people to get to know.

Moreover, all the testimonies of the night crew, in ways large and small, correlated and concurred. Nobody knew how or why or when General Pachaci died. None could recall how his body was discovered or, indeed, who found the corpse. All their actions were for the greater good, i.e., "prepping" the prisoners for interrogation. All agreed that Sergeant Elton got his marching orders from Captain Nate Willborn and Chief Warrant Officer Amal Ashad, the former, the MI team leader, and the latter, the MI linguist who served under the captain.

I was about halfway through Private Andrea Myers's performance in the witness chair when Katherine entered the room and fell into the chair across from me.

She wore a shapely black pantsuit, crossed her legs, and asked, "What are your impressions so far?"

Well, she looked great but I saw no need to mention that. "My bed was lumpy."

"Anything else?"

"Imelda's coffee hasn't improved."

She smiled and seemed to enjoy my complaints. "Imelda was right. You've gone soft, Drummond."

"Can't you talk your billionaire buddy into throwing in a decent coffeemaker? A maid would be nice."

"I'll see what I can do." She obviously wanted to avoid this subject, though. "I meant, any relevant observations on the case?"

"Tell me what you think."

She made no reply for a while, then said, "I think the government jumped the gun."

"You think the evidence is thin?"

"I think the public exposure and outcry forced the army's hand. They needed to fry somebody, and I think they did a hasty investigation, quickly settled on the lowest ranking members, and now they're praying they can get some convictions and that satisfies the public's lust for a hanging."

Rather than debate this point, I inquired, "What's the current status of Captain Willborn and Chief Ashad?"

"I know neither has yet been charged with anything, if that's what you mean. Willborn's current status is witness for the prosecution. I don't know Ashad's status. Only the prison commander, Lieutenant Colonel Paul Eggers, has been punished."

"How was he punished?"

"Relieved of his command." She paused, then continued, "I understand that marks an undistinguished end to his career, but it seems fairly trifling compared to the general court martial these soldiers are facing."

"Is that what you think?"

"For God's sake, Sean, he still gets his military pension. He goes home to his wife and kids, and in a year, nobody remembers he was ever involved in this disgrace. The enlisted types face life in prison."

I pointed out, very reasonably, "He wasn't accused of murdering anybody."

"Maybe he should have been."

"He didn't directly engage in torture, did not strip, did not pee in anybody's face, nor was he stupid enough to have his face circulated in a revolting gallery of photos that give a whole new meaning to the word 'celebrity.'"

She stared at me, and I couldn't tell what she was thinking. Eventually she said, "I want to be sure you have the right mindset for this, Sean."

"What's that supposed to mean?"

"You're a creature of the institution. A military lifer. You buy into the whole rank thing and all that comes with it. I think all of you, after enough time in uniform, come to accept certain institutional norms."

"Thank you for telling me how I think, Katherine."

"Well . . . it's hardly a challenge." She smiled to indicate this was a joke; the smile looked forced and insincere. "I'm just saying that our best defense at this point might be one that makes you squeamish."

"You make me squeamish."

We seemed to be at an impasse here. We had had this discussion many times before, starting as law students at Georgetown and on through all the years I'd known her, and we had never settled it yet. Katherine, to put it mildly, was a power-bashing leftie. I had never been accused of anything close to that.

But I wanted to go on record, and said, "Hard as it might be for you to accept, the army is not a machine and the uniform is not a mental straightjacket. A lobotomy does not come with the oath of service. The concept of free choice is alive and well. Illegal or immoral orders can be refused, and, in fact, the army expects, even encourages you to do so. It doesn't matter if you're the lowest ranking private in the army, if anybody of a higher rank tells you to do something morally or legally repugnant, you have the right and the obligation to tell them to fuck off."

"Did you check Lydia's IQ yet?"

"I wasn't aware she has one."

"Ninety-two. So here we have a young girl with a lousy education, below average intelligence, a backcountry rural upbringing, poor self-image, possibly a few impulse control issues, thrown into something much bigger than she could possibly understand."

"Are we talking about her or you?"

"Screw-off, Drummond."

Two points for me. "Katherine, I understand what you're saying but those fall under the heading of extenuating and mitigating circumstances, issues you raise *after* a conviction. Base your defense on those concerns, and Lydia's going to spend her old age crapping granola in Leavenworth latrines."

"Please expand on your reasoning."

"According to the testimonies, these activities spanned over a month-long period of fun and games—a full month of Lydia, June, and Andrea entering the prison at night and playing hide-the-willy with the prisoners. It wasn't a one-night splurge fueled by alcohol or drugs, or a bout of temporary, collective insanity, nor was it some sudden emotional lapse. It was premeditated, prolonged, deliberate." I looked at Katherine and noted, "The only relevant issue was whether they knew right from wrong."

"And you believe they did?"

"I believe all young girls are taught not to pee on men's faces. They are taught that penises are not toys. They are taught to keep their clothes on in front of males, except when in the presence of lovers and gynecologists. Now imagine, if you will, that these were male guards in a female prison, and they engaged in the same kinds of kinky, degrading, sexually aggressive behavior. In that instance, do you think you could convince seven reasonable men and women that a slightly below average intelligence and a low self-image justified acting out such impulses?"

"Is that what you think?"

"What matters is not what I *think*, what matters is how it will be pitched and received in a courtroom. And I believe we're going to discover even more interesting perversities, more fantasies indulged in the dead of the night. Unless you have some reason to believe that Lydia fails the M'Naghten qualifications, I suggest you drop that line of defense."

The M'Naghten standard, as Katherine well knew, is the old English criteria that remains the foundation for modern legal reasoning regarding moral responsibility. It has two parts: did the defendant cognitively understand that what he or she was doing was wrong; and, two, was the defendant so mentally impaired, by mental disease or profound defect, that he or she lacked the mental gravity to select right from wrong?

Following that line of thought, I asked Katherine, "Has she been psychiatrically examined yet?"

"She's scheduled to be tested the day after tomorrow."

"By us, or by the government?"

"Tomorrow's the government turn. The next day is ours. Dr. Theodore Erickson is coming up from New York City."

"Is he good?"

"Better than good, Sean. He'll be our expert witness. I'm confident he's better than anything the army can drag up on the stand."

I looked hard at Katherine. "Here's a good piece of advice. Don't assume all army lawyers are dumb knuckle-draggers and don't assume all army docs are incompetent quacks. It's no good for our client."

Katherine evaded this subject, perhaps out of consideration to the only army lawyer within earshot. She said, "I have scheduled appointments with a military prison consultant and June Johnston. Want to come along?"

I was tired of reading, and ready to begin meeting the characters directly involved in this case. I got up and followed Katherine out to the Toyota Prius, which was still sitting by the curb, not yet stolen, though I had left it unlocked with the driver's door ajar.

Note to self—next time leave a large, welcoming invitation on the windshield.

Chapter Eight

We drove down the hill and hooked a right, then parked and entered a small eating establishment called Shades. Shades had the look and feel of a neighborhood bar/diner with an eating area, booths, and so forth. It was like a charming jump back in time to the fifties, and the restaurant was filled with a mixture of grizzled locals— many of whom looked like they had been there in the fifties—and a number of clean-cut, short-haired, muscular young men in civilian clothes who were still easily recognizable as soldiers.

Katherine led me to the back where an older-looking gent with short hair was hunched over a table, sipping from an iced tea.

He jumped up as we approached, pushed out a hand, and shook with Katherine. Katherine did the introductions. "Fred Norell, this is Sean Drummond, my JAG cocounsel."

Then to me, she said, "Fred retired last month from the MPs. He was a lieutenant colonel on the staff of the corps commander in Iraq."

Fred and I spent the typical man moment sizing each other up. Truly, men are like dogs; we don't get down on all fours and sniff one another's butts, but probably only because we can't get away with it. Fred was a large man, perhaps 6'4", thin and fit, with a severely cropped crew cut that could only have been inflicted by a military barber. He had what you would call a manly, seasoned face, tanned, prematurely wrinkled skin, narrow, inquisitive eyes, uncommunicative mouth—the face of a man who had seen something of the world.

He indicated for us to be seated, then he and I spent another brief interlude becoming acquainted. He was older than me, closer to fifty than forty, wife, three kids, and had experienced the typical career pattern of a senior military police officer. Troop service in Germany and Korea as a junior officer, then his career veered into penal duties, including several stints at the confinement facilities at Fort Knox and Fort Carson, graduating, eventually, to the big house at Fort Leavenworth.

Katherine interrupted this hale-fellow-well-met moment and shifted us into gear, informing me, "Fred has agreed to be an expert defense witness. Further, he's agreed to be an unpaid consultant to our team."

This was interesting, both that a career officer agreed to testify on Lydia's behalf, and also that he was waiving remuneration for the service.

I asked Fred, "What was your job over there?"

"I was on the multinational corps staff in the operations office. It was a long, hard year. Specifically, I was the planner for prison operations."

"I've never heard of that position. Was it unique?"

"It was created just for me." He appeared to understand that this required an explanation and he provided one. "Understand that everything in Iraq after the initial invasion was an unmitigated mess. Nobody planned for an occupation, an insurgency, or a civil war. If you haven't been there, you've at least read the papers and seen the news. I'm sure you understand. I was one of the firemen."

In fact, I had there been there, very briefly, on a highly classified mission I didn't want to discuss in front of Miss-You-Know-Who.

So I nodded, which Fred took as an indication to continue. "Everything in the theater and the army was in chaos. Iraq exploded in violence. I was the deputy commandant at the Castle, and got overnight orders to proceed to Iraq on the next flight."

As I knew, the Castle was the nickname for the Disciplinary Barracks at Leavenworth, the crown jewel of the army's penal system and its only maximum security prison. Only the hardest cases are incarcerated there, what army authorities call Level III inmates, meaning it takes at least a seven-year hitch to get a room reservation.

Fred continued, "Between the insurgency and the fact that Saddam had emptied his prisons before the invasion, crime and violence spun out of control. Field commanders didn't know how to react and just began rounding up tens of thousands of young men, often indiscriminately. The influx of new prisoners quickly overwhelmed our capacity to deal with it. In just a few short months, the corps had nearly two hundred thousand incarcerated."

Katherine asked, "Where did they put them all?"

"You put your finger on the problem, Katherine. The Iraqi police had been disbanded or melted away. Saddam's old prisons were there, but in terrible condition, and anyway the flood of prisoners was too great. The commanders on the ground were forced to improvise, creating impromptu camps, throwing up barbed wire and hiring contractors to feed them."

I said, "Were there other problems?"

"Guards, Sean. The correct term is corrections specialists. Special training is required for this job, and MP branch has a course for this purpose at Fort Leonard Wood. But the graduates of that school were busy running our stateside penal facilities."

"And what does this training entail?" Katherine asked. She had a notebook on the tabletop now and was taking copious notes. She always was a great student.

"Well . . . screening is a big part."

"Screening for what?" Katherine asked.

"Mentality is part of it. No Napoleon complexes, no power issues, no dangerous insecurities. Most importantly, we look for a low explosion threshold, which roughly translates to a high level of tolerance, and a low level of sensitivity. A lot of prisoners have severe personality disorders and issues. Many are antisocial, some violently so. Dealing with them requires a special mentality."

"That's why they're in prison," I noted, unnecessarily.

"Yes . . . good point, Sean," he said, and somehow managed to even make it sound like he meant it. "They're usually young men, trapped in cells, denied sex or much normal entertainment, and they take this out on the only authority figures within reach. The guards."

Like a lot of military men, listening to Fred was like reading a military manual. Everything tightly organized, clipped, and factual. Cops and soldiers, after enough time in uniform, I've noticed, learn to dispense with unnecessary words and even emotions. I had no doubt he'd make an excellent expert witness.

"What special training do they receive?" Katherine asked Fred.

"Everything from basic prison operations to prisoner treatment to special situations. Bear in mind that prison presents a lot of challenging situations that are unique. Handling riots, prisoners abusing one another, sexually and otherwise, gangs, medical issues, and of course, a number of these people are flat-out insane."

As I mentioned before, Katherine's legal background concerned issues dealing with homosexuality in the military, whereas mine had mostly been spent with criminal cases. I had been to Leavenworth to visit clients a number of times, as well as an assortment of other military confinement facilities. Those trips, however, stopped at the visiting room. Hollywood fantasies aside, neither Katherine nor I had any idea what duty must be like *inside* those places.

Fred continued, "Now throw into that mix that these prisoners were Iraqis. The language problem alone was huge and insurmountable. The cultural chasm was maybe worse. Here we had your typical young American boys and girls, totally blind to issues like touching or staring, which constitutes a severe insult to Iraqis, who are an unusually sensitive people."

Katherine looked up from her notebook. "So you're saying that Al Basari was primed for trouble?"

"No." Fred paused and stared at Katherine. "That's an understatement. I'm saying it was much worse than you can begin to imagine."

I asked Fred, "How so?"

"For starters, the personnel shortages were a doorway to disaster."

"Can you give us specifics?"

"Okay, here's a general rule we use in planning. For every four thousand prisoners, it takes a full brigade of MPs, or roughly nine hundred soldiers, to guard them. I didn't invent that, it's doctrine based on the experience of more than a dozen wars and conflicts." He allowed us a moment to absorb that ratio, then added, "At the time of the scandal, Al Basari contained around eighty-five hundred prisoners, yet there was only one battalion guarding the prisoners."

Katherine did a quick calculation and said, "About three hundred MPs, right?"

"Yes, roughly. Should've been more like three thousand."

I asked Fred a relevant question. "Did you ever visit Al Basari?"

"I did. On several occasions. I couldn't get out of there fast enough. It was a hellhole, a veritable time bomb. The MP battalion was a National Guard unit. Good people, but not full-time soldiers, and the situation was hopeless—they lacked proper training and even a modicum of experience. Many were only recently reclassified as MPs to fill the gaping holes in military needs. Previously they'd been clerks, cooks, or mechanics. They were amateurs being asked to do the work of ten highly trained soldiers."

"The whole theater was undermanned and under-resourced," I noted, just as I was sure the prosecutor would also emphasize in court. "I don't think that argument will elicit much sympathy from a court martial board."

Fred's face grew thoughtful. "You two have to make them understand."

"How? What did the personnel shortages mean?" Katherine asked with her pencil poised to make more notes.

"Look, a cellblock shift typically works about three hours, then breaks for two or three hours, then maybe does one more three-hour shift. The breaks and controlled hours are crucial. You have to relieve the stress, give the guards the chance to blow off steam before they do something stupid or vindictive. Lower security prisons where the inmates are less challenging and aggressive might have longer shifts. But Al Basari was more tense than any prison I'd seen."

"In what ways?"

"Take the temperature. A typical summer day in Iraq can be well over 110 degrees. Al Basari had no air-conditioning and lousy ventilation. It was a sweatbox in there, like working in a sauna. Imagine if you will, spending twelve hours in such an intolerable environment. It smells like human waste, the prisoners are angry and noisy, insufferable conditions for the guards and inmates. And if that weren't bad enough, it was in the middle of a war zone, with occasional shelling and snipers."

"What else?"

"Shifts ran up to twelve unbroken hours, seven days a week. Try to imagine twelve straight hours of abuse from the inmates, of numbing heat and frustration and physical and mental exhaustion." He paused for dramatic effect, then added, "Now ask yourself why Elton, a lowly E-5, was put in charge of an entire block."

Katherine bit. "Why?"

"Just as the guards were overstressed, the chain of command was stretched beyond all human limits. All over the prison you had junior enlisted working way above their paygrades. That ten-to-one ratio was even worse for the officers and senior noncommissioned officers." To be sure we understood, he explained, "Look, a good prison functions on strong procedures, set routines, and absolute accountability. Those are the pillars . . . but none of that was present. The guards do their jobs because they know they're being watched, they know the captain or lieutenant or a senior sergeant will pop in at unexpected moments. At Al Basari—that wasn't happening."

"So the chain of command broke down," I suggested.

"You could put it that way." He shook his head. "But they were set up to fail. They had undertrained guards, were scandalously undermanned, and were given an impossible mission in a night-marish environment. You can't judge Al Basari by any normal standards."

"How would you judge it?" Katherine asked.

"To borrow a sports image, it was like showing up to play the New England Patriots with three high school football players."

While Katherine and I pondered that comparison, he finished with the grim summary, "It's no surprise that we got a scandal. The surprise is why there's only one—and why it's not worse."

Chapter Nine

As much as I wanted to spend more time with Fred, Katherine insisted that it was time to move on to June Johnston, one of Lydia's alleged coconspirators.

This required a drive onto West Point and, at the gate, as per standard security procedures, I hit the brakes to flash my military identification card to the young MP who sauntered over from the guardshack. Since 9-11, security at all military bases had tightened up, and at West Point, where the army's well-earned reputation for anality is sharpened to a fine point, I was surprised when the guard didn't force us out of the car for a cavity search.

He did, however, eye the Prius and ask me, "This *your* car, sir?"

"No . . . absolutely not."

"Then . . . ?" he asked, frowning.

"It's a rental and it's hers," I noted, perhaps with a defensive undertone, pointing at Miss Save-My-Planet in the passenger seat.

He observed, "Got a Ford 150 myself." He then leaned closer and inspected my passenger. "Do you have a military ID, ma'am?"

Katherine replied, "No."

I explained to the MP, "Be careful, she's a terrorist."

He placed a hand on his hip holster and examined her more closely. "That right, ma'am?"

"He's lying."

"Then . . . what is your status?"

"Taxpayer. I'm the one being terrorized."

He looked back at me. I said, "She might be carrying a bomb. You should strip search her."

A hint of a smile appeared on his face. "Will that be necessary, ma'am?"

"I'm also a lawyer." Katherine smiled back. "If you touch me I'll own West Point."

The MP told me, "Says she's a lawyer, sir."

"So what? Are you afraid of lawyers?"

"Well . . ." He examined the JAG emblem on my collar and appeared torn. "I guess, maybe . . . a bit."

"At least body search her, or you're a wimp and a bedwetter."

Katherine chimed in, "I'll own your balls."

"Well . . . that wouldn't be good. My wife sorta feels she owns 'em."

"Women," I said. "They always want what they can't have."

He smiled but it looked forced. "Should I let her in, sir?"

"Oh . . . all right."

He straightened up. "You two behave now, y'hear."

We drove on post, and I didn't want to hear the call he was making to his superiors at that moment.

My father was a proud graduate of West Point, class of '50, and he used to drag little Seanie and big brother Johnny up here for his class reunions every five years. These affairs were part happy and part somber events, as the old boys caught up on life, family, and professional accomplishments, but they always ended up in the West Point cemetery to pay respects to those classmates who'd dropped off along the way. His class had graduated straight into the inferno of the Korean War, then been burned again during the long struggle in Vietnam, so these memoriums were never short affairs or without pain.

I returned once for a legal conference and was struck then, as I was again now, by the nearly mystical beauty of the place. Location, location, location, our realtor friends say, and here the army had an amazing piece of ground. It was founded initially as a temporary fort during the revolutionary war on a strategic perch that overlooks a sharp bend in the Hudson River that leads south to New York City; batteries of artillery were planted on the heights and a thick metal chain was strung across the river. Had any British ships tried to sail past, the bend would've slowed them, then the chain would've forced them to a full stop, making them sitting ducks for the batteries of overlooking guns.

These days the only sitting ducks are the cadets waiting to graduate and then be shipped off to Iraq or Afghanistan, to long wars in uncertain and troubled lands. But it says something that most can't wait to graduate from this rock-bound highland home. As a graduate friend of mine used to tell me, the best view of West Point is in your rearview mirror.

Anyway, we drove in a near-circle around a big field and ended up back almost where we began, and parked in front of a long red brick building, which we entered. By its shape and dimensions it appeared to be a stable from the long-ago era when West Point still trained its officers to lead cavalry charges. The horses are gone now, but a lot of horseshit has stayed around.

Katherine seemed to know where she was going and led me upstairs to the second floor, where we entered a small conference room.

Private June Johnston was seated at the end of a long table as we came in. As per proper military decorum, she rose to her feet when she saw my rank.

I smiled pleasantly and told her to be seated, then Katherine and I sat, me to Private Johnston's right, Katherine to her left.

Similar to her official army photo, June was fairly cute, with short blonde hair, aqua-blue eyes, thick lips, and, well . . . nicely figured, I guess would be the appropriately professional way to phrase it. She was young, about twenty, and though I'm a senior officer and don't notice these things, even beneath her baggy ACUs I could detect that she was hauling a pair of big guns. Heavy on the makeup, and it struck me that, my rank notwithstanding, she was fairly comfortable in the presence of males, or perhaps confident would be a better word.

She smiled at me and offered Katherine a nod that appeared to be afterthought. To put her at ease, I asked a few simple warm-up questions.

"Where are you from?"

"New York City. Queens."

"How much time do you have in?"

"Two years. Joined after high school. Right after."

"Why?"

"Why what?" she asked. "You mean, why'd I join?"

I nodded.

She looked, I thought, like she was wondering that herself. She then said, "Personal reasons."

"Would you care to share them?"

"It wasn't . . . well, I didn't come from a real good home, you might say." She added, after a prolonged pause, "My old man, he kept putting his hands on me . . . and . . . seemed like a good time to get the hell outta there."

"Your father was abusing you?" Then, realizing a more exact verb might help, I specified, "Did he molest you?"

"Never got that far." She shook her head. "But only cuz he was fat and outta shape, and I locked the bedroom door and was careful when I went to the bathroom."

Well, there are many reasons to join the army and I suppose escaping an incestuous predator was as good as any and probably better than most. But I had heard as much as I wanted to know on that disturbing topic. "And you're a personnel clerk?"

She smiled at me and nodded. "Same as Lydia and Andrea, sir. 71 Zulu. We were assigned to the same personnel section."

It was occurring to me that June Johnston did not need to be put at ease in the presence of any male, regardless of the rank on his collar.

She was brighter than Lydia, certainly more self-assured and affable, and she also was more self-contained, looked me in the eye, and had better diction and grammar, though perhaps this wasn't much of an accomplishment. The Queens accent came fast and thick, slaughtering vowels and consonants alike. I recalled a few pieces of strategic information from her personnel file: single, Catholic, and quite attractive.

I was a little wary of diving straight into the issue of her role in the lusty activities in the cellblock, and Katherine, I think, sensed this, because she said to June, "Can you tell us your connections to the other accused?"

"Yeah, sure. Like I said, Andrea and Lydia were in my section. We were friends, I guess," she noted, which was an interesting way to put it. "Week or two after we got there, Lydia introduced me to Danny and Mike. She knew them from before the deployment. I guess that's how it all got started."

"How what got started?" Katherine asked.

"Well . . . we all started hanging out. Danny and Mike, they worked awful hours. Their job sucked. So the three of us, I guess we sort of, y'know, liked to get hooked up."

I was aware that among her generation the term "hooked up" has interesting and variable connotations. It can mean anything from casual making out without any romantic intentions, to down and dirty sex, also without any attachments—or guilt—afterward.

I'm only eighteen years older than June Johnston, but her generation and mine have a different take on these things. I'm in that unfortunate generational bracket that missed both the sexual revolution of the sixties and the totally liberated, uninhibited behavior of her generation. In short, I had to work hard to get into the ladies' panties, using all my charms, which meant I had to work damned hard. I didn't have to send flowers or chocolate the next morning, but it was regarded as good manners to at least stick around for breakfast, and good form to remember the girl's name.

June's generation seemed to have a more interesting notion of sex as a forgettable gratification. I mean, it used to be only guys who dreamed of sex without any lingering complications, and women who thought otherwise. I had to get used to how these people think.

But I didn't want to get into that yet, and instead asked, "What did you think about Lydia?"

"Well . . . she's different, y'know."

"I don't know. Please explain it."

"She's from the south, for one thing. Country girl, y'know. Talks a little slower. Not like where I'm from . . . New York."

"And she *thinks* a little slower?"

"You said it, sir. She can be a little slow on the uptick." She paused and giggled. "Okay, she's slightly dumb."

Katherine leaned closer to June. "Whose idea was it to employ sex as a weapon on the inmates?"

It was nicely put, avoiding more severe phrases like torture, or live porn acts, or even something as sharp-edged as S&M. But of course June knew exactly what she meant, and you could see by her face that we'd now gotten to the yucky stuff. Unlike Lydia, she appeared to possess a stronger moral paintbrush, or at least a sense of decorum, because she blushed slightly, stiffened a little, and looked away. After a long pause, she said, "Hell if I know."

"Come now," Katherine prodded, "It had to be somebody's idea. Think back to the first time it happened. Who initiated the action?"

June appeared deep in thought. And also, totally clueless.

To jog her memory, I recounted to June, "According to Lydia, the first time was your idea. A prisoner was brought back from interrogation, you removed your blouse, started dancing, and before you knew it, your clothes were lying on the floor, and Lydia was measuring his manhood."

"Lydia said it like that?"

"Her words might not have been quite as delicate, but yes."

"Oh . . . gawd, but that's not at all the way it happened."

"All right. Then what did happen?"

"This guy was brought back in by Danny, and he—I mean, Danny—he looked pretty frazzled. And Lydia, she leaned over to me and said"—she paused and did a dead-on impersonation of Lydia's hickish diction and elongated intonations—'Hey, you know what? This Hadji ain't seen no tits and ass in a blue moon. See if you could, maybe, rattle him a bit.'"

"Didn't that suggestion make you uncomfortable?"

"Maybe . . . a little." She appeared to realize that in present company this was an inappropriate response, so she quickly modified her answer to, "Okay, at first, yeah. But then . . . then I thought, hell, what's the big deal? You know?"

Katherine fixed her with a hard stare. "I don't know. "

"Just, well, I guess girls aren't as uptight about this stuff as most guys. So I gave 'em a little flash . . . just a little peek, then a little bit more, and . . . I mean, what's the big deal?"

"Why didn't Lydia do it herself?" Katherine inquired.

"I don't know. Maybe Lydia thought I'd be better at it."

I asked, "What would give her that impression?"

"Sometimes at night, in our tents outside, we'd put some music on, and we'd dance . . . just girl stuff, y'know? Lydia, she had this real jerky way of moving. It was, like, well . . . funny-lookin'."

"How was it funny-looking?"

"I guess cuz she's a country-girl. Probably grew up square-dancing or some such crap. And it was all, like, disconnected, kind've retarded looking. Y'know, like, no sense of rhythm. I tried to teach her some moves, but she just didn't get it. Hopeless."

I suggested, "So she thought you were more of a turn-on?"

"I guess you could put it like that."

Katherine asked, "Would there be another way to put it?"

June did not reply to that antagonistic query for a while. When she finally answered, she looked at me. "Hey, I don't want to sound full of myself or anything, but the prisoners always stared at me a lot."

"Because you're blonde and you're hot?"

Still looking at me, her eyes seemed to change. She brushed a lock of hair off her forehead, her eyebrows arched up, she lowered her chin and pursed her lips together. It was an alluring look, a come-on, a way of asking, do you think you're man enough to handle me?

And this was a young lady who joined the National Guard to escape her father's lecherous groping. I didn't know if this sort of seductive behavior was a response to her father's illicit intentions, or the cause of it, but it struck me that June Johnston was hardly an innocent waif.

She eventually asked me, "What do you think, Colonel?"

Katherine evidently preferred not to hear my answer to this question and quickly said to June, "So your behavior and that of

Lydia and Andrea evolved into role-playing. You and Andrea were the temptresses, and Lydia became the humiliator."

This theory coming from Katherine's lips was fairly insightful. The behavior captured in those pictures did suggest a weird evolutionary process based on their respective kinkiness rankings: June and Andrea being the comely flirts, the seductresses, and physically the hottest, and then, Lydia—poor, awkward, plain, squatty little Lydia—left to diddle with the erections June or Andrea induced. I don't believe this was an angle Darwin considered. But I'm sure it's one he would've found interesting.

The photo of Lydia peeing on the prisoner's face, however, was something else altogether, both literally and metaphysically—but even there, Lydia wasn't a femme fatale; she was a clown, a vulgar show-off, straining perhaps to be something she wasn't, or maybe visually confessing to something she knew she would never be. I made a quick mental note to study those pictures more closely to see how they confirmed or denied Katherine's observation.

June did not look pleased with this assessment, but she replied, "If you wanta put it like that . . . then okay."

Katherine closed her notebook and abruptly announced, "I think we're finished with this session. We may want to speak with you again."

June produced a shrug, and said, with no apparent enthusiasm, "Not like I've got better things to do."

We stood, but June remained seated. Evidently, I had put her too much at ease. I said, "Since you're going to be a witness, we'll have to go through everything. Think about what happened, and we'll speak again."

We left and went outside. In the car, Katherine turned to me and said, in a tone that was clearly disapproving, "I don't think you handled that very well."

"Nonsense. She was eating out of my hand."

"Look, I know you're uncomfortable speaking about intimate matters with attractive females and—"

"Wait a minute, I—"

"No, hear me out, Sean. To get to the bottom of this case, you have to overcome your Victorian prudishness. Sex is at the heart of this case. You should've seen your face when you asked those questions, like you were touching a hot stove. I know men find it easier to ask a plain-looking girl like Lydia these kinds of questions than a somewhat attractive woman like—"

"Give it a break, Katherine. And for the record, she is hot," I said to piss her off even more.

"Oh, for God's sake, she's young enough to be your daughter."

She was trying to goad me, but I knew how to respond. "How old is Nelson Arnold, your billionaire buddy? Does money make men look younger?"

"Watch it, Sean. You're way out of line."

So we seemed to be at a draw. Practice makes perfect, and after all these years of provoking each other, we were getting pretty good at it. Katherine is not as sarcastic as I am; Katherine, however, has excellent aim.

But I thought I knew what lay behind Katherine's outburst and it surprised me—jealousy. As I said before, Katherine is not an emotional person, at least not on the outside, and it can be hard to tell what she is thinking, and even harder to understand what she is feeling.

But it was nice to see that she had enough feelings for me to promote that mood.

I gave her, and myself, a moment to cool down, then asked, "So what did you think?"

"About what? About her?"

"I believe you already vented your feelings about me."

"Okay. I think we'll have a big problem with her on the stand."

"Because of their differing memories about how these activities were initiated?"

"Partly, yes. Mainly, because I know her type."

"I'll bite. What type is June?"

Katherine turned and faced me. "Look Sean, sex is more complicated for women than it is for men."

"I believe I've heard that somewhere. Should I take notes this time?"

"Because it's true. For some women, it's about submission. For some, it's the opposite, about dominance. It's like yin and yang, and sometimes it's a mixture of the two, at war with each other."

"Spare me the lecture, Katherine. Men have two brains. Believe me, that can get fairly crowded."

"No, men have a dominant brain; the other one, the one that's supposed to think and reason, short circuits the moment the unthinking one engages. Women are always thinking, before, during, and after."

"Is this the voice of personal experience?"

She made the wise choice to ignore me. I can be annoying. "Since you asked, June is the barracuda type. I mean that in every sense of the word. She seduces to show the man she can have him anytime she wants. It might have to do with her memories of her father, some suppressed compulsion to reverse the roles between the hunter and the hunted . . . the predator and the prey, if you will. But also, it's a display of superiority to the women around her, a way of saying 'I can have any man I want, including yours.'"

Women have a different take on these things. I mean, men have a fairly impulsive view of sex that pretty much begins and ends with the climax. For women, the orgasm can be faked, and real or not, is only the middle of the story. I don't know which is right or wrong, I only know it keeps things interesting. Also dangerous.

I put the car in reverse and backed out of the parking space. I told Katherine, "I'd like to see the remainder of the pictures when we get back."

"I should warn you, it's best not to look at them on a full stomach."

"Really, Katherine. I believe I've seen the worst that people can do to one another."

"That was only war," she replied. "These pictures are worse."

"I'll hold my nose when I look."

"Okay, tough guy, you'll get them after dinner. There are several hundred to wade through." She added, after a moment, "Incidentally, Nelson Arnold is driving up from the city. He'd like you to join us for dinner. He wants to meet you."

"Doesn't he have a helicopter like every other self-respecting billionaire?"

"You're prejudging him, Sean. Don't."

In fact, I had looked him up on the Internet that morning. Mr. Nelson Arnold seemed to be a classic case of poor kid makes good—or rich, which in America might not be that different—having returned from Vietnam, used the GI bill to attend Rutgers, done a few years in investment banking to learn the trade, then gone into business for himself. He was not listed in the Forbes Top 100, but had he not developed the questionable habit of throwing a billion dollars a year, every year, into an assortment of liberal charities and causes, he'd be somewhere up there. Still, his wealth was pegged somewhere between two to three billion dollars, which, for a guy scraping by on army pay, is what I would call a fairly impressive margin of error.

Though he attended plenty of charity balls and la-di-da soirees in the Hamptons and Palm Beach and Davos, unlike most of his species of hyper-rich, he apparently had an aversion to being photographed or to seeing his name bandied about in the social columns.

The source of his monstrous wealth was a hedge fund named The Old Warrior's Fund, which was an interesting title. He was a widower—his first wife had died ten years ago—and according to several columns that deal in this kind of esoteric trash, he now led a fairly active social life, including a scattering of Hollywood lovelies, a few female politicians, and assorted other prominent ladies who scratched his fancy.

Not for nothing, I have noticed that the ladies are strongly attracted to men who own yachts. They must have seafaring in their DNA.

I asked Katherine, "Who's paying for dinner?"

"Dutch treat."

"Dutch . . . What?"

"It's part of my bargain with Nelson. He pays for the legal services, but that's where it stops."

"Am I bound by this agreement?"

"That's up to you."

"Tell him I like Béarnaise sauce on my filet mignon."

Chapter Ten

Katherine was right, Nelson Arnold was not what I expected but even worse than I feared.

He arrived, for one thing, driving his own car—not a sumptuous Rolls Royce or even a sleek Lamborghini, but a crap green Ford Taurus station wagon, about five years old, dinged and dented. It didn't even have leather.

Nor, as I had expected he would, did he arrive attired in an Italian-made, hand-sewn suit with matching Guccis, or even Brooks Brothers high-end leisure wear, but instead wore distressed blue jeans, a faded flannel shirt, and well-scuffed hiking boots, à la lumberjack chic. If you're interested, I *dress*; the rich are *attired*.

I was aware that he had to be in his very late fifties or early sixties, though he looked roughly my own age with blondish-brown hair, lightly dusted with gray, sharp blue eyes, was very fit, and had enough wrinkles to make his face interesting, without appearing ancient or even worn.

The rich, of course, can afford to be beautiful and preserve their youth, though I had the sense that, with Nelson Arnold, it was less nurture, more nature.

He bounded out of the car, brushed Katherine's cheek, and stuck his hand out to me. "A pleasure, a real one," he said, even managing to make it sound sincere. "Do you prefer Colonel or can I call you Sean?"

I took his hand. "Can I call you Nelson?"

"Actually, my friends call me Nel."

"Right. Can I call you Nelson?"

He smiled, then sort of nodded as if to say, this is going to be a long evening. Indeed it is, Nelson, the longest of your life. He replied, "Call me whatever you like."

Oh, I will, Nelson, I definitely will. We got into his car, Katherine in the front passenger seat, yours truly in the backseat, and Nelson, or Nel, if you prefer, behind the wheel.

I studied him studying me in the rearview mirror. Eventually, he remarked, "You remind me of him."

I took the bait. "Who?"

"Your father. I definitely see a strong resemblance."

"I wasn't aware you were friends."

"We weren't, exactly. I served under him. '69 through '70, in Nam. He was my brigade commander. That was your father, right?"

Our eyes met in the rearview mirror.

"Your old man was a real hellion. Everything by the book, everybody had to dig proper foxholes every night, and he always dropped in unexpectedly. Rumor was he never slept." He chuckled. "Never saw a better ass-chewer."

"I helped him perfect that part."

He ignored that. "I can't say I liked your father, but I certainly respected him. I was only a buck sergeant and I hated digging those damned holes, but it saved my ass two or three times." He then asked, "How is he?"

"Great. He runs a car dealership down south." Apropos of Nelson's fond remembrances, I informed him, "High turnover among his sales people. They're tired of digging holes."

He laughed. It seemed we were into reminiscences, and he remarked, "I remember the night he got wounded. It was pitch dark, cold, been raining heavily for days, a real lousy night for an operation. We were doing a sweep in the Highlands, and he got shot with a . . . a . . . ?"

"A crossbow."

"That's right." He smiled. "A crossbow."

He laughed again and I joined him. Pop had just climbed out of his helicopter, he dropped his map, bent down to pick it up, and some Vietcong with a terrific sense of irony landed one where the sun doesn't shine. To this day, whenever asked what he thought of Vietnam, he answers, fairly bluntly, "Aw, it was a big pain in the ass."

Nelson wheeled the car into a parking lot and lo-and-behold, it was the McDonald's just outside the gate of West Point. He pointed at the arch. "I love these places. I put a few hundred million in their stock back in the late seventies. Haven't sold a share yet. Now worth about three billion. I eat here whenever I get a chance. Anybody mind?"

"I was really looking forward to stale roadkill," I informed him.

Predictably, Miss Preserve the Body and Soul reminded him, "You know I like to eat healthier, Nel."

He parked, and got out of the car. Like most billionaires, he really didn't care what we liked.

We entered the McDonald's and stood in line for a few minutes: Katherine ordered green stuff; Sean, a greasy Big Mac; and Nelson two Quarter Pounders with cheese, a large chocolate shake, a large bag of fries, and then, he dropped five million on the counter and bought the place. Just kidding.

We settled around a small table in the back and dug in. After a moment spent studying my Big Mac, Nelson asked Katherine, "How's the case look?"

"It's too early to tell. We're still in the exploratory stage."

"So you've formed no strong views yet?"

"That I'd hang my hat on . . . ? No. The five accused are all singing pretty much the same tune, with a few minor variations."

Nelson considered that assessment. "So you think they corroborated?"

"Yes, they definitely did," Katherine replied, picking through her salad, trying to find something that wouldn't induce an immediate cardiac coma. "When you read the Article 32 results, it's obvious. Of course, it won't last."

"Why not?"

"The usual problem with conspiracies. They differ in the small details. It hasn't been a problem so far . . . but it will be in court when they're answering under oath for the first time, and five different prosecutors begin digging deeper and picking them apart."

"That how you'd do it?" he asked. He had already started on his second burger. Also, the fries were gone, and the shake was already making that obnoxious slurping sound. What would Miss Manners advise about such a situation? Eat faster so he wouldn't feel like the only glutton at the table, or let him win the eating contest?

"That's exactly what I'd do, Nel," Katherine replied. "Any experienced prosecutor will see the opportunity and exploit it."

"And what's the second part?" The second burger was almost gone and he was eying what was left of my Big Mac.

Katherine advised him, "Somebody's likely to be hung with a murder or manslaughter charge, and the rest will face coconspirator charges. In a week or so, five different defense teams are going to start pressuring their clients to cop a deal and plead out. The closer we get to a court date, the more our clients are going to feel the heat."

"You think one of them will break ranks?"

"It could be the difference between ten years and life. Yes, all of them are going to contemplate their options."

"So what do we do about that?"

"That's not clear. We have a lot more work to do before that stage. For instance, we need to know exactly how vulnerable Lydia is. Especially relative to the others."

It was interesting that Katherine chose the term "vulnerable" instead of "guilty," which was the real issue. Nelson chewed the last of his fries, then looked at me, "That what you think, too, Sean?"

"I think what I think is none of your business, Nelson."

His expression didn't change. "Why isn't it?"

"Because Katherine and I don't work for you. We work on behalf of the accused, and while you might have more money than Midas and you might pay Katherine's bills, my paycheck is signed by my Uncle Sam. Besides, I'm not in habit of disclosing sensitive case information with an outsider." I added, "Lawyer's oath."

His eyes sort of narrowed. "Didn't Katherine tell you?"

"Tell me what?"

"I also have a law degree. NYU Law, and I'm a member of the New York bar." He paused before he dropped the big news. "I'm also listed as a cocounsel."

I looked at Katherine who, for some reason, had failed to mention this small yet not insignificant detail and now found something more interesting to look at on the other side of the room. I said to Nelson, "No . . . Katherine never brought that up."

"So now you know."

"Yes, now I know."

"Is this going to be a problem for you?"

"Did you register with the military's legal affairs office to represent the accused?"

"The moment Katherine got Lydia's permission to represent her, yes."

"Have you ever participated in a trial?"

"I got the law degree more or less on a lark. Figured it would be helpful in business." He hesitated then added, "It has been."

"Please answer the question."

"No. I've never represented a client in court."

"Do you have any experience in criminal matters?"

"Nope. Just corporate law. But every lawyer has to start somewhere."

"Then no, I have no problem at all."

He may have picked up the small note of sarcasm that may have crept into my tone and said, "Relax, Sean. I don't expect to be making any courtroom arguments. I'll leave that to the pros, you and Katherine. I'm not in this for the publicity, nor do I have any pretensions about being Clarence Darrow or Alan Dershowitz."

"Then why are you in it?"

"It's a cause I believe in."

I looked at Katherine, who did not look back; she now was studying the Golden Arch outside the window as if it held the key to the mystery of life. It struck me that she had set up this little tête-à-tête, and was enjoying every second of it. Have I mentioned how manipulative she can be?

I looked at Nelson Arnold. "I wasn't aware it was a cause."

"I suppose I owe you an explanation." He looked back at me and explained, "I was a lower enlisted soldier in 'Nam. I was a volunteer, not a draftee, and I did two tours there, having volunteered for the second one after I served under your dad. He was an inspiring commander. I regarded it as my patriotic duty."

"Good for you, Nelson. Your government thanks you, your fellow citizens thank you, and I thank you. You earned the right to get filthy rich."

"You know, Sean, I believe I did." He leaned forward and added, "I have two Purple Hearts and a Silver Star, and I spent three months in a VA hospital recovering from the Silver Star and second Purple Heart. Now I also believe I have blood rights as a citizen to prevent history from repeating itself, the ugly history I lived through."

"Which part of that history bothered you?"

"A lot of it. The lies, the mismanagement in Washington, the bankrupt strategy. I wasn't aware of it while I was lying in foxholes praying I didn't get my ass shot off. But later, I understood I'd been used and abused. Me and about ten million other guys, some living, some dead."

"And Lydia Eddelston is to be your expurgation?"

"That's not exactly the way I think of it."

"Have you at least given some thought to the fact that she might be guilty? Inconvenient, I know, but the facts, as we currently know them, certainly support that presumption."

"Guilt and innocence might be interchangeable concepts in this case."

"Why her and why now?"

"Why not her, and can you name a better time than now?"

"You tell me, Nelson. What part of your past does she fit into?"

He paused to think about this a moment, as did I. Vietnam produced more brooding regrets than any other war fought in our long, bloody national history; regrets by politicians, regrets by the public, and more deeply than others, regrets by those sent into the jungles to battle determined foes, and experience firsthand the horrors of a war in a faraway alien land that we failed to win.

My own father returned with a ruined colon, a king-size whoopee cushion, and a grudging determination to get on with his life. He took his retirement with 80 percent disability, put the war behind him, and began pushing used cars, hardly the career I'm sure he dreamt of when he strode the majestic plains of West Point.

He never spoke of the war—except quite literally, as a big pain in the ass—and addressed its memories with the tempered stoicism of a career soldier. When he and his military buddies got together they told war stories that normally were quite funny, and often weird, but whatever angst or lingering nightmares they held stayed hidden, smothered somewhere beneath the laughter and old boy bonhomie.

Nelson Arnold, apparently, was from that other school of survivors; his war ended over thirty years before, and in some weird way, he was still fighting it.

Nelson completed his reverie, saying, "Lydia came to me by chance and circumstance when her lawyer died. It didn't have to be her but she's ideal."

"Ideal for what?"

"Oh, for Christ's sake, Sean. She's a young and dumb country girl, at the bottom of the military foodchain, and now she's facing court martial for a scandal brought on by others."

Rather than debate these points, I asked Nelson a more pointed question. "Does she know you view her as a totem, a symbol? She's facing life in prison, Nelson. I think she has a right to know one, and possibly two, of her lawyers have their own agenda."

If this accusation troubled him, he didn't show it. "To be truthful, I don't know what she understands. I have explained my interest in her case to her, directly. She had no complaints or hesitation."

What he didn't say, what he didn't need to say, was that Lydia had neither the brains nor the common sense to understand this Faustian bargain. I doubted Lydia could identify Vietnam on a map, would probably be surprised to learn we had fought a war there, and she certainly had no concept of the demons and ghosts haunting

Nelson's brain. She was the classic pawn, limited to one slow move, easily outfoxed, no doubt dazzled by the word "billionaire."

But Katherine considered this an appropriate moment to chime in and said, "Nel's motives aren't at issue here, Sean."

"They are with me."

"The only issue is the quality of the defense. Nel has committed to funding whatever we need to defend Lydia. The best expert witnesses, the full costs of lawyer expenses, any lab or research needs that would help the case. It's a remarkable act of generosity."

"Did Nelson agree to keep his personal bias and quest out of it?"

Nelson did not enjoy being talked about in the third person and said, "Nelson can speak for himself."

"Then tell Nelson to answer the question."

"I have no intention of polluting the best defense possible."

"That's not what I asked."

"That's as good an answer as you're going to get."

The rest of the meal, brief as it was, passed pleasantly enough except for the one guy who sat pissed off, staring at the ugly walls, totally disengaged from the conversation.

Nelson's vague assurance notwithstanding, it was now clear in my mind that he, and Katherine, intended to use this trial to score points against the administration and the army. Lydia was the public face of the scandal and her court martial would become a media spectacle. In other words it would the perfect showcase for putting the conduct of the war on the docket.

As much as I cared for Katherine and respected her passion and intelligence, I did not always care for her courtroom tactics and I strongly disapproved of her and Nelson using Lydia as an opportunity. A good criminal lawyer plays to only one audience, the jury, and any distraction from that can be harmful to the one person you're supposed to be concerned with—your client.

I watched the interplay between Katherine and Nelson and had the impression of more going on here than I understood. Also, I don't think Nelson enjoyed being talked to in this manner by a lowly army lawyer. Billionaires tend to be treated with inflated esteem, if not abject obsequiousness, for the plain and simple reason that they have all the toys. But also, I think, people tend to think—maybe even *believe*—that the accumulation of vast wealth equates to wisdom, just as army people conflate general's stars with brilliance and sound leadership. Both are flawed assumptions. A general's stars might as easily result from being Uncle Sam's nephew, or from rare political instincts—e.g., a gift for sucking up. And a billion dollars in the bank often only means the owner is just greedier and more ruthless. Or luckier.

Nelson dropped me off back at the house and he and Katherine sped off to "take in the sights," a euphemism for sneaking off, alone, to talk about my favorite subject—me.

Katherine had called ahead and Imelda met me at the door with an ambiguous expression and an expandable folder crammed with pictures that were anything but ambiguous.

It was my first chance to have a word with Imelda, alone, so I asked her, "How long have you been working with Katherine?"

"Why you askin'?"

"Small talk. Old friends catching up."

"Uh-huh. Answer is, a while."

"What do you think about this case?"

"A clusterfuck." She chewed on her tongue a moment, shuffled her feet, then modified that perspective. "A big clusterfuck."

I nodded. The appellation "clusterfuck" is an old army aphorism that roughly translates to . . . well, who needs an explanation? But discipline is to the army what oxygen is to the body, and when discipline flags, the army becomes rabble, boys being boys—and in this case, I suppose, girls being girls—but not confined to some dark o-club basement.

I thanked Imelda for providing me with a proper orientation, grabbed the folder, fixed a cup of coffee, and went to my bedroom for a firsthand look at the clusterfuck.

Somebody had made the decision to organize the photographs by date and time—Imelda, with her typical Prussian-like efficiency, I suspected—and it was quite helpful. I started at the beginning, and the activities were disturbing, but all in all, not really that bad: June or Andrea dancing or disrobing, or taunting the inmates with sexual gestures, and our client, Lydia, mostly assisting in the inmate degradation. But as time wore on, the activities grew more lurid, more sexually provocative, and well, for want of a kinder term . . . more sexually bizarre.

By night ten of fun and games, it was less fun, more games, if that term could be applied. Many of the inmates now wore makeshift costumes, ranging from loincloths to short skirts, and many wore makeup heavily applied, à la the Roman skits of ancient yore. The girls became more physically and sexually brazen and Lydia had become a more direct participant, frequently joining with June or Andrea in disrobing and playing the tart. There was a lot of fondling and people putting hands where they shouldn't be.

Another observation: In the earliest photos, these activities were focused on one inmate, one poor soul who bore the brunt of their collective tormenting. Night by night, the number of inmates grew and, by the end, it became seven or eight prisoners, small mobs of men with unhappy, fearful expressions.

With the final three nights left to view, I took a break and mulled this over. Despite the altruistic protestations of all five of the accused, judging by the prisoners' expressions and the gleeful expressions of their tormentors, the purpose and scope of these nightly assaults had grown beyond any attempt to "soften-up" the prisoners for interrogation, if indeed that had ever been a motive, which I doubted. They now were engaging in all-out orgies. These were carnal fantasies acted out by five young Americans with no restraints and no other purpose than to play out their own weird desires, fixations, and obsessions.

A third observation: It was becoming harder and harder for the five participants to get off; not in any physical sense, though certainly that was also possible, but in the more subliminal, psychosexual department. Like a timid married couple who start with the missionary position, then decide a little variety might be nice, then progress from position to position, a journey through all 236 pages of the Kama Sutra, until pretty soon the whips and chains come out, and then they are making S&M porn flicks and posting them on the Internet. And in line with that thought, for the opening nights at Al Basiri there were only a few pictures, but as the sessions wore on, the production increased to as many as thirty photos for one particularly ribald evening.

The question was why? As in why, as their behavior sank to more perverse levels, did the desire grow to record it? Certainly, these people did not have their heads screwed on right.

Danny Elton and Mike Tiller were always behind the camera, or cameras. One or the other was included in some shots, but never both at once. Several times I noted photos of the girls engaged in some particular activity, but with shots of the same activity taken from different angles, so definitely there were two cameras, with two photographers, at work.

Indeed, I was not looking forward to the final three nights for, as I mentioned, the level of perversity had already reached nauseating heights. Nonetheless, the worst time to see these images for the first time would be gaping, with my mouth open, in the presence of a court martial board, so I continued.

The ladies were now bringing in toys and instruments, and forcing the inmates to actively engage in increasingly disgusting behavior, from oral sex, to humping one another, to jamming playthings into various orifices. Some of the participants had bloody noses, bruises, and contusions, evidence that when persuasion and verbal coercion failed, brute force replaced them. The aforementioned shot of Lydia peeing on a man's face occurred with two nights left, which tells you something about what followed.

It was clear that the charade had now come full circle, from the girls as performers to the inmates as the main show. Less clear was what Lydia was doing during these final two nights in the chamber of horrors. She was not visible in any of the pictures. Andrea and June appeared sporadically—pointing out various activities, screaming in inmate's ears, smiling, laughing, mugging it up—but Lydia was nowhere in sight. Hopefully this meant she was not present, though I suspected otherwise.

I stuffed the last picture into the expandable file, then I leaned back to get a breath. The total ran to 406 photographs—406 moments in time from which you could try to extrapolate what happened in between.

A picture is a snapshot, absent dialogue or any enlightening script, but here we had an entire collage of arresting imagery that told a story, if only it could be interpreted. But if a picture is worth a thousand words, then 406 pictures is sensory overload, countless small mysteries that compound and complicate a giant mystery.

I placed the folder on my bedside table, turned off the lamp, and mentally addressed this mystery. Nothing in the personal or professional backgrounds of Andrea Myers, June Johnston, or Lydia Eddelston indicated a proclivity toward such aberrantly appalling behavior. A country girl, a city girl, and a girl from the suburbs of Cincinnati—culturally, socially, and physically, as different as three young ladies could be.

But in a long career practicing criminal law, I had learned this: what you see usually is only the shadow of the truth. And in this case there were too many images and too many crimes—torture, physical assault, rape, various violations of the Geneva Convention—and murder.

I lay down, counted sheep, and tried to wipe the 406 images from my mind before I floated off to sleep.

I don't think I succeeded, because when I awoke the next morning, the sheep were all sweaty and tired.

Chapter Eleven

I'm not a breakfast person and Imelda knows this, yet she had assembled a large feast of omelets and cheesy fried potatoes and greasy grits, southern style. I made a quick mental note to call my cardiologist just looking at it. "You look like crap," she said as I came downstairs to the kitchen.

"Thank you."

"Just sayin'." She played with something on the stove a moment. I could hear the sounds of Katherine banging around upstairs, dressing, primping, and whatever else women do in the mornings. Imelda turned around and asked me, "What'd you think about them pictures?"

"I think our clients are toast if they get entered into evidence."

This was the correct legal response, however that's not what Imelda meant. I knew that, and she acted as if I annoyed her. "I mean, why do you think them little girls acted like that?"

I answered truthfully, "I have no idea." I then threw out a few of the theories that Katherine and Nelson seemed to believe in, ending with the ever-popular, "Because they were ordered to? Because they caved into high level pressure to force the prisoners to talk?"

"Hmmpf. Bullshit."

"Right." I crossed my arms and leaned against the breakfast table. "Can you elaborate on that thought?"

I should mention here that Imelda spent nearly thirty years as an enlisted female before she traded her spurs for a life. She is not particularly attractive, she is slightly heavy, spare with the makeup, probably has never been to a professional hairdresser, and her taste in civilian attire, as with many soldiers spoiled by a lifetime of uniforms, was somewhat questionable. For example, at that moment, she wore baggy blue sweatpants with a shapeless army sweatshirt, white socks with sandals, and her hair was shorn close enough to her scalp that she could be mistaken for a frumpy male with two misshapen lumps glued to her chest.

But the army has never been fully comfortable with women in its ranks, and the regulations concerning female appearance, attire, and adornments—regarding such items as earrings, makeup, proper hair length and style, and the wear of uniform skirts—reflect the ambiguity of a claustrophobic institution with a strong masculine ethos, mutating uncertainly to adapt to a new germ. During my seventeen years in service, the regulations regarding female appearance have changed so many times they should be written with quick-drying ink. And like many female lifers, Imelda eventually decided that her appearance and her attire were irrelevant, and she adapted to the masculine mores that became her life.

But she is still a woman, with all that implies—one who experienced the same frustrations, burdens, and mixed expectations as Lydia, June, and Andrea. So I was anticipating some kernel of insight, some enlightening clue about female drives and perspectives that would break the entire mystery wide open.

After banging around a few pots and pans in the sink, she said, "What happened in them pictures was sick."

"I certainly understand that. But why did the girls engage in such obscene behavior?"

"Dumb question. Girls ain't *that* different from boys."

"Meaning what?"

"You best get to know them girls better. Especially your client."

She turned back around and began washing something in the sink. In her uniquely polite way, this session was obviously over.

And at that moment, Katherine appeared, dressed—uncharacteristically—in a short skirt, black pumps, and a dark, low-cut blouse. She was also going heavy in the blush and lipstick department, and whatever gook girls put on their eyes these days. It was the sexiest I had ever seen her look—I mean, she looked *really* sexy—and my mouth hung open, but she was staring at her watch and said, "We've got an eight o'clock with the prison commandant. Come on, we have to hurry."

At the gate to West Point, the same diligent young MP was on duty, and he peeked in at Katherine, apparently seeing past her attractive camouflage and politely observed, "You look mighty nice for a terrorist today, ma'am."

Katherine smiled back just as politely and announced, "Today I'm a hostage."

"Uh-huh . . . well, you look good for one of them, too."

"I'm not joking. This man kidnapped me."

He looked at me and asked, "That right, sir?"

"She's lying."

He looked at her. "What about that, ma'am?"

"Would I be with him otherwise?"

"Well . . ." He bent forward and examined me more closely. "You know, she's gotta point, sir."

"She got me shot," I informed him, truthfully. "In Korea."

"Ah . . . well . . . that sounds pretty serious."

"In the stomach," I clarified. "It really hurt."

"Okay . . . uh . . . she ever apologize for that?"

"She thanked the man who shot me."

His face formed a frown and his eyes turned to Katherine. "I did not," she insisted, very emphatically. "He's mistaking envy for gratitude." He waved us through and saluted me, though I don't think he meant it.

I said to Katherine, "Your sense of humor is improving."

"It's being with you, Sean."

"Thank you."

"It wasn't a compliment."

"Thank you."

"Did you hear me?"

"Thank you." This time, she heard *me*.

So we drove in silence to the cadet area, where I found a place to park on the roof of the academic building.

We walked from there along a sidewalk and quickly became engulfed in a sea of gray-clad cadets rushing to change classes. I couldn't get over how young, how bright-eyed, and how sharp they looked. You could almost believe that West Point was a normal college campus until you see the cadets, who look like the last preserved specimens from some earlier, prehistoric era, clean-cut, fit, earnest, almost startlingly uniform in both dress and appearance.

Like much of the rest of the army, it's all an illusion, of course. The boys and girls at West Point are no different than, no better and certainly no worse, than thousands of other students at campuses spread across the country; they share the same youthful lusts, the same confused ambitions, the same impatience to graduate and get on with their lives. But they have chosen to do something entirely different afterward, which is what sets them apart from the rest of their generation.

Anyway, as per regulations, every cadet felt the need to salute me; saluting back quickly became tedious, then tiresome. The salute is a quaint custom unique to the military, the army's equivalent of a secret society handshake, or the pat on the ass that football players use. It is both a gesture and a symbol, one that dates back a thousand years to an age when warriors were called knights, a title that signified rarified qualities of virtue and courage and nobility. They wore armor and helmets then, and they would reach up with one hand to tip the metal visor open so they could identify one another's faces as they passed. It would always be the right hand, the sword hand, suggesting that the passing warrior's intentions were nonthreatening and peaceful.

The army, being the army, of course, turned this good-mannered gesture into a requirement—a regulation—and, by compelling the lesser ranks to always initiate the exchange, a sign of subservience. But nobody seems to mind very much, until, like me, you are caught in a hailstorm of saluting cadets.

We were passing now through a bunch of large, gray stone buildings and ended up in an office complex where the academy administrators were housed. With all the lawyers, accused, and witnesses running around, the academy was having to shuffle all available spaces to handle the conferences.

The building and its interior were right out of a nineteenth-century gothic novel—large, arched windows, a forest of aged mahogany, high ceilings, and quaint, ancient lighting—as was the lady who met us by the entrance and escorted us up a long stairway and down several hallways. She was quite slender, with a severe, puckered face, a beehive hairdo, and . . . well, who cares?

A pudgy, bespectacled lieutenant colonel with thinned gray and blond hair on his head, Eggers on his nametag, crossed MP pistols on his collar, and a world of anxiety on his face awaited us at the end of a shiny, long conference table. I had briefly perused his personnel record the night before and recalled that his first name was Paul, he had been the commandant at Al Basari, was a West Pointer from the class of '82, who had resigned from the active army after five years of service, remained with the National Guard, and now, was facing a career, a reputation, and possibly, a life, in the toilet.

Katherine and I quickly introduced ourselves and settled into the seats directly in front of him. We engaged in inconsequential chatter for a few minutes. Paul Eggers was listed as a witness for the prosecution for all five court martials, and from his hunched posture and guarded tone, it seemed evident he did not regard Katherine or me as hale fellows well met.

After enough time wasted on phony cordiality, I said, in a prosecutorial tone, "Could you please describe your career after you graduated from West Point?"

"After I was commissioned in 1982, I went to the Air Defense Artillery course, then a Hawk battalion in Germany for three years . . ." and so on. The details weren't all that exciting or pertinent, so the condensed version is this: Paul married his high school sweetheart in the cadet chapel three days after his graduation from West Point, neither he nor she enjoyed the army, he got out, stumbled through a few jobs here and there, finally matriculating to become a software engineer in Cincinnati, which remained his civilian occupation. He continued in the reserves for four years after he left fulltime service, then transferred to the National Guard, he claimed to continue to serve his country, though I suspected the chance for a monthly retirement check and full benefits might've factored somewhere in the equation. Like many guardsmen of that era, I doubt he thought he would ever see a deployment to a combat zone, and I'm sure it came as a surprise about as welcome as a big throbbing hemorrhoid.

Paul came off as bright, slightly mentally disorganized, and, to be blunt, he had a fairly flat, lackluster personality. He was, in the contemporary lexicon, a nerd. It struck me that if I went back and examined his record as a cadet, I would find that he was an exemplary student academically, never experienced any disciplinary problems, was somewhat anonymous among his peers, and his only real challenge was in the gym. He had narrow shoulders, skinny arms, and a large rear end matched by a heavy paunch that rolled over his belt—he resembled, I thought, a marshmellow swathed in tan camouflage.

In fact, Paul had as much command presence as a lop-eared beagle. Even his voice was soft and lispy and lacked inflection.

He continued through his rise up the National Guard ranks, culminating with his selection to command a military police battalion with troops scattered across dozens of communities in three different states, which would be completely unacceptable in a regular army unit, but was a fairly common arrangement in the Guard.

Before he bored us to death, I interrupted to ask, "How much notice did you get before your unit deployed to Iraq?"

"Uh . . . well, uh, about sixty days." He inhaled heavily as though the memory was too painful to recall. "It was all such a mess."

"How was it a mess?" Katherine asked.

"In the beginning, it was mostly screening. And you know . . . a lot of mixing and patching. About a third of my battalion failed to qualify for combat deployment." He stared off into space. "Yes . . . I think that's accurate . . . about a third."

"That sounds like a large percentage. Why so many?"

"The usual stuff for Guard people. Health problems, pregnancies, family situations, and because we were slated for male prison duty, all the female MPs got reassigned."

"So you deployed with a lot of people you didn't know?" I suggested.

"Put it this way," he replied, edging his plump rear forward in his chair. "They were still throwing last-minute fillers on the bus as we left for the airport."

I asked, "Had you ever performed prison duty before? I mean, you personally."

There was a long pause as he seemed to stare off into space again. It struck me that LTC Paul Eggers, despite being in command at the time of the scandal in question, was not currently facing any formal charges or serious disciplinary issues. Though his career and his reputation were sinking fast, he had his twenty years in, and would leave military service with his rank intact, a considerable accrual of lifelong benefits, and without the stain of an Article 15, or worse, a court martial, to blacken his tombstone.

But it did not escape my knowledge, nor I am sure his, that this comfortable arrangement could be changed at the army's whim. In polite terms, Paul Eggers was in one of those situations where loyalty to the institution equals loyalty back—more bluntly, the army had its big green vise on Paul Eggers's balls. He had to tread carefully or the conditions of his retirement would change, and he would be publicly disgraced, booted out on his ass, sans any of the goodies America awards its veterans in good standing.

He did not confess this directly, but instead said, "I would say the army gave me a good foundation for the job. A West Point education, over twenty years of solid leadership training and experience, and I had the benefit of superb MP training courses."

Utter bullshit. This sounded like exactly what Eggers had been told to say by some public relations flack or a mealy-mouthed army attorney—in other words, exactly what I would've advised him to say. I was tempted to peek behind him to see the ventriloquist's hand stuffed up his butt.

Katherine couldn't resist stating the obvious. "Bullshit."

This blunt assessment appeared to surprise Eggers and he asked, "What did you say?"

"I'm sure you heard me, Colonel. Neither you, nor your unit, were at all prepared to run a military prison in a combat zone. Your battalion was jerryrigged together at the last minute, and you were thrown into a mission you personally were totally unprepared to undertake."

Paul Eggers was already shaking his head at Katherine. "You don't know what you're talking about. Yes, there were a few soldiers who weren't all that experienced, but I had a fine unit." As if we needed elaboration, in his most sincere tone, he added, "Good officers, capable sergeants, excellent soldiers."

As only she can, Katherine looked ready to jump down his throat, but I interceded and asked Eggers, "How well did you know Sergeant Danny Elton?"

He looked both relieved to be reprieved from the earlier topic and unhappy to be on this one. "Not very well," he said, then quickly expanded on that, saying, "To be honest, Elton was one of those soldiers who were assigned to my battalion at the last minute."

Katherine opened her mouth and started to go back to the earlier topic, so I raised my voice and asked, "Before the scandal came to light, had you ever met him?"

"I suppose I had."

"Is that a yes, or a no?"

"A . . . a yes." After a moment of squirming, he added, "But I didn't recall him. He's the type of soldier . . . well, he really didn't make much of an impression."

"According to his personnel file, he was a troubled soldier with a well-documented record as a disciplinary problem with big attitude issues. Who promoted him to be shiftleader of an entire cellblock?"

"I don't exactly remember."

"Try harder."

"His platoon leader, maybe, or his first sergeant. I don't know. Those decisions occurred far below my level."

"Didn't you have to approve it? Controlling an entire cellblock is a big responsibility, one normally assigned to someone two paygrades higher than Elton's. You were the prison commandant."

"Oh, well, I'm sure I did. It was sort of pro forma, those temporary assignments. A piece of paper floating through my in-box. Never had much time to investigate the individuals."

"Why didn't you?"

He looked at me. "Have you ever run a prison in a war zone?" The question was specious, as was his expression, and he went on, "On a daily basis, we had nearly nine thousand prisoners. I had a full battalion of three hundred and eighty men to command, in addition to the prison facility. I had to feed them all, house them, process those coming in and those leaving. I had to arrange for electricity in a country without power. And without workable plumbing or sewage or running water, I had to arrange latrine facilities for ten thousand people to take a shit, and potable water to brush their teeth. These simple things and many others occupied whole days of my time. I had to oversee our contractors, attend frequent command and staff meetings in Baghdad, handle personnel issues, coordinate with the military intelligence people . . ." He paused, then asked me, I think facetiously, "Should I go on?"

"It was tough duty."

"Tough? On an average night, I was lucky to get three hours of sleep. Same for my chain of command. We were all walking zombies. And of course there were those things that came up unexpectedly, the unscheduled mortar attacks, or a prisoner died, or one of my soldiers died, or got badly wounded, or a sudden influx of hundreds of new prisoners had to be . . . well, let's just say things were never dull." He awarded me a sarcastic smirk. "So no, Drummond . . . no, I didn't pay a lot of attention to an E-5 running one of very many prisoner sections under my control."

"What about the three women involved? Lydia Eddelston, June Johnston, or Andrea Myers? How well did you know them?"

"The God's honest truth . . . the first time I ever heard their names was when this thing broke."

"But they had free access to the prison. Isn't that unusual?"

"What do you mean?"

"I should not have to describe what I mean, Colonel Eggers. Three female personnel clerks, not even assigned to your battalion, yet they were free to come and go, at all hours, to roam at will throughout a male prisoner cellblock. This suggests a remarkable laxness, a clear breakdown in proper prison procedures and discipline. They were present in your prison, late at night, engaging in shockingly unrestrained behavior and yet, nobody ever dropped in to check on them."

Rather than respond defensively, or in any meaningful or constructive way, he simply shrugged.

"Should I rephrase that as a question?"

With a look of pure irritation he replied, "Okay . . . yes, I suppose there was a lapse in proper procedures."

Katherine asked, "Why?"

Again, he shrugged. "It wasn't an ideal situation. Nobody had a right to expect perfect results. Ninety-five percent of prison operations functioned well . . . uh, reasonably effectively . . . and here, uh . . . in this instance . . . well, human error . . . common oversight . . . Look, I still don't know how those three girls pulled it off."

When neither Katherine nor I replied to that stumbling, halfhearted confession, he stated, "I have three daughters myself. My two oldest are about their age." He turned and looked at Katherine. "What would make girls behave like that?"

Indeed, what would? I worked up a deep frown and warned him, "Colonel Eggers, you should be aware that as a prosecution witness, you will be cross-examined by us on the stand. We have done considerable research into the conditions at Al Basari, and the results are a bald contradiction of what you're telling us now. We have expert witnesses who can and will attest to the genuine circumstances at that prison. Neither Miss Carlson nor I will go easy on you on the stand. Do you understand what I'm saying?"

"Yes . . . uh . . . I believe I do."

"Then I encourage you to do some serious soul-searching before the trial. Your career is already ruined. And while the conditions of your retirement might be in jeopardy, so is your reputation as an officer, your integrity as a West Point graduate, and your self-respect as a husband and a father."

"I don't need lectures from you on my integrity, my duty, or anything else, Drummond."

"Yes, I believe you do." I leaned across the table. "That these five soldiers conducted themselves reprehensibly isn't in question. What remains very much in question is how much the command environment, the scandalous lack of resources, and possibly command interference contributed to their actions."

As it was intended to, this lecture annoyed him and he came forward in his chair until his face was two inches from mine—his face grew tight, his eyes became slitty, and for the first time his tone conveyed a world of genuine intonation. "Those three fucking bitches weren't even in my chain of command, Drummond. They ruined my career and brought shame and dishonor on all the good soldiers who were doing their jobs under the most terrible circumstances imaginable."

I stood up. "You've been warned, Colonel Eggers." I looked down at him. "We can and will call as many witnesses as we wish. There are a lot of soldiers who did duty at Al Basira, and who experienced life under your command. You can't stop the truth from coming out."

He stared back a moment, then looked away.

Katherine did not appear ready to leave, but I had left her little choice, so she stood and joined me, though she definitely did not look happy about it.

I nodded at Eggers who stayed in his chair looking like a man who had just learned that he had an inoperable brain tumor.

The moment we were outside, Katherine turned to me and in a very cold tone, said, "The next time you decide to take over an interview, have the courtesy to let me know in advance."

I continued walking and said nothing.

After a moment of silence she remarked, "Why do you look so angry?" She then observed, "You were on the right track, Sean. You shouldn't have backed off."

"Why not, Katherine?"

"You know why. Because he's getting a free ride for failing to come out with the truth."

I looked at her. "What did you do after September eleventh?"

She mulled that question before she said, "I suppose what everybody did."

"And what did everybody do?"

"I mourned, I wanted somebody punished, and I prayed for my country. I actually applauded when we attacked Afghanistan."

"But that's not what everybody did, Katherine. Soft, chubby little Paul Eggers left his wife and his three young daughters, his nicely tended home in the suburbs, and all the luxuries and conveniences America has to offer, and he deployed to a combat zone, probably for a fraction of the pay, to do a miserable job in a hellish place where your whole life hangs on whether an insurgent mortar-man decides to change the deflection of his tube one degree or two, or whether you choose to drive down the wrong street at the wrong time, and end up on the one with the big bomb planted there with your name on it."

"I understand that, Sean . . . but—"

"No buts, Katherine, hear me out. You or I may tear him apart on the stand, but we don't have to feel good about it. In fact, we should feel ashamed because he's a real patriot and though he might have fallen down on his job, he was there, and he was probably trying his best in a position nobody in his right mind would want."

"All I ask is that he tell the truth."

"No, you want him to tell the truth as you want to hear it. You want him to say conditions at that prison were deplorable. You want him to confess that he failed to run a good prison and that caused three young girls and two guys to do what they did. You want him to say that the military *wanted* Lydia to do what she did, and that Lydia was not responsible for her own conduct, sexual ethics, or actions."

"And what if that's true?"

"Then it's only part of the truth."

"Don't go naive on me, Sean. Our job as lawyers is to expose those truths that are advantageous to our clients."

"I know my job, Katherine. Spare me the lecture."

We walked on in silence a while longer, nursing our opposing grievances, then Katherine asked, "Why did you give him a free ride on the prison conditions? Or the failure of his chain of command?"

"Did I?"

"You know you did."

"All right. Because he's facing an impossible quandary, and he hasn't yet been called on it. He's under crushing pressure, personally and professionally, to paint the best portrait of his operation. His balls are in the hands of people above him, and he hasn't yet figured out what's more important, his self-respect, or his ass." I concluded, "Anyway, we don't know enough at this stage to break him."

"You mean, you prefer to do it on the stand?"

"I mean, if we have to, and it will help our client, yes. And I don't want to cue him on the direction we'll take."

After considering that for a moment, Katherine said, "Good call." She then informed me, "I actually look forward to getting him in the witness chair. He doesn't impress me. I could see him as a staff officer, but he doesn't seem to possess the qualities of a solid commander."

"I'm not sure it mattered, Katherine. I'm beginning to get a picture of complete chaos over there. George Patton would've been shellshocked."

"Welcome to the party."

Which was an appropriate introduction for what happened next. An older, seedy-looking gentleman popped out of a doorway directly to our front, exchanged a quick look of recognition with Katherine, and headed in our direction.

He stopped and Katherine gave him a brief hug and an air-kiss on the cheek. She remembered her manners and said to him, "Mel, this is my cocounsel, Lieutenant Colonel Sean Drummond." Then to me, "Mel Cramer. He's the journalist who broke the Al Basari story."

All of Katherine's new pals seemed to be into truncated names.

He put out his hand to shake, but I must not have been paying attention—I think I was preoccupied studying the air quality—because, after an awkwardly long moment, he withdrew the hand.

In truth, the name was more than familiar, though not the face, which was heavily lined, pockmarked, large-nosed, and ugly. In his late sixties or perhaps early seventies, with a full head of wooly white hair, he was dressed beneath both his station and his age, in faded dungarees and a worn safari vest, à la Crocodile Dundee, as if he was about to wrestle a bull rhino to the floor, or topple a president with an in-house scandal. I wondered if he was wearing a diaper for incontinence.

I was also aware that Cramer was an old-timer who had broken military scandals and exposed military secrets going back to the Vietnam War. He had one or two Pulitzer Prizes on his shelf and was still going strong, still exposing secrets, still igniting scandals, and, as his presence here indicated, was now angling for another shimmering trophy to add to his collection. In his circles he was an admired legend for getting the inside scoops, and for turning molehills into three days of front-page outrage and fat book deals.

In my circle, he was a lowlife, scumsucking hack who would sell his soul and undermine his country for a byline. I recalled the old saw about why reporters always whistle when they are on the toilet; it's the only way they can remember which end to wipe.

Anyway, Mel and I exchanged brief eye contact and instantly decided we loathed each other.

He turned to friendlier company, Katherine, and announced in a loud, theatrical tone, "Boy, this place is in high cover-your-ass mode."

"Not getting much openness and cooperation?" Katherine commiserated back.

"No shit. I just wasted two hours with some pathetic public relations twerp they brought up from DC to handle this. He jerked me off so hard I might have to see my urologist." He laughed at his own bad joke, which is another habit I find annoying.

Katherine, in an effort to explain my bad manners, mentioned to her pal, Mel, "I can't even get my cocounsel to tell me what he had for breakfast this morning."

Mel laughed, slapped his side, then replied, "Hey, you know the difference between talking to an army lawyer and a lobotomy patient?" He then howled out the answer to his own riddle. "At least the lobotomy patient has half a brain."

I was going to tell him the one about how to save a reporter from drowning—take your foot off his neck. But I summoned all my willpower and courtesy, then said, very respectfully, "Fuck off, Melvin."

But I sensed that Mel was one of those men who enjoy irritating you, so to piss him off I smiled, and even produced a laugh, like I didn't mean it. Au contraire—I meant every syllable.

Katherine said to her buddy, "Forgive him, Mel. He's not a big fan of the First Amendment."

To which Mel replied, "Probably can't count that high." Apparently, this was another big ha-ha, because Mel nearly soiled his pants he laughed so hard.

Well, the flaming lefties were having a good old time at the expense of yours truly, and they continued in this vein for a while, tossing around jokes.

But it suddenly struck me that perhaps I was being too harsh, possibly even unfair. Mel and Katherine, after all, were dealing with some serious displacement issues. I mean, sometimes you have to put yourself in their shoes, empathize, try to understand their feelings. Here they were, brothers and sisters in leftie arms, trapped behind enemy lines, so to speak, in West Point, the citadel of military correctness and professionalism, literally and figuratively the birthplace of all they detest about the green machine. Really, it was only natural for them to blow off a little steam, and I should be man enough to swallow my pride.

As I said, they *were* being complete assholes.

And at the first pause, I asked Melvin, "Are you really the one who first broke the story?"

"I was," he replied in a tone that revealed a gargantuan ego. "I published the first article and distributed the pictures."

It was time to teach Katherine a lesson and I knew how to do it. "Could I ask how you got the pictures?"

"Of course."

"Good, then . . . who gave them to you?"

"I said you *could* ask, Drummond. Didn't say I'd answer." He cackled so hard I thought he was choking. That would be a treat.

I smiled back. "Good one, Melvin. Were they e-mailed to you?"

He decided to humor me. "Might've been."

"From Iraq?"

"Possibly."

"From a guy or a girl?"

He shook his head. "Don't bother asking, Drummond."

"From someone in their chain of command?"

"Stop wasting my time."

"Did you get any additional information from this source?"

"Yadda, yadda, yadda."

I hate that phrase. Strike Two. "Do you know *why* they were e-mailed to you?"

"Well, I suppose I have a certain . . . well, a reputation for pursuing and exposing the truth." He assumed an air of false modesty. "I like to believe that's why I was chosen."

"But there could have been other motives?"

"How would I know? I can't account for what's in the minds of my sources."

"So who sent you those pictures? And what additional information and insights did they give you, Melvin?"

"There you go again, Drummond. The First Amendment, try reading it," he answered with a smug smile and a light flip of the hand. Strike three.

"Oh, I have, Melvin. I also read the rest of the constitution."

"What's that supposed to mean?"

"The Fifth and Sixth Amendments. Freedom from unfair prosecution. The right to a fair trial, the right to directly cross-examine their accusers. Chain of evidence issues. So you got this packet of pictures and then you did your best to get them, and yourself, on every front page in the world. And only you know where they came from. Do you see where I'm going with this, Melvin?"

"I'm not sure I do." In fact, Mel in the rumpled safari jacket now was shifting his feet and looking at his watch as if his underpants had just shrunk three sizes.

Katherine took my arm and started to protest my boorish behavior, but I ignored her and leaned forward until I was about six inches from his face. "It's very simple, Melvin. You're their main accuser—you put them in their cells, and you placed them on the court docket. Without you, nobody would ever have known about their activities. You fingered them and you provided the evidence that will get them hung. So I'm asking if you'll be a man and come forward to clarify how you got those pictures, from whom, why, and what else you were given."

Melvin now looked as if he just remembered an overdue White House scandal he had to attend to—and was edging away from me.

I grabbed his arm. "Tell me you're not going to be the little chickenshit I think you are and hide behind the First Amendment. I mean, gee, Melvin, you probably notched another Pulitzer, and maybe a book deal, and with any luck a movie deal, and, as the price of getting you a little more fame and cash, five young people are facing life in prison. Is it right to throw them to the wolves without knowing who ratted them out and why? Is it really right to throw out the Fifth, Sixth, and Fourteenth Amendments, just to protect the First? You wouldn't be such a total selective prick, would you, Melvin?"

Katherine released my arm and said to me, "Back off, right now Sean. He has every right to protect his sources."

But Melvin had heard enough, and he jammed his face forward. "Listen to me, Drummond. I was spitting out punks like you when you were still in diapers."

I said, "You know what bothers me most about guys like you?"

"I really don't care." He tried to loosen himself from my fingers, so I tightened my grip and pulled him closer, almost on his tiptoes.

"That's right—you *don't* care," I told him. "You lit the match that ignited this bonfire, and now you're sneaking around watching the bodies being thrown into the flames, acting like your only responsibility is to record the mayhem. You get your story, another notch on your legend, and screw them. You trample on their rights to protect yours. You're a chickenshit, Melvin."

On that note, I released his arm, and Melvin scampered away, rubbing his arm, and sort of stomping, or doing some kind of silly half step. I wasn't expecting an invitation for drinks any time soon, unless a tasty cup of hemlock was involved.

Katherine and I stood in silence, quietly nursing our separate grudges. Finally, she said to me, "That was totally uncalled for. You were incredibly rude."

I faced her. "How do you know him?"

"He covered some of my trials, and wrote excellent, very accurate stories about them. He's a great reporter. You acted like a horse's ass, Drummond."

"Doesn't it bother you that he knows facts about our case that might benefit our client and that he's too much of a selfish prick to tell us?"

"No. Why should it?" she replied, in a self-righteous tone. "This is exactly what the First Amendment's about and for. It serves the greater good by protecting the anonymity of the sources."

"I knew you were going to say that."

"Here's a newsflash—the Supreme Court said it first. Mel is under no obligation . . . No, in fact, he has the honored duty not to disclose privileged information. You're asking him to betray his professional ethics."

"Have you thought how hypocritical you are, Katherine? It's fine for some reporter pal of yours to withhold vital information that might benefit our client. But if an army officer does it, for reasons every bit as valid and even more noble and defensible, you want to gouge his eyes out."

"It's not at all the same thing."

"The problem with you, Katherine, is you can't even see the double-standard."

"It's still not the same thing," she reiterated.

"You're right, it's not. His right to fame and fortune behind the shield of the First Amendment, versus protecting vital national security secrets. The obligations of a reporter as opposed to the disgraceful obligation and loyalty an officer feels toward his comrades, his service, his nation."

Well, it was déjà vu all over again. We hadn't resolved this problem in three years of law school nor in all the years I had known her. It did not look like we were solving it now.

She gave me a cold look then walked away, leaving me alone in the long hallway. Two points for Drummond.

I smiled at her back.

I had the car keys. Three points.

Chapter Twelve

As soon as we got back to the house, after a short, tense drive during which neither of us spoke to the other, I went into my bedroom and called Terrence O'Reilly, the watchdog protecting my and her highness's asses.

I identified myself and inquired, "Where are you now?"

"Across the road from you, right across. We rented a small room in the ratty-looking bungalow with ugly blue shutters."

I pulled aside the window curtain, quickly picked out the only house with blue shutters, and O'Reilly waved at me from a second-story window. I responded to his gesture by giving him the bird.

He laughed. "I always said lawyers got class."

"So have your boys been keeping an eye on us?"

"Every minute."

"I haven't seen them."

"They're good boys, you're not supposed to. They drop off when you go through the front gate—the MPs on post pick you up there—but they're on your ass every minute of everywhere else. How was dinner at McDonald's? A Big Mac, right? Watch your arteries."

"I'm reassured," I told him. "Any updates on the murders?"

"Not really. Everybody's frustrated and tossing theories around."

"What's the most popular theory?"

"That would be the Arab-with-the-hard-on hypothesis. Y'know, like these five kids insulted the faith and degraded a bunch of Mohammad's boys, so, since the five kids are too protected to whack, their lawyers pay the price."

"Do you like that theory?"

"What's not to like? Kill all the lawyers. Shakespeare, right? Literary justice."

To be polite, I laughed.

"Thing is," he continued, "this theory posits that they snuck in an assassin, or activated a sleeper, to handle this holy revenge mission. If it's the right theory, you're all toast."

I thought I knew the answer but asked, "Why?"

"Cuz then this guy's a pro, possibly with a suicidal disposition. He's a guided missile. He's gonna be a bitch to stop. He won't make no stupid mistakes. He'll have a great legend, perfect creds, possibly some help here in-country from a terrorist cell. Add all that up and he'll be a bitch to find." He then added, unnecessarily, "And even harder to stop."

"Do you give it credence?"

"Two perfect murders, no clues, no witnesses, no leads . . . just that note left at Major Weinstein's murder site that suggests some kind of religious grudge. Hey . . . looks pretty good to me."

I observed, "I don't like that theory."

He laughed.

"Try another."

He laughed again. "Well, here's theory two. It might help you sleep better."

"Let's hear it."

"We call it the nut-chasing-the-flame. Your more-or-less typical serial killer looking to make a big splash, instant fame. I mean, here we got the biggest story on the planet, these kids molesting prisoners, right? So the idea is, some whacked-out ghoul decides to hitch a ride on the publicity train."

"Who came up with that idea?"

"FBI profiler folks down in Quantico."

I considered this theory a moment. "Do you know the old story about the two hunters out to shoot some deer and one of them falls over, apparently dead?"

"Nope, tell me."

"Okay, so the other hunter scrambles for his cellphone and frantically calls 911. He screams that he thinks his friend is dead, and the lady on the other end tells him to take a deep breath, and, first thing first, make sure his friend is dead. After a moment there's the sound of a rifle going off, then he gets back on the phone and says, okay, I just blew his fucking head off so I *know* he's dead. Now what?"

O'Reilly chuckled. "Okay, I know, it sounds a little fizzy, but think about the nutjob who killed John Lennon, or that lunatic punk who nailed Reagan to show off to some lady movie star he had the hots for. These serial killer guys, by definition, they're nuts. Who knows how the marbles align inside their heads, right?"

I replied, "Any other theories?"

"Plenty. And if you don't like that one, believe me, you don't want to hear 'em."

"Maybe I do."

"Trust me, Colonel. Everybody's throwin' crap against the wall to see what sticks. Frankly, they're all so loopy, you'll lose confidence in the people protectin' you."

"Who said I had confidence?"

There was a long moment of silence then O'Reilly yelled, "Hey . . . who the fuck is that?"

"What?—Who?"

"Listen, you guys are supposed to inform us when you're expectin' a visitor."

"I wasn't . . . What are you talking about?"

"On the front porch . . . dark, swarthy guy . . . Oh shit . . . he's got a gun."

My heart jumped through my chest, and I pushed open the curtain and peeked down at the porch, but saw nobody there. I looked across the street and saw a single finger pressed against the window.

He laughed and I joined him. I mean, it was funny, right? I said, "You know a guy named Chief Rienzi?"

"Tommy? Sure, I know 'em. Why?"

"He handled the investigation into the death of General Palchaci, the corpse found in the cell at Al Basari. What's the read on him?"

"Good guy. Older, by the book, always been on the criminal end of things."

"He got a brain?"

"Not Einstein . . . but yeah, Tommy's got a head on his shoulders. Why . . . you meetin' with him?"

"About thirty minutes from now."

"Here's a tip. Tommy loves pizza. Anchovies and pineapple."

"Seriously?"

"I know. A goombah but he's got a Hawaiian grandmother. Weird, right?"

We exchanged farewells and I hung up. Katherine and I did not seem to be on the same page when we conducted our interrogatories and, as I said, our approaches to the trial strategy appeared to be wildy divergent, so I thought I would conduct this interview alone. I knew it would piss Katherine off if she discovered my free-lancing, but I needed to get the straight story out of Chief Rienzi without Katherine veering into her favorite territory—how the army screwed up.

Thirty minutes later, I was back at the same red brick building Katherine and I had visited the day before. Rienzi was waiting for me on the front steps when I parked and got out carrying two big pizza boxes from Domino's.

I had also ordered six pizzas with everything for delivery to O'Reilly and his crew. It's never a bad idea to make sure the guys protecting you are happy and content. Incidentally, Nelson was paying for it.

We shook hands and he led me inside and down a hallway to an office on the back side of the building. It was an antiseptic office, furnished rather sparsely, a temporary place to hang his hat while he waited for the trials to begin. He settled in behind the gray metal desk, I pulled a gray fold-out metal chair to the front of the desk, I straddled the chair, and we both opened our pizza boxes.

He appeared surprised and mildly delighted at the anchovies and pineapples. "Wow. How did you know?"

"O'Reilly is my security guy."

He stuffed half a slice in his mouth and between chews asked, "You got Terry, huh?"

"He any good?"

"Yeah, he's okay." Between noisily chewing and swallowing, he looked thoughtful for a moment. "He's only lost two . . . no, make that four protectees."

I looked to see if he was joking, but he maintained a perfectly straight face. He said, "Terry did two years of protection duty in Baghdad." He tackled another slice. "Nobody's perfect."

"Speaking of which, how were you notified about the body in Al Basari?"

"Late night call." He took another large bite and talked as he chewed. "My office was located in the Green Zone . . . ordinarily about a thirty-minute drive from Al Basari . . . assuming you had an escort convoy, and there were no known bombs en route." He took a moment to swallow, then observed, "Iraq poses lots of unique traffic issues."

"Who notified you?"

"Commandant's office." He finished off a slice, then overlapped two more together and resumed eating. He seemed to know where I was going with this and explained, "The body was discovered by a Sergeant First Class Haley. He was making the rounds, looked in the cell, and at first he thought Palchaci was asleep. Lots of those prisoners slept nearly all the time . . . but then he noticed Palchaci's hand hanging out the sleeping bag, and the smell . . . I mean, the whole place reeked like old shit, but this odor was even worse." He looked at me. "The guy had been dead two days."

"Did Sergeant Haley touch anything?"

Rienzi knew this question was coming and suggested, "You don't wanta go there, counselor. Everything was handled by the book. Haley's a career MP . . . this wasn't his first homicide. He unlocked the cell and entered, felt the wrist, confirmed that Palchaci was dead, then backed out, posted a guard, and arranged for us to be called."

Now halfway through the pizza—it was a large—he closed the lid on the box and leaned back into his chair, wiped his lips on a paper napkin and patted his stomach. Watching this guy eat was not a pretty sight. "Could you please describe what you did when you got there?"

"First, I went to the commandant's office and reported my presence. This was about the fifteenth killing I'd had to investigate at the prison, so everybody was familiar with the—"

"The fifteenth?" I interrupted. "Is that what you said?"

He nodded. "Look, Al Basari was a real mess. Almost indescribable. It's an insult to call it a prison. For one thing it was mortared and shot at every week. The majority of prisoners lived in tents, outside. Sometimes they'd lose five or ten prisoners in a week to mortars that crashed through their tents. Then there were plenty of prisoner-on-prisoner homicides."

"What caused those?"

"Lots of reasons. Some of 'em probably got it cuz the insurgency ordered the hits. Like, maybe a guy was ratting out his buddies, or was a member of some competing jihadi faction, or he knew too damned much and they were just generally worried that he'd spill his guts. Not unlike our own prisons, the Iraqis organized themselves in gangs and cliques, and it was easy enough to smuggle word into the inside—and even easier to find someone willing to do the hit. I'll tell you, the price of a hit in Iraq is dirt cheap, a few hundred dollars. Some of it was just the typical vendetta crap you always get in prisons. But this is Iraq, a society founded on grudge justice, so it was even more prevalent than you'd find here. A few times, a prisoner just went nuts and started killing guys. Remember, Al Basari was a mess, so you had total crazies and certifiable psychopaths mixed in with the normal population."

"So is that what you thought when you first entered the prison?"

"Yeah, pretty much. That was usually the case with my earlier visits."

"Can you describe the scene when you entered the cell?"

"Godawful," he said, grimacing to underscore that assessment. "No other word will explain it. There was the stink . . . by then . . . My God, the corpse had been there almost three days. In that heat . . . in a closed room, the gases had already blown the stomach open exposing the intestines . . . and . . . uh . . . just say it was as bad as any corpse I ever smelled." His face was contorted from the memory, or maybe the aftertaste from the pizza. For a guy who likes anchovies with his pineapple, the smell must've been monumentally nasty.

I asked him, "Did you know who the victim was?"

"At first, I didn't have a clue. The commandant's office just said it was a body."

"So what next?"

"Warrant officer Lennie Blazer was with me. She handled the forensics while I interviewed the personnel."

"And what did she find?"

"The victim was wrapped in a US Army–issue sleeping bag. He was dressed in underwear that was heavily bloodstained. Jenny took samples . . . all the blood was his. Indentations and scrapes on his wrists and ankles indicated he'd been tied up with a coarse rope when he died. Whoever put him in the sleeping bag had removed the restraints, postmortem."

"How do you know he didn't put himself in the bag?"

"Simple deduction. The beating Palchaci took was too severe."

"Explain that."

"Both his legs were broken, one snapped in multiple places, both kneecaps shattered. Six, maybe seven ribs were fractured. His face was so destroyed, it was if he'd been hit by a truck. Most of his fingers were broken, as was one elbow."

I had already read the autopsy results and his inventory of injuries accorded with that report, minus a few additional injuries to his internal organs and a number of contusions. But I had a reason for taking him down this path, getting him into the routine of automatically answering my questions. "So you're assuming he was too physically damaged to maneuver himself into a sleeping bag."

"I'm assuming the pain was excruciating . . . more than enough to prove disabling. Two ribs were sticking in his lungs. Two of the leg breaks were compound fractures. The man died in agony."

"And you're assuming it was torture?"

Without hesitation, he said, "Torture . . . yeah, certainly. The man was beaten methodically, and deliberately pummeled with a blunt object that might've been a baseball bat. Why? You got another name for it?"

I ignored his obvious attempt at sarcasm and suggested, very coldly, "So based upon the extensive damage to his body, you're suggesting his death was a premeditated and controlled act. Torture in your words."

Tommy Rienzi was a senior CID officer with long experience dealing with lawyers. He did not like me putting words into his mouth, though in this case, I was merely repeating his own words, and he instantly objected, saying, "That's not what I said. I told you—"

"You said it was torture."

"I said it *might've* been tor—"

"No, Chief, your stated conclusion was unequivocal. Torture, without hesitation or doubt. And more specifically, you described it as methodically applied, as in, the damage done to Palchaci wasn't haphazard or impulsive. It was cool and systematic, the product of hard logic." I allowed him to digest his own words, then said, "Torture. How did you arrive at that causative noun?"

"That's the way it looked to me."

"I see. Not the way it *was*, the way it *looked*. Not an objective description, more like a half-assed subjective conclusion based on how you felt that morning."

"Do you have a problem with the word torture?"

"I do, as will you, on the stand. It's too late to change it now, because that's the exact noun you used repeatedly in your crime report. But you don't really *know* it was torture, do you, Chief?"

151

"I know it sure as shit wasn't suicide."

"Since we're into conjecture, let's try out a few other theories. Try revenge. Or uncontrolled fury or rage. Or, if you don't like those, try the act of a fellow prisoner, somebody totally deranged and unhinged from reason. You said yourself that the prison at Al Basari was full of nuts, schizos, and psychopaths."

Chief Rienzi was now annoyed enough to begin rubbing his forehead. He'd just gone from a fairly content man with his tummy stuffed with free pizza to a distinctly unhappy individual holding an untenable position. He had made a kingsize blunder—the cardinal sin of conjecture—and just been given an alarming preview of how that gaffe would be shoved up his ass at the trial.

Worse, it would be a legal gang rape as all five of the accused were tried and all five of the defense lawyers copycatted one another.

Trying to look composed, he said to me, "Why are you bringing this up now?" as in, why are you firing your big gun prematurely? He knew, as did I, that I could've withheld this ammunition till the trial and used it to discredit him on the stand.

"Honest answer?" This query, of course, is always the prelude to a lie.

"Sure."

"You were doing a hard job in difficult circumstances and I have no interest in burying you on the stand. What would that help?"

He did not appear to buy this claim; he seemed, in fact, to assume I was jerking him off. Smart guy. After a moment's hesitation he said, "And you'd like a favor in return?"

"How understanding of you to ask, Chief."

"All right, what is it?"

"You did the investigation and had the first look at the crime scene and suspects. Who did you think did it?"

"I had no idea."

"Go on."

"How much do you know about General Palchaci?"

"Assume I know nothing," I replied, failing to clarify what an excellent assumption that was.

He leaned back in his chair and crossed his legs. "Palchaci was one of Saddam's favorite generals. He was from the region of Tikrit, Saddam's home town, and commanded one of the revolutionary guard divisions, a singular honor reserved for Saddam's most trusted lieutenants."

"So he was not one of the good guys?"

"Oh, he had quite the well-deserved reputation as a miserable bastard. Over the years, he'd done a lot of dirty work for his patron. And by dirty, I mean that in every literal sense of the word. He was particularly hated and feared by the Shiites and Kurds. He was a key figure after the first Gulf War, putting down the insurrections. The record indicates he obliterated three entire Shiite villages, then had them flattened and buried in dirt—not because they were guilty or implicated, just to dissuade others from rising up in opposition. An example. Old men, women, children—he buried all of them. That gives you an idea of his style."

"So he had a lot of enemies?"

"A lot?" he mimicked. "Try about three quarters of the country. After the invasion he went underground. The intel folks surmised he was designated by Saddam to help inspire, organize, and lead the insurgency. That's what he was doing when he was captured. Not number one, but certainly top ten."

"How was he captured?"

This question seemed to amuse Rienzi because he chuckled. "His own cousin turned him in."

"Family always comes first."

"He was using the cousin's house for a hideout, and he raped his host's daughter. Dumb shit. The girl was only twelve, and she was his blood relative, for God's sake." He added, in a sentiment I probably agreed with, "Palchaci deserved to die the way he did."

This of course was very valuable knowledge, as it would go a long way toward persuading the court martial board that Palchaci was a murderous monster long before he became a murderer's victim. Murder is murder, in theory, but in reality it comes in many flavors. It did not in any way alleviate the fact of Palchaci's murder, but offered a powerful argument in favor of leniency—after a conviction, that is.

Unfortunately I was no closer to knowing my client's guilt or innocence, and in that light, I asked, "Do you think any or all of the accused guards had anything to do with his killing?"

He gave me a long hard stare. "Understand, Colonel, that at the time I was investigating the crime I was unaware of the . . . well, the extracurricular activities of your client and her friends. But knowing what we all know now—that Elton and his crew were going collectively nuts in there—yeah, I'd put them near the top of my list." After further reflection he got a little more specific. "The very top."

"There's a big difference between sex games and murder. There was no physical evidence connecting them to his death."

"Not exactly accurate. There was proximity, there was motive, and there was the unusual fact that he died in a prison block they controlled. Remember, they had the keys to his cell. And they certainly were displaying . . . behavioral issues."

"All of which falls under the heading of circumstantial."

"You asked what I think and I'm telling you. You've seen the pictures. Things were spiraling out of control in that cellblock. Compare the activities of night one to the shit happening on night twenty, and you get the distinct impression that it was getting harder for this happy little band to get their rocks off. Look at those pictures—study their faces, Colonel."

"And what will I see in their faces, Chief?"

"Look, if you haven't read a book called *Lord of the Flies*, I highly recommend you do. That's what was happening in that cellblock. A bunch of kids were marooned in there, absent any adult supervision, and away from civilization. They reverted to their own rules. The more they got away with, the more they tried, and . . . Look, based on the stuff they were doing in the last pictures . . . yeah, I could see them taking the next step up the ladder of insanity."

I wanted to disagree with this logic, but the truth was I found myself in total agreement. And the larger truth, I thought, was so would a board of good and earnest soldiers in a military courtroom. It was the same unsettling thought that had kept me awake the night before after reviewing the whole disgusting tableau of pictures.

As a group, and as individuals, Lydia and her friends had gone on a journey together, a journey into darkness—a journey that escalated without any moral breaks or intervention by the authority figures above them. Rienzi was right—they were like kids breaking the rules, surprised they were getting away with it, and thus, they acted as though they created the rules.

But did they break the cardinal rule, the sixth commandment? I wasn't yet willing to accept that they did.

But neither would I rule it out.

I thanked Rienzi for his clarifications and candor, then said, "I may want to talk to you again."

"Whoopee. I'll look forward to it."

Actually he looked like he wanted to be anywhere but here. I went to the door and left Chief Rienzi and the smell of overbaked anchovies that now permeated his small office.

It occurred to me that a lot of careers were hanging on this case, the five accused certainly, but also those in the chain of command, those who investigated the crimes, and probably the lawyers on both sides of the docket—and last, though certainly not least, the attorney I care most about.

In fact, the asses on this post were so tight you could ship in a little coal and run a diamond factory here. But I was relieved to learn that I probably didn't have to worry about the murder charge. Rienzi had as much as admitted that the government lacked anything beyond broad circumstantial evidence, and certainly there was nothing directly connecting my client to the death of General Palchaci.

My cellphone rang. I checked the incoming number and it was Katherine, obviously checking on my whereabouts. I punched receive and said, in a mildly aggrieved tone, "I just finished with the investigating officer. Where were *you?*"

"What? . . . What are you talking about?"

"I just talked to Rienzi. Once again, where were you?"

"You . . . what? Obviously without me. That's—"

"Didn't you get my message?"

This of course was not a lie but a lawyer's nimble way of not telling the truth.

"Don't try that bullshit on me."

Well, time to change the subject. "I have happy news to share with you."

"Don't try to change the subject. I won't have you freelancing—"

"Rienzi doesn't know who committed the murder. They have no physical evidence."

There was a brief pause, then Katherine asked, "What?"

"All they have is that Lydia and her friends were the guards, they had the keys, and were already behaving badly. It's circumstantial with a large *C.*"

"Rienzi said that?"

Note that she had forgotten her little problem with *moi*. I can be very clever. "Nearly word for word."

"Then what's it doing on the charge sheet?"

"Don't ask questions that have obvious answers."

"Make it more obvious for me."

"It would've been impossible *not* to include it, Katherine. A senior Iraqi officer died in a horrible way in a cellblock controlled by a few soldiers who were about to become pinup idols for the Marquis de Sade star of the month club. The army couldn't shove his murder under a rug, and our clients had already signed up to be perfect suspects."

There was a long break in the conversation as she thought about this. "But . . . if the charge is this weak, they risk undermining the other charges, right? No competent prosecutor would take such a dumb risk."

"Is that what you think?"

"Don't play stupid, Sean. If a jury sees that the prosecution case for murder is sloppy and flawed, that bleeds over. They could discredit their entire case."

She was getting it. "It certainly would, and my bet would be that the prosecutors were dragged into it kicking and screaming. But the commanding general wanted to avoid a public relations flogging by allowing a murderer to go free, insisted on throwing it into the mash, and left the prosecutors no choice but to proceed."

"That's stupid."

"Maybe."

"So are there other options?"

"One, and it's not necessarily exclusive, is that they have no intention of dragging the murder charge into court. It's a ruse—leverage they're holding as barter for a deal." I added, "If nobody bites, they drop the charge before they embarrass themselves in front of the court martial board."

"Which works only if *we* don't know it's a bluff, right? What's two?"

"An ongoing investigation. They're still digging, still hoping for a break, or a Hail Mary, before it gets to trial."

"Not likely. If they haven't found a smoking gun yet, they won't."

"You might be right, Katherine."

"It sounds like there's a 'but' to that sentence."

"Here's a novel thought. You also might be wrong."

"You know . . . that *is* a novel thought." I think she was being tongue in cheek, but with Katherine, you can never be sure.

"Well, for the sake of our client, let's consider it."

"Because you believe in the possibility that our client or one of her friends killed Palchaci?"

"Don't you?"

I found it interesting that she failed to answer that portentous question. She asked me, instead, "What more could they be looking at? What other leads do they have?"

"Katherine, I've been on this case two days. I don't even have dirty laundry yet." I suggested, "Maybe it's something we should talk to our client about."

"That's a good idea. Just not today."

"Why not? I'd like to get this out of the way. If we can discount the murder charge, we can focus our energies on the lesser charges."

"She's got her pysch exam with the government expert today."

"And you don't want to overload her mental circuits, right?" I asked, without mentioning that this could probably be accomplished by asking her if there was a state in the union called Montana.

"Well, to be frank . . . she has a limited ability to concentrate on more than one issue at a time," Katherine admitted, then added, more curiously I thought, "Like somebody else I know."

There was a subcurrent to that statement but I didn't pick up on it: perhaps I didn't want to.

Chapter Thirteen

I made the five-minute drive back to our home/office, picked up my cocounsel, and drove her back to the front gate. The same young MP was back on duty—he took one look and frantically waved us through with an expression of immense relief when we obeyed his instruction. I think he wanted to avoid Katherine. She can be tiresome.

From there, we drove back to the cadet area, and I parked on the same rooftop again.

We then hoofed it back to the same building where we had earlier met LTC Paul Eggers, but we moved up the stairs to a different floor, a different conference room, and a different prosecution witness, Captain Nate Willborn.

I pushed open the door and ushered Katherine inside, then, a beat behind, I entered. Captain Willborn was seated at the long table, right next to a lovely female JAG officer, and I didn't even have to check the rank on her collar or the letters on her nametag to know she was titled and named Major Mary Ingle.

I had met Mary twice before, once in a courtroom encounter that led to her defeat, and once on a dance floor, that led to dinner, and that led to drinks, and that led to . . . well, a real gentleman doesn't kiss and tell.

But, yes, it led to that, too.

Apropos of that night, I recalled Mary's rather brusque revelation to me over coffee in her townhouse the next morning: "My fiancé, Pete, is coming over any minute." She further revealed, "He's a member of Delta, one of their top gunslingers." She then asked, "Would you care to stick around and meet him, or be a perfect gentleman and slip out the back door now?"

I hadn't seen an engagement ring, and apparently informing me about this little detail must've slipped her mind, so *I* had done nothing wrong and had absolutely nothing to fear from Deadeye Pete—though I wasn't betting he'd see it that way. Anyway, never let it be said that Sean Drummond is not a perfect gentleman, when the situation calls for it.

If you're interested, this was one of those occasions when a gentleman is not expected to send flowers or chocolate the next day.

Anyway, Mary was smiling as I entered the room and it was obvious she was expecting me, though I had no foreknowledge that she was involved with this case. I had studied the roster of opposing counsel and was confident her name wasn't on the list.

Also, it was interesting that Captain Willborn had chosen to arrive for this meeting lawyered-up, for, as I mentioned, he was merely listed as a witness.

Katherine introduced herself to Nate Willborn and to Mary, then said, "And this is my cocounsel, Sean Drummond."

Willborn rose like a proper gentleman and we exchanged brisk handshakes. He was slight of build but made an obvious effort to produce a strong grip. Mary chose to remain seated and mentioned in a forthright manner, "Sean and I are already acquainted."

"I see." Katherine took this in, then said, "Sean does get around, doesn't he?"

Mary smiled at Katherine, who smiled back. Regarding this awkward situation, Mary remarked, "Small world."

Well, the temperature in the room instantly cooled about a hundred degrees. How do women know these things?

I thought for a moment about the appropriate response to this prickly situation, and quickly decided that I didn't owe anybody an explanation, appropriate, or, more in character for me, otherwise. While I had known Katherine for well over a decade, the standard protocol of coital disclosure applied: I hadn't slept with Katherine, so who I had slept with was none of her business. Then again, had I slept with her the issue of disclosure would have become even more interesting.

And regarding Mary, whatever the advisable protocol is for a regrettable one-night stand wasn't in my copy of the *Service Etiquette*, Fourth Edition.

We all sat, and Sean, Katherine, and Mary tried to pretend like this was not an awkward moment. Nate Willborn, at least, looked absolutely clueless. Men have no instinct for these things.

I said to Mary, "What are you doing here?"

"For this meeting, consider me the counsel for Captain Willborn."

Katherine asked the logical question I was about to ask. "Why does a witness for the prosecution require a lawyer?"

"He doesn't, necessarily. I'm only here to keep you honest."

Setting aside the obvious oxymoron of lawyers trying to keep lawyers honest, I asked Mary, "Are you on the prosecution team?"

"I am."

"Since when?"

"Yesterday, today, and tomorrow."

"Funny, I didn't see your name on the scoresheet."

"Because there are five different trials, it was felt that there should be an overall coordinator. That would be me."

Katherine and I exchanged looks. This was a smart move from the government's point of view, as it gave the five prosecutors a big advantage the defense could not share. Among the accused it was every man/woman for him/herself as we all clawed and scrambled to get the best deal for our clients, even if that meant, as it so often does, that the other accused got the short end of the stick, or the long end of the sentence.

In military parlance, the tactic is divide and conquer, and Mary's role was to act as a clearing house, to probe our weaknesses and vulnerabilities, to coordinate the activities of the prosecutors, de-conflict any damaging issues, and to bring back as many scalps as possible.

"Congratulations," I said to Mary, "General Fister chose well."

"I'll assume that's a sincere sentiment and say thank you, Sean."

"Assume whatever you want."

Well, the sexual tension in this room could be cut with a fat slice of salami. I never understood why Mary chose to seduce me, or why I chose to succumb to her charms, but I suppose it had something to do with the usual pressures of getting married, the queasiness about whether she'd chosen the right mate, a last-minute fling—or maybe she was just horny. Ordinarily I don't mind being the antidote to that last itch, but not when my partner is married or engaged, especially to a certified member of the army's most elite killing unit.

But the main reason behind the tension was Mary's army-issue maternity blouse. She appeared to be more-or-less eight months pregnant, which roughly corresponded to the aforementioned time I had snuck out her back door.

About that, I remembered to say, "Also congratulations about the wedding."

This was a polite way to acknowledge the gold wedding band on her finger without saying something less clever, like, Is there a paternity suit in the room?

"Again, thank you," Mary replied. "It was a beautiful ceremony. I would've sent you an invitation but . . . I seemed to have misplaced your address."

"And congratulations on the child," I remembered to add—how's that for subtlety?

"His name is Little Pete." She patted her stomach and offered me a matronly smile. "A boy, obviously. He's going to be named after his father."

I nearly jumped to my feet and yelled whoopee over this slyly worded revelation, but settled instead for a pale smile I hoped didn't betray too much relief. If you're wondering, this really is how you spell relief. Nothing alleviates male anxiety more than the simple phrase, the baby is not yours.

Poor Captain Willborn, the presumptive subject of this unhappy little get-together, was beginning to look like a third wheel.

Fortunately Katherine brought this meeting away from *Days of Our Lives* and into a safe focus, and asked Mary, "Are there any ground rules for this session?"

"Quite a few." She added with a look in my direction, "Don't worry. I'll let you know if you violate any of them."

Katherine considered that rather amorphous threat, then without further ado, said to Captain Willborn, "Will you describe your duties at Al Bazari?"

He glanced at Mary, who nodded, indicating, apparently, that it was okay to risk an answer to this perfectly innocuous question. "I was a section leader in the 315th Military Intelligence Battalion. I was in charge of—"

"A section leader?" Katherine snapped. "What does that mean?"

"I was about to—"

"How big was your section?"

"It was a standard interrogation te—"

"Standard? What's that supposed to mean?"

"Uh . . . there were three of us."

Katherine had her notebook out with her pen poised, and her mind, and her tongue, sharpened to a fine point. Clearly, with these rapid-fire interruptions, she was trying to rattle him, but so far he seemed cool enough.

Military Intelligence is an interesting branch, whose main purpose is to study the enemy, interpret the enemy's intentions, and provide ample forewarning to the troop commander to eliminate any unwelcome surprises, like defeat in battle. MI officers tend to be bright, highly organized, and essentially staff officers rather than leaders, which usually means their personalities are more bureaucratic, which often equates to being stuffy and hyper-cautious about saying things that might be proved wrong. They are often described as the two-handed branch due to their propensity to start conversations with "Well, on the one hand, this, and on the other hand, that."

Clearly, in this case, Captain Willborn regarded Katherine and me as the enemy, and I could almost see his mind churning to try to determine our intentions and our tactics.

"Name the other two," Katherine said in a severe, distrustful tone.

"Chief Warrant Officer Amal Ashad and Sergeant Kenny Waylon."

"And where are they now?"

"KIA. Killed in action."

"Thank you, but I know what KIA means, Captain. Are you saying both were killed?"

"Yes . . . both."

"How? When?"

"In Iraq. About two months ago." He paused and looked at her, apparently awaiting another rude eruption, but when none materialized he continued, "I wasn't there, but I understand the Humvee they were riding in got hit by a roadside bomb. An IED, it's called, which—"

"I also know what an IED is."

"Right," he said but didn't sound like he meant it. He was making a deliberate effort to get on Katherine's nerves with these little insinuations about her civilian status and lack of military knowledge. "Well, it was a big one. They died instantly. They were both blown into mist."

Katherine exchanged eye contact with me. Two months ago was right around the time the scandal first broke.

I said to Captain Willborn what we both were thinking. "Two of the key witnesses kick off just as the investigation kicks in. A little odd for a coicidence, don't you think?"

"Yes. It was most unfortunate."

As an attorney, I don't particularly like coincidences, particularly when they are not to my advantage. It's not that I don't believe in them, for, on rare occasions, they do happen. More often, however, the word can also be a synonym for "cover-up" or "bullshit" or the even more interesting "erasure of a big problem."

Willborn seemed to know what I was thinking—it wasn't hard—and quickly remarked, "Look, there is a war going on over there. Shit happens. The choice of who dies is not ours, it's the enemy's."

"Not always."

"No . . . maybe not." He then added, with an attempt at certainty, "In this case, it was *definitely* the enemy."

"I thought you said you weren't there."

"As their team leader I was informed of the circumstances and included in all the paperwork and documentation regarding their deaths. It was definitely an IED. Like I said, Colonel, shit happens."

"You don't sound all that choked up about their deaths."

"It happened two months ago. The grieving period is over." He apparently recognized how brutally callous that sounded and informed us, "The truth is, we weren't all that close. They were assigned to my team after I got in-country. Amal Ashad was pretty standoffish, and I don't buddy-up with sergeants under my command." He further added, unnecessarily, "The army discourages fraternization between the ranks."

"I see." I then asked, "What were their responsibilities as members of your team?"

"Our mission was interrogations. Ashad was an expatriot Iraqi. Born in Baghdad, he immigrated to the States when he was a young teenager. So he was a native-level linguist and had a lot of helpful insights into the local culture. Waylon was our driver and did administrative work for us."

"Meaning what exactly?"

"He kept our files in order and mostly did odd jobs."

"Did you perform a lot of interrogations?"

"We were drowning in prisoners to be interrogated. So the answer's yes."

"Who decided who your team would manage?"

"Headquarters . . . usually the colonel or the operations office. Mostly it was haphazard unless there was a direct line of connection."

"Explain that."

"It's a routine goal in interrogations. Say we were making headway on a particular insurgent cell and a new prisoner was suspected of involvement with that cell, or say a new prisoner had a relation-ship to one of the targets already assigned to our team. In those cases, it made sense to assign that source to our team. The idea was to maintain continuity. Of course, it wasn't always possible to achieve."

"Why wasn't it?"

"Because we were getting so many prisoners, a ceaseless deluge, it was like a never-ending conveyor belt. We were thinly spread. Of course, speed was always an issue."

"Speed?"

"Speed . . . yes. The target is most vulnerable and mentally dis-organized immediately after apprehension. Initiative and momen-tum are everything in interrogation—you can't afford to spend weeks or days, or even hours, debating who will handle the prisoner. Lose that psychological window, that brief moment of confusion, fear, and dislocation—that fleeting psychological advantage—and you might never recover."

"Is that how your team ended up with General Palchaci?"

He was opening his mouth to answer that question when Mary barged in. "That question is out of bounds."

I looked at Mary. "What does that mean?"

She looked at Katherine. "What level is your security clear-ance?"

To which Katherine replied, "Don't be facetious."

Mary directed her eyes back at me. "General Palchaci's disposi-tion and how that decision was made are classified."

I asked, "Classified by who?"

"By whom."

"You're starting to piss me off, Mary."

"The command in Baghdad, Sean. Captain Willborn is not authorized to disclose sensitive or compartmentalized information, and you will refrain from asking any questions that might compromise or jeopardize ongoing operations in the war zone."

"This is a joke, right?"

"Do I look like I'm laughing?"

I studied her face a moment. No—not on the outside, though she couldn't suppress how much she was enjoying herself on the inside. Note to self: it's always a mistake to sleep with opposing council.

I asked Mary a reasonable question. "How will we know when we're asking a question that will lose the war?"

"I'll be sure to let you know."

This was a good time to give her the bird, but I had a better idea. I turned my attention back to Captain Willborn. "I'm not very familiar with how you people work. Could you please explain the tactical nature of your efforts with Palchaci?"

This was a white lie, of course. In my Special Forces days, I had once received a full month of training on interrogation techniques, but I thought it might make the captain more comfortable not knowing that.

"Well . . . he wasn't what we call a cooperative witness. Officially speaking, he fell under the classification we call hostile and antagonistic, though . . . I . . . uh, I suppose that misstates things a bit."

"Why would that be a misstatement?"

"He wasn't exactly antagonistic. In fact, he could be very congenial. Charming, actually . . . or, I suppose paternal is the right word."

"*Paternal?*"

"He'd been a senior general and I was only a captain, for God's sake. He certainly didn't feel inferior or intimidated by my rank and position. From our opening session he seemed, I don't know, fatalistic, or, resigned . . . yes . . . resigned." He amplified on that thought and suggested, "You know, I think he almost expected it to end that way, with him in a prison camp."

"I would think a fatalistic mindset would make a prisoner more likely to talk, Captain. A spirit that is crushed and demoralized is like an open doorway to a skillful interrogator. But he wasn't cooperative?"

"No, he refused to give anything up. Actually, he would lecture me about the stupidity of the invasion, about how arrogant and naive America was, about how the insurgency would inevitably win. It didn't matter what I asked, or how. He always found a way to twist it to what he wanted to talk about."

Katherine asked a very good and leading question. "And did this frustrate you? Make you angry?"

He looked at her like a parent would a misbehaving child. "I am a trained professional, Ms. Carlson."

"Please explain what that has to do with my question."

"Effective interrogators don't get emotionally involved. We don't get angry or abusive or frustrated. We go into a session *expecting* to get nothing and we remain perfectly sanguine when that's the result."

We made eye contact and it was hard to tell what he was thinking—like whether he was telling the truth or throwing enough bullshit to paint the walls brown. After five minutes with Captain Willborn I had the uncomfortable impression that he was, indeed, a formidable interrogator. His voice was steady, steely, and modulated, conveying no emotion or animosity; he sounded, in fact, like a spokesman for Dramamine. He had shrewd blue eyes, thin, tight lips, immobile eyebrows, and aside from that disparaging look directed at Katherine, his expressions so far had ranged from nothing to nowhere. The man looked like he had ten tons of Botox pumped into his face, and maybe his brain. In general appearance he looked, I thought, like a choirboy: he was slender and fit, and his uniform and accoutrements were meticulous. He looked like he was ready to jam toothpicks under somebody's fingernails or teach Bible study without the slightest change in demeanor or moral ambivalence.

Thinking back to his too-aloof carriage when he described the untimely deaths of Chief Ashad and Sergeant Waylon what I had first mistaken for an attempt to hide his true emotions, now struck me for what it was—his innate emotional default of detached indifference.

I also had the unnerving sense that this interrogation was going exactly how he wanted it to go, versus how we wanted, or, more accurately, how we *needed*, it to go.

It was time to take the game up a notch, so I asked Captain Willborn, "Were all your team's sources incarcerated in Cellblock One?"

He glanced at Mary and her response was telling. She looked at first mildly befuddled by this question, then she nodded, but hesitantly, like it was breaking her neck.

Actually, it wasn't safe. Not at all. Of course, neither of them knew that yet.

"No, not all of them," he answered.

"How many, Captain Willborn? A lot, or a few?"

"I really don't know. Probably no more than a few."

"Be more specific, Captain. Would you say half your cases were in Cellblock One, or more than half?"

"I don't really know."

"So it could've been more than half?"

"I doubt it."

"According to Sergeant Elton's testimony, his cellblock was reserved for hard cases and malcontents. Yet you just informed us that General Palchaci was, in your own estimation, not antagonistic . . . he was congenial . . . almost paternal." I allowed him a moment to absorb his own contradiction, then asked, "Do you see the paradox here? How do you explain his incarceration in Elton's wing?"

"You know, I have no idea who assigned him there, or why. Those decisions fell under the prison commandant's purview and authority."

That was patent bullshit, of course, but I decided not to challenge it, at least not here, and not now—and instead asked, "Were you aware of the cellblock's reputation?"

"No, not really." He could see we weren't buying that easily disprovable lie, and quickly amended that statement. "I mean, sure . . . I guess I heard some rumors about Cellblock One. But Al Basari was a factory for bullshit. Eat a meal in the unit mess and you were kneedeep in braggarts and war stories. You know how men in a war zone are, right, Colonel? All the cellblock guards liked to think they were the roughest."

Katherine saw where I was going with this and quickly asked, "Did you know Sergeant Danny Elton?"

"Yes, of course."

"How well did you know him?"

"There was daily interaction between the interrogators and the guards. We saw them when they delivered the prisoners to us, and when they picked them up for return to their cells. And, right out of the manual, we often traded insights and observations about various prisoners."

"Was he working for you?"

"No . . . absolutely not."

Katherine asked, "Did he *think* he was working for you?"

"I don't see how he could get that impression."

"You're a captain and he's a buck sergeant. I've never been in the army but I've been told that officers can tell enlisted soldiers what to do. Was I misled?"

In response to Katherine's rare burst of sarcasm he awarded her a slight smile. "If you've met Sergeant Elton, you'll understand that he does not have particular regard for anybody with a higher rank." In a rare moment of truth, he added, "He's got a huge chip on his shoulder."

"Did you ever tell him how to treat the prisoners?"

"I don't understand the question."

Katherine played with her pencil a moment—I thought she was going to snap it in half—but she wisely chose instead to rephrase her query. "Sergeant Elton and the other members of his crew have testified that you employed their services to soften up various prisoners. They claim you told them to give certain prisoners special treatment, to 'prep them' for interrogation in your own lexicon, that you thanked them when it made the prisoner talk, and you encouraged them to turn up the heat when it didn't. They claimed you gave them a camera to record these activities so you and Chief Ashad could review the effects."

"That's a lie."

I allowed that revelation to sit for a moment then inquired of the captain, "Which one is a lie?"

If this question irritated him—it was certainly intended to—he didn't let it show. "I had no idea what they were doing in there. I was as shocked as anybody when I learned about it."

"Shocked? Really?"

"Yes, that's the right word. And let me add disgusted as well."

"Why would they lie about it?"

"Isn't it your job to find that out?"

"Well, somebody is lying. My job is to discover if it's you or them." I asked, "Why would you lie, Captain Willborn?"

Mary, in a harsh tone, interrupted, "That's enough, Sean. You'll stop this line of questioning right now."

"Give it a break, Mary. I didn't ask if him if he killed Palchaci." Now that I thought about it, though, that seemed like a terrific idea. I looked at Willborn. "Did you?"

Mary did not like this question either, and quickly informed me, "This is not a cross-examination, Colonel Drummond. You will refrain from making hostile comments or insinuating suggestions."

"Is that another of your arbitrary rules?"

"Yes, a big one. And if you break it again, I will break this off. I remind you that Captain Willborn is here as a courtesy."

I was getting tired of Mary and her endlessly expandable rules and her belligerent interjections and her interrogatory roadblocks and answered accordingly, "He's here, Mary, because my client and four other soldiers are facing life imprisonment for a crime they may not have committed. Captain Willborn is here because any judge will rule that since Miss Carlson and I have been brought into this case late, after the Article 32 hearings, we have the right to question him before the court martial." I then suggested, "But if you continue to be a pain in the ass, I can go find a judge and I can get a court order."

"That won't . . ." She reached up and adjusted her hair, and her expression. "Just rephrase your question."

I looked at Captain Willborn. "Regarding the reason the accused are all pointing their fingers at you, certainly you must have a suspicion, or at least a theory about what's behind it?"

He seemed to ponder this, then said, "Of course I've thought about it. They're trying to use my team as an alibi. They have to justify their nauseating activities and hide their real motive. That's obvious, isn't it?"

Katherine snapped, "It's not obvious to me."

Willborn leaned far forward, nearly in Katherine's face. "Then I'll make it clearer. Those people are sick. You've seen those pictures.

They're perverts, plain and simple." He couldn't resist adding, "Especially your client. A real sicko."

The way he treated Katherine pissed me off and I decided it was time to draw a little blood. I asked, "You disapprove of what they were doing?"

With an air of haughty righteousness, he replied, "Yes, I absolutely do."

"Had you known of their activities prior to the outbreak of the scandal would you have reported them to higher authorities?"

"That would be my duty as an officer and I . . . yes, I certainly would have. Gladly."

"Were they molesting any of *your* prisoners, Captain?"

Willborn was apparently unprepared for this somewhat predictable question, and in a rare lapse of self-control, he threw another curious look at Mary, who also seemed to have been caught off-guard. When a long moment passed without any helpful visual cues from Mary, Captain Willborn replied, "I think I did see several of my cases in the pictures . . . so, yes."

I informed him, "By my count, a total of forty-three different Iraqi men were included in the 406 pictures in my files. How many of those men were your cases?"

"I have no idea."

"You seem to be a bright guy. Approximate, Captain Willborn—was it closer to three, more like ten, or upward of twenty?"

"I told you I had no idea."

"Yes, you did say that. It's just not convincing."

Mary started to interrupt again, and I ignored her and pushed through with my next line of inquiry. "Was it your practice during interrogation sessions to observe the physical and psychological condition of your subjects?"

This was another question he seemed to have trouble answering. I decided to offer him a little assistance, so I glanced at my notes and read to him, verbatim, "The interrogator must be constantly aware of the shifting attitudes which normally characterize a source's reaction to interrogation. He notes the source's every word, gesture, and voice inflection. He determines why a source is in a certain mood, or why his mood suddenly changed." I looked up and asked Captain Willborn, "Do you recognize those words?"

"I suppose they do sound . . . vaguely familiar."

"I would hope they sound more than familiar, Captain. That excerpt was from Chapter One of Field Manual 34-52, the US Army bible on interrogation. I'm sure you're aware that the manual stresses repeatedly that the interrogator must be acutely observant and vigilant about any changes in the mood or attitude or mental state of his cases."

He looked pained, like he knew what was coming. "I'm familiar with the doctrine, Colonel."

"Good, Captain. The sessions in Cellblock One always occurred late at night. The prisoners were dragged out of their cells and forced to participate until the early morning hours. Over a month-long period, not only were they physically abused and mentally and physically raped, they were severely deprived of sleep. Didn't you ever notice any mood changes or swings? Maybe they appeared unusually exhausted?"

He pretended to think about this and remained perfectly expressionless and impassive; I've seen ice sculptures exude more vitality, more interest. Eventually, having exhausted the thoughtful routine, he said, "Not that I recall. I mean, sure, there were days when certain prisoners seemed worn out." He smiled like this was a big joke. "Hell, there were days when Ashad and I had to use toothpicks to pry our eyes open. We lived on caffeine over there."

I did not smile back. "Did you ever see any bruises or abrasions?"

"No, none."

"Signs of depression?"

"Remember these men were in prison. Their usual mental state was depressed and dispirited."

"Ever detect any evidence they'd been sexually molested?"

"Well, to be truthful, I've never raped or sexually abused anyone. What might that evidence look like . . . sir?"

It was a small room with only enough room for one obstinate wiseass. This guy was starting to get on my nerves. "Maybe they complained about the night sessions?"

"Oh, inmates complained all the time. It was the Al Basari anthem."

"What did they complain about?"

"About the food, about the smell, about the heat, about medical care, about the lousy accommodations . . . Hell, we complained right back at them." He paused to smile at me again. "Let me let you in on a big military secret, Colonel—Al Basari sucked."

"I asked if they complained about the night sessions."

"No, never."

"Maybe they displayed some signs of trauma, physically or psychologically." I recalled some of the activities from the photos and suggested, "Maybe they had difficulty sitting."

"Look, I'm embarrassed to admit that I saw nothing. Nothing tangible, nothing visible, nothing suspicious. In retrospect, sure, I wish I had been more attentive . . . more . . . Hell, I still don't know how I missed it . . . any warning signs . . . whatever."

"Regulations also mandate that you keep a log of all interrogating sessions annotating your observations. Did you maintain such logs?"

"Yes. As you said, it was required."

And that's when Mary erupted again. "Those logs are off-limits."

"Why, Mary?"

"Because they're filled with highly classified material. You can't touch them and you may not ask about any material or observations they contained."

Katherine, who had not previously known about either the requirement for, or the existence of, such logs, did not take Mary's injunction well. She replied with a rare show of genuine agitation and indignation, "Give me a break. You're kidding, right?"

"Didn't I sound serious?" As if we weren't getting the message, she answered her own question. "They're strictly off-limits."

"Those logs go to the heart of this case, Major. You cannot deprive our clients of possibly exculpatory material."

"Oh, watch me. I can, and I definitely will."

And they went back and forth, tossing threats and counter-threats at each other as Nate Willborn and I sat back and watched the badminton match.

Like Katherine, Mary was a very good lawyer, just not as good, though she didn't have to be; not today, and not later, before seven members of the court martial board. Since 9-11 the courts have sided with the government on a lot of these conflicts where the rights of the accused clash with the government's claims about the limits of privacy, about prolonged incarceration, and about security classifications.

I don't know which is right or wrong; I only know that government lawyers now have a big stick, and when you give them a stick it very often ends up inside your butt. I mean, government bureaucrats these days can slap a "Top Secret" label on a grocery list and the courts will usually back them up, which is like giving a kleptomaniac the back door keys to Macy's.

Katherine knew this, of course, but was using Mary to vent her frustration, which was emotionally gratifying, I'm sure, and was getting us nowhere. Katherine has a thing against the government and usually we're on opposite sides of the aisle, but in this case I agreed with her—though if I were sitting in Mary's shoes I would probably agree with her, too. This case was really conflicting.

After about two minutes of this, I became tired of the verbal ping-pong and interrupted to say to Mary, without notable enthusiasm, "We're going to file a motion for the logs and see where it goes."

Captain Willborn, he of the usually stoic demeanor, could not restrain another smile. "Well, you could do that . . . but . . . I wouldn't want you to waste your time."

I asked him, "What does that mean?"

"It would be pointless." After a pause, accompanied by a regretful frown, he informed us, "The logs are missing, I'm afraid."

"Missing is an ambiguous word, Captain."

"Yes, I know."

"Then be more specific. Missing as in, stuck in a thick safe in the basement, or missing, as in they accidentally fell into a big bonfire?"

Now with a perfectly straight face, he replied, "As I told you earlier, Sergeant Waylon managed the administration for the team. At the end of each day, I gave him our log sheets, and . . . after he died, I went looking for the logs . . . and"—he produced an almost convincing shrug—"well, they were all gone."

"Just gone?" You can imagine how much I love being jerked off like this.

"Hey, I know how suspicious this might sound to you. Remember, though, that the conditions at the base were primitive and hectic. There was no safe, so Waylon stuffed them in a large, expandable, paper file box. The box had disappeared."

"How could a box filled with classified material get up and walk away?" I asked, making no effort to mask my anger or my skepticism.

"That's a good question."

"I know, so answer it."

"I can't."

"Can't or won't?"

"Look, what we believe is that after Waylon died, as per regulations, a team of soldiers went through and inventoried his personal effects. Then his stuff was packaged and shipped to his family back in the States. The same with Chief Ashad's personal effects. Everything was shipped to his wife. The logs may have been shipped by accident. Plus there's always some crap left over, like porn, or dirty magazines, or official papers that are either inappropriate, irrelevant, or of no value to the family. As per procedure, the inventory teams separated those materials and destroyed what was left. It seems quite possible that the team that performed the inventory found the classified material and, not recognizing its military importance, destroyed it as well, or perhaps shipped it by mistake." He paused for a moment then added, "This was a serious loss of national security material. Naturally, I reported it to my chain of command."

"Was there any mention of the file box on the inventory forms?"

"You know, that's another odd thing."

I remarked, "Odd seems to be the byword of this case."

"Yes, well . . . there wasn't."

"No kidding. How do you account for it?"

"It's possible that Waylon stored the box somewhere else. Or perhaps Ashad had it. I really don't know. We searched for it, but it was hopeless."

He was definitely lying; we knew he was lying, he knew he was lying, and according to Mary's rule, we all were supposed to pretend he wasn't. I knew it wouldn't do any good but I said to Captain Willborn, "You're not even a good liar."

He produced a slight shrug and mumbled, "Sorry," though it wasn't clear if his apology applied to the missing file box, that he was lying, or that he wasn't even a good liar.

Chapter Fourteen

It seemed an opportune moment for what I assumed was an impromptu legal conference, and Katherine decided to kick it off the moment we got back in the Prius, away from prying ears, and after I pushed the stupid button that turned on the ignition.

She turned to me and asked, "How are we doing so far?"

"I'm doing great."

"There are two of us on this case."

"Good point. Well, I'm not so sure about you."

"So what's new?"

"Every question you ask has to do with whether our client was influenced or pressured to behave the way she did."

"And after all you've learned and heard, you still think that's the wrong track?"

"That depends. Do you want to win this case, or lose it to make some political point and embarrass the administration and the army?"

"You make it sound like an either/or proposition, and it's not. If Lydia and the others were behaving that way because they were ordered to—if they were even nudged in that direction—their responsibility and personal guilt is alleviated, if not abnegated. The

White House and the Pentagon were rewriting the rules on interrogation and torture. If a bunch of junior enlisted took it too far, the administration still bears blame."

"Listen to yourself, Katherine. You make it sound like they took a tiny, tentative step across a smudgy gray line. But that's not what happened here, was it? Peeing on a man's face? Is that a small step too far? Are you going to try to argue some bizarre link between that and waterboarding? Between forcing a prisoner to stand for uncomfortably long periods and stuffing objects up a man's rectum? How about—"

"I know what they did, Sean. When you light a match, don't act shocked when it ignites a forest fire. Once you move the restraints on human behavior, don't be surprised if a bunch of immature junior enlisted forget where the lines are."

"I hope this isn't a preview of your court summation. Really, Katherine."

"Given those damning pictures, do you have a better alternative?"

"No, I don't. Not yet," I replied. "But neither LTC Eggers nor Captain Willborn is going to confess they ordered or in any way encouraged the soldiers to behave that way. Chief Ashad and Sergeant Waylan are keeping their mouths shut because they're dead, which may be suspiciously convenient, but is still a fact. And everything on paper seems to have come in contact with a blowtorch. Whatever's left after that has been classified—we can't touch it. And anyway, it'll never make its way into court."

"Thanks for pointing out the difficulties I already knew." She paused to take a deep breath, then turned in her seat, put a hand on my arm, and asked, "What I meant is how are *we* doing? You and me?"

Uh oh. When women ask a question like that, it's usually a prelude to something men don't want to talk about. I replied, somewhat evasively, "A few big philosophical differences aside, I think we're doing fine."

"So do I, Sean." She looked me in the eye. "So . . . after Korea . . . why didn't you call me?"

"Well . . . I was in the hospital for a few months."

"I know. I visited you, remember? I left my number on your table."

"Was that you? Say, you weren't the one who slipped the liquid ex-lax into my IV line, were you?"

"Why didn't you call me, Sean?"

"Given the severity of the head wound, I was having a lot of memory issues."

She gave me a punch in the arm. "You were shot in the stomach."

"Oh." I rubbed my head and observed, "See, I forgot."

"Be honest with me, Sean. I won't get mad. It's important that you tell me the truth."

Well, the conversation had just progressed from "uh oh" to "oh shit." When a woman utters those words, she's either lying to you, or to herself, because she *definitely* will get mad. But I couldn't think of a convincing fib at that moment, so I answered, lamely and perhaps truthfully, "I thought about it, Katherine. I wanted to."

"But you never did."

"No, I never did. I'm just not sure it would work out."

"Neither am I. Tell me your reasons."

"We would kill each other."

"True." She shrugged. "But hardly relevant. Any others?"

"Your turn."

"All right." She thought about it, then said, "That first year at Georgetown I hated you . . . at least I thought I did. The other girls in the class were all smitten with the handsome war hero, the tragically wounded vet, the cool, confident, brilliant student . . . you should've heard the talk behind your back. They really put you on a pedestal." She laughed.

I didn't comment.

Katherine continued. "So I decided I would be the contrarian, I wouldn't flirt or fawn over you as so many others were doing. I would become a burr in your side. Every time you gave an opinion in class, I raised my hand and tried to make you look stupid. I tried to guess the position you would take on case studies, and I would research and take the opposing position. I almost killed myself studying, trying to do better than you."

"I was hoping you *would* kill yourself."

She smiled. "It wasn't until the third year when I had a revelation."

While she paused to think about her revelation, I tried to get my arms around the fact we were having this discussion in the first place. In all the years I'd known Katherine, we had never really had an intimate conversation about anything but the law, politics, and our opposing views on everything from the creation to the second coming, conversation that normally evoked homicidal imaginings—conversations about everything, that is, except sex and the way we felt *toward* each other, versus how we made each other feel.

She continued, "Well, that truth is, I had a big crush on you. I actually was nuts about you. I used to sit in class and just stare at you . . . when you weren't looking, of course."

"Oh, I saw you. I thought you were trying to bore holes through me with your laser eyes."

"Well, now you know. But, unfortunately, I had already set the pattern of our relationship. Every time you laid eyes on me, your face would turn this funny shade of red, and get tight all the sudden." She paused and did a quick, really stupid imitation of me, held breath, clenched fists, flexed jaw, snorting nostrils, and all. It didn't even look like me. Really. She said, "I set out to be a real pain in your ass, and I became very good at it."

"I had no idea." Well, I knew she was a pain in my ass but I had no idea she found yours truly attractive.

"So . . . eight years later, I decided to try again."

"Korea."

"Yes, Korea. Enough time had passed, I thought. Enough to put it behind us . . . enough to make a fresh start."

"You should've informed me, Katherine." I decided not to mention that it wasn't until the end of our case in Korea that I realized she was batting for the right team.

She said, "And maybe I wanted to see if I still felt the same way about you."

"And what did you decide?"

"You hadn't changed a bit. You were still incorrigible, stubborn, opinionated, coarse, violent, pushy—"

"I didn't want to mar perfection."

She couldn't let that one go without comment. "The thing is, you're the last man I would've . . . I mean, face it, Sean, you're not exactly an exemplar of progressive male virtues. You're such a throwback, the original tough guy, slightly chauvinistic, totally insensitive, mulish . . . and—"

"Katherine, that's no way to talk to a wounded vet."

"All right, my feelings hadn't changed. Maybe I didn't make that clear when I left you my number. But when you never called, I moved on."

If I was honest with myself, I had always felt a strong attraction for Katherine, as well. I think there is something about a woman who is cool and professional and unapproachable that makes her more alluring; it's the sexy librarian thing, or lusting after your first grade teacher. I should grow up and rise above that, but I haven't yet. I asked her, "Why are you bringing this up now?"

"Well, I don't want to pressure you . . . but Nel."

"So you and he are . . . ?"

"We are. In a committed relationship, romantically involved . . . whatever they call it these days." She added, somewhat coyly, "I think you already figured that out."

"For how long?"

"Nearly a year. We met in New York City, at a fundraiser for a cause we both believe in."

A picture formed in my head of Nelson calmly dropping a cool million or two to build lovely underwater resorts for humpback whales just to show off and slip into her panties. For some reason, that really pissed me off.

But of course, I was being silly; Katherine would not be impressed by wealth. She was the least materialistic person I had ever known.

Then again, a few billion dollars is enough to make anyone blink.

Anyway, Katherine seemed to hesitate for a long time before she dropped the big bombshell. "Nel asked me to marry him."

"I see." After taking a moment to absorb this announcement, I asked her, "And did Katherine say yes?"

"Katherine said, 'Give me some time.'"

"Because of me?"

"Partly, yes." She then clarified, "Largely, if I was honest with myself."

"Do you love him?"

"Maybe. I think I do."

"I believe the appropriate response for a long, happy union is yes, without question or doubt. I'd even leap off a cliff for him."

Actually, getting married *is* jumping off a cliff with no bottom, but this didn't seem like the right moment to bring that up.

"We're good together, Sean. Nel and I, we believe in the same things."

"So do Dallas and New York," I replied. "That's what makes the football so interesting."

"Are you describing Nel and me? Or you and me?"

"Good point." I looked away for a moment. "He's much older than you."

"Check the mirror, Grandpa."

"I'm old enough to be your big brother. He's old enough to be your great grandfather."

"Don't exaggerate." She cleared her throat, then said, "I seem to be attracted to older men. Maybe I just find dinosaurs sexy. I find *you* attractive."

"Plus he's filthy rich. Your hippie parents will boycott the wedding."

"Mom and Dad have finally grown up. Dad got his CPA license two years ago."

"A CPA? He really went over to the dark side."

"I know. He cried when the license arrived in the mail." She smiled, then informed me, jokingly, I think, "I can have fun giving it all away. Seriously, we can do a lot of good together."

"I'm sure the dying whales and endangered snails will be over-joyed. Be sure to invite them to the wedding."

"That's not fair, Sean. I like Nel, and I certainly respect him."

I was opening my lips to address that claim when I looked at Katherine and asked myself an alarming question—what was I saying? Only two minutes before I was ready to wrap my hands around her lovely throat and throttle her till her ears rattled; now I sounded like a jilted lover.

I thought of that old Chinese maxim that if you save a man's life, you are responsible for the rest of his life. What if you talked a woman out of a wedding? I could already feel the concrete drying around my feet.

I asked Katherine, "Is this why you asked for me as cocounsel?"

"No, I asked because you're the best choice. This is a tough, very challenging case and I admire your intelligence, your military acumen, your . . . well, your legal ingenuity." She played with her purse, then added, "Those reasons just happened to coincide with the personal ones."

I asked Katherine a very good question. "Does Nelson know about me?"

"I haven't told him . . . no."

"But he has an idea?"

"He's not an idiot. Yes, I'm sure he suspects."

"Do I have to worry about poison in my quarter-pounders?"

"He's a grown-up, Sean."

"Good for him. I'm not. Tell him to keep an eye on his brake line."

"How sweet. I've never had two men fight over me."

"You know this is crazy, Katherine?"

"Believe me, I'm well aware of that."

"This is the most publicized trial on the planet and we have the most sensationalized client, and she's possibly a moron, and it's an uphill case, the government is stacking the evidence—did I mention our client is almost certainly guilty?—and you want me to sort out my feelings for you."

She looked thoughtful, then said, "I suppose that about sums it up."

"I want to talk to Lydia again," I told her, which was my way of saying I didn't want to talk about *this* anymore.

Katherine looked slightly annoyed and checked her watch. "She should be done with the government psychiatrist by now." She flipped open her cellphone, punched in a number, and spoke to somebody about making Lydia available. She signed off and looked at me. "The same red brick building where we met with June Johnston."

I slipped the car into gear and we made the short drive back to the other side of the post. Neither of us spoke during the drive. I mean, you could tell somebody in the car was unhappy with somebody else in the car.

Lydia was awaiting us in the same small conference room where we had met with June, and this time her nose was stuffed inside a magazine called *Celebrity Fashions for Prison.*

Okay, not really; she was actually reading *Time* magazine, and at first, I thought we might be witnessing the dawn of a great intellectual awakening before I noticed her picture on the front cover, and the heading wasn't "Person of the Year."

Chapter Fifteen

Lydia looked up at us and smiled, and for some reason she looked inexplicably happy and remarkably healthy, with cheeks that were surprisingly ruddy for one who had been locked up indoors for the better part of two months. She reminded me of somebody else, but I couldn't seem to put my finger on who.

Katherine moved around the conference table and hugged Lydia, then they did the cheek brush thing, while I remained stiffly on my side of the table. Colonels don't hug and kiss privates unless they are courting a sexual harassment charge. And in a similar vein, a lawyer and client are expected to keep a certain distance, both physical and emotional. I was not sure what was going on between Katherine and Lydia, but whatever it was smelled like trouble.

Then we all sat and Katherine asked Lydia, "How are you feeling?"

"Okay. Still real bored, though."

"How did your meeting with the psychiatrist go?"

"Okay, I guess." She seemed to have second thoughts, though, and her lips got all scrunched up. "He sure asked lottsa funny questions."

"That's part of the routine, Lydia. Anything in particular that bothered you?"

She looked at me and seemed uncomfortable discussing such intimate matters in my presence. In my most comforting tone, I assured her, "It's okay, Lydia. I'm not judgmental and anything you say is strictly confidential." Actually, I'm very judgmental, but Lydia had exposed enough of herself in the pictures that I couldn't imagine what verbal disclosure or intimacy could possibly bother either of us at this point.

After a moment Lydia confided, "Sure asked a lotta questions about sex. The guy was weird."

Katherine asked, "What kind of questions?"

"He asked how old I was when I got my cherry popped, and he asked me to talk about near ever' time I got laid." She studied the tabletop, then corrected herself. "'Course he didn't put it like that. He used all kind of classy words, like coitus and cunnylingus and such."

Classy? I bit back a smile as I pictured the doctor having to explain the definitions of those more formal sexual terms to such an uninformed mind. When you put A into B that's coitus; and when A goes into C that's cunnilingus. This was assuming that Lydia knew the alphabet as well as she understood anatomy; probably not a good assumption.

Katherine also seemed to have difficulty controlling her expression but had enough presence to ask, "Did he focus on anything in particular?"

Lydia produced a clueless shrug. "Seemed mighty interested in my family, too."

"I think that's natural, as well. Some psychiatrists believe all mental issues are rooted in early familial relations."

If this Freudian revelation meant anything to Lydia she chose not to show it. "Ask me, he's the one who needs help. He's a real nutjob."

Goes without saying, Lydia—he was a shrink after all—but I did not really care about this, so I changed the subject. "Lydia, Katherine and I have interviewed the prison chain of command, and the military intelligence folks. They claim that nobody told Sergeant Elton to torture or abuse the prisoners."

She stared at me, in her slow way apparently trying to catch up to the shift in topic, then replied, in a very aggrieved tone, "Never said they did."

"Yes, you . . ." Her obtuseness was already getting on my nerves, and I took a few breaths, backed off and asked her, "Remind me. What did they tell you to do?"

Unfortunately, her mind was still stuck on what I had just said. "Wusn't nobody torturin' nobody," she insisted, sounding now whiny and petulant.

I ignored the triple negative and asked, "Then what would you call it?"

"Havin' fun is all."

"*Fun?*"

"Nobody got hurt or nuthin'. We was jus' playin' games. Wasn't harmin' nobody."

Actually somebody did get hurt. Palchaci was dead. "Just games?"

"That's what I said. Lotta them prisoners, they had as good a time as us."

I glanced at Katherine who was pretending she wasn't disturbed by the twisted nature of Lydia's logic. I held the stare.

Eventually moved by my look, Katherine did inquire of her client, almost hesitantly, "Why would you say that, Lydia?"

"Cuz it's true, Katherine." Lydia had slipped into full pout mode now—she had crossed her arms like a huffy little girl signaling the onset of a full-blown tantrum. "Guys pay dang good money to see strippers. Them Iraqis, they got all the looks and peeks they wanted. All fer free, too. Didn't cost 'em nuthin'."

When Katherine made no response to that bizarre rationalization, Lydia continued. "I mean, they wuz stuck in prison, bored outta their wits. And let me tell you, they got off on it."

"Got off?" I asked. "You mean they were enjoying themselves?"

"I mean they got big boners and jizzed all over the place."

"Oh."

"So ask me . . . yeah, damn sure they enjoyed it," Lydia insisted.

It was no use debating the point—Lydia was obviously the type who made up her own mind, presumably not a difficult task, as small as it was. I did warn her, however, "That may be your opinion but you will not express it in court."

"Why not? When men get a big woody and git their rocks off, don't it mean they're havin' a real swell time?"

I really wanted Katherine to straighten out this circuitous sexual logic, woman to woman, so to speak, and I looked at her but she was too busy enjoying the expression on my face.

Well, somebody had to, so I said to our client, "You induced these men to aroused states, Lydia. They were not participating on their own volition, and their expressions in the pictures suggest that fun was the last thing on their mind. Many were terrified."

Lydia still looked confused, so hoping to clear this up I informed her, "Technically, what you did to those men was rape. And perhaps, in a legal sense, as well, it was rape. If you raise the specious argument that it was as enjoyable for them as for you, you invite the prosecutor to delve into this issue and you will definitely antagonize the jury." Then, hoping against hope to get off this topic I asked her, "Did you ever actually meet, or see, Captain Willborn or Chief Ashad in person?"

"Yeah."

"When?"

"Well . . . Ashad, I guess I saw 'im once or twice."

"All right, where?"

"In the prison."

Getting a direct unequivocal answer from this girl was like debating with a herd of politicians. "Be specific, please. I'm asking *where* in the prison?"

"The cellblock. He paid us a visit a coupla times."

"At nighttime, or during the day?"

"I already tole you I wasn't there during the day."

"Right. So it was night?"

She gave me a look like I was one who was dense. "Well, yeah." She hesitated, then added, "I remember, cuz he came once when we was havin' one of our ST sessions. He didn't say or do nuthin', though. Just stood there . . . in a corner. Sorta watched for a while."

I glanced at Katherine. "And do you remember what you were doing that night?"

"Oh . . . well, I recall that real good."

Now we were getting somewhere. "Why do you recall it so clearly?"

"See, one of the Hadjis, he didn't seem to be gittin' with the program. And one of them other Hadjis, he spoke real passable English and he tole us this guy was pretty educated'n all. A college professor, a real uppity sort. So Danny, he tole us we hadda break this guy."

"Because he was educated?"

"No . . . well, not exactly. See, this fella, the others all looked up to him . . . I guess on account of his education'n all. And he'd mumble a bunch of stuff at 'em in Iraqi and break the mood. We couldn't never understand squat he wuz sayin', but it sure looked like he wuz tellin' 'em to stand up to us."

"So Danny wanted you to break him. Get him to knock it off, right?"

A quick nod. "Anyways, that night we tied 'im to a chair and ole June climbed aboard, and she give 'im a lapdance liable to make a rooster faint. Danny, he was playin' some music, and I mean, that June, she ground away 'bout ten minutes and . . . well, nuthin'. It was weird. The Iraqi guy, he just sat there with this funny expression—y'know, like he was bored, or it was all a big joke or somethin'." Lydia was shaking her head now, as she recalled that night. "When June got off she tole us the guy didn't even pop a boner."

"Some men have more self-restraint than others."

"Nah, wasn't like that. Let me tell you, when June's naked and grindin' away, any reasonable pecker in the world's gonna get harder'n a chainsaw." She looked at me to see if I comprehended what she was saying.

"I understand." A chainsaw?

"So Danny, he called Chief Ashad and he asked 'im what he wanted us to do 'bout that. That Ashad, he wuz a real clever fella. He tole Danny that maybe we wuz lookin' at the problem backassword."

"And what came next?"

"Well, 'bout five minutes after that, Ashad showed up. And Danny, by then, he had another prisoner all lined up and he made this guy git naked and then git on this professor's lap and start twistin' and grindin' and wouldn't you know . . . that professor . . . well, he wasn't smiling no more. He 'bout burst outta his pants."

"So he was gay?"

A big nod and a bigger smile. "A real faggot." She then came full circle and informed me with a knowing smile, "Now, I got nuthin' agin faggots, but no wonder June didn't git no rise outta him."

"Yes, no wonder. And what happened after that?"

"That was pretty much the end of that ST session, so Danny, he tole us to put ever'body back in their cells. But, well, turns out them Iraqis got somethin' fierce agin fags, cuz the next night when we got this guy outta his cell, he was beat up somethin' awful. I mean, them other Hadjis . . . well, they jus' lumped his ass real good." She added, sounding very satisfied, "Didn't give us a lick of trouble after that."

"And Ashad witnessed this?"

"I tole you he did. He didn't say nuthin', it was jus' like he was sorta checkin' to see we was handlin' it okay. Good officer."

"And this was the only time?"

"Well, there wuz this other time . . . I wuz purty sure it wuz him, tho' I couldn't swear to it or nuthin'."

"When was this?"

"Purty near the end, and the lights would get real dim in there. I was real concentrated on what I was doin', but I seen this figure . . . sort of standin' in the shadows, y'know, like watchin' us real close."

As I recalled from the pictures, "near the end" would mean Ashad was a witness to some of the worst depredations. "Did you see his face?"

"Not exactly . . . but I wuz pretty certain it wuz him . . . Ashad, I mean. The guy I saw was real skinny'n all, with big shoulders, like Ashad"

"Any other reasons to believe it was him?"

"I guess so. Cuz Danny, he kept glancin' over there, like it was somebody he wanted to make a big impression on. Danny really looked up to that Arab officer."

Katherine asked her, "But it could have been somebody else?"

She contemplated this with a funny expression. "Katherine, I tole you I couldn't swear to it or nuthin'."

To avoid the onset of another petulant tantrum, I said, "Yes, so you did. Did any other members of the team see him?"

"Guess you oughtta ask them."

Then I quickly changed the subject to another topic. "Did you ever give the Special Treatment to General Palchaci?"

Sometimes with clients, a sudden, unexpected shift in topic like this will unveil a welcome response—like truth—but Lydia's mental circuits were so lethargic, I wasn't optimistic. I studied her face, and her eyes, as she considered this question and, as expected, it took a long moment for the question to ooze through the ear canal, to rumble past the mental lint and litter, and sink into the deep recesses of her brain. And, during that moment, her expression shifted quickly from surprise, to something resembling alarm, before it matured to her usual countenance of dulled awareness. "Nope. He didn't never get no ST," she replied, sounding absolute about that.

"You're sure?"

"Said I wuz, didn't I?"

"Did you have any dealings with him? In any form whatsoever?"

"I dunno. Coulda happened, I guess. We never really knew their names, y'know." She added in an unfortunate aside I hope she didn't repeat in court, "They wuz all jus' meat to us."

"Well, Palchaci was older, in his sixties. Do you recall any dealings with an elderly gentleman?"

"Most of them guys wuz older than me."

Good point. I withdrew Palchaci's photo from my briefcase and held it up for Lydia to observe. "This is General Palchaci. Take your time, study his face, and tell me if you remember him."

She got another of those funny expressions and she rubbed her temples. "Don't guess I do, nope." After another painfully long moment, she added, "But I ain't fer sure."

"This is important, Lydia. Did you enter his cell after his death?"

"Oh . . . no, fer sure I didn't. No way."

"You're certain?"

"Why you askin'?"

To annoy you. "Because you're likely to be asked the same questions on the stand, and Katherine and I need to be certain there's nothing that ties you to the General, or implicates you in his death."

"Well, I had nuthin' to do with any of that."

Katherine asked a few more questions about Palchaci, about whether Lydia heard any of the others discuss his murder, and so forth, then a few more queries regarding the statement Lydia gave the MPs when she was arrested. Lydia finished up by saying, "Y'know, they had all them pictures'n all, so it seemed real stupid to try'n deny all the stuff we did. I wouldn't, anyways . . . no siree. I'm proud of it. I mean, a lot of them Hadjis, they tole the intel folks all kinds of stuff. We wuz savin' lives. Helpin' win the war."

The odd thing was, she appeared to really believe it. I had this weird thought, a foreshadowing of Lydia, in fifty years hence, seated in her rocker with a large passel of her grandkiddies gathered at her feet, looking up at her, and curious little Billy-Jo asks, "What'd you do to win the war, Granny?" Well, boy, plug your ears because your ole granny really went above and beyond.

I looked at Katherine and neither of us had any more questions for Lydia at that moment. But it was a relief to confirm that we had nothing to fear regarding Palchaci's murder, on either CID's part, or Lydia's. We bid Lydia farewell and walked out to the hallway.

Once we were far enough away that we couldn't be overheard I said to Katherine, "We're going to need a major coaching session before the trial."

"I'm not so sure about that."

"Katherine, she thinks she was the life of the big party and the guests had the time of their lives. She thinks it's okay to force a man to orgasm. She thinks Uncle Sam owes her a big hug and maybe a medal or two. And those are just the idiotic delusions we know about."

Katherine did not reply. Finally she asked, "Can you think of a way to make the pictures go away?"

"Didn't we already go over this?"

"Remind me, what did we say?"

"We agreed to select the worst ones and submit a pretrial motion to the judge for exclusion on the grounds that they're superfluous and prejudicial. Don't play games with me, Katherine."

"So you don't intend to challenge *all* the pictures?"

"What's your point?"

We were out in the parking lot now, walking through the rows of cars. Being an army post, there was only one Prius in the entire parking lot, one quirky yellow oddball tucked in among all the pick-ups and SUVs and cheap sedans. I pulled the bill of my hat lower and hoped nobody saw me walking toward this thing. Katherine was saying, "The court martial board will see enough pictures to establish Lydia's guilt firmly in their minds. We can't avoid it. But they can also hear from her own lips how incapable she was of making sound moral judgments. I'm thinking of putting her on the stand. If she sounds like a delusional idiot, that might be our only hope."

"That's a terrible idea."

"I knew you would say that."

"Katherine, I—"

"Sean, I'm really not in the mood for another argument right now."

Well, she got her wish because that was the moment when we reached the car—and whatever thought I was about to express, immediately vanished.

The first thing I noticed was that the driver-side window was broken, completely shattered as though somebody had driven a crowbar or hammer through it.

The second thing was the pair of human ears on the middle of the driver's seat, two mildly shriveled appendages from a human head—just sitting there.

With one hand, I grabbed Katherine's shoulder and pulled her down to the tarmac and, with the other, I reached behind my back, beneath my army blouse, and withdrew my .45 automatic.

I looked around for a moment to see if anybody was watching us, then, from my pants pocket, I withdrew the amulet Chief O'Reilly had provided and squeezed it as hard as I could.

During the four minutes it took for a response unit to arrive at our location, I asked myself some very good questions: Whose ears were in the car and what were they doing there?

Chapter Sixteen

The initial response crew was comprised of two burly young MPs whose job was merely to secure Katherine and me until Chief Terry O'Reilly showed up, nearly three minutes afterward, with one of his security people.

Terry shot out of his sedan, peeked in the window and said, "Oh . . . shit."

Katherine looked over his shoulder at the ears and asked, "What's going on here?"

O'Reilly looked at her, then at me, then said, "Look, there's something I didn't tell you about the murder of Martin Weinstein."

"Let me take a guess," I said. "The perp cut off Major Weinstein's ears."

O'Reilly shrugged, but without any hint of apology or embarrassment. "We were keeping it secret. You know, to determine at the next crime scene if we're dealing with the same guy."

We collectively gawked at the ears a little longer; obviously this was the same guy. O'Reilly finally remarked, "The FBI profilers had a theory that we had a trophy hunter on our hands."

"Wrong," I said. "You have a perp who likes to send messages. You have a killer who thinks ahead. A planner."

"Well, I guess we know that now."

"And even as he killed Weinstein," I continued, "he was thinking about us, or his next target. So what's the message here, Chief?"

"Ears, right?" He stared at the inside of the car. "So it could have something to do with listening—either too much or not enough. Or maybe to the wrong people."

"Or," I countered, "he just wanted to scare the shit out of us, and it could be that Major Weinstein's ears were the nearest things to chop off with a knife." I pointed at his ears. "They come off really easily. Some American soldiers in Vietnam used to take them as war trophies."

O'Reilly shrugged again, as if to say, yes, it could be that, too. What he did not say but should have said was the truth: O'Reilly didn't have a clue.

Katherine was standing beside the car, gawking at the gory sight. "One of those ears looks like it has something stuck in it."

We all stared at the pieces of poor Martin Weinstein on the car seat and it *did* look like something was tucked inside one of them. O'Reilly reflexively did his gumshoe thing, snapped on a pair of latex gloves, reached inside and carefully withdrew the piece of paper, unfolded it, and held it by a corner for us to see. Scrawled in bold crayon were the words, "BE CARFUL. YOU DON'T KNOW WHO YOUR MESING WITH."

The writing, which was block-like and messy, looked as if it had been scrawled by a child, and the infantile spelling and grammatical errors suggested a low level of education or perhaps a foreigner who lacked familiarity with the English language.

O'Reilly asked us, "Any idea what it means?"

Katherine observed, "Somebody is watching Sean and me. That's what it means."

"I mean what's he warning you about?"

Katherine looked ready to say something, but before she could get any words out, I gave her a look and said, "If we knew the answer to that, Chief, we'd tell you."

O'Reilly decided it was a waste of time to question us further and he shooed us away, then he and his assistant began the standard forensics ritual, bagging the ears and glass debris, applying powder for fingerprint traces, and so on. But I think we all sensed that they were empty motions. Considering the skills the killer had shown at both earlier crime scenes, would he really be dumb enough to leave any helpful breadcrumbs at this one? Not likely.

Katherine and I used this moment to engage in a candid exploration about why we had been targeted, and by whom, and for what. O'Reilly seemed like a pretty good guy and I trusted him and his people to do their best to keep us alive—but did I trust him not to share insights of our legal strategy with his friends in the opposition? That was another question altogether. Always remember who signs the guy's paycheck.

So, after wasting a few minutes on all the things we didn't know, Katherine told me, "Our predecessor was murdered. And now we've been targeted for this warning, assuming that's what it is. I don't think that's a coincidence."

"No, it's not."

"What's that about, Sean?"

"For some reason the defense of Lydia Eddelston seems to be a matter of significant interest to the killer. Plus he killed Danny Elton's lawyer. We should assume that's what is called a clue, a connection."

"Definitely. But what do Elton's defense and Lydia's have in common? We haven't even talked to Elton yet."

"Do they share a secret?"

"Maybe. But I don't see what it is."

I considered this and it still didn't make sense. So I did what I usually do when faced with a head-splitting quandary—I changed the subject by asking Katherine, "When was the last time Lydia had a full medical workup?"

"I would think you have a better idea of that than me."

"Before the deployment would be my bet."

"Okay, so what?"

"Get a doctor to give her a short exam. Today, Katherine. Tell Lydia it's a standard follow-up to the psych exam, and tell the army we're worried about her general health."

"What has this got to do with the ears in the car?"

"Forget the ears. Think about what your eyes are telling you."

Chapter Seventeen

Sometimes, not often enough, bad news comes wrapped in good news. The bad news was that Chief O'Reilly, in an effort to be thorough and diligent, called his FBI contact in the area, who also wanted to have a look-see at the missing pieces of Major Feinstein in our car. The FBI guy was fifteen minutes away, which meant we couldn't use the car for at least thirty minutes.

The good news was that this left us thirty minutes to kill—though I suppose that was an unfortunate choice of words—and it turned out Sergeant Daniel Boone Elton was inside the long red brick building, having just finished an interrogatory with another defense team. This case was getting to be like a game of musical chairs between all the legal teams, witnesses, and accused.

The trick was you had to remain alive long enough to end up in a chair.

So Katherine and I marched back inside, this time to a cramped conference room on the second floor where we found Sergeant Danny Elton with his defense attorney, an army Captain named Bill Delong.

Elton, I was surprised to see, was actually quite clean-cut, and fairly good-looking, with a strong jaw and a lean, muscular build.

His BDUs were well pressed, and his army boots, which were black, instead of the new vogue loam desert boots, were buffed and lacquered to a high sheen.

He looked, in fact, like a recruiting poster soldier, a martial Beau Brummel, which was proof once again about the pitfalls of judging by appearance. Either his defense attorney had cleaned him up nicely, or Elton had a few edges that I hadn't anticipated.

Delong, to the contrary, looked like one of those army lawyers who give rise to the suspicion that all of us are hiding from a malpractice suit or disbarment. He was overweight, for one thing, with a soft, chubby face, recessed eyes, and blubbery lips. His uniform, for another, looked like it hadn't been cleaned or pressed since the Battle of the Bulge, a battle he had clearly lost in more ways than one.

Like most officers in the technical branches, I am not a stickler for regulations. But you can push it too far. I assumed that Captain Delong was either so good at his job that he didn't need to worry about it, or so far gone that he still didn't have to worry about it.

To continue with the poor first impression, from his posture and his expression, which was an annoying combination of drollness and smug haughtiness, Bill Delong appeared to think a great deal of himself, and not so much of us. There's a fine line between cocky and insolent. I, for example, am sometimes cocky; this guy was kissing his own ass. He didn't even come to his feet when a senior officer entered the room, which the army would not approve of, nor for a lady, which his mother would frown at. Aside from a generous imagination, I could not for the life of me see the source of this guy's tapestry of arrogance. Well, maybe he had a big dick.

Anyway, Katherine gave a nice smile as she performed the introductions and graciously thanked both Delong and Elton for making themselves available on such short notice.

Katherine, when she chooses to be, can be quite diplomatic; obviously, she wanted Danny Elton in the proper mood, which I approved of. From his testimony in the earlier Article 32 hearing, Danny appeared to react about as well to confrontation as I do.

She and I sat, side by side, at the table across from Elton and his attorney, while I forced a smile on my face that hurt. I don't enjoy smiling at assholes.

Captain Delong wanted to get the opening shot and quickly announced, "I intend to remain here for this meeting." He added, with no attempt at sincerity, "I hope that isn't a problem for you two."

Katherine smiled nicely. "And if it is?"

He shrugged back. "Live with it."

Katherine lied and said, "I was going to ask you to stay anyway." She then withdrew a small recorder from her purse and placed it in the middle of the table. With an air of contrived formality she announced, "Interrogatory with Sergeant Daniel Elton in the presence of his attorney, Captain Bill Delong. 1430, February twenty-third." Katherine then looked at Elton and asked, "Sergeant Elton, how long have you known Lydia Eddelston, and how did the two of you become acquainted?"

"Well, best I can remember . . . 'bout a year now."

"Okay, that's when. Now how? And where?"

"We was doin' a weekend drill, in Indianapolis, if I recall right. And one night after training, a bunch of us went to a local joint for some suds and a little booty call. I got pretty ripped and I thought the night was gonna be a pussy blowout, then this chick walks up to me, and, without no howdy-do or nuthin' says, 'Hey stud, how about you and me go fuck.'"

Katherine didn't blink an eye. "Just like that? Lydia approached you, out of the blue?"

"I know, right?" Elton gave her a leering wink. "Hell, I didn't even know her name . . . but it ain't like you really need one to fuck." He turned to me and with a guy-to-guy smirk, confided, "She wasn't that good-lookin' or nothin', but I figured, hey, she's got a pussy and that righteous attitude, right?"

When neither Katherine nor I responded to that uncharitable assessment, he leaned far back into his seat and let loose a loud chortle. "Tell you what—that chick was crazier'n hell. Once she turns on, she's like that Eveready rabbit. Wasn't nuthin' she wasn't willing to try. Hell, I couldn't walk right for two days."

Well, he may have looked nicely dressed and coiffed, but beneath that rehabilitated veneer Danny Elton was every bit the coarse asshole suggested by his personnel files and by his earlier Article 32 testimony.

Katherine paused for a moment and, though her demeanor and expression remained indifferent, I was sure her insides were in a high boil. For Katherine, who obviously is into the whole women's lib thing, I didn't think the lady reversing roles issue would shock or appall her in the least. But Katherine is still every inch the lady, with all the personal rectitude that entails, and Danny Elton, with his vulgar disclosures and masculine brutality, was waving a red cape at a bull.

I mean, even I felt like driving a fist down Elton's throat.

Captain Delong, however, apparently found his client's humor irresistible, because he chuckled.

Katherine said, a little coolly and stiffly, "So the two of you developed a relationship?"

"A . . . *relationship*?" He frowned.

"Do I need to spell it for you?"

Elton studied her a moment with narrowed eyes, obviously trying to fit Katherine in some sort of mental box. I don't think he spent a lot of time around women like Katherine, educated women of higher intelligence who did not find his company enthralling or his humor titillating. He said, "We screwed a lot, if that's what it means."

"I suppose that's one definition of a relationship."

He slapped his sides and laughed. "You gotta point there, girl." He stopped laughing. "Anyway, when we all got to Iraq, Lydia became my fuck buddy. She—"

"What do you mean by that?" Katherine interrupted.

Elton gave her a sarcastic smirk. "Do I need to spell it for you, honey?"

"A definition would suffice."

"Jesus, where you been? My fuck buddy—if I needed to get my rocks off, she was there, legs behind her ears, ready'n able."

Katherine, to her credit, did not blink or even blush. "So your relationship was sexual, not romantic?"

"What'n the hell kinda question is that? Christ, that girl's nothin' more'n a life support system for a vagina. She's stupider'n dirt."

Neither Katherine nor I replied.

Once again he seemed amused by his own insults, however, and couldn't resist going one step further. "Mind you, I ain't complainin' or nothin'. In Iraq, the other guys was all watching porn and whackin' the donkey to get their rocks off. I was getting my lights balled off anytime I got the itch."

He turned to me. "Tell you what, pal. That chick's pussy ain't got no off switch."

I was not his pal before, and I was becoming less so by the second. Elton laughed again, as did his lawyer, while I considered jumping across the table and kneeing them both in the nuts. But Katherine gave me a look I interpreted to mean, their balls are off-limits.

So instead I leaned forward and asked, "Whose idea was it to use the women in the special treatments?"

"Shit, man, wasn't nobody's *idea.*"

"Come now. It had to be somebody's idea. I thought you were . . . a man . . . a leader, Sergeant Elton. I didn't realize you were such a wimp that you allowed your visitors to take control over your cellblock."

As I suspected he might, he did not like this dig at his personal virility. His eyes narrowed and he cleared his throat. "Well, y'know, sometimes, you just gotta let shit happen. Go with the flow." He hesitated then added, "See, ole Lydia, she's got what I'd call a real imaginative mind."

"You're saying it was Lydia's initiative?"

"I'm saying her and June was there one night when I brought a prisoner back from interrogation. And Lydia, with her, she's such a slut . . . everything's about fucking, about how she can get off. So she talked June into doing this stripper act. At first, I went whoa, put the clothes back on, girl—but when I saw it was workin', y'know, I went, well . . . what the fuck?"

"Working? What exactly does that mean?"

"The prisoner was flipping out, man. Screaming, crying, waving his arms, like, totally freak. Christ, it was even better'n beatin' the shit out of the guy." He paused for a moment to mull this trade-off between force and libido. "Thing is, Iraqis have this thing about pussy." He thought about it a moment longer, then expanded on his sociological theory. "Shit, they're all momma's boys. Y'know, afraid of snatch. That religion really fucks with their heads, man."

Katherine ignored his scatology and his brawny take on Iraqi sexual pathologies, and asked, "And Andrea, what was her role in this?"

"Christ, she's as much stuck on stupid as Lydia. It's a miracle she remembers to breath."

"I did not ask you to describe her, I asked what her role was."

"Yeah . . . I heard that. Another chick willing to lend her twat to the cause is all. Anything you asked, pretty much, she'd do."

Katherine asked, "And what was your relationship to Captain Willborn and Chief Ashad?"

He slumped back into his chair with an amused expression. "That relationship word again, huh?"

"It's a straightforward question. Please answer it."

"Well, they was tryin' to get information from the prisoners and I knew how to make 'em squeal. They didn't have the balls to do what it took. I did. That was the relationship, all right?" He then added, "Call it a ball swap."

"Technically, you were not in their chain of command, and technically, there was supposed to be a firewall between your activities as a jailor and their responsibilities as interrogators. So what I'm asking is this—Did you and Captain Willborn and Chief Ashad formalize this arrangement?"

"Formalize?" He looked at Katherine like that word did not compute. "Lady, what world are you lawyers livin' in?"

Good question, but Katherine explained, very patiently, "I'm asking if you and the interrogators worked out an arrangement, if they gave you orders, if you and the girls were doing their bidding."

Elton came forward in his chair and began using his finger to talk. "Tell you what . . . Ashad tole me he *liked* what we was doin'. He gave me a camera. He asked me to take pictures so's he could see what worked, and how it worked. I debriefed him every mornin' after our little sessions and since I don't know shit about computers I gave him the camera to put the fuckin' pictures in his. He figured his whole daily interrogation strategy on what I told him." He looked at Katherine. "That fuckin' formalized enough for you?"

In an effort to confirm what Lydia had told us, I asked Elton, "Did Chief Ashad ever directly witness your prep sessions?"

"Sure."

"You're positive?"

"Oh, he popped by a coupla times."

"How often?"

"Like I said, a few times. More, maybe . . . I ain't exactly sure." He paused for a moment, then he winked at me. "He didn't like to interrupt the flow, so he hadda hidey place where he liked to sneak peeks."

"Where was this place?"

"End of the cellblock. He'd disconnected the lightbulbs there, y'know, so's he could hide in the shadows."

I thought about what he'd said so far, and what Lydia and June had told us, and it was interesting that only Ashad was mentioned as the overseer of the group's activities, and only Ashad had actually visited the cellblock during the nightly sessions. "What about Captain Willborn?" I asked. "Was his involvement as deep as Ashad's?"

"He was Ashad's boss," he replied as though that answer was enough to ensure the captain's culpability. "Oh, yeah, he knew everything goin' down. And don't let 'em tell you no different."

Katherine quickly informed him, "In fact, he has denied it. We spoke with the captain earlier this morning and he emphatically told us he had no idea what was going on in the cellblock."

"He said that? Well . . . he's a big, fat liar."

"But neither Lydia nor June ever met Ashad or Willborn. That leaves only *your* word that they knew what was happening."

Elton's face had gone redder. "I *know* Ashad told him what was going down. A coupla times when I was briefing Ashad, Willborn came into the room. But he wanted to keep his distance. You know the type—he wanted all the credit but he didn't want to stick his hands in the shit." Elton's face scrunched up with disgust. "That guy's a ballless a-hole. He bolted like a scared jack rabbit as soon as it dawned on him what we was talking about."

213

Katherine asked, "So would it be safe to say that most of your dealings were with Ashad?"

"Look, if you're talkin' about who gave me the instructions, and who I briefed, and who I talked to . . . yeah, Ashad. All Ashad, all the time. But if you're sayin' Willborn wasn't in on this, you're suckin' a hundred gallons of horseshit through a straw, lady." He added, "Don't you let that asshole weasel out of it."

When neither Katherine nor I responded to that charge, he insisted, loudly and with great vehemence, "He *knew* what we was doin' in there. Damn sure, he did."

"Okay," Katherine said in a placating tone, obviously having heard enough on this subject before she moved the interrogatory to the next topic. "Who do *you* think killed General Palchaci?"

Captain Delong awoke from his languorous slumber to insist, in a forceful and rude tone, "My client had nothing to do with Palchaci's death. If you're implying he did, this session is over right now."

Katherine shot me a glance I interpreted to mean handle this officer-to-officer, or idiot-to-idiot, and, in my most reassuring tone, I responded, "Relax, Captain. We're not implying that Sergeant Elton had anything to do with Palchaci's murder. Katherine merely asked his view on who did."

Actually, in my mind, and probably, a great many other minds, Danny Elton did seem the most likely candidate for Palchaci's murderer. He was hot-tempered, had volcanic ego issues, no moral boundaries I could discern, and in a physical sense, certainly he possessed the strength and bulk to beat a man to death. Not to be overly chauvinistic, no matter how sexually libertine their behavior, I simply could not picture Lydia, June, or Andrea pulverizing a body with such obliterating force, abandon, and fury. Women, through-out time, have been known to employ sex as a weapon, and that is exactly what these girls did, in their own minds, and certainly, in the physical sense, as a weapon of war. Brute force, on the other hand, tends to be the provenance of men. As Chief Rienzi observed, the beating inflicted on Palchaci had been surreally brutal and, after five minutes with Danny Elton, there was not a doubt in my mind that he possessed both the thoughtless cruelty and moral laxity to inflict such severe carnage on a human body.

In fact, for a man like Elton, I thought, a man who detested authority in any manifestation, killing a general officer of any army would be a treat.

But Delong seemed to buy my reassurance, and he signaled with a jerky nod to Elton that it was all right to proceed. Actually, Elton seemed to welcome the opportunity. He grinned at me. "You know, you're the first guy to ask me that fucking question."

"Well, Sergeant, here's your chance to answer it."

"It was me, damn sure, I'd be lookin' at Ashad and Willborn."

I couldn't resist replying, "Because you don't like them? Because one is dead and the other is getting off scot-free? Why are they your prime suspects?"

"Cuz fuckin' Palchaci, that guy drove 'em nuts. He wouldn't give 'em the time of day. They was taking big heat over him."

Katherine leaned forward on her elbows and asked, "How do you know this?"

He slumped down in his chair. "Okay if I smoke?"

This was a government building and it was definitely not okay, but I just nodded my approval—which drew a dirty look from Katherine, who did not appreciate my insensitivity to the environment or to her lungs.

He withdrew a pack of unfiltered Camels out of a pocket, tapped it a few times on the back of his hand, tough guy style, dug out a cigarette, lit it, and took a long, slow drag. He said, "Willborn tole me he and Ashad were ordered to do whatever it took to get him to crack."

"Ordered by who?" I asked.

He took another drag and shrugged. "You had every flavor of spook in them trailers on the FOB. MI, CIA, NSA, all the alphabets was there. They tried all kinds of stupid shit to blend in and act like they was soldiers, but they stuck out like boils on a baby's ass."

Something went off in the back of my head, and I filed it away. I asked, "So *you* don't know?"

"Specifically, nah . . . tell you what, though. They had big pull. I sure-as-shit know that."

"Why do you say that?"

"Cuz Willborn, he was a pretty cool customer, and *he* was rattled."

"How was he rattled? What rattled him?"

"Look, I broke a lotta those guys. I made Ashad and Willborn look damned good, but it was never enough for them assholes in the trailers. They really wanted Palchaci to spill his guts. Willborn and Ashad was catchin' big-time heat. So they got Palchaci transferred to my block, and Willborn made me a promise that if I got the guy to sing, he'd arrange an instant transfer to Hawaii for me."

"You didn't like Iraq?" I asked.

"What can I say?" He smiled. "The beaches suck and raghead chicks don't put out."

"Shallow reasons."

He laughed.

Regretting that I had amused him, I waited for his smile to wear off, then asked, "So did you try to get Palchaci to open up?"

"A few times, sure. And let me tell you somethin', that old geezer had woodpecker lips for a hide."

"What did you do?"

"A little rough stuff—just shoving him, maybe knockin' him around a bit . . . but like I said, I coulda rubbed his dick with sandpaper and he wouldn't of told me shit. We put him through the special treatment a few times and you know what?"

I took a guess and suggested, "He enjoyed it."

"That old coot had a blast. Kept laughin' and hollerin' at the girls to step it up, make the show more lively. He really got into it. Thought he was directing a porno flick or somethin'. Wanted 'em to use dildos and make out with each other."

"And did you report this to Ashad or Willborn?"

"Oh, they was following Palchaci's progress real damn close. Yeah, yeah, I told 'em. Showed 'em the pictures, too."

I paused to make another mental note to myself, then asked, "And how did Ashad react to that news?"

"How do ya think?"

"Sergeant, I already know what I think. I'm asking what you think."

Elton took another drag and leaned forward, nearly across the table. He was the type who likes to get close to share confidences. "He detested that son-of-a-bitch. Wanted to kill him."

"Those were his exact words?"

"He hadda lot of ways of sayin' it, man. Oh, he really hated that guy. Him and Willborn thought the guy was the devil." He leaned even closer and confided, "Ashad told me once, he actually dreamed of beating the shit outta him so hard he choked to death on his own blood." He raised his eyebrows. "That's how the old bastard died, right?"

"So you believe he followed through on that wish?"

"Maybe." He shrugged. "He definitely had bigger balls than Willborn."

I thought about this a minute. Clearly in Elton's claustrophobic view of the world, it all came down to balls. A real man had to be willing to beat, to torture, to kill somebody to gain his respect. A pecker contest with this man would be dangerous.

I looked at Elton and said, "Palchaci was in a locked cell, under constant surveillance and supervision from your shift. You see where I'm going with this, Sergeant? How could Ashad get in there without your knowledge or willing assistance?"

"Yer forgettin' somethin'."

"Am I?"

"The day shift."

"Good point. Who was in charge of that shift?"

"Three or four guys. None of 'em ever lasted that long. Couldn't handle it, y'know. If you haven't heard, my block was a real roach hotel. But I think . . ." He paused and tried to remember. "Yeah, it was Jimmy Martin round the time Palchaci got whacked."

Katherine did not appear interested in this and asked, "You know that Ashad is dead? He was killed by a roadside bomb."

"Yeah, I heard that." He chuckled. "Pretty convenient, if you think about it."

Katherine observed, "Not if you think about Ashad's or Sergeant Waylon's families or loved ones."

Elton took a hard last drag on his cigarette and then snubbed it out on the floor. With smoke dribbling out his nostrils, he responded, "Yeah, but if you really think about it, him bein' gone'n all, everybody gets a get-out-of-jail card."

I noted, "Not everybody."

"Yeah," he agreed. "I'm totally fucked."

That seemed like an appropriate truth to end this session on, and I turned to his attorney, Captain Delong, and asked, "Bill, can you step outside with us for a minute?"

"I have a full schedule. I'm very busy."

"I'm sure you are . . . it'll just take a minute. Please, it's important or I wouldn't bother you."

He looked annoyed but he got up and we all three stepped out and gathered in the hallway.

He looked at me. "Make it quick. What's this about?"

I began by saying to him, "I understand you've just been appointed as Elton's counsel. Congratulations."

"A few days ago, that's right." He offered me a smug smile. "I was personally handpicked by General Fister."

"Hey, me, too."

"Well, if that's all—"

"So what did you do to piss him off?"

"What? I . . . uh . . . I have no idea what you're talking about."

"Personally, I hate getting the job after your predecessor got whacked. You know? Here's a tip—get your life insurance up to date."

Captain Delong took a deep swallow. "That has nothing to do with me."

"Right. Hey, I sure hope the killer sees it that way. So . . . what kind of gun are you carrying?" I pulled out my big .45 automatic and showed it to him.

He stared at the gun like it was biological waste. "I don't carry firearms."

"Really? I love guns."

"Lawyers have no business carrying weapons." He looked at his watch and prodded, "If you have a point, then make it."

"Well . . . I don't want to alarm or upset you . . . but well . . . we just found Major Weinstein's ears downstairs. In our car."

His eyes suddenly became large. "What? . . . I . . . uh . . ."

"I know, right? Seems the killer has a real hard-on against your client's lawyers." I paused to allow that to sink in, then expounded a bit more. "I mean, less than an hour ago, the killer was right here. A few more steps and . . . Wow, those could've been *your* ears, Bill."

"My . . . uh . . ."

"Think he knew you were up here?"

His face had turned pasty white, and he was sort of staring at the floor. "Oh, Jesus. Oh . . . his ears?" He then went speechless.

"I know, a real sick puppy. So how many security guys did they give you?"

He seemed to be preoccupied, contemplating how close his brush with the grim reaper had been, then his eyes jerked up. "Uh . . . three."

I raised an eyebrow.

"What? . . . Is something wrong with that?"

"No . . . it's just . . ."

He grabbed my arm. "It's just *what*?"

"Well, Katherine and I . . . we have twenty."

"Oh . . . shit . . . oh, shit."

I patted him on the arm, then we left Captain Delong mumbling to himself and we walked down the hallway to the stairs. Katherine waited till we were almost at the bottom before saying, "You're a heartless jerk. That was unnecessarily cruel."

"Nonsense. I was merely raising his alertness level."

"His . . . Sean, you scared the shit out of that guy."

She started to say something else, thought about it a moment, apparently changed her mind, then laughed. "He was pretty full of himself, wasn't he?"

"I believe *was* is the operative tense."

Chapter Eighteen

The moment we got back to the house, I told Katherine that she, Imelda, and I needed to once again give the collected pictures a complete visual scrub, a suggestion that did not attract an enthusiastic response.

Katherine, in fact, inquired, "You've already seen the pictures, right?"

"I want to see them again."

"Are you going strange on me, Sean?"

"Take a break, Katherine."

Specifically, Elton had mentioned a group of photographs he had forwarded to Ashad and Willborn showing Palchaci undergoing Special Treatment. While I had reviewed the pictures only two nights before, I was nearly certain Palchaci had not been in any of them, but it wouldn't hurt to be sure.

Also I wanted to see if we could locate any shots showing that little sneak, Ashad, standing in the background, snatching peeks of Elton and the girls in action.

I flashed a portrait of Palchaci to Imelda, allowed her a long moment to study his profile, told everyone what we were looking for, divided the shots into three roughly equal groups, and we all three dug in.

But if you think it's fun studying these kinds of pictures in the presence of two stunningly judgmental women, try reading a *Penthouse* while sharing cucumber sandwiches with your mother's knitting group. I was the personification of a pregnant silence.

It took nearly ten minutes of prudish silence, and the occasional disapproving glance, before Katherine said, "I think I have . . ." She paused to stare at the picture harder, "Yes . . . here . . . take a look at this one."

We were seated side by side, and I leaned over for a closer examination of the photograph in question. The theme of this particular shot was Lydia holding a man's Mr. Johnson as June and Andrea pranced around in birthday suits like a couple of Shakespeare's less modest forest sprites. The lighting was dim and presumably Mike Tiller was wielding the camera as Danny Elton also was included in the shot, standing about five feet from Lydia, staring, but not at her, or at the prancing girls, or even at the prisoner having his puddly girl-handled, but off to his left where, if you looked hard enough, you could vaguely make out a figure standing in the shadows, right around the location Elton had described to us earlier.

Had I not known what to look for, or more specifically, where, I would never have noticed him. It looked like one of those hoax pictures with an eerie ghost in the background—the only things showing were his feet and legs; the rest of him was submerged in darkness. I said to Katherine, "Good catch."

"No, it's too vague. We can't be *sure* that's Ashad."

"Right. Must be another Peeping Tom." I assured her, "It's Ashad, Katherine."

"Damn it, I know who it is, Sean. But it's too blurry, too indistinguishable to take into court." She slid the photograph off to her left side. "At least we now know *exactly* where to look. Maybe we can find others."

After another ten minutes of rooting through pictures we found two more, but in none of the shots was it all that clear that the figure in the shadows was Amal Ashad. In the most revealing one, you could make out his whole body up to his shoulders—as Lydia described, he had a long thin torso and broad shoulders—but he was stripped down to his army brown undershirt, thus there was no nametag, no other identifying patches or sew-ons, and his face was still obscured in darkness. Also, the pictures were all a little grainy and, because he was in the background, they were also unfocused at the point where he was standing, so I asked Katherine, "Can we get the originals of these shots?"

"I believe we have the same copies the prosecution has."

"But you aren't certain?"

"No, I'm not. But remember the photographs were all stored in a computer. I was told all of us have the same file and thus, the same pixels."

Imelda, always quick on the uptake, looked at Katherine. "If Mr. Arnold will pay for a lab, there's ways to sharpen them pixels to make that dude clearer."

"Good idea." I nodded and said, "You follow through on that, Imelda." Then, to both of them, I asked, "Now who did we not see in any of these pictures?"

"Palchaci," Katherine answered, confirming that she, also, had been paying close attention to what Danny Elton told us during our interview. She then looked at Imelda and explained about Elton's claim regarding the pictures of Palchaci he forwarded to Ashad.

Imelda took that in. "So somebody's got more pictures."

Katherine nodded. "But we know all the pictures were stored in the same computer file."

I said, "So now we also know the file was sanitized prior to its dissemination. By extrapolation, somebody deleted certain incriminating pictures before they forwarded the remainder to your friend Melvin."

In truth, this was what I had expected to find when I first heard Elton mention that there were pictures showing Palchaci undergoing special treatment.

I looked at Katherine. "So what do the missing pictures mean?"

"That whoever leaked the file exercised a little damage control first."

"Controlling the damage to who? Answer that question and we will know who sent the pictures."

"To everybody."

"No, he, or she, definitely meant to screw Elton and our client. I don't think it's accidental that they didn't forward anything that might incriminate Ashad or Willborn, or anyone else in the chain of command. And somewhere, there might be even more pictures of Ashad, not to mention Palchaci."

Katherine responded, "That's exactly what I've been trying to tell you all along, Sean. Lydia and the others are being scapegoated, while the people who are truly responsible are being protected."

Before I could address that charge, or its tone and implications, Katherine's cellphone began rattling—a tune from a Joanie Mitchell song, naturally—and she withdrew it from her purse and flipped it open, and thankfully, stopped the damn music. I've never really been into protest music. I'm the one the protests are about.

After she identified herself, the conversation went something like this, "Yes, I appreciate your reacting on such short notice . . . Uh-huh . . . Yes, I, see . . . I . . . Oh, shit . . ."—her face turned sort of pink—"Uh-huh . . . All right . . . How far along did you say? . . . Okay, thank you."

She punched off and stared at the tabletop.

Acting on a strong hunch, I asked her, "What did the doc have to say?"

"How did you know?" She stopped staring at the table and looked at me. "About Lydia . . . how did you know?"

"How pregnant is she?"

"You either are, or you aren't, Sean. It isn't measurable by degree."

"Thank you for the explaining that. I was wondering." Obviously this news had put her in a snippy mood. I gave her some time to cool down then asked, "Do we at least know the name of the proud papa?"

"You can relax." The look on Katherine's face did not indicate she had cooled off. "You're not a suspect . . . not this time."

I decided to let that taunt pass. How do women know these things?

Katherine shrugged her shoulders, then said, "It's obvious Danny Elton is the probable culprit."

What was your first clue, Katherine? I commented, "But I wonder if he knows his fuck buddy is now eating for two." Then, considering our own client's general air of blissful ignorance, I asked Katherine, "Was Lydia aware of her condition or did the doc get to break the happy news?"

"Of course she knew."

"Well, that's not always the case."

"What are you talking about?"

"I've read stories about women who ended up in the delivery room and that was their first clue they were knocked up."

"Stop getting your news from *National Enquirer*. Of course women know. Monthly periods come to a stop. The body changes. Many experience morning sickness."

"Really? I've had worse hangovers than that."

"That's . . ." Katherine did look impressed by my observation. "Let me ask again, how did you know about Lydia?"

I had a funny answer to that but Katherine did not seem to be in a light mood, so I canned the flippancy and instead explained, "Well, she's packed on a few pounds, and even after two months of incarceration, I thought she looked . . . suspiciously healthy, rosy-cheeks . . . You know, knocked up."

She examined my face. "I think it was something else. Or someone else. That bitchy lawyer of Willborn's . . . Margaret . . . or Mabel . . . whatever."

"You know her name, Katherine."

"I don't care about her, or her name. I think after you saw her condition you got the idea."

Imelda was watching us, and made the wise and timely decision that she really didn't need to be here for this conversation, so she quickly mumbled something entirely unconvincing about the need to make a fresh pot of coffee, and bolted for the door.

Katherine waited until Imelda was gone and, the moment the door shut, complained, "This case is a mess."

"Just imagine how poor Elton's going to feel when he gets the update about little Danny. Or is it Danielle?"

"Stop being a jerk. This is not the time for your sarcasm."

Obviously there was more going on here than the news that Lydia had the proverbial bun in the oven. I mean, I'm not totally unaware, so I guess I knew what was behind it, and it pissed me off. I wasn't getting on Katherine's case about Nelson, a man she was currently involved with, who had recently made a marriage proposal, one she had yet to turn down. And yet, here she was climbing up my ass over a lady with whom I had a shallow one-night affair, and with whom I hadn't spoken in nearly nine months.

Boy, just imagine if I had actually been sleeping with Katherine.

But I'd had enough of this nonsense and I said to Katherine, "You're not being rational . . . or fair."

"Well . . . this case is really bothering me."

"And *you* volunteered for it, remember? I don't recall being given a choice."

"I see. And do you regret it?"

There were two ways to answer that, and I chose survival over truth. "No, I'm having a great time. I can't remember having such a—"

"You're lying. This case sucks."

Yes, and getting worse by the second. I asked Katherine, "This case or being with me?"

She thought about that. "You're really getting on my nerves."

"Then I'm sorry, Katherine. But after ten years, you just told me how you feel . . . and I . . . I need a little time to digest that . . . to adjust and—"

"You shouldn't, Sean. You either care for me, or you don't."

"All right . . . I do . . . " Suddenly a frog got caught in my throat, and I took a deep swallow and continued, "I do . . . well, I care for you."

"That sounded forced . . . like it hurt."

I tried to put a little more enthusiasm and confidence into it this time "Katherine, I care for you."

"Oh, for God's sake, Sean. I shouldn't have to squeeze it out of you."

So much for trying to say the right thing. Sometimes it's not you; it's them.

But in all the years I'd known Katherine, she was always the cool, cerebral, serene, composed one, while I was the bull in the china shop, emotionally and otherwise. I wasn't enjoying the role reversal.

I took Katherine's hand. "Don't press so hard. I'm confused. I need time to make up my mind."

"Sean, if you haven't . . . Look, you're thirty-eight, single, never been married, probably never even had a serious long-term relationship—"

"And no children," I interjected.

She placed an accusatory forefinger against my arm. "You need to think about your commitment issues."

"What's that supposed to mean?"

"Be honest with yourself. The moment it gets serious, the instant a girl expresses interest in you, you slap on the track shoes and make for the highway."

"Katherine, I'm not the one holding a marriage proposal and straddling two men."

"Well, you wouldn't be, would you?" She added, "You would volunteer for a tour in Iraq long before the marriage word came up. You'd rather take the chance of getting your head blown off, then the chance of a long-term commitment."

See what I mean? "Look, I don't like being put on the spot this way."

She looked at me a moment, then said, "You're right. I'm . . . I'm sorry . . . I . . ."

"I don't—"

"Wait. Let me finish, Sean."

She leaned back, away from me, which is never a good sign. "I think you're still confused about your life, wrapped up in the army, and maybe you're not ready to commit to someone else, or anything else. I understand that." She paused to offer me a weak smile. "Maybe I even empathize a bit. But I'm thirty-four years old, I want to have children, and I don't intend to wait around for you to sort it out."

I almost replied, I'm not asking you to, but I had learned my lesson and kept my mouth shut.

She said, "This is not an ultimatum"—which of course was exactly what it was—"but I'm not being fair to Nel, leaving him hanging this way. I'm giving myself two days to make up my mind."

Chapter Nineteen

I went upstairs to engage in a little philosophical jujitsu about myself, about life, and about women. I sat on the bed and, after about two seconds, I became bored with it. So, looking for something better to do—actually giving myself a kick in the balls was preferable to this—I realized I had not read, much less studied, Chief Ashad's military record because I had assumed a dead man was unlikely to be a big factor in this case. Wrong, wrong, wrong. As I was learning, his ghost was becoming more and more of a spectral presence and germane influence regarding what went down in the dead of the night in a dreary place called Cellblock One. So I opened his file and began correcting that.

As Captain Willborn had informed us, Ashad's place of birth was Baghdad, and apparently, after arriving in the States sometime during his teen years, he'd done well enough, because his undergraduate college degree was from Cornell University, suggesting he was a model immigrant kid, a good student, and an upright citizen. According to his record he was commissioned as a warrant officer one at the age of twenty-two, shortly after graduation. Why he chose warrantcy over a full commission as a lieutenant and the chance to become a general was an open question. He was branched military intelligence, and as I read through his initial assignments, I thought it seemed a little out of whack, though his Iraqi background and his native fluency in Arabic and Farsi perhaps accounted for an unorthodox career path.

Specifically, he attended the basic course at Fort Huachuca, Arizona, where all young MI officers and warrant officers go to learn the rudiments of their trade, then upon graduation was immediately reassigned to Washington, DC, specifically to the National Security Agency, which struck me as highly unusual for a virgin warrant officer. The army typically consigns brand new officers to a lower level tactical unit, to an intel shop in a combat arms brigade or division, or to a military intelligence battalion, the basic idea being to learn the trade from the ground up.

Three years later he was assigned to the Central Command, the major headquarters for the region that includes Iraq and Iran, remaining there for seven years in a series of positions that ranged from interpretation to strategic analysis.

Then, in 2006, three years after the war in Iraq broke out, he wound up assigned to the 315th Military Intelligence Battalion, as a member of Captain Willborn's tiny interrogation team, where he found himself at the end of the universe in a shithole called Al Basari Prison, and then to his ultimate destiny, traveling down a dusty street with a big bomb with his name on it.

His religion was listed as Moslem, and his age at the time of his unfortunate passing, as thirty-seven. Just how an Ivy League stud ended up as a lowly warrant officer, and why a highly experienced strategic analyst ended up pigeonholed in an interpreter slot for a small tactical interrogation team, were mysteries to me. I put a little more mental grease into it and my conclusion didn't change. Does not compute.

So I closed the file, and carried it downstairs to my dining room office, where I used my cellphone to call LTC Mark Hertling, an old buddy who these days happened to be a military intelligence officer working in the bowels of the Pentagon. Mark and I had done a tour together when we were younger officers, both of us bachelors. He liked to drink and womanize, as did I, so we hit it off pretty good.

A female lieutenant commander named Hernandez answered with her rank and her name, then said, "Office of Middle Eastern Threat Analysis."

"This is Lieutenant Colonel Sean Drummond and I need to speak with Colonel Hertling."

A few moments later Mark was on the line, sounding slightly annoyed. "So what do ya need?"

"Ever hear of a guy named Amal Ashad?"

"Yeah, sure, just . . . give me a minute . . . I'm having trouble remembering if he's Al Queda Iraq, or Pakistani Taliban."

"Try Chief Warrant Officer Three, United States Army. Military intelligence type."

"Oh . . . *that* guy?" Then he informed me, "Nope." He then asked, "What's this about?"

"The Al Basari case."

"You got a piece of that?"

"I didn't run fast enough."

There was a brief pause before Mark asked, "Which one is your client?"

"Lydia Eddelston . . . she's—"

"I know, I know, the idiot who likes to play with their little ding-a-lings."

"Well . . . everybody needs a hobby."

He laughed. "Shit, you really got the runt of the litter, pal. Who did you piss off?"

"Have you got a pad of paper and an hour?"

"Yeah, figures. Hey, who got that blonde hottie?"

"I have no idea who you're talking about. They all look the same to me, Mark. Says so in the manual."

"Yeah, right." He laughed.

I said, "I need you to look at something, okay? Give me your fax number."

He did, and I faxed him the first three pages of Ashad's military personnel file, which included his basic biographic data and the summary of his assignments, then gave him a few minutes to look it over.

Eventually he said, "This looks a little funny."

"Okay, tell me what looks wrong with it."

"What looks right? How about an Ivy League egghead becoming a warrant? Doesn't fit. And his career progression . . . it's possible . . . but . . ."

I suggested, "Maybe because of his Iraqi birth and childhood, the army decided he posed a security risk and an officer's commission was ruled out."

"Okay . . . that happens . . . Except your guy passed a special background investigation, has a Top Secret clearance and is in about five I'd-have-to-kill-you-if-you-knew compartments."

"It's important, Mark. I need this guy checked out."

"Quietly, right?"

"Don't even chew before you swallow."

He thought about it, then said, "Thirty minutes. If you haven't heard, Middle Eastern threats is a growth business around here. I'm analyzing my ass off. Be standing by the phone."

We hung up and I wasted about half an hour swigging coffee, watching CNN recycle old news stories, thinking dark thoughts about Amal Ashad, and avoiding Katherine, before Mark called back. He said, "Okay, here's the deal. I called George Harrit who was the executive officer to the J2 at Centcom headquarters during the years Ashad's record says he was assigned there." Having explained that, he went on, "Harrit's the Rabbi type. He knew everybody in intel down there, and I mean, *everybody*. Okay? And . . . he never even *heard* of your guy."

"Right."

"So I called another pisan, Billy Kline. Billy worked intel officer assignments during those years. And he called three or four old buddies, and they called . . . Want the long story short?"

I told Mark, "Well . . . I know you're busy."

He laughed. "Okay, your guy Ashad is a fuckin' ghost."

"What does that mean?"

"Means his name's in the system . . . he's listed as deceased, so he's in the personnel computers, right? . . . But . . . guys who should definitely know or remember him from when he was alive, definitely don't. Capisce?"

"Is it possible Ashad was working in sensitive compartments with covers that shielded him from normal channels? They do that with certain clandestine units, like Delta, right?"

"Possible? Sure. Likely? Nah. Anyway, I went down that route. The assignments guy who handled special compartments says your goombah wasn't one of his boys. Got it?"

"Got it. I owe you one."

"Yeah, you do," he said and we rang off.

I drank another cup of coffee and thought a little more about CW3 Amal Ashad and did not like what I had just learned. I had a growing apprehension about what was behind this—or rather, who—but it wouldn't be easy to confirm, and definitely shouldn't be tried long distance.

Even more definitely it shouldn't involve, or even be revealed to Katherine, at least not yet. For if my suspicion was correct, this case was about to take a turn into truly weird territory and become even more complicated, not to mention dangerous, than it already was.

But also Katherine, and her new pal Nelson, had a different agenda than the mere pursuit of justice: to wit, they wanted to use Lydia's trial to convict the administration and the army for condoning and even propagating the use of questionable interrogation techniques.

Anyway, Katherine could not enter the places I might need to go to, and the people I might need to talk to would clam up in her presence.

So I scribbled what I hoped was a maddeningly obtuse note to Katherine saying I might be back tomorrow, without fully explaining why I would be gone, or where.

I then went upstairs to my room, packed some civvies, a fresh uniform, my overnight kit, and my gun, got in the car and headed off to DC, and hopefully some answers.

Chapter Twenty

As I expected she might be, Phyllis Carney, my putative CIA boss, was seated behind her desk at the offsite location of the Office of Special Projects in Crystal City, Virginia, when I dropped in unexpectedly at 9:00 p.m.

I used my magic CIA passkey to enter the facility, and nobody stopped me, or even noticed me, perhaps because the building was dark and empty. The sole defense of Western Civilization was a crack of light coming from beneath Phyllis's office door. I opened that door without knocking and entered, then moved straight to the long conference table in front of her desk, where I took a seat, and waited for her to react.

She was reading a memo, then without greeting, or even the mildest manifestation of alarm or surprise, she looked up and remarked, "You're supposed to be in New York."

"Aren't you supposed to be home? It's nine at night, Phyllis. A lady your age needs her beauty sleep."

Rather than respond to my age-insensitive query, Phyllis replied, "I hadn't expected you . . . not this early."

"But you were expecting me?"

"Let's just say I had a premonition that you would find your way down here. Eventually . . ."

I thought about this mysterious premonition, then came right to the point. "Why did you release me to this case?"

She shuffled some papers. "How I answer that depends on who's asking. Is this Sean Drummond, an auxiliary member of the CIA? Or Lieutenant Colonel Sean Drummond, an army JAG officer seeking a favorable verdict for his client?"

I understood the distinction she was making and chose not to address her query, but to keep the ball in her court. "Answer my question, Phyllis."

"Well . . . I suppose you deserve one."

"You're damned right I do."

We looked at each other in silence before she continued, "Several reasons come to mind. Because I thought you were becoming bored and grumpy, and a break from this office might be good for you." She paused, then confessed, more accurately, "Actually, *I* needed a break from you. Also, it's a vitally important case. The army should have its best lawyers attending to it."

"Try again, Phyllis."

Phyllis casually brushed a strand of white hair off her forehead and leaned back in her chair. I had not expected her to blush or shudder, but neither had I expected her to react in a manner that could only be described as blasé and aloof. I had underestimated her, and reminded myself not to do that again.

I should mention here that Phyllis is, in every sense of the phrase, a tough old bird. She joined the OSS when she was a teenager near the end of WWII, and has been kept around, in one capacity or another, long past any sane retirement age, primarily because every CIA director has been scared shitless of her. The joke around the office is that Phyllis knows Victoria's Secret, which might be an exaggeration, but she definitely knows Uncle Sam's secrets, which means Uncle Sam's balls are on her keychain. But, in fact, I could not imagine a woman like Phyllis relegated to a retirement home in Florida, passing her sunset years cheating at bridge, and worrying about what terrible trouble the nice young doctors on *General Hospital* will get into that day; I don't think she could either. Nor could I imagine that her masters in the Agency would find serenity in the thought that Phyllis, combatting the boredom, would be sitting down in Florida composing her memoirs and revealing seven decades of screw-ups and scandals they thought were long-buried and forgotten. She told me once that she will leave this job her own way, on her back, in a coffin. Also, she happens to be very good at her job, though I'm not entirely certain what that job is, and here we had a case in point.

She gave me her old schoolmarm frown. "If you remain civil, Sean, we can have a fruitful conversation. Otherwise, show yourself to the door right now."

I wasn't about to back down, which meant it was time to get a few points on the board. So I looked back at her and asked the last question she expected or, indeed, wanted, to hear. "Who is Amal Ashad?"

It took a moment for her to answer that question and, when she did, it was to ask, rather coldly, "What makes you think I know who he is?"

"That's not the answer I'm looking for, Phyllis."

"Maybe because you're asking in the wrong place. But I'm being rude. Would you care for some coffee or tea?"

When I made no response to that obvious diversion, Phyllis stated, "That was meant to be a hint, Sean . . . perhaps I was too subtle." She added, with a slight smile, "Subtlety is never the right tact with you. I prefer Earl Grey."

So I got up and went to the corner where she kept two large metal stand-up urns, one filled with coffee, from which I poured myself a lukewarm cup, the other filled with steaming hot water, from which I made her a cup of tea, with two bags, and two squirts of honey, sans cream, just the way she prefers it.

It didn't escape my notice what she was doing or how sly and indirect she could be; she was using this petty show of servitude to remind me that she was the boss, and I, the compliant underling.

You have to know that, with Phyllis, every conversation is like a game of chess. There are no idle or wasted words; she always starts two or three moves ahead, so, as long as you play by her rules, you always end up on the short end of the stick. But you also have to pay attention because she shifts pieces around the board when you aren't looking. She will say something seemingly harmless and innocuous like, isn't the weather here unbearably chilly today, and you nod—and the next thing you know you're on a fast plane to the searing climate of Iraq.

I brought her the tea, then, carrying my lukewarm coffee, returned to my seat. I said to Phyllis, "May I be blunt?"

"Regrettably, I believe that's the only way you know how to behave."

"Look at me, Phyllis." She looked at me. "There are two ways this conversation can end. One, you can tell me the truth, or two, I can call Melvin Cramer and he can root around, find out who Amal Ashad really is and we can both read about it on the front page." We made eye contact. "You know this is not a bluff, don't you?"

Phyllis stirred the tea bags with a spoon, then put the cup down. She replied, typically without replying, "What makes you think Ashad isn't who he's supposed to be?"

"The better question is how did anyone believe he *was* who he was supposed to be? For one, here's some advice for next time—have somebody who spent a day in the army create the phony personnel files. Two, nobody from the previous assignments listed in that file ever heard of Amal Ashad. And three, at Al Basari prison, guys from outside agencies, like this one, for instance, were sneaking around, dressing, talking, and trying to act like something they weren't—soldiers."

"Sometimes, I forget just how smart and resourceful you are."

"Oh, I think you knew I would figure it out."

"You might be right, Sean. I'll admit that when General Fister called to ask for you, I had . . . well . . . reservations about releasing you to this case." That didn't match Katherine's account, but Phyllis fingered her teacup and added, "You know, an army of military investigators have been digging through this case for months. You've been on this case only a few days, but you're the first one to smell this out."

"Rats leave a trail of droppings. Ashad had diarrhea. You're avoiding my question, Phyllis."

She tested her tea with a small sip, then withdrew the teabags with a spoon and, with exaggerated care, placed them on her plate. I knew what she was doing: reappraising the situation, and me, and figuring out her next move—in other words, it was time for me to keep my eye out for the moving pieces. She said, "You say you want the truth, and I'm willing to give it to you. But first I need your word."

"My word about what?" With this lady you never respond to an unconditional request.

"Much of what I'm about to say is classified and extremely sensitive. It cannot be disclosed, under any conditions—certainly not to the public, not in court, not even to your cocounsel, or your client."

"Phyllis, do I look stupid?"

"No, you're bright enough, Sean. Maybe too bright."

"Tell me what I want to know, or I'll tell *60 Minutes* what I do know."

Phyllis did not look happy with that threat—the CIA enjoys publicity about as much as men enjoy visits to the proctologist, which actually isn't such a bad metaphor. Anyway, she ground her teeth for a few seconds, then relented. "I don't think I should have to explain to you, of all people, the importance of reliable and actionable intelligence to the wars in Iraq and Afghanistan. These kinds of conflicts are settled by who knows what, and when they know it. Early in both conflicts we underestimated . . . or, no, we forgot that, I suppose. The price was awful and getting worse. Both wars going off the rails. Thousands of body bags returning home."

"Who's we?"

"It doesn't matter."

"It matters to me. Answer the question."

"The military, this Agency, the Defense Intelligence Agency, senior people in the government, certain opinionated members of Congress. Everybody who matters, and quite a few who don't. We slid into these wars with an intelligence apparatus built for other purposes. It proved a wrong fit . . . a catastrophically wrong fit."

"What does this have to do with Ashad?"

"Stop barking at me, Sean, and I'll get to that. A year into the war, the army was complaining bitterly about inadequate support from the Agency. And the Agency, in turn, was criticizing the army's intelligence efforts as too amateurish and unsophisticated. The situation became . . . intolerable."

I didn't really need this bureaucratic gibberish lesson. "The question was, what does this have to do with Ashad?"

"I'm getting to it, Sean. After the usual symphony of teeth gnashing and fingerpointing, an accommodation was worked out. The Agency would step back from the big picture and get more involved at the granular level. We decided to place certain assets in the army, for example, to advise field commanders on local conditions and channel raw intelligence to them before it sprouted cobwebs being massaged and debated by the bureaucracy here in Washington. We also decided to place some of our more promising interrogators on the front lines . . . at the grassroots level, if you will."

"And Amal Ashad, was he one of your people?"

"*Our* people, Sean. And you already know the answer or you wouldn't be here. About fifteen years ago, we recruited him out of Cornell where he majored in Arabic studies . . . he was fluent in Arabic and Farsi . . . had spent his childhood roaming the streets of Baghdad. He was a perfect catch." In a transparent attempt at gaining my sympathy she told me, "He was married with three young children, if you're interested."

"I'm really not, Phyllis. Why did you disguise him as a soldier?"

"Many reasons, all them good. But protection, for the most part. Some . . . in fact, most of those attached to this program have been NOCs or served in some undercover capacity. We didn't want them exposed and compromised."

"So you had them march around like toy soldiers? Did you teach them to salute, and how to use a bayonet? Really, Phyllis."

She snapped, "You make it sound dumb, and it's not." She then took a deep breath—Phyllis prided herself on self-control, and I tended to test it a lot—then continued in a more composed tone, "Take our friend, Amal Ashad. Living in a military prison, associating with the worst scum of Iraqi society, and who knows how many foreign jihadists trying to make their creds by killing Americans. On a daily basis, he was face-to-face with dozens of insurgents. Why hang a sign around his neck that says CIA? His future value in any overseas capacity would be lost forever."

"So the uniform was intended to hide his identity?" I asked, perhaps allowing a tiny note of cynicism to creep into my tone.

"That was one consideration. Now here's another. Had the people he was questioning known he was an Agency man, they would've been less vulnerable . . . less forthcoming. They would've clammed up."

"I definitely get that."

She was used to my sarcasm and knew how to react to it—she ignored me and said, "Don't be insulted, but army interrogators are not particularly feared or respected by the insurgents. It's not exactly a promising career track in the military. Many of your army interrogators have shallow experience, limited training, and questionable talents. Some can't even speak Arabic, for God's sake—they have to rely on interpreters. Ashad not only brought his linguistic and cultural fluency, he also had a masters degree in psychiatry from Johns Hopkins, a degree paid for by the Agency before he spent years interrogating for us. How many of your army interrogators can match such credentials?"

The question was obviously rhetorical, and I gave her the rhetorical courtesy of not answering.

She acknowledged my nonresponse and continued, "The people Ashad interrogated at Al Basari had no idea they were being massaged and manipulated by a pro. That army uniform . . . well, you might say it put a wolf in sheep's clothes." She was into the metaphorical analogies now. "Think of a grandmaster playing chess against a rank amateur, an amateur who has not a clue who he's up against."

I looked at Phyllis and wondered if she was talking about Ashad and his targets, or herself and me.

"But, in fact," I noted, "it also gave the Agency perfect deniability. Any abuses would be blamed on the army. I'm sure your people considered that. I'm also sure they loved that part."

"Stop saying *your* people, Sean. We're on the same side."

"Are we?"

I saw a little squirming from Phyllis, an uncharacteristic show of emotion. "I'm telling you that wasn't the intent, Sean. Nobody was playing the blame game."

"If not the intent, it is, in fact, the reality. The army is caught in a shit storm, and Ashad flushed the toilet."

Phyllis smiled condescendingly. "You don't know that."

"Don't I? My client and her friends—"

"*Your client?* Oh, for God's sake, Sean, don't tell me this is the first time you ever had a client lie to you."

"Maybe, for once, I don't believe my client is lying."

"Then grow up. She and her friends will say anything to wriggle out of this. And Ashad's death makes him the perfect fall guy. He's not around to deny or refute their accusations, is he?"

"Ashad knew what they were doing, he encouraged it, he provided instructions and advice, and on several occasions, he even dropped in for a visit." I added, "He gave them a camera. If he missed the evening matinee, he enjoyed drooling on the pictures over his morning coffee."

"Just because your client and her friends say so, you expect me to believe that? Don't take me for a fool."

I didn't know if Phyllis believed what she was saying herself— she was the ultimate institutional chameleon, able to lie so adeptly and with such certitude and conviction that even she believed it. Maybe.

But it was time to put a new piece on the board, so I reached into a pocket, withdrew one of the incriminating pictures, and tossed it on her desk.

Phyllis lifted up the photo, carefully using the tips of only two fingers, as though it might carry a sexually transmittable disease, and casually examined it. Her face formed a really distasteful scowl. "Is *that* your client?" she asked, pointing at Lydia, who, with a particularly stupid look on her face, was fondling a man's dick.

"Forget about her. Upper left corner . . . the guy lurking in the shadows. Recognize him?"

Oozing disbelief, she asked, "You're saying that's supposed to be Amal Ashad?" She peered closer at the picture. "This man has no face . . . no name on his uniform . . . no identity I can detect."

"He disconnected the lightbulbs, and tried to hide, but yes, that's the pride of the CIA taking in the sights." I stretched the truth a bit in time, and informed Phyllis, with a dose of unbridled optimism, "This picture, as well as a few others, is in a lab right now having the pixels expanded and clarified to get a clearer look at our voyeur." I then offered, "Let's make a bet. Is Mr. Ashad smiling or drooling?"

She put the picture face down on her desk. I didn't know if Phyllis was aware that somebody had clipped certain pictures from the original computer file, and I didn't know if the CIA had a hand in that clipping, but if they had, and she did know about it, she was probably saying to herself at that moment, Oh shit, how did those morons let this one slip by?

She fixed me with a severe look. "Even if that *is* Ashad—and I don't for a moment believe it is . . . but even if you *can* show beyond reasonable doubt that he was present, what does it prove or disprove?" She then answered her own question. "Nothing, not a damned thing."

"Thank you. When I want opinions on courtroom strategies, I'll go to somebody with a law degree."

"What do you think it will accomplish?"

"How about showing the world that the army doesn't have a monopoly on perverts and sadists?"

"I don't appreciate your sarcasm."

Nobody does, Phyllis. I looked in her eyes. "Ashad was there. He was present for some of the worst of the nightly depredations—he not only knew about it, he witnessed it, and he actually offered advice on some very peculiar perversities he thought would be help-ful." I then asked her, "Would you care to hear some of his sugges-tions?"

Apparently not, because she snapped, "And will that get your client off?"

Obviously she, or a team of Agency lawyers, had thought this through. I decided it was best not to answer that question.

She said, "Expose him, Sean, and you will unmask and thereby undermine the entire program. And for what? The program will almost certainly have to be scrapped. You know the mood in Con-gress. They go after the CIA like a pool of convicted rapists at an orgy. You'll be building a scaffold for them. What will that accom-plish?"

"Justice."

"Justice?" she asked as if it were some vulgar foreign word like menage à trois or *fick dich*, which roughly corresponded to my sen-timents at that moment.

"Sounds fair to me."

"Fairness has nothing to do with this."

"Sure it does. The army might even enjoy having a little com-pany as it's getting the crap kicked out of it on every front page in the world."

"Don't be crazy."

"It's lonely at the top." I added, "Hey, we could carpool to the congressional investigations. Save gas."

Phyllis hesitated, then leaned forward and said, "Sean, let me offer you some good advice."

I looked at Phyllis.

"Drop it. Forget everything about Ashad."

"And if I don't?"

"I'll return to my opening query—which Sean am I speaking with?"

"There never were two Seans, Phyllis. I took an oath to look after the interests of my client, and I took an oath to protect and defend the Constitution of the United States, not the CIA," I told her. "Have I made myself clear?"

It was time for a fresh approach, and she rolled her eyes. "Your client's behavior was so abhorrent it can't be justified by anything Ashad did, or said. This picture tells the whole story." She held up the picture and directed a finger at Lydia. "Look at her face, Sean. Look closely . . . she's having the time of her life. This was all about her and her sick desires."

I was getting tired of having the pictures rubbed in my face. "I'm not so sure about that."

She raised an eyebrow. "Surely you're not serious?"

"It doesn't matter whether I'm serious. It's irrelevant, here, between you and me, but it becomes very relevant in a court of law. Ashad, as you said, was the proverbial wolf in sheep's clothing. I have no idea how well his guise worked with the prisoners, but I know it worked wonders with five easily corrupted American soldiers. He manipulated these five soldiers into the behavior you so colorfully described as wicked and abhorrent. He gave them the ticket to act out their darkest fantasies, to see the prisoners as playthings, as objects for their sexual gratification. Worse, he led them to believe it was in the national interest, that the more twisted and perverted they became, the more they were helping win the war."

Phyllis got up from behind her desk and she walked around it, then sat in a chair at the conference table, ending up right beside me. She placed her hand on my arm and, in a soft, maternal voice, said, "One of the things I most like and admire about you, Sean, is your soldier's ethics and sensibilities. So here we have a young man who died defending this country. He died in a horrible way, on a lonely street, in a terrible war. My God, there weren't even enough pieces left to bring home. Right now, his grieving family . . . his wife, and his three young children, have only one thin solace to hold on to, one irreplaceable thought: Amal Ashad died a hero." She tightened her grip. "Think of his family, Sean. Don't ruin that memory."

"That has got to be . . ." I paused to shake my head. "Really, Phyllis, couldn't you at least arrange a little Wagnerian background music to accompany your bullshit?"

The hand fell off my arm. She smiled and shrugged. "Not working, I take it?"

I did not smile back. Phyllis is not a sentimental person and that she had resorted to such a mushy, saccharine stab at changing my mind indicated she was reaching the end of her repertoire. That meant either that she was done, or it was time for the threats.

She leaned back in her chair and said, "All right, there are . . . other considerations."

"There always are, Phyllis. I really don't care."

"But you should, Sean. You really should. You're getting in way over your head. A great deal more rides on this than you know. There are people who will go to some length to keep you from exposing this."

"Who are these people?"

"I don't know." My expression might've indicated some skepticism about her claim because she felt the need to reassert, "I'm telling the truth—I really don't."

"Are *you* one of those people?"

"I'm not part of this effort, no. And it goes much higher than me."

I wasn't sure where Phyllis stood in the Agency's line chart, but I knew her direct boss was the director himself. By extension this meant the big honcho himself was involved, and possibly his boss, the occupant of the White House.

I looked at Phyllis and, as usual, I couldn't tell if this was total bullshit, or if she was being perfectly sincere. Her face did convey an expression of worry and concern, like one of her children was about to do something terribly stupid that would bring a world of hurt and misery down on his head. But this was Phyllis; more likely, she was fretting about her tea getting cold.

Still looking at her, I asked, "Is this a threat?"

"I don't understand the question."

"Let me simplify it. There are already two dead defense attorneys. Is there going to be a third?"

"Don't be silly. Nobody's contemplating anything so drastic."

That reassurance aside—with its understated yet implied threat—the question was, what did the CIA consider less drastic? A quick trip to the most Taliban-infested archipelago in Afghanistan? A plane that takes off and never lands? The thing about paranoia is, it's a game two people can play: your worst nightmare might understate their favorite option. I gave Phyllis a hard look. "I'm trying to decide where you're coming from."

"I'm your boss and . . . I'd like to believe I'm also your friend."

"Friends don't let friends get hurt."

"It's out of my hands, Sean. I'm just passing on a warning. I told you I'm not part of this."

"Then give your other friends a message from me. If I find the slightest evidence of obstruction or tampering with this case, I'll blow the top off this agency."

Phyllis made no reply to this macho claim, but she did get up and return to her desk, and her tea. I had the feeling that she'd done her job, which was figuring out how Sean Drummond was feeling that day.

As both an army officer and a temporary employee of the Agency, I had just made it clear which side of my split personality

I came down on; it wasn't hers, and it definitely wasn't theirs, whoever they were. She sat quietly and sipped from her tea, while I sat and watched her sip and contemplate what to do about her favorite recalcitrant employee.

But also, I wondered if Phyllis was now in some jeopardy because of me. I was her subordinate, after all, and it was Phyllis who had voluntarily released me to serve as cocounsel for Lydia. Her agency, in retrospect, would consider that a miscalculation, and her inability to enlist my cooperation now would be perceived as a failure to correct that misjudgment. Like most government institutions, the CIA can, and regularly does, forgive failure in the course of routine business, but it draws the line when that mistake tarnishes the reputation of their beloved Agency.

Eventually she said, "I'll tell them that I can't control you. But that you've been advised that Ashad's status is a highly sensitive, classified matter, and you promised you'll tread lightly."

"Tell them whatever you want. Just be sure to add that if they take the first shot and miss, the next shot is mine and I won't miss."

She nodded, but I noticed that she didn't look overly anxious or even mildly impressed by my threat.

I got up and left, thinking that maybe I was making a big mistake; maybe it was a dumb idea to let them take the first shot.

Chapter Twenty-One

The rule of investigations is, when you have a lead, you follow it. Especially when you have only one lead, which really clears up any maddening ambiguity about which lead to pursue. Or, as somebody clever once said, never miss an opportunity to have an opportunity.

Specifically, Captain Willborn had mentioned during our discussion that the interrogation log kept by him and Ashad may have been shipped home to the surviving families. And though odds were he was lying, no other lead had any odds, good, bad, or otherwise. Simply put, there were no other leads. Besides, I was in the Washington area with nothing to look forward to but a long, exhausting drive back to West Point and Katherine.

According to his military records, Amal Ashad's home of record was 3822 North 38th Street in Arlington, Virginia—as the crow flies, only about five miles from CIA headquarters.

Had the CIA been smart, the name Amal Ashad would be an alias, the home address would be a sham and, had they really been smart, Sean Drummond would right now be grabbing his ass and dodging mortar rounds in some backwater shithole in Afghanistan instead of sticking his nose up their backside here. But the Agency hadn't been smart when it composed Ashad's ersatz military records, nor when it released me to this case, and there was a chance that the lazy bastards had taken the easy way out, and used his true name and his real address.

Actually, until I came along, it hadn't really been a problem.

After a short thirty-minute trip, I found myself driving down an archetypal suburban street lined thickly on both sides with small homes, mostly brick ranches constructed sometime in the fifties or thereabouts. Ozzie and Harriet would call it paradise.

I pulled up to the front of 3822 and idled at the curb for a minute. The home was compact in appearance, essentially a two-level ranch built of red brick with a minimalist smattering of stone face, and though North Arlington, due to its proximity and short commute to DC was prime real estate, the home did not look impressive or overly expensive. I could easily imagine a mid- or high-level government employee and his family squashed into this small, drab place, especially if his wife worked, so I decided to throw the dice and go to the front door.

It was well after eleven at night, and the lights in the home were out, but I'm good company and I was sure Mrs. Ashad wouldn't mind.

I stood on the doorstoop and pushed the buzzer. About two minutes passed—with me jamming the stupid buzzer every thirty seconds—before the door cracked open. I hoped the lady of the house hadn't been awakened by my impatience—actually, I hoped she had been in a very deep sleep cycle and was susceptible to my bullshit and lies.

An attractive woman, about thirty, long black hair, slender, and clearly of Arabic extraction, peeked out the crack. She examined my face, then my uniform, then said, "How can I help you?"

She was not smiling, so I smiled at her, and she managed a slight smile in reply. Polite lady. "Mrs. Ashad?" She produced a quick nod, and I lied and informed her, "I served with your husband in Iraq."

"Oh . . . I see."

"And I just got back and wanted to stop by and extend my condolences. He was a good man."

She looked confused for a moment, then recovered a bit. "I'm sorry . . . I didn't catch your name." She then felt the need to observe, "It's very late."

I widened my smile and mumbled as incoherently as I could, "Drummond . . . Harry Drummond." Because I did not want the CIA to know I was rooting around in Ashad's life, I did not want Mrs. Ashad to know my true identity, but I was still in uniform, with its accompanying nametag, so this stupid, impromptu half-lie was the best I could come up with. I could picture somebody saying, let's see, Harry Drummond . . . Sean Drummond . . . could this be the same guy? It might confuse the average person for about two seconds. Then again, this was the same CIA that was still looking for nukes in Iraq. Never overestimate the opposition.

I said, "My apologies for dropping by so late. Are the kiddies in bed?"

She nodded, somewhat impatiently. "They have school tomorrow."

To show her I wasn't a total stranger, I noted, "There are three of them, right?"

"Three . . . yes. And I have to work." In the event I wasn't getting the message, she emphasized, "Early. I have to drop them off at school and be in the office at seven."

"Right. Well, I'll just take a moment of your time." I rubbed my arms to remind her that it was cold outside and she was being rude. "Can I step inside?"

"That would inappropriate. I'm not wearing a dressing gown."

"I'll wait. I've traveled a long way. Please, Mrs. Ashad. Your husband and I were friends."

She appeared indecisive, so I blew on my hands and shivered a little to subtly remind her again of the near-Arctic conditions. She was obviously a nice, well-mannered lady, and eventually she said, with obvious reluctance, "I'll be back in a minute."

So, as I stood there and with nothing better to do, I made a quick survey of my surroundings. A heavy, wet snow had fallen that morning, and the sidewalk and driveway were already cleared, and the all-weather bushes along the side of the house looked neat and well-groomed, suggestive that Mrs. Ashad was a good grounds-keeper, and that the recent death of her husband had not caused her to fall off on the job. Some newly minted widows go completely to pieces and ignore everything; others go to the other extreme, trying to fill the sudden void in their life with unrelenting work and activity, no matter how useful or useless. I didn't know which of these categories applied to Mrs. Ashad, but she had a full-time job, three young children, and she appeared to be keeping her life in order.

The door swung open and Mrs. Ashad beckoned me to enter. She now wore a long, fluffy pink robe that went nicely with her long black hair and dark complexion. She led me down a short hallway, then we hooked a left, passed through a small, wood-lined study, and entered a kitchen that was so small that the family better really love one another, or at least be good diplomats.

From what I could observe of their home, the Ashads, Americanized as they were, retained the furnishing tastes of their heritage. As with the home's exterior, the interior also was neatly kept—no toys or kiddie bric-a-brac in sight—with enough Oriental rugs and tapestries to outfit a souk, plenty of brass tables and elaborate floor cushions, and Mohamedian paintings and whatever. On the outside, the home looked like a piece of Americana, circa 1950, where

Ted and Wilma could be found knocking back cocktails and flipping burgers in the back; inside, Ali Babba and the Forty Thieves could be huddled around a hookah, planning their next heist.

She sat at a small table next to the big, black refrigerator, and indicated I should join her. So I did and she announced, "It's late so I won't offer tea or coffee."

"I don't mind."

She came right to the point and asked me, "What's this about?"

In my most nonthreatening tone, I replied, "The truth, Mrs. Ashad, is I never was in Iraq with your husband, nor did I ever know, nor have I ever met him." Before she could become overly alarmed or invite me to show myself out, I added, "I'm an army investigator on official business." I reached for my wallet, and pinched my ordinary military ID card. "Here . . . I'll show you my credentials."

As I hoped she would, she waved it off and replied, "That won't be necessary."

"Thank you." I leaned back into the chair and inquired, "Are you aware of your husband's professional activities in Iraq?"

"I was aware of his job. I don't know the details, however."

"Then you know he was actually an employee of the CIA?"

"Of course. I know a lot of people believe that Agency employees keep it secret from their spouses, but we do know, Colonel Drummond. Of course, he didn't share the particulars with me. He wasn't supposed to, and Amal respected that." She then asked, "What's this investigation about?"

I offered her my most reassuring smile. "Don't worry, your husband wasn't in trouble or anything." Though if I had anything to do with it, his balls would be dragging from my rear bumper.

She appeared relieved to hear that.

"After he died, some documents were lost, or perhaps misplaced. Very sensitive papers we wouldn't want to fall into the wrong hands," I mentioned, without also mentioning how much her husband's employers wanted to keep them out of *my* hands. "It's my job to plug the security leak."

She had a refined accent, was obviously highly educated, and she carried herself well, despite the bathrobe and the late hour. In better lighting, in fact, even without makeup, I couldn't help noticing what an attractive woman she was—and exotically sexy—with large, round, black eyes, high, sculpted cheeks, a long patrician nose, and thick black hair. Also, despite the bulky, fluffy robe, she appeared to have an excellent figure—not that I was looking.

She replied to my mission, stating, "I'm afraid . . . I know nothing about any missing documents."

She started to get up before I quickly inquired, "Were you aware that your husband's job in Iraq required him to impersonate a soldier?"

"No." With a slightly annoyed expression, she sat back down. "I thought I told you I know nothing about what Amal did over there."

"Then you might be interested to know he worked in a military detention facility. He interrogated enemy prisoners and provided intelligence to our forces." I offered her an appropriately sad smile. "According to the reports, he was ingenious at finding ways to make the prisoners talk."

This news did not seem to surprise her. In fact, she nodded thoughtfully. "I suppose, given his language skills, it makes sense."

I said nothing and allowed her the opportunity to ask some follow-up questions. Surely she must've had considerable curiosity about the final months of her husband's life, about what he actually did for a living that led to his death. Perhaps a little more about his contributions to the war effort she could one day pass on to their children.

But she just stared straight ahead—maybe the CIA programs its wives to do that—so I eventually skipped past the fibs I was prepared to tell and asked her, "After his death, did you receive a package from the army containing his personnel effects?"

This question appeared to confuse her because there was a long pause before she answered. "Yes, I . . . I believe it was a month or so after his death."

"Good, but according to our records, closer to two weeks after his death. The postal service always gives us a receipt."

"It may have been . . . Yes, yes, two weeks sounds more accurate," she quickly corrected. She then added, with an appropriately forlorn expression, "Frankly, everything in those days was a horrible blur."

"I'm sorry . . . I know this must be very painful for you, but I assure you it's necessary. Now do you happen to recall what was in the package?" I gave her a brief explanation of army procedures regarding the handling of a deceased soldier's personnel effects, and ended up, by saying, "Perhaps you saved the inventory sheet. If I could see it, it would save a lot of time and trouble."

She bit her lip and looked bothered. "Inventory sheet?"

"Yes ma'am. It's a standard military form. A commissioned officer signs it, in duplicate, and the original copy of the form is included in the shipping container."

"I . . . well, to be truthful, Colonel Drummond, I don't recall seeing any such forms. Maybe it got lost, or . . . Oh God, could I have failed to notice it before I threw the box away?"

As a lawyer, I work with liars for a living. Mrs. Ashad seemed sincere and above board, yet something about her was giving me an uneasy feeling. I suggested, "Some idiot on the other end probably forgot to include it. You know how the army is."

"Well, I don't, not really. But I'll take your word for it."

I smiled. "Let's see how good your memory is."

She smiled back. "Without that inventory form, how will you know if my memory is accurate?"

"As I said, it was filled out in duplicate. I studied a copy before I came over," I fibbed. "I have a good memory."

"How fortunate."

"We don't screw everything up, Mrs. Ashad."

"With two wars going on, I should hope not."

"Me too, Mrs. Ashad, me too. But to be sure we're talking about the same box, did it include a set of green prayer beads? On the form, they were described as having these little gold squiggles."

This was another lie, of course, but I needed to test Mrs. Ashad's credibility and see if *she* was lying.

"That's right." She looked at me and elaborated, "The beads were a gift . . . from Amal's uncle, I believe. They meant a great deal to my husband."

"Ah . . . well, perhaps I can see them? It won't hurt to be sure we're talking about the same beads, and the right box."

"I'm afraid not." She hesitated, then with a solemn expression, informed me, "I gave the beads to one of the children. To Amro, who was so distraught over his father's death, and I thought . . . well, I hoped it might console him." A cute pout came over her face. "A schoolyard bully beat him up and stole it. Little boys can be so cruel."

"Big boys are even worse."

"Yes," she said, looking at me, "I suppose that's true."

"Now please think hard because this is important. Amal kept a journal at the prison, probably about four hundred pages in length. It may have been typed or it may have been handwritten. Do you recall seeing it?"

It was obvious that if she answered yes, I would want to see the journal and, if no, I would still want to see it, but I would have to go away. "I'm sorry," she answered. "There was no such journal. Is that what you're looking for?"

"It is. Are you certain?"

"Did the inventory form indicate it should've been there?"

I feigned a look of disappointment. "Unfortunately not. But one of the soldiers who participated in the inventory swore he included it in the shipment, so I thought I'd give it a shot. Sadly, this isn't the first lie we caught him in"—or you, I might've added, except I didn't want to hurt her feelings.

She shrugged. "I'm sorry you had to come all this way in the dead of night."

I stood and looked down at her. She didn't look sorry, she looked relieved. "You've been very hospitable and helpful, Mrs. Ashad. Thank you."

She also stood and began escorting me to the door, quite happy that this was over. But about halfway through the study I slapped my forehead and said, "Oh . . . one more question."

She looked at me with an expression somewhere between annoyed and quizzical.

"Did your husband ever mention Kenny Waylon? Perhaps in conversation or in a letter?"

Again there was an interesting pause before she replied, "The name might ring a bell . . . I'm afraid, though, I don't remember it."

"They died together. Waylon was driving the Humvee and Amal was in the passenger seat." And, actually they ended up blurred together in the same bloody mist, though it might be poor taste to mention that part. But I decided to take another throw of the dice and informed her, "Kenny and Amal worked in the same section at the CIA. There were partners in Iraq. I'm told they were quite close."

It was her turn to feign a look of surprise. "Oh, you mean Ken?"

"Same guy." I nodded. "Good ole Ken."

"Amal always called him Ken, never Kenny. Yes, they were good friends. What about him?"

I did not really want to answer that question and I replied, "How tragic that they died together. How was the funeral, Mrs. Ashad?"

We were at the door, which she was holding open, no doubt intending this to be a strong hint to not let it hit me in the ass. "Sad . . . very sad. All of Amal's friends were there, as was his family."

"Where was he buried?"

"Why does it matter?"

"It doesn't . . . if I've been too intrusive, I'm sorry."

"No, I . . . Well, the funeral was in the town where Amal grew up . . . in California."

She was obviously thinking on her feet—she chose the farthest location from here she could get—so I couldn't just pop over and confirm the gravesite. Smart lady.

Well, maybe not that smart; according to Amal's military records, which had, so far, checked out, Ashad's home of record was Aberdeen, Maryland.

My right foot was wedged against the door, so she couldn't shut it in my face. "Incidentally, what was his boss's name?"

I produced a quick yawn to prove how exhausted I was and explained, "We spoke just a few hours ago . . . in fact, that's how I got your address. I promised to call when I finished up here."

She looked at me and said, "So much for your excellent memory."

"I'm sure I said I have a *good* memory."

She smiled back, a bit patronizingly. "I see . . . good, not excellent."

"Well, I'd better get along . . . I have to make the hour drive back to the office and get the number from my Rolodex. I hate to wake his boss at two o'clock in the morning . . . but . . ."

She made no reply for a few seconds, but apparently more conflicted about interrupting the fitful sleep of Amal's boss then inconveniencing me, she eventually informed me, "I suppose since you already know her, it won't hurt anything. Margaret Martin."

"Well, thank you again, Mrs. Ashad."

"I hope I've been helpful."

"More than you know," I said—and meant it.

I waved farewell and walked back to my car.

I climbed into the Prius, pushed the starter button, turned off the automatic headlights, then turned on the radio and listened to the local news while I lingered and kept an eye the house. The kitchen light went out first, the front hallway lights next, then a bedroom light went on—and stayed on for the next thirty minutes. Interesting. What was keeping Mrs. Ashad awake at this late hour? For sure, she had acted and looked tired; but maybe I bored her. Anyway, I hoped she wasn't on the phone making an alarming report about the strange man who had popped by to ask a lot of inconvenient questions.

Mrs. Ashad had lied about the box of personal belongings, and she lied about the location of her husband's grave. She was not a natural dissembler, but neither had she engaged in any of the schoolbook giveaways: no shaking hands, no trembling lips, no outbreak of sweat, no eyeballs inverting to her left. Indeed, I thought, she looked and sounded rehearsed. But rehearsed by whom, and more importantly, why?

I put the car into gear, drove about five miles to a Dunkin' Donuts in a worn-down strip mall, picked up a box of a dozen glazed, a large carry-away carton of coffee, and then returned to

38th Street, where I parked at the end of the block and settled in for a long vigil.

If I was going to engage in a stakeout like a cop, why not go all the way?

Chapter Twenty-Two

The home's garage was located on the lower level, at the bottom of a steep driveway and, at 6:30, a silver Dodge minivan crested the rise, took a right, and drove at a slow speed past me. I was just stuffing the last of the donuts in my mouth, and was parked directly below a street light as she passed—I could see Mrs. Ashad staring straight ahead from behind the steering wheel, and I could see kids' heads bobbing up and down in the back. And on the far side of the van, I thought I saw the vague outline of a male seated in the passenger seat.

Maybe Mrs. Ashad had moved fast and already found a replacement for her dearly departed hubbie, or maybe she had purchased one of those blow-up dolls carpool lane cheaters use.

I put the car in gear and followed. We drove up a big hill, then crossed Glebe Road, drove a few more blocks, took a left, and she pulled into the large circular driveway of Williamsburg Elementary School. The middle doors of the van flew open and three kids piled out, hauling their backpacks and mauling one another by the curb. I watched a man step out of the front seat. He pointed a finger like a dagger and said something sharp enough to make the kids quit the horseplay, he gave each kid a hug, then got back into the car.

Despite being thoroughly overcaffeinated and tripping on sugar-logged donuts, I was still running a little short on gas, but I definitely recognized the physique, and the face—Amal Ashad.

And to think I had thought he was dead and buried. Okay, I had sat in the car all night and was following them now because I hadn't thought that at all; Mrs. Ashad had lied about the package, she had lied about the prayer beads, she had lied about the funeral, so the really big lie wasn't all that hard to figure out.

As I watched, the kids skipped off in the direction of the school's entrance, and mom and pop hit the gas and left. I waited half a beat, then followed them back to Glebe Road, where they took a sharp left, then they drove for a few more miles over Military Road, then through some more twisty roads and up a big hill until we were crawling through dense traffic down Route 123, in McLean, Virginia, about half a mile from CIA headquarters at Langley.

I watched them hang a right into the headquarters complex and decided to use my Agency pass and follow them inside. I don't usually talk to corpses, but I was really looking forward to a lively conversation with Amal Ashad, who seemed to have rematerialized from a death-strewn street in Baghdad and transported himself here. I believe in resurrections, but only as the aftermath of an immaculate conception.

When I got to the gate, however, I realized I had made a big mistake. While the gate guard in the blue uniform walked toward my car, two dark sedans pulled in and came to a screeching halt behind me, totally blocking in my little Prius. I had been so preoccupied with tailing the Ashads that I never noticed the cars tailing me. The army has an astute technical term for this—rectal defilade, i.e., having your head up your ass.

A very tall man in a light gray suit with a narrow gray face, and a beak like a swollen cashew nut, walked to my door, bent over, and tapped on the window.

I pushed the button, brought the window down, but only a bit, so there was a large enough crack to speak through but not enough for him to get his big hands on me. I smiled at him and said, "Park it where it'll get no scratches, or dings . . . or no tip."

He did not appreciate my insouciance. "Unlock your doors now."

"I don't think so. I've seen everything I want to see."

"You think you're smart?"

"I know I'm smart. I'm just not certain about you."

He seemed a little pissed off, and I don't think my surly mouth was the cause, though it was not helping matters, nor was it meant to. Probably, like me, he had just spent a long, cold, boring night parked on a suburban street, and I was definitely the cause of that. He looked tired, with bloodshot eyes, and a little disheveled, and, as I said, very pissed off.

On the other hand, Sean Drummond was seated behind the wheel of a cute little yellow Prius, which I could not imagine James Bond being caught dead in.

He said, "Look, Drummond, if you want to be a pain in the ass, I can have a tow-truck up here in about five minutes, and make you." He sort of snorted. "Now who's the smart one?"

This guy had obviously not read the warning that when you argue with an idiot, you have to get down his level, where he has more experience. I said, "Hey, was that you parked on Thirty-Eighth Street all night?"

"You never saw us, Drummond. How does it feel to be caught with your pants down?"

I don't think we were bonding. In fact, it was start-time at CIA headquarters and the traffic was really beginning to pile up behind us as this bully and I engaged in our juvenile taunting. I'm good at this. And I enjoy it. Or, as my army infantry buddies like to say about themselves, when you wrestle with a pig, everybody gets dirty but the pig actually has a ball. Anyway, it was a major intersection and a bunch of cars had shot through the green light toward the guard point, and were now backed up behind us and blocking the intersection. A few people were honking. The gate guard gave him a look and shouted, "Hey buddy, can you two cut the crap? I gotta get this moving."

"In a minute," he barked. Then, looking at me, he sort of opened his coat a little so I could observe the big black pistol hooked to his belt. He said in a low, authoritative tone, "Drive down to the building. Now, or else."

"Or else what?"

"I'll make you."

"Am I under arrest?"

"Maybe."

"Show me your police badge and your warrant, then I might come along peacefully."

His face turned really red, and his right hand moved down to his holster.

Now I knew he wasn't a cop, or an FBI agent, and he obviously didn't have a warrant; even more obviously, he was not happy with the situation, or, I suppose, with me. It's always a stupid idea to provoke a man with a gun, but I was pretty sure shooting me in the presence of so many inconvenient witnesses was not in his instructions. But his jaw was now very tight, and his hand looked shaky.

Two more men suddenly emerged from the government sedans to our rear, and walked toward my car. One, a short, chubby fellow in a nice blue suit that resembled a well-tailored tent, smiled nicely at me, and inquired, "What's the problem here?"

"The problem," I replied, not smiling in return, "is your Gestapo goon here, who keeps giving me orders and showing off his gun."

Short guy said to tall guy, "That true?"

"Absolutely not," tall guy insisted, quickly closing his coat. "I merely made a polite request for Drummond to accompany us down to the headquarters."

"He's lying," I informed short guy. "He said I better get moving before the fat runt got here, or he'd shoot me."

Short guy was apparently sensitive about his height and his weight, because his lips sort of became sucked into his mouth and then he turned back to the goon with the gun. "You've mishandled this. Go back to the car."

Tall guy glowered at me and said, "This isn't over," then turned on his heels and stomped back to the car.

Short guy smiled at me. "I apologize for any misunderstanding."

"Which misunderstanding are you referring to? Following me for the past ten hours, or blocking my car, or having that big idiot threaten me with a gun?"

We regarded each other a moment, sort of taking each other's measure. I don't think he liked what he saw. "All of it . . . whatever," he replied, with a distinct note of impatience. "Please, Colonel Drummond, we need to talk."

"Will Amal Ashad be present for this talk?"

"Well . . . maybe that could be arranged."

I turned off the engine and leaned back in my seat. Route 123 was now a parking lot filled with very pissed off people.

We were at an impasse here. He wanted me to drive onto CIA property where I would be subject to arrest and possibly detained in the basement and forced to endure some mind control experiment that would turn me into one of *them*. I, on the other hand, wanted to get my hands around Amal Ashad's throat and find out why he wasn't nearly as dead as he was supposed to be.

But Ashad was obviously the hook, and he said, "All right, you'll get your crack at Ashad. You have my word."

I knew it was a bad idea to trust this guy, but I pushed the start button and drove down the hill into the parking lot in front of CIA headquarters. I pulled into an open parking space with a sign that claimed it was reserved for a deputy director—in the palace of lies and deception, you can't trust a simple sign—put the car in park, and switched off the engine. I got out and stretched; inside a minute, short, fat guy and a few of his friends showed up, including tall guy who was looking at me like he was measuring a coffin.

Mr. Short approached me and, with his hand held out, put a name and a job to the body. "Mark Helner, internal security."

I shook his hand and asked, "Why was I under the misimpression that the CIA is barred from operating inside the borders of the United States?"

He shrugged. "That is the law, yes."

"So . . . ?"

"So . . . it appears we have a misunderstanding." He then explained the nature of this mix-up. "You invaded the home of a CIA employee, which brought this matter under our jurisdiction." He paused. "Mrs. Ashad called us late last night. She was distraught about an intruder who misrepresented his identity, impersonated an army investigator, lied his way inside, and began pressuring her to answer questions that violate our national security."

This sounded, in fact, like a fairly accurate rendition of what I had done the night before, but, as a lawyer, of course, I wasn't stupid enough to confirm this story. I relied, instead, on the old legal adage that when a sound defense is impossible, be offensive, or go on the offensive—I can never keep that straight—and replied, "And did she remember to mention she was hiding a corpse inside her home?"

"I have no idea what you're talking about."

"Unless she enjoys necrophilia, Amal Ashad is alive and was in her bed last night."

He either did not know the meaning of this exotic word or chose to remain on the offense himself. He stuck out a finger. "You have a big problem, Drummond. You violated several federal statutes, not to mention sticking your nose where it doesn't belong."

"Fine, charge me. Let's sort it out in court."

"Good idea. I just might."

"A good bluff has an odor of truth, Mr. Helner. All I smell is bullshit."

Staying true to my olfactory theme, he replied, "Sniff again. Don't underestimate me, Drummond, and don't misjudge the seriousness of this situation." He then put a finger against my chest and stated in language I could understand, "Your ass is in my hands."

"In court, you get to explain the little mystery of how Ashad, who's supposedly dead and buried, ended up in his home, back in Arlington." I plucked his finger off my chest. "I'll invite every reporter I know and be sure to raise my voice when I get to that part."

"You're mistaken . . . or mistaken again." It looked like he was dying to tell me how mistaken I was, so I chose not to address that charge.

"The man you saw this morning is Mrs. Ashad's brother-in-law." In the event I wasn't getting the message, he embellished on this lie. "Amal's little brother, Rashid. I'll admit the family resemblance is quite striking" He added a little more bullshit to the recipe and said, "He was worried about Mrs. Ashad and decided to spend the night."

"Then bring him out and let me talk to him. We can clear up any confusion and I'll go away."

"I don't think so, Drummond."

"I'd like to see him now."

"I'm afraid that's not even a little possible."

"Then I'll go get a little subpoena and make it possible."

"You better get it fast." He smiled again—it was one of those smiles Snidely Whiplash would produce, if he had a plump, churlish face, and no mustache he could twirl. "He has a plane to catch. An international flight. I hear he plans to be away for a long time."

I said, "What are you going to do? Arrange another unfortunate accident? Don't you get tired of killing this guy? Doesn't he get tired of it?"

His smile broadened. "You know, that's an idea with possibilities. An accident . . . of course, it would be a terrible coincidence, both Amal and his brother killed. So much tragedy to befall one family, don't you think?"

"You promised I could talk to him, and now you're planning his funeral."

"I'm with the federal government, Drummond—trust me is just another way of saying I'm lying." The smile hardened. "You'll never talk to him, Drummond. Never."

I did my best to look disappointed and pissed off at this news. "Then I guess . . . I'm . . . well, I'm just wasting my time."

"I couldn't have said it better. Amal Ashad died two months ago. He's not coming back to life."

The tall guy with the hatchet face was smiling and found it impossible to resist saying, "Like I said, Drummond, who's the smart guy now?"

I ignored that comment—and him—and said to Mr. Helner, "Now that everything's cleared up, am I free to go?"

"First, I've got some news for you. As I said, you've violated any number of Agency regulations, not to mention several federal statutes, Drummond. Impersonating a military investigator is a serious offense. You should be aware that, early this morning, your security clearance was revoked. Also I'll have to take your Agency passcard."

"What if I want to keep it?"

"Won't do you any good. Your passcode has also been erased from the system. It's CIA property. I insist you give me the card."

I pulled out my wallet, withdrew my card, and threw it on the ground. "Does this mean I won't be coming back to the CIA when this case is over?"

This thought seemed to make him happy—but not nearly as happy as it made me. "I think that's a good guess," he informed me.

"Do I have time," I asked, "for one farewell gesture?"

"If you wish."

I raised my middle finger and pointed it at the Langley headquarters building, aiming specifically at the top floor, where the Lord of the Manor hung his hat, and I could swear I saw him looking down at me and waving back, a big goofy wave. But it's possible I imagined that.

Mr. Helner laughed. He surprised me and said, "I always wanted to do that. How does it feel?"

"Therapeutic. Give it a try."

He seemed to shrink. "The whole parking lot is under camera. I've got three more years till I retire."

I got in the car, started the engine, and drove away, out the gate first, then took a right and proceeded about three miles to the town of McLean, where I pulled into the crowded parking lot of a Rite Aid and put the car in idle.

I pulled out my cellphone and brought up the pictures I had taken only thirty minutes earlier, at Williamsburg Elementary School. I hadn't had time to check them yet, so I did—and there, front and center, two times, I had Amal Ashad with his forefinger pointed at his kids, then once, in a third shot, just before he climbed back into the van, he turned and appeared to be looking directly at me.

The pictures were a little off-centered and gauzy, but all in all, they were good enough for government work, or more relevantly, for making a very damning impression on a jury—especially that third shot. The expression on his face said everything that needed to be said.

Obviously, he knew I was there, and obviously this scared the shit out of him.

Chapter Twenty-Three

Next, I placed a call to my old office, specifically to Lila, the security agent at the front desk who pretended to be a receptionist, and had a gun in the top drawer, a black belt in her past, and probably knew ten ways to kill you using sesame seeds. She was quite pretty, and also happily married, but she liked to flirt, as do I, so in a building of tight-lipped, tight-assed bureaucrats, we made an interesting couple.

I identified myself, to which Lila replied, "Drummond? . . . Drummond? Sorry, I don't know that name. He's been wiped from human memory. A nonperson."

I replied with false innocence, "I don't know what you're talking about."

"Really, Sean? When I came in this morning, there was a firmly worded directive on my desk stating that your security creds have been yanked, and I should spank you if you try to enter."

"This is a joke, right?"

"Did I mention it's signed by Phyllis? I believe the last joke she told was in 1923."

"Oh . . ."

Lila laughed, then went silent a moment, then said, "Look, I'm really going to miss you around here."

I said, "I need a favor."

"Gee . . . I don't know. Your name's really mud around here. I don't want any trouble with the thought police."

"Just a phone number. Margaret Martin."

"Where does she work?"

"Somewhere in the puzzle palace. What office oversees torture?"

"The office of professional ethics?" She giggled.

"Lesser forms of torture."

"I guess a simple phone number won't get me in any trouble, right?" When I did not respond to that questionable assertion, Lila told me, "Hold on."

I held, while Lila looked up the number.

"Got it," she said. "She's in the Directorate of Operations. Her title says Director of Support Services."

"Support Services? Is that the Agency's euphemism for yanking out fingernails and playing squash with your balls?"

"Now, now, Sean, you know we don't do that stuff."

No, you have somebody else pull down their pants and play with their wee-wees. Of course, I didn't say that—instead I said, "No, you ask them politely who's planning on bombing New York and wait patiently until they tell you."

"Well, sometimes a knee in the nuts improves the male memory. Take my husband, for instance. So . . . you want the number or not?"

She gave me the number and I wrote it down.

When she finished she warned, "Be careful, Sean. Powerful people are pissed at you."

Thanks for the newsflash, Lila. "Speaking of which, you know a guy named Helner?"

"Mark Helner? Sure, I used to work with him."

"Tell me about him."

"Well, he's short and fat and obnoxious and—"

"I know all that."

"You've met him, huh? Well, I was about to add very sly, brutally ambitious, and totally ruthless. And efficient—he's the type who smiles as he sends a boxcar full of people to reeducation camp . . . or, to take another example, the type who can pull your security clearance overnight and end your career. I hope he isn't one of the people after you."

"Worry about him, Lila. This is me. Mothers warn their kids to be good, or big bad Sean will get them."

There was a long pause before she remarked, in a noncommittal tone, "Uh-huh. Well . . . watch your ass anyway. Helner doesn't play fair."

"Right." I hung up and pondered what to do next. I started with a brief inventory of my problems, or, as a less congenitally cynical person might say, the minor challenges I had to overcome.

One, somebody was still out there, still trying to kill me, possibly. No progress had been made toward finding out who the killer was; so far, the only meaningful progress was scraping up the bodies this guy clipped. Were the severed ears only a harmless warning, or official notice that Katherine and I were next on the grim reaper's list? This seemed like a not inconsequential question. But only the killer knew the answer, and I didn't want to learn what he was thinking the wrong way.

Two, we were no closer to deciding how guilty our client was, or was not, or on solidifying a trial strategy, which hinged very much on getting a grip on the former issue. Our interviews with two other members of the night crew indicated Lydia was, indeed, very guilty and further, that the other members planned to pin the rap on the dumbest, most vulnerable participant. This was a contest Lydia won hands down. They seemed to be claiming that it was her willfulness, her brainchild, and they had merely followed her lead. In the sentencing lottery, Lydia was being lined up for the long stretch.

And if all that weren't enough, three, I now had the CIA on my ass. I knew the big secret, and their only hope of covering it up was covering me up. I could picture the meeting going on at the top floors at Langley at that moment, Amal Ashad wracking his brain about how to go back to being dead, and his bosses scratching their heads about how to make me dead.

Handling the Drummond quandary was apparently Mark Helner's issue and I recalled Lila's warm and eloquent description of him—ruthless and brutally ambitious, and he doesn't play by the rules. I regarded Lila as a sound judge of character—she liked me, right?—and it struck me that it would not be a waste of my time to worry about Mr. Helner. Pulling my CIA easy pass was probably not the only thing he had up his rather ample sleeve. As our Mafia friends like to say, the best witnesses are the dead ones.

And last, though not least, Katherine. Dear, sweet Katherine. Did I love her? Despite her maddening qualities and our promiscuously contentious history together, yes, I was pretty sure I did. Enough to marry her? Well, that was a different question. She had not exactly given me an ultimatum as much as she had given herself one, which, in this case, added up to pretty much the same thing.

So, worst case. I could lose this case, lose Katherine, and lose my life, none of which were mutually exclusive. Best case . . . well, I could win the case, outlive the killer, and still end up with a life sentence. Said otherwise, could Sean and Katherine move past a decade of venomous bickering and incestuous competition to build a happy, blissful union? This did not sound promising. This sounded, in fact, like either the plot for a particularly rancid soap opera, or the formula for a mutual homicide pact.

Anyway, I pushed that troubling thought aside to focus on a more pressing question; specifically, why would the CIA cook up the phony death of Amal Ashad? To hide and/or cover up something, obviously. But what? What secret could be so big and so bad to merit such an effort?

And on a more selfish note, was my beloved institution, the army, involved in the cover-up? Now that I had made myself persona non grata with the CIA, it seemed like a good time to consider whether I still had a paycheck and a checkered career to return to. Regarding the army's connivance in this conspiracy, I thought not. The CIA was genetically addicted to conspiracies. But that wasn't the army way. The army is too incompetent and systemically clumsy to be conspirational, for one thing. As the saying goes, military intelligence is an oxymoron. For another, the fact that the army was taking all the heat over this affair did not imply willing or, as I was learning, even acknowledged participation.

No, I thought, the army was being cuckholded by the Agency. Amal Ashad had been brought in to help out, then, once that help turned toxic, and the cat was leaving the bag via the leaks to Melvin Cramer, the Agency got cold feet and left the army to take the bows from the stage.

For, if I believed Danny Elton, Amal Ashad was the Svengali behind the twisted shenanigans of the night crew. Serious, for sure, but was his involvement really shameful and scandalous enough for the Agency to construct such an elaborate charade just to conceal his role? Perhaps. Never underestimate the lengths a public institution will go to get out of the way of an incoming shitstorm. Yet my instincts were telling me there was something more here, that whatever Ashad did was far more sinister and portentous than merely prodding and encouraging a few corruptible soldiers to do naughty things in the dead of the night.

I thought about that a little more. Whatever it was, why didn't the Agency just write Ashad off and let him take the fall? Describe him to the press and to congressional investigators as a formerly reliable agent who snapped, went rogue and off the reservation, burn any documents that might implicate anyone else at the Agency, and follow the Agency motto: deny, deny, deny.

Said otherwise: What did Amal Ashad have on the Agency?

Answer that question and Sean Drummond, too, would have the Agency by the balls. And as with life, so it goes with big institutions: once you have them by the balls, their hearts and minds follow.

Only four days ago I was sitting in an o-club bar with nothing more pressing on my mind than figuring out how to get into the knickers of a comely college teacher; now I was overdosing on plotlines, any of which, or all of which, could prove hazardous to the career, not to mention the health, of my favorite hero—me.

Chapter Twenty-Four

I decided, before making the long trek back up to West Point, to pay a brief visit to Justin, West Virginia, birthplace and home of record of PFC Eddelston, and the one place where, I hoped, I could get a bit more background, and some clarity on young Lydia before she matriculated into the dominatrix of Al Basari.

After nearly three hours of driving, I ended up in a small burg in the middle of the Appalachian Mountains, a place that seemed to match in every respect the dyspeptic description Lydia had provided me earlier.

According to the Internet, Justin had a total population of 723 with an average family income of $22,354, which placed it somewhere down there on the socioeconomic pole. The average home value was $65,000, a mixture of freestanding buildings and trailers, the latter apparently the domicile of choice. They could rename this town shithole and be accused of putting on airs.

I had the address of Lydia's family in my pocket but decided to do a little noodling with some of the locals before I dropped in on her ma and pa, who I did not anticipate would be all that forthcoming or revelatory about their troubled daughter's childhood. In my experience, all parents regard their parenting skills as above reproach and their children-gone-astray as misunderstood angels, even when that child has matured into a child-molesting serial killer. Take my own parents, for example.

Anyway, I pulled into the small square in the middle of Justin, a crossroads, really, with a mom-and-pop grocery store, a disheveled-looking bar that was already open with a parking lot full of rust-coated, banged-up pick-ups, and, across the road, the prestigious 7-Eleven described by Lydia the night I met her.

I had changed into jeans and a red polo shirt before I left Washington, and decided the bar was a more promising venue for my purposes than the 7-Eleven; someone needed a drink.

I parked and entered through the front entrance and, much like the small restaurant back in Highland Falls where Katherine and I met with Fred, our prison consultant, it was like stepping backward in time, with dim lighting, chipped and filthy linoleum floors, a bunch of ancient tables in the middle of the floor, and even older-looking booths lining the walls. The style of the décor was impoverished wreck. Apparently the federal smoking ban had not made it to Justin, because the air was nearly gray with smoke. It was three in the afternoon, and I could see why the average income in this town was so meager. Half the male residents, it seemed, had already kicked off from work, if indeed they had done any work that day.

In my clean polo shirt, and with all my teeth intact and brushed, I was badly overdressed and immediately drew every eye in the establishment. I sauntered to the bar where an older looking gent and a middle-aged woman whose profession wasn't hard to guess were hunched over their drinks. I squeezed between them and the bartender wandered over and asked, "You old enuff to drink, fella?"

I looked at him and answered, "Scotch, neat."

"Any particular brand?"

I was fairly certain Chivas Regal was above the waterline for such an establishment and replied, "Something that leaves my eyesight intact."

He apparently found this humorous because he laughed before he wandered off to squirt a little hooch into a hopefully clean glass, which he deposited in front of me at the bar.

The woman seated beside me appeared to sense a business opportunity and asked, "New in town, aren't ya, fella?"

What was your first clue, honey? She was somewhere between thirty and fifty, though it was difficult to be precise. Triple coating of makeup, blown-out hairdo circa 1980, and she was moderately attractive, or at least had once been before life and a serious addiction to either drugs or booze had given her looks a weather-beaten patina. But if you're looking for insights in a small town, the local whore beats the town librarian any day. I informed her, West Virginia style, "Just passing through, ma'am."

"Uh-huh. Well, where you from?"

"Nowhere," I answered. "I'm in the army."

"Oh . . ." she said, as though I had just asked for a quickie for God and Country.

"I'm a lawyer," I clarified, and that seemed to perk up her interest.

"Well, I always like lawyers. Got business here?"

"I'm representing a girl from Justin. Lydia Eddleston. Know her?"

"Guess ever'body knows ever'body hereabouts." She added, with a scowl, "Sure got her tits in a wringer."

"How well did you know her?"

"Used to see her around. I know her daddy much better," she admitted, a statement that revealed something about the marriage between Mr. and Mrs. Eddelston, not to mention the social limitations of this lady's trade. She looked perplexed, then informed me, "That guy next to you, I'll bet he knows her 'bout as good as anybody."

"Does he?" I glanced at the man to my left.

"More'n likely. Ole Hank was the principal of Justin High 'fore he retired last year."

Preoccupied as he was with his drinking, Hank did not appear to be paying attention to our conversation. To get his interest, I stuck my hand in his face, in the space between his lips and his glass. He turned and stared at me. "What do you want?"

"A quick conversation." When this did not elicit an enthusiastic response, I amended that to, "Let me buy you a drink."

I didn't have to ask twice, because he accompanied me to a booth on the wall, where I quickly introduced myself and explained my purpose for visiting Justin.

To break the ice I asked him a few questions about himself. His full name was Henry Livingston, and though he preferred to be called by his given name of Henry, the locals had a hankering for Hank. I hate to generalize, but in small backwater towns such as this, multisyllabic names tend to be equated with putting on airs.

Anyway, Henry had been the high school principal for twenty-six years, which included duty as the science teacher and guidance counselor. He had not been born and bred in Justin, but in Wheeling, and he noted in a disapproving tone that only 3 percent of the town residents had been to college, and only 35 percent had matriculated from high school.

He had a West Virginian drawl, but it lacked both the country thickness and careless vernacular I associated with Lydia's speech. Physically, Henry appeared to be in his early to midsixties, though as with the lady at the bar, albeit hopefully for different reasons, he had aged unkindly with a large gut, sparse though messy hair, and a face that had set into a deepset scowl that I thought reflected a mixture of resentment and disillusionment. It was, as I implied, a face of discontent, of a man living only because he wasn't yet dead. To underscore this impression, it took three glasses of gin to plow through to this point in the conversation. At this rate, it won't be long, Hank.

Before he could become incoherent, or his liver give out, I asked Henry, not Hank, "How well did you know Lydia?"

"The high school's only got like 180 students so I guess I got to know all the kids pretty well." After a brief reflection he informed me, "Troubled girl."

"Troubled in what way?"

"Messed up family for starters. Her folks ain't exactly the kind of parents you'd call ideal."

"Ah, I see."

He stated, "Her Daddy's a real mean cuss, and her mom's a rotten drunk," oblivious to the fact that he was working his way through his fourth gin since we'd sat in this booth. He shrugged and added, "Always suspected she got abused a lot as a kid."

"Abuse is a broad term. What kind of abuse?"

"She had . . . well . . . she had a few what you might call behavioral issues at the school."

"Can you be more specific?"

"Hard to describe. Lydia was a pretty poor student. Her teachers thought she was dumb, and maybe hampered by some mental disability, ADHD, or something like that. Her test scores certainly suggested somethin' wasn't right. Tell you what, though—she ain't nearly as dumb as she appears."

"Was that the issue?"

He took another long sip and appeared to contemplate my question. He leaned forward and lowering his voice, whispered, "Look, what I'm about to tell you is on the down-low, okay? I was the guidance counselor so it was my job to check these sorta things."

"Of course," I replied—which is lawyer-speak for "I will respect the confidentiality until it suits my purposes to do otherwise."

"I guess there ain't no polite way to say this. Lydia was banging a few of her teachers. And she was real aggressive about it, guess you'd say. She'd go visit their homes late at night, and nearly rape 'em." His face folded into a deep frown of regret. "Hadda fire one of them teachers. Ole Ted Ebersol. Too damned bad, too. That Ted could teach a dog to meow. Would've fired the other two I found out 'bout, 'cept then we'd of had nobody to teach geometry or social studies."

"Okay. Was this known in the community?"

"As a fact, nope." He leaned his head back and took a deep sip. After a long swallow, he admitted, "Oh, there was rumors, of course. Small town like this, folks are always yakkin'. Course I spoke to her Pa about it."

"And how did he react?"

"Hollered at me to git my nose outta her affairs. Said it was her pussy and how she chose to use it was her business." He raised his eyebrows and tipped his glass at me. "Funny thing was, cain't say he was all that surprised by it."

"So you suspected he was sexually abusing his own daughter?"

"Well . . . I ain't no expert or nothin'."

"But I sense that you formed an opinion, Henry. Would you care to share it?"

Apparently so, because Henry confided, "Well, I spoke to some of her grade school teachers and they tole me little Lydia did lots of inappropriate things in school."

"What kind of things?"

"Sexual stuff you don't much see from little kids. You know, touching, showing off her privates, that sort of thing. The boys in the school took to callin' her Nurse Lydia, on account of her slut-tiness." He got a pained look in his eyes. "Guess you know them's all tell-tale signs of a girl who got raped, or molested at home. Tell the truth, I wasn't the least bit surprised to see Lydia's pictures in all them newspapers and news shows, doin' that awful stuff they say she was doin'. Ask me, that girl was bred to be like that."

"And did you report these suspicions?"

"To who?"

"The police. Social services. To somebody with the authority and resources to investigate and intervene."

"Couldn't," he replied. "Didn't have no proof. Hell, her folks wasn't likely to change, anyway. Like I said, her ole man is a real mean cuss."

Henry put down his glass and looked at me. Despite that easy rationalization, he obviously knew that he should have reported his suspicions regarding the perversities occurring in Lydia's home and, had he done so, maybe the authorities would have intervened, and maybe Lydia might have gotten professional help, and maybe Sean Drummond wouldn't be sitting across from him now.

A man has to have illusions in order to become disillusioned. I had the sense that at one time Henry had tried to run a good school and push his students to graduate and make something of themselves, to escape from a town with maybe ten college graduates and where only one of four adults hadn't dropped out of high school and life. I'm sure he had some successes, some bright, shining kids who beat the odds and pulled themselves out of the wreckage of poverty and alcoholism and hopelessness that seemed to permeate this sad community. Just as I'm sure he had his hopes crushed hundreds more times by kids who never had a chance, no matter how hard Henry tried to fix their lives. I wasn't here to judge him, but it looked like he was judging himself, and he did not like the results.

Somehow, I doubted having Lydia Eddelston as his most famous graduate was going to wash away his regrets.

But a visit to Lydia's parents now seemed less like a waste of my time. I should get a look at the monsters who'd sent their child like a guided missile into the army.

I dropped a fifty on the booth table, then stood, content that Henry, or Hank, if you prefer, could keep drinking for another hour on my dime. I thanked him for his help and started to walk away before I remembered one other small matter he might be able to help me with. I looked down at him and said, "Incidentally, Lydia married a kid out of high school. It lasted only a few months before they got divorced. Do you recall the name of the boy she married?"

Henry was shaking his head long before I finished that explanation. "Willy Packer. Weren't no divorce though."

"Right. Then what was it?"

"A funeral. Car accident. Willy drove off a cliff."

A warning bell went off in my head, but I did my best to appear merely curious, rather than alarmed. "Why would Lydia tell me it was a divorce?"

"Guess you'll hafta ask her. But I should'a warned you that Lydia and truthfulness, they ain't even mildly acquainted. I never knew what went through that girl's head." He knocked on his own head a few times. "Tell you what, though. She ain't all right up there."

I left Henry and got back in my yellow Prius, then punched her parent's address into the navigation system, which drew a blank. I leaned out the window at an elderly lady passing by on the sidewalk, and inquired, "Could you please tell me the way to 313 Hollowbrook Road."

She shrugged.

I modified my request to, "I'm looking for the home of Silas and Lenore Eddelston."

"Then why didn't you say so?" she asked, not all that kindly. She then gave me directions, which I followed, ending up on a dirt road about two miles outside of town, a rustic, unpaved trail that I followed for nearly a mile off the paved road, until I ended up in a junkyard of dead cars and rotting refrigerators and long-defunct washing machines, and, amid all these industrial corpses, a double-wide trailer on cinderblocks that seemed to be leaning awkwardly to the left. It was like driving to the end of the world, where all of the carcasses of the planet's greatest consumerist nation came to die.

I climbed out of the car and went to what passed for a front porch where I knocked on what passed for a door. I heard what passed for a voice holler, "Lenore, you git that."

Then a woman's voice in reply, "Nah . . . git off your fat ass and you git it."

"Stupid lazy bitch. Awright, but next one's yers."

The door opened and there stood a large fat man in baggy jeans and a filthy white T-shirt that was stretched tight at the belly. "Who're you?" he asked by way of greeting.

I offered him my name and my rank, as well as a brief explanation of what I was doing there.

"No shit?" he asked, leaning on the doorjamb. The first thing I noted about Silas was the odor, which was as foul as it was pervasive. He did not appear to be a frequent bather, or even an infrequent one, nor was vanity one of his vices, as his unkempt hair hung down past his shoulders and his scraggly beard down to his chest. Perhaps I was responding to the suggestion already planted in my brain, but this guy actually *looked* like a child molester. He was now inspecting the cut of my jib and asked, "You ain't got no uniform on. You sure you ain't another of them damned reporters been comin' around here lately?"

"Do I look like a nosy asshole?" When the expression on his face appeared ambiguous on this issue, I withdrew my military ID card and allowed him to study it.

He finally looked up at me. "You takin' care of my little girl?"

"Trying to." Apparently he was experiencing a lapse of manners, so I inquired, "Mind if I come in?"

"Place is a little messy," he warned, stepping aside, which I took as permission to enter.

Silas Eddelston also had a gift for understatement. I stepped over toys and broken furniture and bits and parts of machinery until I entered what was supposed to be a living room, though it looked more like a storage bin for chaos.

Lenore yelled out, "Well, who is it, fatass?"

"Some army lawyer," Silas bellowed back. "Says he's defendin' our little girl."

A door in the back flew open and Lenore waddled down a narrow hallway, squeezed through a skinny doorframe, then entered the living room, which instantly shrank in size. She was, well, I suppose the most charitable way to put this is, a lot of woman. About four hundred pounds worth, though I doubted she kept count, as a precise weight was long past the point. Neither was she particularly attractive, with a small, upturned nose hidden somewhere in a large, fleshy face accentuated by a greasy, unwashed, and unfashioned mess of brown and gray hair. Her eyes were small, brown, and glinted with distrust. Though the floors were cluttered, she moved confidently and with surprising deftness, as if she knew where every piece of junk lay, stepping glibly over broken furniture without even glancing down.

"He talkin' 'bout you?" she demanded in a low smoker's voice.

Who else? "Lieutenant Colonel Sean Drummond, ma'am. I dropped by to ask a few questions about Lydia."

She contemplated this announcement a moment, and me. "Should'a called ahead."

Why? "Yes, ma'am, I suppose I should have."

"Well, what do you want?"

To get the hell out of here. I smiled at Mrs. Eddelston and asked, "You're aware of the charges being brought against your daughter?"

"Course I am. Ever'body in the friggin' world knows the terrible lies bein' spread 'bout our Lydia."

Silas, who had momentarily disappeared, reentered the small room carrying a can of hillbilly champagne, aka Miller beer. "Lydia didn't do none of that shit they're sayin'," he remarked, echoing his wife's sentiments. "I ain't never seen such a bullshit contest," he added, eliminating any mystery about the origins of Lydia's grammatical propensity toward double negatives.

I asked both of them, "You've seen the pictures in the news?"

"Hell, course we have," Lenore answered with a disapproving scowl. Her husband raised his beer can, which seemed to be his way of replying in the affirmative. "So what?" Lenore demanded. "She might'a done a few little naughty things, but it don't amount to nuthin'."

"Mrs. Eddelston, the pictures you've seen actually account for a small slice of Lydia's activities at Al Basari prison. In all, the prosecutors have over four hundred photographs of Lydia engaging in acts over more than a month-long period that you describe as naughty, any one of which could get her convicted of very serious crimes. And there may be even more photos."

Lenore grew quiet, which was a treat. But Silas took over. "Aw, fuck that. Ain't it yer job to git her off?" He cocked his head to the side, squinted, and added, "Don't sound like yer doin' shit to help our little girl."

I'd been here less than a minute and already I was resisting the impulse to pull out my gun and pop Silas and Lenore Eddelston.

Regarding his rude query, I replied, "My responsibility, Mr. Eddelston, is to provide your daughter the best defense I can, which in this case might amount to a plea of guilty and a pretrial bargain that allows her to walk out of prison before her AARP card becomes an antique. Your daughter is in a great deal of trouble, and no, my job is not to get her off, as you simplistically and erroneously put it, but to try my best to convince the court martial board that Lydia's crimes do not merit their most severe sentence. Do you understand what I'm telling you?"

While Silas considered my words, I decided to throw a little fuel on the fire. "My visit here relates to that intent. There is evidence suggestive that Lydia was abused from a very young age, that she was sexually molested here, at home, that she exhibited sexually inappropriate behavior throughout elementary school, and that, in high school, she seduced several of her teachers. I am told you were informed of this by school authorities."

Silas Eddelston was now staring at me with an expression that veered between shock and confusion; Lenore merely looked dully preoccupied, like she couldn't recall whether she had included sanitary napkins on her shopping list.

I continued, "I raise this because it speaks to the issue of extenuating and mitigating circumstances, as to whether your daughter's decisions and actions at Al Basari prison were motivated, or perhaps even precipitated by, her childhood experiences, the result of sexual trauma inflicted here, in her home."

Neither Silas nor his wife appeared to fully comprehend what I was saying, so I recast my multisyllabic explanation into an easier vernacular that might sink in. "What I'm saying, Mr. Eddelston, is that by diddling your daughter you fucked up her head. This caused her to reenact what you did to her on the prisoners. Now, do you understand what I'm telling you?"

Apparently, it did register because Silas cocked a fist and ran toward me. I'm no longer the lean, mean fighting machine I was in my days as a Special Forces stud, but Silas was hauling at least one hundred pounds of pure lard and, anyway, he made the bar-brawler's mistake of signaling his intentions.

I took a step to my right just as he yelled, "Why you somna-bitch, I'm gonna—," and with my left arm I clotheslined him, then with my right fist I popped him hard on the right ear, which is more painful than a punch in the kisser. Silas's feet kept going, but his ass and his head bolted straight for the floor, and he let out a loud *ooompf* as he landed, then grabbed his ear and began rolling around and howling.

His wife looked at me, then down at him and said, "You fat-assed idiot. You couldn't've made it more easy for him to kick yer ass."

I gave Silas a moment to let some of the pain wear off, and his squealing to subside, then said to him, "If you care about your daughter, you'll tell me the truth, Mr. Eddelston. It might be her only hope of persuading the jury that she wasn't entirely respon-sible for her own actions at Al Basari prison. Did you diddle your daughter?"

Silas looked up at me. "You bastard. You broke my ear."

"That looks like it hurts. Does it?"

"Hell, yeah . . . feels like a bunch'a hornets are stinging the crap outta me."

Satisfied that Silas was now in the proper frame of mind, I told him, "Then answer my question, Mr. Eddelston. Did you diddle your daughter?"

Still seated on the floor, he shook his head a few times in an effort to make the pain lessen. "Hell, no," he squealed. "I ain't never touched little Lydia." He then amended that to, "Well, sure,

I spanked her plenty . . . but I never once touched her in that sick way yer sayin'."

"He's tellin' you the truth," Mrs. Eddelston interjected. "Silas loves that little girl. But in a God-fearin' way."

I looked at Lenore. "I'm having trouble believing you, Mrs. Eddelston. Lydia exhibits all the symptoms and behavioral characteristics of a young woman who has been sexually traumatized. She's promiscuous, a sexual exhibitionist, sexually predatory, and at the prison, she was modeling her peculiar activities and behavior on something." I did not state that Lydia had neither the physical imagination nor sexual creativity to invent such behavior but I was sure they got the point.

While Lenore Eddelston pondered this charge, I decided to make her situation a bit more complicated, and revealed, "Oh, by the way, in the event you aren't on the notification list, you're about to become Grandma and Grandpa."

Mrs. Eddelston's eyes popped up. "What?"

"Your daughter is pregnant, Mrs. Eddelston. About three months now, which means the father is probably someone she served with at Al Basari. I'll leave it to your daughter to tell you who the proud father is, but there's a very good chance your first grandchild will be born in prison. I thought you should know this."

Lenore and Silas were now exchanging looks and expressions that shifted from surprise to horror. There was a great deal communicated by those looks, a shifting collage of emotions that was hard for me to sort out, just as it appeared difficult for them to settle on a final communal verdict. But the prominent emotion wasn't elation that a new generation of Eddelstons was about to be brought into the world—aside from horror, it was guilt and fear.

Silas, in fact, said, "Well, I'll be . . . You gotta be shittin' me."

"She got herself knocked up?" Lenore asked, though I thought it was more along the line of an observation than a question.

Silas, by now, appeared to come to his senses and said something I would've said long before. He pointed a finger at me. "You git yer ass outta here."

I looked down at him, still seated on the floor, still rubbing his ear. "I think you're telling the truth, or at least some version of the truth about you not diddling your daughter, Mr. Eddelston. But I think you're hiding a different truth. Something happened to Lydia in this house, and you and your wife know what it was, and are trying to keep it secret. I think you feel some guilt about this, and I think that if you don't come clean about what happened in the past, you are going to compound that guilt and make the situation infinitely worse for her, and for yourselves as well."

"Git out."

"Have a good day," I told him and left, picking my way back through both the material debris piled up in their cluttered yard, and the muddled swamp of the Eddelston's sorrow, secrets, and shame.

Chapter Twenty-Five

On the drive back up to West Point I pulled off Interstate 95, into the Maryland House Service Area, where I reached into my pocket and withdrew the slip of paper upon which I had written the office phone number for Margaret Martin, the CIA Director of Support Services, and apparently, Amal Ashad's boss du jour.

It was nearly six o'clock in the evening, but I was betting that Margaret Martin's workday had been spent trying to figure out how to handle a big problem called yours truly, and she would still be in her office trying to work her way through the other issues in her inbox.

She answered on the third ring.

"Mrs. Martin, this is Sean Drummond."

There was a long pause before she replied, "Who?"

I nearly lifted my feet off the ground to avoid the bullshit. "Let's not play that game, if you don't mind. Listen, Mrs. Mar . . . Can I call you Margaret? "

"If you wish."

"Good. Now that we're friends, you and I need to have a little talk."

There was another long pause, and I could picture Margaret frantically punching a button to a switch that could record and trace this call. Margaret's voice, if you're interested, was what I would classify as bureaucratic baroque, as there was absolutely no intonation or variation in pitch, as though someone had taken a steam iron to her vocal chords. It was a cool, impersonal voice that radiated impartiality; the only clue you weren't talking to a machine was her breathing, which sounded like her lungs were hooked up to a metronome. Where did they get these people? She eventually observed, "I believe you called me, Sean. Why don't you talk and I'll listen."

In fact, she sounded like a younger, sprightlier version of Phyllis—which tells you something about Phyllis's vocal range—so I decided not to beat around the bush. "This morning when Mark Helner took away my magic pass, I think I forgot to mention to him that I took several adorable pictures of Amal Ashad dropping off his kids at Williamsburg Elementary School. The photos are date- and time-stamped, so there won't be any unnecessary confusion about whether these were taken before or after Ashad never died."

"I—"

"Wait, I'm not finished." The best way to get Herr Helner off my ass was to show these people how badly he'd screwed up, so I informed her, and whoever else was listening, "When I get back to West Point, I intend to have the pictures entered into evidence, and to share these photos with the prosecutors and other defense attorneys. I further intend to give copies to Melvin Cramer, who I am confident will find a way to get them on the front pages of many newspapers. Then I will take them to a military judge so I can obtain a subpoena that will be issued to your agency compelling Ashad to testify." I paused, then asked her, "Do I have your attention?"

"I would say you do." As I expected she would, she insisted "You really don't want to do this, Sean."

"Well, Margaret, yes, I really do."

"Listen . . . you have no real idea what you're getting into."

In the event my former boss Phyllis, was, or would soon be, listening to the tape, I replied, "I was already told that once in the past twenty-four hours. It didn't work then, and that was before you people decided to screw with me and interfere with the conduct of a legal investigation."

There was another brief pause, and I could picture Margaret Martin taking a deep breath, now realizing how badly Mark Helner had mismanaged the Sean situation. Still in that same flat tone she said, "I'm sorry if Mr. Helner mistreated you. That was . . . unfortunate. He has some rough edges."

"You mean you're sorry he didn't scare me off." On the chance that Mark Helner was also listening, I felt the need to add, "And if rough-edged is a euphemism for saying he's an asshole, I won't argue with you."

She had obviously chosen a placating tact over a defensive or antagonistic one, which showed she was a realist. "I can certainly see where you'd feel that way, Sean."

"Quit trying to jerk me off, Margaret. It didn't work this morning and it's not working now."

She realized this appeasing approach was falling short of the mark and fell back on her earlier warning, telling me, "There's a great deal more going on here than you know."

"That's what I love about you people."

"I wasn't aware you love anything about us."

"It's your predictability, Margaret. Every time you get caught with your hands in the wrong place, you think you can make it go away by claiming you're the only grown-ups in the room." I told her, "We'll let the American people know. Let them decide."

"You're mad right now, Sean. You're not thinking clearly. Don't do anything stupid or precipitous."

"The only stupid ones on this line are you, Margaret, and the people working with you. You should have known Ashad's activities at Al Basari, once they blew up in the army's face, couldn't be covered up and concealed no matter how much camouflage you threw on it. But to let five soldiers take the entire responsibility for what happened at Al Basari is more than stupid. It's criminal."

My use of the word "criminal" was intended to fling down the legal gauntlet, and Margaret was obviously savvy enough to pick up on it, with all the ugly implications it conveyed. Ashad's activities were demonstrably prosecutable, but now that the Agency had engaged in a cover-up, everybody who had knowledge of or fingerprints on that conspiracy was a candidate for a perp walk. And if this thing went as far and as wide as I was beginning to suspect, the perp walk would look like the Macy's parade and it would begin at a well-known address on Pennsylvania Avenue. The government would have to rent a coliseum for the trial.

She needed a long pause to consider how to reply to this troublesome insinuation. I suspected there was someone else in the room with her, because I couldn't even hear her breath, meaning she was either experiencing a serious coronary event or she had a hand placed over the mouthpiece.

When she did not drop dead, it was to insist, "Sean, you and I need to talk."

"We are talking, Margaret."

"What I have to say to you cannot be breached over an open line. I can only convey this to you in person."

"You could've seen me in person this morning. Remember? I was just outside your building."

She displayed admirable self-restraint and responded, "Please, Sean, that's all I ask. Let's discuss this, and . . . afterward, if you still feel the need to expose Ashad, we won't try to stop you."

"You couldn't stop me if you tried."

"I . . ." Whatever Margaret was about to say, she changed her mind and inquired, "Do we have a deal?"

"Tomorrow, not later than 1000 hours. Come alone."

"That's not acceptable. I'll be accompanied by one person. You'll understand why tomorrow."

"If it's more than one, I'm gone." I then warned her, "I'll be armed."

"That's fine, but totally unnecessary. We won't. I promise."

"And I'll be bringing my cocounsel. She has the right to hear this also."

"No, you . . . I'm afraid that's . . . Look, that's not part of the deal."

"Why not?" I lied and informed her, "You'll like her." I then told her an even bigger lie. "She's more reasonable than I am."

"Regardless of Ms. Carlson's personal proclivities, she doesn't have a security clearance. What you're going to hear is on a need-to-know basis."

This seemed like a good opportunity to remind her, "I don't have a clearance either."

Margaret also was into lies and deceit because she responded, almost managing to make it sound sincere, "That was a stupid mistake. Nobody told Helner to do that. I'll get it reinstated right away."

I thought about Katherine's earlier admonishments to me about not flying solo—not to mention that two corpses are harder to dispose of than one. "Wave your magic wand and give Ms. Carlson a temporary security clearance. You can do that, Margaret. I know you can."

"You'll understand why I have to insist on this when we talk. This is nonnegotiable, Sean. Please, don't be difficult."

Whatever she had been briefed about me, she obviously did not know me very well: difficult is my middle name.

But it sounded like Margaret Martin was offering to let me in on the big secret shared by Amal Ashad, and though it went against my better survival instincts, I decided to accede to her demand that we meet alone. Why not? In the memory chip of my cellphone was all the evidence I needed to blow the lid off this case—as long as she couldn't destroy it, or me, I had enough protection to survive a meeting.

Apropos of that thought, I told Margaret, "Just so we're clear, I've already taken precautions to ensure the pictures survive in the event I don't."

I hadn't yet. But now I thought about it, it didn't sound like a dumb idea.

"I understand," Margaret replied. She then added, for the first time with real conviction in her voice, "Please do drive safely, Sean."

The moment we rung off, I punched Imelda's number into my phone. Before I could identify myself, Imelda inquired, "Where you at?" in a tone that did not sound all that friendly.

"I took a wrong turn leaving the neighborhood yesterday, and ended up in DC, of all places. I'm on my way back."

"Uh-huh. Shoulda tole somebody. Them security folks across the street's been going nuts."

"It's in their job description to go nuts."

"And everything's goin' nuts with this case."

"What are you talking about?"

"Cuz them little girls is pregnant."

Despite possessing two master's degrees and a razor-sharp mind, Imelda's diction can often be confusing, even to me. For instance, I thought she said pregnant, plural. I replied, "We learned that Lydia is pregnant before I departed."

"I know that. But that other little girl's pregnant, too."

I took a stab. "Are you referring to June Johnston?"

"Well, it ain't me."

"And we learned this, how?"

"Private Eddelston called Katherine. Her head was all messed up."

This seemed to be a reliable clue as to who the father was; actually, times two. I definitely wouldn't want to be in Danny Elton's shoes when the night crew got together for veteran reunions.

"Where's Katherine right now?"

"With the client. When Eddelston learned Johnston was pregnant, she flipped out. Katherine is calmin' her."

"I see." I then told Imelda, "Don't tell Katherine where I've been. Also, I'm about to forward you some pictures I took this morning, but you are not to show them to anybody. Not even Katherine." I emphasized, "*Especially* not Katherine."

There was a long silence before Imelda said, "You two got to cut this crap out. It ain't good."

I replied, perhaps untruthfully, "I have no idea what you're talking about."

"Don't be playin' that with me. You'n Katherine, you two like a pair of dogs in heat, pissing on everything around you."

Now I was sure what she was talking about, and I didn't like it. I cleared my throat. "Imelda, it's none of your business."

"You two makin' it my business. You gotta a client whose head is so messed up, she needs her lawyers to have their heads on perfectly straight. You two best straighten your shit out."

Imelda rarely uses profanity, and it is even more rare for her to stick her nose into the personal lives of those around her. She had a good point, though. "I'll work on it."

"Didn't ask you to work on it. I said straighten this shit out."

I informed her, "I should arrive in about three hours," and rang off.

Chapter Twenty-Six

My stomach was rumbling when, at 9:00 p.m., I rolled into the somnolent village of Highland Falls. I knew of a few burger and pizza joints nearby, but my favorite animal is steak so I decided to hunt for a more substantial meal at the Thayer Hotel, on post, just inside the front gate. Besides, I needed some time to think, and, knowing what I now knew, I didn't really want another confrontation with Katherine. As both an attorney and a career military officer I have spent my life keeping secrets and I'm good at it. Katherine, however, doesn't play fair. She has an annoying tendency to know what I'm thinking.

I parked in the lower parking lot, hoofed it uphill to the grand old hotel, entered through the impressive front entrance, then hooked a left and went downstairs, where I knew the dining room to be located.

It was late on a weeknight so there wasn't much of a crowd, just two or three couples, though the receptionist made a big deal of asking if I had a reservation.

To which I replied, "Are you kidding me?"

"No, I am not. Did you call ahead to book a table?"

"Does it matter?"

She awarded me a snooty look, spun about on her heels, then, without another word, led me to a seat in the back room where I was the only customer.

But at least from this rear room I could gaze out the window at the conspicuous splendor of the Hudson Valley and its accompanying river. In early fall, when the trees and vegetation are kaleidoscopic in color, the scenery is worth selling your soul for, though I would recommend settling for the price of a ticket on the Hudson River cruise. In the dead of winter, on the other hand, when the trees are bare and skeletal, it tends to be gray and bleakly depressing.

Thankfully it was nighttime. It was just dark.

A comely waitress appeared and I ordered a steak, well-done, and a Scotch, sans ice, sans water, sans anything that might weaken the brunt. About two minutes later an officer in uniform entered the back of the dining room, and it was Captain Nate Willborn who, apparently, had failed to book a reservation as well. He was alone, as was I, and his face revealed his initial surprise at seeing me, followed by a lame attempt to not recognize who I was—no doubt accompanied by an urge to bolt from the room.

I quickly stood and put on my most winsome smile. "Good evening, Captain Willborn." This forced him to acknowledge me with a limp wave. I asked, "Would you care to join me?"

He quickly surveyed the room as though he was searching for a party he was expecting, which, under the circumstances, was a contest between phony and ridiculous. "Relax, Captain. This is personal, not professional."

A look of resignation came over his face and he moved toward me. I stuck out my hand and he shook it. Avoiding my eyes, he told me, "I'm not sure this is a good idea. Isn't there some kind of legal stricture about personal interactions between witnesses and an attorney you will meet in court?"

"Trust me, I'm a lawyer," I answered, and even managed a perfectly straight face. "If such a rule existed, I would certainly have heard of it," I informed him, forgetting to mention that I had heard of it. "We'll keep it safe. The first one who mentions Al Basari buys the drinks."

He shuffled his feet, then sort of fell into the chair across from mine.

I asked him, "Can I call you Nate? It is Nate, right?"

"That's right, sir. If you wish. What should I call you?"

"Sir will be fine." I laughed and he joined me.

I told him, "But for tonight, I prefer Sean."

"Sean . . . fine." Many regular officers regard those of us in the specialty branches—military doctors, shrinks, lawyers, and so forth—as civilians in uniform and it is not uncommon to use first names instead of the formality of ranks. There are even days when I think I am a civilian.

He recovered a bit of his composure and confidence. "I wasn't aware you were a guest of the hotel."

"Neither was I." I signaled the waitress to come over, then explained to Nate, "But I stayed here a few times as a kid. My father was a grad. He dragged me up for a few reunions and we always stayed here. I thought I'd relive my youth tonight."

The waitress arrived and Willborn ordered a gin and tonic and, for dinner, pork chops. He relaxed back into his chair, and I had the impression that he already had the benefit of a few drinks under his belt, which is how I like my witnesses. He confirmed this suspicion, telling me, "I just left the tavern. A few of us got together for drinks."

"All veterans of the prison?" He nodded, and I asked, "What was that like?"

"In a word . . . weird." He looked down at his silverware. "It was real different over there. There wasn't time for socializing. Besides, everybody was compartmentalized. Jailors, intel people, security people, contractors . . . you work in the same place but might as well be in different worlds."

"Do you see them in a different light back here?"

"You know, you do. Take Colonel Eggers, for example."

"What about him?"

"Over there, he was *the man*. He might not look like much, but he walked in the shadow of God. He was the commandant of the prison, the commander of the MP battalion, and when he spoke, the ground trembled."

"How does he look now?"

"Like a flabby, balding, middle-aged man scared shitless that his ass is hanging out in the wind." He shook his head. "He was drunk on his ass when I left him. Kept whining about how he's being screwed." He added, "Your name came up in that conversation."

I smiled, and Willborn smiled back. It's always nice to know you put a scare into the opponent's witnesses. The waitress arrived with our drinks, and I told her, "Bring two more."

So we chatted awhile, mostly about personal stuff that was totally inconsequential and irrelevant, but was good cover while I worked on getting more booze into Willborn. He was from a small town outside Boston, attended Boston College, was commissioned via ROTC, like me, and was still single, a status, he informed me, that was not likely to change as he was under orders to return to Iraq the moment the trial was over for another year-long tour.

I wanted him relaxed with me, and with himself, and the next three gin and tonics took him not quite to three sheets to the wind, but judging from his speech, which was becoming slurred, and his physical mannerisms, which were clumsy, two definitely were fluttering in the breeze. Willborn was slick and obsessively self-controlled, but alcohol was not permitted in the war zone, and, after ten dry months in Iraq, he obviously had lost some of his tolerance. Personally, if I had to spend a year without booze I would go looking for an IED. These people are real patriots.

I eventually asked him, "Are you going to be a lifer?"

"I was," he answered. "I'm not so sure anymore."

"What changed your mind?"

He seemed to think about this, then informed me, "The war. Al Basari." He added, after a moment, "The way the army's hanging us all out to dry over this case."

"You were the first one to say Al Basari. Drinks are on you, and I'm thirsty."

He shrugged.

I signaled the waiter and ordered two more. Nate took that as an invitation to finish off his gin and tonic, which he emptied in one long slug.

I looked at him and figured it was either make my move now, or watch him get too shit-faced to speak coherently, so I casually mentioned to Willborn, "I was in Iraq for a while."

"Were you?"

"My travel agent fucked up. I distinctly told her Bermuda."

"You should fire her."

"Instead, I referred her to everybody I don't like at the office."

He chuckled. "Where were you assigned?"

"Baghdad. I didn't mind the insurgents nearly as much as the brass. War brings out the micromanager in all of them. It's like they tell you how many shakes to give your dick after you piss."

"Tell me about it." He was looking around for the waitress hauling his next drink. "They were squeezing my balls so hard at Al Basari, I—" He spotted the waitress and stopped midsentence while she placed his drink on the table. He took a long swig, then completed that thought. "Like, we'd get a new prisoner, and the next morning the Colonel was already busting our balls. What do you have, why haven't you broken this guy yet?"

I feigned ignorance and said, "I know very little about interrogations. Is that unreasonable?"

"Absurd. Most people over there don't understand what we do, how interrogations work, and they demanded overnight results, like you give us a prisoner and we have some mind-reading machine and we can empty their brains. It doesn't work that way. But I'm sure the colonel was getting his balls busted by the people back in the Green Zone—shit flows downhill, right?"

"And Al Basari was the gutter."

"Not true. We had to get on our tiptoes to look up at the gutter." He watched the cute waitress for a moment, then said, "Thing is, Ashad and I were getting the ringleaders of the insurgency. Hard men. They were usually older, more self-confident, definitely more dedicated and tougher than the foot soldiers."

"So they were more difficult to break?"

He took another long, deep swig. I had the sense that he knew what I was up to, getting him tipsy enough to break down his pathological reserve, but maybe he was past caring. Or maybe, being an interrogator himself, he was enjoying the role reversal, the thrill of being the prey in the chase for a change.

I recalled how I always felt when I came back from war zones where life seems to move at a thousand miles an hour, where every little thing becomes a matter of life and death, you wonder if every drive is your last, every road, every building, and every dead dog looks like a host for the grim reaper, as, too often, they are. It's exhilarating, the ultimate test of manhood, the biggest adventure a human being can experience. But also, it scares the shit out of you.

Then, suddenly, you are back in the good ole USA where the greatest concern is whether Britney Spears is wearing her underpants that day, or which stupid rock star or movie star overindulged in drugs and made a trip to the morgue. The human mind is a remarkably adaptive organ, but unlike the human body it does not slow down the instant it crosses the finish line; nor does it adjust well to the sudden decompression from praying you don't get your dick blown off, to the pointless chatter and trivialized garbage that is modern American culture.

There is a period, a sort of turbo-lag in reverse, where the mind is still on the razor's edge, overly attentive, hypersensitive, and ultra-starved for a burst of testosterone.

Indeed, I found it curious that Nate Willborn was already on orders to return for another tour of duty in Iraq, for the only way for that to happen was that he volunteered for a quick turnaround. This suggested that he either felt out of place here, or left unresolved issues back there, or both.

He finished contemplating my question and replied, "Every one of them was a bitch to break. Ordinarily, it could take months of methodical, back-breaking effort."

"But surely, there had to be a reason the command assigned so many tough cases to your team. Don't be modest, Nate. You were good at it."

"It's not about modesty," he answered. "Ashad broke them."

"But you and Ashad were a team," I told him. "Ashad worked for you. Whatever successes he had, you both get credit. You both *deserved* credit."

"Look, it wasn't like that. We were a team in name only. He did his thing, I did mine."

I took a sip of Scotch. I couldn't tell if Willborn was sober enough that he was still trying to get his distance from what Ashad did over there, or if he was venting something deeper, something definitely more interesting. What I could tell was that he didn't have a fucking clue that Amal Ashad was still alive, which seemed to confirm what he was saying; Ashad had been a solo act, and vice versa.

I told him, "Well, it's too bad Ashad died."

"Is it?"

"I wish I had a chance to meet him. The impression I have is that he could get anybody to squeal." I smiled and added, a bit disingenuously, "I could use some pointers."

Willborn put down his drink, planted his elbows on the table, and leaned forward. "He was a dangerous asshole!" he replied with a burst of vehemence I found surprising. "Arrogant, conceited, selfish, manipulative. He looked down at the rest of us because we weren't born in Iraq, and didn't graduate from some Ivy League tower. It was all about him. He didn't believe in sharing. He took all the credit for everything."

"Come now, Nate. He couldn't have been that bad."

"Of course, you never had to work beside him, so you have no way of knowing how . . . he could seem very nice and even charming, but he had his own agenda. He didn't really care about anyone else but himself. He was—" whatever Nate was about to say, he seemed to realize that he was going on and he halted midsentence. He broke eye contact with me and looked around the room for the waitress. He even yelled, "Hey . . . what do I have to do to get another drink around here?"

But he was also self-aware enough to recognize that he had exposed a little more than he wanted about the relationship between himself and Ashad. After a moment, he said, in a quiet voice, "Look, I was very sad when he died. Getting blown to pieces that way . . . I guess . . . you know . . . well, nobody deserves to go like that."

Actually, it sounded like Willborn thought Ashad got exactly what he deserved. Anyway, the waitress arrived carrying my steak dinner in her right hand, his pork chops in her left. She was just setting them on the table when he looked at me and complained, "I . . . uh, I'm not feeling very well."

"Relax, Nate, the cure just arrived. Food will make you feel better."

"I'm sorry." He got to his feet. "I . . . I have to go back to my room. I think I'm going to be sick." And with that, he spun around and rushed out of the restaurant.

The waitress looked at me. "Will your friend be returning?"

"He's not my friend."

"Oh . . . well—"

"And no, I think somebody disagrees with his stomach."

She looked confused.

"Wrap it up in a doggie bag, and have it delivered to his room. His name is Willborn." I added, "Let me put a note on it."

While she packed Willborn's dinner in a Styrofoam container, I scrawled out a quick note on a napkin to him, handed it to the waitress, then ate my dinner.

Chapter Twenty-Seven

I was up at 5:00, after a troubled sleep, showered, shaved, dressed, and alert enough by 5:30 to notice that I was the only one stirring. I had not expected Katherine to awaken so early, but Imelda was a different story; her new civilian status was taking the edge off. I had sneaked in the night before, removing my shoes at the doorway, and tiptoed upstairs to my bedroom to avoid a late-night confrontation with Katherine, or another crusty lecture from Imelda. I have earned ribbons for fearlessness on the battlefield, but women are a different story.

I nearly walked past the doorway to Katherine's bedroom, which was open, before I peeked in and saw that she was sound asleep. I did not want to awaken her, but I did want to see her, so I slipped quietly inside and stood and watched her, feeling somewhere between a guilty voyeur and a lovesick teenager.

She was on her side, arms akimbo, her long dark hair splayed out, framing her beautiful face, which was directed toward me. I noted that she did not snore: two points. Also, she slept on the left side of the bed, as did I: minus two. Her choice of sleep attire was a ratty old T-shirt and I did not even peek beneath the covers to discover if there was a commando under that outfit—minus two points for me.

But in repose, as she was, she looked serene, untroubled, and chaste, in fact, angelic, proving, once again, that those with an unsullied conscience are granted the gift of real rest.

I recalled the night we had shared a meal with Nelson Arnold, and the way he and Katherine had looked at each other. Clearly Nelson was totally infatuated with her, though I did not detect a reciprocal level of ardor emanating from Katherine. Still, despite the very large differences between them in age, wealth, social status, and background, they did appear to be entirely comfortable in each other's presence. There were none of the difficulties or tensions that seemed to ignite every time Katherine and I laid eyes on one another.

Essentially, Katherine is a more cerebral person than she is a passionate one, at least in how she behaves and comports herself professionally. I have always suspected, however, that, in her case, it is more a product of self-control than libido. On the courtroom floor, she can be hot-blooded and fiery, and it would interesting, not to mention, fun, to find out which is the true Katherine.

But people are endlessly complex and there are no laws of nature to sort out romantic relations. Unlike magnets, opposites do not necessarily attract; sometimes they merely bash one another to death. But neither is absolute harmony necessarily a formula for smooth relations; very often, it only leads to emotional stagnancy and boredom.

I wanted to shake her awake and ask what she saw in Mr. Moneybags. But having now met him, he was everything most women dream of—handsome, filthy rich, smart, filthy rich, principled, filthy rich, and with a very pleasant personality. I wanted to demand that she pick up the phone and tell him that in a contest between an army officer who barely had a pot to piss in, who could offer her nothing but constant moves, frequent separations, lousy pay, and the ever-present chance of becoming a young widow, he, with a pot large enough for the whole world to piss in, could take a flying leap.

I looked down at her face and tried to imagine Katherine as an army wife. Indeed, the army is hard on the soldier, but it is murder for the wives or, these days, their husbands. Those mates who survive a full career tend to be strong-willed, resourceful, independent, and hardy. Katherine had all those qualities in abundance, yet I could not picture her wearing white gloves to the officer wives' tea party, kowtowing to bossy generals' wives, or enduring the petty politics and ritual ass-kissing that are as much a part of army life as parades and military funerals. Then again, the modern army is different than it was for my mother's generation. The white gloves are gone, and while most of the generals' wives I have met are humble and wonderful, a few are insufferable, and they do test you. But the army has long since adapted to the pushier mores of a new generation of ambitious, independent women like Katherine, who do not stand behind their man, but rather beside him. Still, Katherine being Katherine, I suspected she would push this newfound tolerance to its limits.

If Katherine were a more practical woman, there would be no contest—she would already be fitting Nelson's yacht with new curtains and filling out the wardrobe closets with the newest French fashions. But the words Katherine and practical do not belong in the same sentence.

I blew her an air-kiss and wandered back downstairs, where I gathered some files, then down to Main Street where I found a restaurant that served breakfast, and awaited the CIA's call.

It came at 8:00 a.m., and it was Margaret, still speaking in her asphyxiating monotone. I was in neither a chatty nor a convivial mood and abruptly named the place for our meeting, then rang off and spent the next hour reviewing the office log of Captain Howser, my deceased predecessor, before I got into the pukey yellow Prius and drove on post. A different MP was at the gate. I could swear I saw him laughing as I drove past.

I drove to, then parked in the lot directly to the rear of the small, picturesque Catholic Chapel, where, half a century before, Ma and Pa Drummond got a life sentence together, then I walked up a steep hill to the much larger and more visually impressive Cadet Chapel, where the Prods perform their pagan rituals. In the old days, chapel was mandatory for cadets, so every Sunday morning they were formed up like stiff-faced prisoners and marched to the morning service of their particular predilection. These days they are free to go or to sleep in, as they wish. But I have heard that attendance is not an issue. There are no atheists in the foxhole, the saying goes, and since most of these young men and women know they will graduate and march off to war, it probably doesn't strike them as a waste of time to get an early jump on things.

I entered through the imposing wooden doors and walked down the broad center aisle, about midway to the altar. I had chosen this somewhat unconventional venue for our meet because it was public, but not entirely. It was a cavernous cathedral, gothic both in design and scale, capable of seating well over a thousand, and thus, three people could conduct a perfectly discreet discussion in plain sight, as long as the conversation didn't become overheated—and no gunfire was involved.

Also, I hoped this comingled monument to religious and patriotic ardor would stimulate my guests to be on their best behavior. I could not imagine even the CIA would whack a US Army officer with the aroma of the pulpit filling their nostrils. On the other hand, if I was overestimating their moral sensitivities, at least it would be a short trip to my funeral. Last but not least, such a pious setting seemed ordained to be a place where only truth was spoken.

I was seated at 9:55 and, at 10:00 a.m., I heard the large wooden doors open.

I stared straight ahead, with my back turned to my punctual guests. I could hear their steps as they moved quickly toward me, a pair of high heels making quick clacking sounds like a malfunctioning machine gun, the other pair, much heavier and louder, like the clump of approaching artillery shells.

They eventually progressed to the middle pew where I was seated with my .45 pistol pointedly positioned in my lap.

A mellifluous male voice to my rear informed me, "You won't need that gun, Colonel."

I looked up and directly into the snub-nosed, saturnine face of Thomas Bernhardt, National Security Advisor to the president. He offered me a friendly wave and requested, "Please put that away. It makes me nervous."

The woman beside him put out her hand. "It's a pleasure to finally meet you face-to-face, Colonel Drummond. I'm Margaret Martin."

So much for my illusion about an ambience conducive to integrity—it was anything but a pleasure to meet each other face-to-face. I stood and stuffed the .45 into my waistband, then shook her hand. "Have a seat," I offered.

While Mr. Bernhardt and Ms. Martin took a moment to squeeze into my pew, get seated, and arrange themselves, I used the opportunity to study my guests.

Thomas Bernhardt, as I knew from press coverage, was a corporate lawyer by training and by profession, who had advised the president about foreign affairs during the campaign and was rewarded with his elevation to his current position of West Wing Mandarin. This meant he either had something on the president, or he had the president's ear, respect, and confidence.

His reputation was as a behind-the-scenes, fingerprintless fixer, a guileful troubleshooter, who, unlike many of his predecessors, eschewed the Sunday morning press circuit and kept himself off the front pages. I didn't know if this was a commendable personal trait or a slick survival mechanism to allow his boss to hog all the press clippings. I had the thought, however, that this explained his presence here—to wit: make the Sean quagmire disappear without raising any waves.

I shifted my attention to Margaret Martin, who appeared to be about my age. She was dressed in a cool blue blazer, a shimmery white blouse, and a tight red skirt that went down to her knees— the standard attire of a life-long bureaucrat, which conveyed that she was feminine by gender without evoking any untidy male sexual fantasies. The red-white-and-blue color coordination seemed to be designed for me.

She also was moderately attractive and would've been more so had she chosen to wear makeup. She had what I would characterize as a pleasant face, only contradicted by a pair of narrow blue eyes that sparkled with calculation and worry. Those eyes had puffy black circles underneath them, indicating that she hadn't gotten much rest, and the half-hearted, forced smile was because she now was looking at the festering boil that caused her insomnia.

As the senior official present, Bernhardt decided to kick things off, observing, "I think it's fair to say that you've stuck your fist into a hornet's nest, Colonel."

I wasn't sure where he was going with this, but I had half a mind to remind him that they were the ones with their dicks in a wringer—and I had my hand on the handle. Given the professional sloppiness I had uncovered, they had to know one other truth; they were now less than a banana peel away from complete disaster. But instead of mentioning this unpleasantness, I merely nodded.

He continued, out of the blue, "How familiar are you with the history of the Second World War?"

"It occurred after the First, right?"

"Good guess." He smiled and winked. "Have you ever heard the tale about Churchill and the town of Coventry?"

"Can you come to the point?" I replied, not really in the mood for a long-winded history sermon.

"Bear with me, Colonel . . . please. There is a point to this, and it's relevant to what we're here to discuss, I promise."

Well, he did have a pleasant smile, and he said please, so it would be churlish of me to develop attention deficit issues. Also, he was about thirty paygrades higher than me. I can be easily influenced that way.

He cleared his throat. "The accuracy of this tale is questionable, but the British had broken the top secret German military codes, a program called Ultra, and two days before, they had intercepted a German transmission indicating that the city of Coventry was about to be bombed. The dilemma this presented Churchill had to be excruciating. If he took action based on this intelligence, say by ordering a hasty evacuation of Coventry, or amassing his air defenses around the city, he would've tipped off the Germans that we had broken their code, which would've altered the course of the war." He paused for dramatic effort before he informed me, "He allowed the city to be bombed."

"And did the survivors of Coventry erect a monument to his good judgment?"

"Probably not."

"You said there's a point to this story."

"Yes, and you seem like a smart guy so I'm sure you didn't miss it." But he apparently had second thoughts about that assessment because he then explained, "In war, Sean, you often have to make difficult decisions . . . even distasteful choices. You have to weigh the larger picture against the small actions that, in comparison, and in hindsight, pale into insignificance."

I looked at Thomas Bernhardt and replied, "And as an attorney, I'm sure you also recognize that's the same greasy moral reasoning that led to the trial docket at Nuremburg."

"Yes, and . . . well . . . I must confess I have some ambivalence myself about the choice we're here to discuss. But I assure you, I will still sleep soundly at night." He turned to Ms. Martin who definitely was not sleeping well. "Margaret, I think it's time Sean learns what really happened at Al Basari."

Margaret clearly was expecting this hand-off of the baton, so to speak. She cleared her throat, then quickly asked me, "How much have you learned about Amal Ashad's role in the interrogation team?"

"A great deal, and the more I learn, the worse it gets."

"Do you believe what you've learned?"

"You people always bring a lot of smoke and mirrors to the party. I thought we were here so you can clear up any confusion."

She shifted gears and observed, "I hear you've done an interrogatory with Captain Willborn."

"Correct."

"And how did that go?"

"As it was supposed to go. He jerked me off with sandpaper."

To Margaret's credit she did not act shocked or take offense at my off-color metaphor. In fact, she smiled. "Phyllis said you have a way with words." She then added, "I enjoy candor, however."

Not so fast, Margaret. "What was, or what is, Captain Willborn's role in this?"

"Captain Willborn, as I think you already surmised, was a figurehead. As Phyllis told you, we went to great lengths to conceal the roles and involvement of our interpreters. He was nothing more than camouflage for Amal Ashad."

"And I told Phyllis what I thought of that Potemkin stupidity. Would you care to hear me repeat it?"

"No . . . that won't be necessary," Margaret responded. "Understand that based on Amal's experience and expertise, it would have been limiting and counterproductive to put a young, ill-prepared captain in charge."

"I think what you're trying to say was the army got to bear the blame and Ashad got to call the shots and walk away scot-free. If this is an inaccurate representation, please explain why."

"Regrettably, that may be the way it works out, Sean . . . I assure you, though, that was not the intent," she replied, trying to paper over that self-contradiction.

"At this point, do you really expect me to accept anything you say as truth?"

"The lies and evasions are over, Sean. You've already uncovered enough of the truth."

"So the truth will set you free to tell the truth."

"Something like that."

I looked at her. "You have one chance to get this right, Margaret. Don't lose it."

"There's no need for threats." She squirmed in her seat. "We made a mistake. A simple mistake. Through the rearview mirror it looks like an incredible act of stupidity, but at the time nobody factored it into the equation."

I took an educated guess and stated, "Amal Ashad is a Shiite."

I don't think Margaret expected me to put this together, as obvious as it now was, and her face showed her surprise. "Yes, that's . . ." She regained her composure, and continued. "In fact, Amal's family fled Iraq because of Saddam's persecution of their religion. Many members of his extended family suffered terribly under Saddam's Sunni rule. Some died . . . a few horribly. His uncle, his father's favorite brother, spent a year in one of Saddam's prisons. His body was returned to the family so disfigured they didn't recognize him. Amal grew up being fed a steady porridge of hatred toward the Sunnis."

Bernhardt leaned toward me and confided, "Our boy went over there harboring a poisonous grudge. He had always been a motivated, reliable agent, but in retrospect . . . well, his stability and tolerance had never been tested under such conditions. No hint of his bias toward the Sunnis had ever surfaced." He shook his head. "In retrospect, Al Basari was the worst place in the world to put him."

Margaret amplified on this observation, explaining, "The army intelligence officials at Al Basari were cowed by his abilities. A review conducted afterward showed that all of Amal's targets were Sunni. In fact, he was cherrypicking men who were involved with the Sunni insurgency that has been ripping the country apart."

I thought for a moment about these disclosures. If Amal Ashad had gone to Iraq to avenge the miseries and persecutions inflicted against his family, and his faith, Bernhardt was right—It would be hard to imagine a worse place to assign him. It was a prison, and worse, a military prison in wartime, where the normal checks and procedures to avoid abuses were strained to the point of nonexistence. Further, his status as a CIA officer comingling within the army meant even less oversight, as the army chain of command would take a hands-off posture toward an employee of a different agency.

Indeed, Ashad's nocturnal visits to observe the activities of the night crew, and his weird arrangement for them to photographically record their debaucheries acquired a whole new narrative. Amal Ashad wasn't a twisted voyeur sneaking in to leer at the depravities, nor was he there to monitor the efforts of his amateur charges to ensure that their unique techniques met his inquisitory standards. He was, instead, a purveyor of vengeance who wanted a firsthand look at the retribution visited upon his enemies.

Bernhardt said, "I see by your expression that it's coming together for you."

I ignored that. "So knowing this, how could you cover up his activities?"

"Good question." Bernhardt cleared his throat, then answered my good question. "Ashad gave us no choice."

"Bullshit."

"Is it?"

"Yes, and you know it is. In a pissing match between the US government and a lowly CIA employee, there is no competition. You had a choice, Mr. Bernhardt—you chose not to exercise it."

Bernhardt looked away from me, and he shared a quick look with Margaret, who seemed to flinch. Bernhardt said to me, "Maybe you need to hear the rest of this before you pass judgment." He forced a smile. "You might say his interrogations bore some unusual fruit."

This seemed to be another cue for Margaret, who told me, "A number of the men in that cellblock were key ringleaders in the Sunni insurgency. They disclosed to Ashad that there is growing dissension, what you might term a widening schism, within the insurgency. Certain factions and tribes are becoming disheartened. They believe there are too many foreigners fighting in Iraq. Members of Al Qaeda, in particular. They feel the foreigners are taking over their war, turning it into something they did not ask for, and don't want."

I was starting to feel like I was with a tag team of well-oiled newscasters. Bernhardt chimed in, "The foreigners have a different mission—and a different mindset—than the native Sunni insurgents. They're trying to instigate an all-out war with the Shiites in Iraq. A civil war, a religious war . . . an internecine armageddon. Fighting us is becoming an afterthought."

Both of them were now looking at me, probably wondering if I was buying this bullshit. I waited a beat, then told them, "This is interesting, but hardly a revelation. Even the press coverage suggests that the Sunnis and Shiites are becoming bored with killing one another. Most of the neighborhoods in Baghdad are already purged of one sect or the other. They're running out of reasons to kill one another. And targets."

"We certainly understand that," Margaret conceded. "You might even say that understanding lent credibility to the claims Ashad was making."

"All right, what were his claims?"

"He . . . well, he claimed he had a list of tribes who were willing to break with the insurgency. More importantly, he got the names of various tribal leaders and influential men, the very people we would need to talk to if we want to exploit this fissure in the insurgency. Do you understand how invaluable this is?"

I had a good idea but suggested, "Explain it to me."

Clearly we had gotten to the important part, and Bernhardt leaned in close to me and placed a hand on my arm, an insincere intimacy at best. "It's an opportunity, Sean. A historic opportunity."

"Go on."

"It's a chance to break what has become a bloody stalemate. A chance to get those tribes and factions to come over to our side. A chance for a whole new strategy. Call it a variation on divide and conquer. We can win this war."

Over his shoulder, Margaret said, "There is no quick or easy way to obtain those names without Amal. His lists are the product of eight months of constant, unrelenting interrogations. By good fortune, some of the men in that cellblock knew exactly which tribal leaders are disenchanted . . . it was a perfect set of circumstances that just came together. "

"Not to mention the unmentionable," I mentioned, "Ashad tortured his subjects to get that information."

"We're not blind to that," Margaret snapped in a rare moment of annoyance.

Bernhardt's lawyer instincts kicked in, and he chimed in, "For God's sake, this is war, Sean, not a courtroom. In our legal system they would be called Fruits of a Poisoned Tree, and the knowledge obtained through those techniques would be verboten. But that procedural nicety doesn't apply here, does it? War has its own rules. Exploiting Ashad's lists will save many, many thousands of lives. American lives . . . Iraqi lives."

"Amal hid those lists," Margaret continued. "Now he's using them as leverage—we protect him from any legal liability and he promises to turn them over. It's a simple deal."

This certainly explained how and why the interrogation logbooks went missing—Ashad purloined and then hid them to use as leverage to save his own ass. I looked at Margaret, then at Bernhardt, "Since you appear to be verbally confused, the correct term for the deal you're describing is blackmail."

Bernhardt had his fingers formed into a steeple below his chin now. "Can the indictments, Sean. The situation is more morally complicated than that. Ashad is offering us a roadmap to win this war."

"Amal is offering you a way to cover his ass."

Like the good corporate lawyer he was, Bernhardtt responded, "Isn't that the definition of a deal? Both sides stand to benefit."

I asked him, "Who made the decision to let Amal off the hook?"

They looked at each other. Bernhardt replied, "Who gives a shit?"

"Me. The American people."

"It's none of your damned business, Colonel."

Actually, his nonanswer was the answer. With the way things work in Washington, the fact that the National Security Advisor

323

to the President of the United States was seated beside me was an indication of who made the decision. The presence of a senior officer from the CIA, on the other hand, conveyed a different message: plausible deniability. If Sean Drummond did drum up a shitstorm, Margaret Martin and her bosses in the Agency were the ones without an umbrella. No wonder she had bags under her eyes.

I looked at Margaret, who was trying not to appear nearly as desperate as she was. I then looked at Bernhardt who now had his hands crossed in his lap, and appeared to be studying the cover of a hymnal in the rear shelf of the pew in front of him—he looked like a choirboy discovered in a brothel, though a whore discovered in church was a more accurate characterization.

I addressed them both and asked the question they were waiting to hear. "Now that I know what I know, what do you expect me to do about it?"

In keeping with the theme of plausible deniability, Margaret addressed this question. "We *have* to honor this deal, Sean. I know you don't like it, and . . . my God, it's far from satisfying to us. But it must go through."

"A deal struck under coercion is not a deal, Margaret—not in a courtroom and not in the real world. Ashad committed very serious crimes. Let a jury of his peers decide if he spends the next twenty years sleeping with his wife, or with Big Earl at Leavenworth."

"For God's sake, Sean, Amal's career is already ruined. We agreed we would keep him on the payroll for one year, then he'll be retired on a medical disability. But his professional life is over. His career is finished."

"His career? My client is facing life in prison."

Margaret appeared annoyed to be reminded of this reality. But she replied, as calmly as she could, "We're all aware of that, Sean."

Bernhardt apparently thought it was safe to weigh in again. "Look, Sean, an operation has already been designed to exploit the information Amal possesses. The president has the deployment order sitting on his desk ordering a surge of forces, an influx of sixty thousand additional troops to bring stability to the country while we exploit this opening. But it's conditional. He's waiting on Ashad to give us these lists. The tribal list will be the roadmap, and the list of names the blueprint for dismantling the insurgency." He reached over and squeezed my arm. "It's all on your shoulders now. The president is waiting on you, Sean."

"And five soldiers are awaiting their day in court. Ashad needs to join them. That's on your shoulders."

He acted like he hadn't heard me and continued his pitch. "The generals in Baghdad are elated. Forgive me for expressing another stale euphemism, but this is the light at the end of the tunnel they've been waiting for."

I looked at Bernhardt. "But you don't have the lists yet?"

"Not yet, no. Ashad will turn them over only when he's confident he's not going to be prosecuted." He felt the need to inform me, "Your unexpected visit to his home upset him greatly."

"Then you have a big problem."

"It doesn't need to be a problem, Sean."

"You're not hearing me, sir. Amal Ashad is a material witness to everything that transpired in that cellblock. He was the recipient of photographic evidence, and, on occasion, a participant, and a coconspirator. He has exculpatory knowledge that will benefit my client, as well as the four other accused."

"Amal Ashad won't make a damn bit of difference in that trial," he assured me. "Oh sure, it'll make a big news splash, and drag the CIA through the mud. But your client will not be exonerated." After a moment, he suggested, curiously, "Actually his testimony would be a disaster for your client."

"You have no way of knowing that."

"Don't be so sure of yourself." He nodded at Margaret who picked her briefcase off the floor and placed it on her lap. Fearing the worst, I immediately reached to my belt and started to draw my .45, when Bernhardt told me, "Relax, Colonel. What Margaret has to show you will hurt, but it won't kill you."

Instead of a gun, Margaret withdrew a compact DVD player, with the DVD already inserted and ready to play.

Margaret said, "Watch this before you make your final decision."

She might as well have reached for a gun. She reached down and pushed play.

Chapter Twenty-Eight

The golden rule for a seasoned litigator is never ask a witness on the stand a question you don't already know the answer to. As a lawyer himself, I had walked straight into his trap, and Bernhardt couldn't resist a smile as I watched the screen come to life on Margaret's lap.

The video began playing. The lighting was better than I expected, as was the audio quality. Not quite on par with a high-definition Hollywood production, but everything was clear enough, so I assumed Margaret had run the video through the CIA's equivalent of technical enhancement.

It opened with four Iraqi males seated on wooden chairs, lined up almost like schoolchildren waiting for the exam to begin—or considering the setting, like sitting ducks waiting for the shotgun blasts to tear them apart. They appeared somewhat frightened, but expectation had yet to jell into all-out dread.

A male voice I recognized as Danny Elton's yelled, "I hear you turds ain't givin' my buddy Ashad what he wants to hear. That's fucked up, boys. *Real* fucked up. Now yer gonna regret it."

A soldier in BDU trousers and a sweat-stained brown T-shirt stepped purposely into the frame. Though his back was turned to the camera, he was obviously black, and I assumed this was Private

Mike Tiller, one of the accused I hadn't yet met. He walked up to the line of men seated in chairs, then appeared to spend a moment selecting which one was worthy of victimization; after some indecision he settled on the ugly, skinny little man on the right side. He lifted the man and the chair together, and repositioned them both about six feet toward front and center, so the victim could be easily observed by the three other Iraqis.

He then stepped aside, and turned and faced the camera, smirking as though he had just accomplished a difficult task. Private Tiller was a handsome man, and well built, with thick, powerful shoulders and sculpted arms that had obviously benefited from a weightroom.

Elton's voice yelled, "Great pick, Mike. Yeah, yeah, that's good . . . start out with that skinny little fucker . . . then work our way up to the heavyweights." After a pause, Elton's voice asked, "What do ya think, Lydia? How're we gonna bust his punk ass?"

There was the sound of two women laughing, then a female entered the frame.

In the event I was confused, Margaret informed me, "That's your client, if you're wondering."

My brain didn't respond for a second. Lydia was dressed in G-string panties with a tight, white halter top covering a pair of breasts that appeared lumpy and saggy. A riding crop was in her right hand, and her hips were moving in an exaggerated sashaying motion. "Sure, I got some ideas," she announced in a more self-confident tone than I had heard from her lips before. "You . . . git off yer ass'n git on yer feet," she yelled at the skinny little Iraqi. He did not appear to comprehend English—or maybe it was her thick country vernacular of it—and stayed where he was, with a clueless expression on his face.

The riding crop in Lydia's hand lashed out and caught him on the side of the head. The man's head whipped sideways, and he jumped to his feet, howling something in Arabic at Lydia.

Lydia waited until he finished wailing, then she spun around and addressed someone out of camera range. "What's he yakkin' about?" she asked.

A voice easily recognizable as Elton's replied, "Oh, he's jus' beggin' for a *little* special treatment. Wants you to give it to 'im, bad."

This elicited a chuckle from Lydia, who then turned back around and faced the prisoner. "Okay, but I guess I gotta see how *little* he is, first." She then bent over, unzipped the man's trousers, and pulled out his Mr. Johnson. The prisoner's face was somewhere between shocked, dismayed, and fearful—and, judging by the size of his weaponry, perhaps ashamed, as well.

Lydia was laughing loudly now. "Anybody here got a looking glass? How 'bout some tweezers? This guy's pecker is teenier'n an inchworm's." She shrugged at her specators as though she was confused. "Dang, I had no idea these things came so small."

She was now holding the prisoner's member in her hand; she was bent over, examining it closely. Suddenly, she gripped it tight, stood up, and began dancing small circles around the room, dragging the prisoner around by his member. Several voices from outside the frame were laughing and yelling encouragement. A female voice was screaming, almost hysterically, "Faster . . . faster . . . hey, Lydia, see if you can pull his cock off . . . go faster."

Elton yelled, "Wooee . . . now that's what I call a handjob."

This went on for nearly a minute, it quickly became tedious, and I actually began to lose interest. I looked away and into the face of Margaret Martin. Her expression was ominously inscrutable, though I thought I saw a hint of self-satisfaction.

My attention was drawn back to the video when Elton yelled, "Now see if you can give him a big ole woody."

Lydia stopped in her tracks, let go of the man's organ, and shoved him back into the chair. She looked back over her shoulder and hollered, "Hey, gimme some mood music. Make it somethin' nice'n sassy, and I'll turn this guy's wiener into a friggin' telephone pole."

A moment later, Phil Collins's rendition of "In the Air Tonight" was booming full blast. I've always loved that song, a melody whose every note is either smoke or sexual sparks, a song saturated with seduction—but I did not like hearing it now.

On the screen, Lydia was swaying from side to side, with her eyes shut, apparently getting into the proper mood and mindset. She tugged off her halter and slid off her panties. Completely in the buff now, she began gyrating her hips, pinching her nipples, and taking some small mincing steps like a prowling stripper.

But June's description of Lydia's physical and musical nimble-ness proved to be farcically accurate, if not understated—her limbs looked disconnected from her chunky torso, her rhythm out of sync, her body neither lithe nor supple, her movements both too slow and too frenzied in all the wrong places, at all the wrong times. It looked, I thought, like a really awful slapstick of a burlesque.

Strip joints should have a sign hanging over their entrance warning women that this should definitely not be tried at home—obviously, Lydia offered a shining example of why not.

After a minute of this, Lydia turned around and faced some-body off-screen. She was full frontal nudity now, her back to the prisoner, her naked butt nearly in his face. I now had a clear view of Lydia's expression—her eyes were closed, and she was doing something incredibly stupid with her tongue, sticking it out of her lips and lolling it around like a spastic windshield wiper. I had the impression she had seen this routine in a movie, perhaps had even studied it with an ambition to replicate it. She then bent forward and shook her shoulders, her breasts hanging low, swinging from side-to-side like a pair of saggy watermelons.

Clearly, this imbecilic corruption of erotica was intended for somebody offscreen—and, no doubt, that somebody was Danny

Elton. She finally looked up at somebody off-camera and taunted, "How do you like this, huh?" and I nearly laughed.

In fact, I *could* hear someone laughing; it was Danny Elton, and the tone was cruel and derisive. Lydia shook her shoulders harder, becoming spasmodic, as though trying to make up for her deflating lack of sensuality with energy and speed, before Elton's voice bellowed at her, "Shit, look at that Arab—that guy's still limp as a wet noodle."

Lydia's movements suddenly ground to a halt. Her eyes opened and any trace of a smile left her face. Elton's voice said, "June, get yer panties off. Git in there'n show this brain-dead bitch how to give a guy a woody."

I could hear collective laughter and, a moment later, June leaped into the frame, wearing her birthday suit and twirling a brown T-shirt in her right hand. Somebody started the song over, and June began moving. She had a perfect body, well toned, full-breasted, and sinewy—and, worse for Lydia, she knew exactly how to use it. In perfect pitch and sync with the song, she began languorously, almost snakelike, exerting minimal energy to achieve a fantastic effect.

I turned to Margaret. "That's enough. Punch stop now."

"It's not nearly enough," she replied. "You need to see the rest." She offered me a clenched smile. "I want you to get full exposure to your client."

That unfortunate choice of words aside, I looked back at the screen. Lydia had made the foolish decision to keep dancing, turning it into a competition—but only in her mind. In fact, June's response to this thrown gauntlet was to turn up the heat, and the Iraqi prisoner was responding in the most visible way possible—his puddly had swung from half-mast to full glory waving in the wind.

Poor Lydia, dancing now with even more frantic gawkiness beside an effortless temptress like June, looked somehow even more ineptly vulgar.

Elton was crudely, and sophomorically, yelling, "Hell, yeah, baby. Shit, yer givin' *me* a boner. That's it—shake that fine ass, June."

The prisoner was now an afterthought, though even he couldn't take his eyes off June, as was the case, as well, with the three other prisoners still seated in the wooden chairs who now looked like three gawking statues with their eyes frozen on one spot.

June began employing the T-shirt in her hand as a matador would a red cape. Both the song and her dance were now reaching a crescendo, and Danny Elton jumped into the frame. He had removed his shirt and his trousers, and was stripped down to his undershorts.

The man was powerfully built and well-toned, and wearing nothing but his whitey-tighties, it was apparent that he also was well-endowed, and in a state of arousal. June wrapped her arms around his neck, pulled him into her, and they began grinding together.

I turned my focus to Lydia. She had stopped dancing, and was standing, now as naked emotionally as she was physically, watching the man she thought was both her lover and her boyfriend simulating the dirty deed with another woman. I felt sorry for her, but also disgusted, and, I suppose, embarrassed in that way you get when you witness somebody humiliating herself.

Elton noticed the pouty look on her face and, over his shoulder, yelled, "Yo Mikey-boy, put down the camera and git in here'n dance with ole Lydia," apparently to Mike Tiller, who was still off-camera.

"Are you fuckin' kidding me?" Tiller laughed, then yelled back, "I'd sooner dance with a cow."

The song ended and Danny Elton, June Johnston, and Lydia were just standing there, three people under a metaphysical spotlight, with all their unhappy and dysfunctional dynamics on full display. Elton still had his arms wrapped around June's shoulders, his loins still pressed into her groin. June had an expression I could only describe as satisfaction, or perhaps, exultation.

Lydia simply looked lost, dazed, and despondent—as though somebody just pulled the plug on her life.

Clearly they had forgotten they were in a war zone, forgotten they were in a prison, forgotten they were soldiers—they were totally engrossed in playing out their raunchy love lives in the presence of the prisoners they were supposed to be guarding.

I reached across Margaret's lap and punched stop. "That's enough, Margaret."

"Does it bother you? Just think what those Iraqi prisoners were thinking as they watched this."

I did not need to wonder; I knew exactly what they were thinking—Americans are crazy as hell. But my chief concern wasn't with four anonymous men in a faraway land, but with what the seven members of the court martial board would think. It wasn't all that hard to figure out. Lydia Eddelston was toast.

Margaret, however, wasn't finished and she again stabbed the play button. The screen popped back to life, and once again, there Lydia was, still standing perfectly nude, still staring at Danny Elton, still with his crotch buried in June's groin.

Suddenly her expression changed from childish resentment to fury. She walked over to the skinny little prisoner who was sitting with his Mr. Johnson awkwardly sticking out of his trousers.

She got two inches from his face. "What's yer problem?" she yelled. "Don't you like pussy?"

As I said, I don't think he understood English because he responded with a silly grin, which, under the circumstances, might not have been the most diplomatic response.

Lydia's riding crop flashed and struck him straight across the face. In his aroused state it was the last thing he expected—his head whipped sideways, and he yelped at the top of his lungs. Lydia then announced to all concerned, "Okay. Since you don't seem to cotton to girls, let's see how ya cater to boys."

Clearly none of the Iraqi prisoners understood English or had any idea what she was saying, but you could tell by their expressions that they got the basic idea; the shit had really hit the fan and they were about to get splattered with the product. Lydia was glowering at the three men in the chairs now, appearing to examine them as though they were specimens. "You," she yelled—she was pointing her riding crop at the one on the left end.

He reluctantly stood up, and was looking down into the faces of the other two men seated beside him, who were looking back as though he had two feet planted on the gallows, about to feel the snap of the noose. I had the sense that these four Iraqi prisoners had been through this before, or at the least, as most prisons tend to be hothouses for rumors, they had heard enough crazy stories to have an idea about what was coming. The standing man now had tears streaming down his cheeks. His knees were actually wobbling.

I said to Margaret, "Turn it off."

"Getting a little atrocity fatigue?" she asked. She pushed stop, then looking at me, commented, "Why don't I spare you and describe what transpired?"

It wasn't really a question. I said nothing.

"Your client made that man get down on his knees and perform oral sex on the little skinny man."

I still said nothing.

"Maybe you'd like to guess where that riding crop ended up?" When I did not respond to that provocative mystery, she informed me, "After she stuck it in his rump, she rode him around, forcing him to make braying sounds like a donkey."

Holy shit. To their credit, Bernhardt and Margaret withheld further comment and allowed me to form my own opinions about what I had witnessed. Why explain it, anyway? Everything that needed to be said was on that nauseating video.

Clearly, it was the end for Lydia—I pictured myself in the prosecutor's shoes, and was confident I could get at least twenty years—a life sentence wasn't out of reach. There was no explaining away, or excusing, or diminishing, what that video showed. Clearly, my client was the prime instigator in the most depraved activities of the night crew.

For sure, Danny Elton was the ringleader and the director. He was the senior ranking soldier, the dominant male, and he kicked things into motion. And maybe he knew that by pitting Lydia against June, he was unleashing Lydia's most resentful furies. But I don't think Elton was smart enough to comprehend that Lydia was the vehicle through which he could get into June's pants. Danny Elton wasn't the type to employ Machiavellian artifices, or anything that might be described as subtle methods for wooing the opposite sex. For a man like Danny, bluff, menace, and straightforward force were his preferred methods.

He only knew he wanted to fuck June—he didn't care how it came about.

As for June Johnston, I recalled Katherine's unflattering portrait of her—and this video was a reminder to never underestimate the acuity of feminine intuition. Katherine had indeed been emotionally astute; for whatever reasons, memories of a parental predator, circumstance, crossed circuits in her brain, or all of the above, June *needed* to dominate. The moment Lydia disrobed, and began dancing, June perceived it as a challenge and she knew exactly how to rise to the occasion—or, more accurately, how to get others to rise. And knowing of Lydia's romantic fixation on Danny Elton, she had chosen the most brutal, and the most public, way to show how easily she could take her man away.

As for my client, Lydia Eddelston, this was, I thought, a very troubled young mind. She should have known that she wasn't equipped—not by bodily architecture, not by sexual artistry, certainly not by her ill-formed libido—to compete in a sexual rivalry with June. But she chose to try anyway, and June chose to bury Danny Elton's groin in her own crotch.

Instead of Lydia licking her own wounds, or directing her anger at those who perpetrated her humiliation, as any sensible woman would do, she instead turned her anger, her frustration, and her shame on the prisoners.

Apropos of that insight, Margaret interrupted my ruminations. "Several of our Agency psychiatrists reviewed this DVD and arrived at some very chilling opinions regarding your client. Would you care to hear them?"

"No, but I'm sure you're going to tell me."

She nodded as though pleased to confirm my suspicion. "The technical term is transference—projecting her jealousy, her rage, and her vexation with Sergeant Elton against the prisoners. Further, they classified her specific behaviors as a classic example of penis envy."

The pictures of Lydia dragging that prisoner around by his willy suddenly acquired an interpretation I did not want to even think about, much less talk about, so I changed topics and asked Margaret, "What are you going to do with this DVD?"

"Right now?" She allowed that conditional question to linger, before she explained, "Its existence is known only by a tiny handful of people. We'd prefer to keep it that way." She paused again, resisting the urge to explicitly ask me, *Wouldn't you*, and more tactfully inquired, "Don't you think the world has already seen enough of your client?"

I answered, literally, "*I've* seen enough of her."

Bernhardt, a bit smugly, stated, "We thought you would feel that way."

Good guess, pal.

He added, "Now, just imagine, if you will, what would happen if that video ever got out to the public. The Arab world that already went into a paroxysm of violence over the photographs would go completely berserk. Burning embassies and murdered diplomats would be the least of our problems. The entire Middle East . . . the entire Moslem world, in fact, would become totally unhinged."

Margaret apparently thought further elaboration would be helpful and stated, "The war in Iraq will almost certainly be lost. No Moslem in the world will want to align with the United States. Our coalition in Iraq will collapse. All our allies will try to get their distance from us. We might lose all our current basing arrangements in the region. Strategically speaking, this video is the equivalent of a nuclear bomb."

I'm not an expert in international relations, but I certainly knew enough about hair-trigger Arab sensitivities to suspect the truth in these assessments. I mean, these people get all worked up at the sight of a brassiere strap or a cartoon making fun of Mohammad. I couldn't imagine the response to a video of Lydia riding a braying Arab prisoner with her riding crop stuffed up his rectum.

I looked at Margaret first, then at the National Security Advisor to the President. "Once again, what do you expect from me?"

It occurred to me that the video in Margaret's hand might be poison for my client, but it was infinitely worse for them—as Margaret herself had just suggested, it was a nuclear bomb, and even that might be an understatement. Said otherwise, I had their balls in my hand, which always is the best time to make a deal.

Then again, if the situation were reversed, we wouldn't be having this discussion.

Bernhardt exchanged a quick look with Margaret before he turned to me. "Forget Amal Ashad. Forget the pictures, and I'm talking about the ones you sent to the lab for enhancement, and the ones you took of Ashad with his kids. As far as you're concerned, as far as anybody is concerned, Amal Ashad died on that street in Iraq."

"This is a joke, right?"

"No, this is the answer to your question." He rubbed a hand across his chin, like a rug merchant. "The bigger question is what you expect in return. What will it take for a deal, Sean?"

"My client may be guilty, but I can't walk away from the only chance to alleviate her guilt in the eyes of the court." I looked him in the eye. "Lydia Eddelston may have done some very despicable things, but Amal Ashad's hand was on her ass every step of the way."

"I already know the difficulties you feel in making this decision, Colonel. Once again, what do you want in return for losing your witness?"

This sounded like an invitation to discuss either my place on the next promotion list, or three years of light duty in Hawaii, or both. But that isn't how I, or the army, or the law, work. I think he knew this. But dealmaking is part of law, and in that vein, I responded, "How I answer that question depends on how much influence you have with the prosecutors and the judges."

He turned to Margaret, who appeared undecided about how to answer this implied question, but then he realized the question was addressed to him. As much as he did not want to get his hands dirty, he admitted, "The prosecution team has not been briefed about Amal Ashad, nor can we ever inform them."

"That's not my problem."

"In this case, my problems *are* your problems, Colonel Drummond. Ordinarily, we could sway the sentences they're requesting from the courts. This time, it's different."

"How is it different?"

"There is a charge of murder that needs to be considered."

"I'm aware of that. I'm also aware how easy it is to change the charge of murder to manslaughter in the third degree, and to let the conspiracy charges disappear, and to negotiate mild sentences in advance of a trial. I've done this hundreds of times before, and I damn well know how much flexibility the prosecution has in cases like this."

"Then I hope you're also aware that your client is one of the prime suspects," Bernhardt commented, as if I hadn't said anything. "In some minds, she is *the* prime suspect."

"Then somebody has been drinking too much Kool-Aid. The list of Palchaci's injuries is so severe, only an idiot would conclude he was murdered by a female, particularly one who is only five foot two and maybe one hundred thirty pounds. While she may be sexually aggressive, she has neither the physical strength nor the psychological inclination to commit such extreme violence."

"Really? She struck that man with her riding crop."

"Have you seen Palchaci's autopsy results? A speeding truck would have done less damage." I noted, "Anyway, it isn't Lydia's style."

"You mean," Bernhardt summarized, "she'd rather fuck them to death then beat them to death."

I made no response. But, yes.

"That's a unique defense, Colonel."

I shook my head. "She didn't kill him."

"You're arguing before the wrong jury. The murder and conspiracy charges are handcuffs, legally speaking. It's in the public realm and I cannot wish them away. Be reasonable, Sean. I'm sure you understand this."

In fact, I did understand what Bernhardt was saying. For as long as Lydia was regarded as a suspect in Palchaci's slaying or, at the very least, as a willful coconspirator in protecting the identity of his killer, the prosecutors weren't going to show any leniency or leeway. Danny Elton, as I mentioned, had once been my number one suspect in the murder of Palchaci—and I suspected, he remained theirs as well. Lydia was pregnant with his baby and she still had strong romantic feelings for him, albeit feelings that had apparently grown more complicated since learning that she didn't have a monopoly on producing his heir, all of which represented demonstrably strong motives to cover up his crimes.

I asked the president's national security advisor, "What if I can prove that she wasn't involved in the murder or the cover-up?"

"That's a mighty big if."

"I do this for a living, sir."

"As do the large number of investigators who have been exhaustively looking into Palchaci's murder for the past two months."

"I'm aware of that."

"Then you're also aware they have found not one fucking iota of evidence as to who killed that man."

I did not mention that those same investigators had also spent two months assuming that Amal Ashad was a red spot on the pavement back in Iraq, while, in fact, he was resting comfortably at home less than twenty miles from CID headquarters in Quantico.

I suggested, "Maybe what this case needs is fresh eyes."

"And what if your fresh eyes don't solve the case?" he asked, without mentioning what he was really thinking, which was that I was on a fucking goose chase. "We're on a tight timeline here, Colonel. The president is waiting on you—the deployment order for an additional sixty thousand soldiers is sitting on his desk, conditional, as I mentioned, on Ashad's lists. The airplanes and ships to get them over there are on standby. Every day we delay means more of our troops are getting killed."

"Give me three days."

He looked at me, but did not commit.

I upped the ante and said, "If I can't prove her innocence by then, I'll resign from the case, and nobody will ever know Amal Ashad is still sleeping with his wife."

I thought I saw the hint of a smile when I mentioned the word *resign*. He said, in a nonnegotiable tone, "One day, no more."

"And I want the assistance of the CIA."

"I think I can arrange that. They want the killer found." He turned to Margaret. "Will that be a problem?"

"Not at all."

Time to drop the bombshell. "Also, I want to talk with Amal Ashad."

"No, absolutely n—" He paused midsentence and asked me, "Why?"

I did not want to tip him off to where I was going with this, and replied, somewhat ambiguously, "He's the one person who has not been interrogated about the circumstances that led to Palchaci's death. Who knows? He may have insights that will help break the case."

He awarded this statement the skeptical rise of his eyebrows it deserved. He then asked a very good question. "Do you regard him as a suspect?"

"Everybody who was present at that prison on the night of the murder is a suspect, Mr. Bernhardt."

"Is that a yes, or a no?"

"There is nothing to suggest that Amal Ashad is any more or any less suspicious than any one of the other ten thousand people at Al Basari on the day Palchaci died."

He and Margaret Martin exchanged looks. They should not believe this, and they obviously did not believe it. Of course Ashad was a key suspect. Certainly he had stronger motives for killing Palchaci than any other suspect—he possessed a deep hatred against the Sunnis who oppressed his people, perhaps a maniacal animosity, and nobody held a greater claim to that bitter loathing than General Palchaci, whose crimes against the Shiites were as monstrous as they were legendary. Further, if you applied the same incriminating logic that had been assumed against the members of the night crew—to wit, they had already crossed a moral divide by beating and sexually torturing the prisoners, so what was to keep them from escalating to murder—well, that same line of reasoning applied to Ashad. The only reason he wasn't the lead suspect on anybody's list was because everybody assumed he was dead.

To my surprise, Margaret, however, did not appear overly concerned by this request. She nodded at Bernhardt. "That's acceptable to me."

He turned back to me. "We'll have him here at five o'clock. You'll have one hour with Ashad. Not one minute more. Is that satisfactory to you?"

I nodded.

He paused a moment, then asked, "Now, is there anything else the President of the United States, or his national security advisor, can do for you, Colonel?"

I detected a new tone of annoyance, bordering on snippiness, and I didn't want to press my luck. When you tug on the king's cape, be careful your hand doesn't slip and end up on his ass.

"Margaret will call you to arrange the meeting with Ashad." He handed me his personal business card. "Call me directly in twenty-four hours. Good luck, Colonel."

Chapter Twenty-Nine

I had turned off my cellphone for the meeting, and when I turned it back on, I found three messages from my cocounsel who, possibly, was wondering where I had disappeared to, and what I was doing during my absence, which I really did not want her to know.

I punched in her number and, when she answered, I informed her, "I'm on the post."

"Doing *what* on the post?"

"This sounds like the fifth degree, Katherine. Change your tone."

There was a pause before Katherine asked, only moderately less coldly, "Where were you yesterday, and what have you been doing?"

She sounded very stiff and unfriendly. It may have been the situation or it may have been that she had thought about our future, and I wasn't in it.

Love and war have much in common; in war, however, at least you know when you're a casualty.

I said to her, "So what are *you* doing?"

"I'm on my way to a meeting with the other defense attorneys. At noon, on post. I tried to tell you . . . unfortunately you were out-of-pocket and your phone was turned off." She added, "Don't ever turn off your fucking phone on me again."

Katherine does not swear much, so I think she was pissed.

"I'm sorry, Katherine," I answered, trying to sound appropriately chastised.

She said, "Imelda told me you were in DC. "

I distinctly remembered telling Imelda not to inform Katherine about my whereabouts. There was a time when Imelda would take a bullet for me, and I for her. I suppose, though, that asking a woman to keep a secret from another woman is a male fantasy.

But had Imelda also clued in Katherine about the images in my cellphone, the shit was about to really hit the paddles.

I asked Katherine, "Didn't Imelda also tell you what I was doing in DC?"

"She said she had no idea why you were down there. Neither do I." She asked again, "So . . . ?

I nearly exhaled with relief. "I was visiting the army personnel center."

"Were you trying to arrange a quick transfer?"

"That's not fair, Katherine. I thought a little more background on some of the prosecution witnesses might be helpful in court."

"And I thought the materials Captain Howser left us included their personnel files."

"Their official files, yes. The army keeps more extensive files at the center. Sometimes there is a classified file. You never know unless you ask."

"Okay. And did you find anything of significance to the case?" Absolutely. "Nope."

"All right. Are you coming to the defense meeting at noon?"

"I can't make it. My day is already mapped out. Besides, I have confidence in you, Katherine."

There was another long pause, then, "Look, Sean, I realize that I may have complicated our relationship and our work on this case. It was a mistake, a bad one. My timing was lousy."

Right. "Nonsense."

"I need your head in this case, and I need my own head clear. I hope you're not moping around, trying to avoid me."

It sounded like Imelda had also had a word with Katherine about our romantic silliness. I informed her, "I have a noon appointment with Lydia."

"About what?"

"Just a few details I want clarified. Maybe start rehearsing her a bit. If she repeats on the stand some of the outlandish things she said to us, she won't need a lawyer, she'll need a straightjacket."

"Go careful on her, Sean. She's brittle."

"I'll wear my best velvet gloves," I lied.

"When can we meet?"

"Not until tonight. I'll call you." And with that, I pushed disconnect.

Chapter Thirty

Lydia was seated at the table in an interrogation room on the second floor of the military police station. Her nose and her mind were stuffed inside a trashy romance novel when I entered, and it took a long moment before she disengaged from the book.

She looked up, then looked around, then it appeared to dawn on her that I was not accompanied by Katherine. When I had called Lydia to set up this meeting, I may have forgotten to mention that Katherine would not be in attendance.

I took the seat across the table, and fixed her with a hard, uncompromising stare, while saying nothing.

She put down the paperback, but avoided my eyes. As I had anticipated, Katherine's absence was unnerving for Lydia.

Despite her tough professional exterior, basically Katherine is a large-hearted person with an almost magnetic attraction toward the underdog. Her legal career as an advocate for gay service members has imbued in her what I would regard as dangerous levels of warmth and regard toward her clients for any normal criminal defense attorney; but, since nearly all of Katherine's past clients were accused of nothing more odious than a failure to conceal their sexual identity, it hadn't been a problem for her, so far.

As for Lydia, she has some serious attachment issues, a lifetime as a victim, and a neediness so neurotically intense that it's a miracle she didn't attract flies.

So Katherine had naturally fallen into the role of her protector, legally, as her lawyer, which was right and proper, and on a subconscious level, as the protective big sister Lydia never had, which was not.

I, on the other hand, long ago learned that in a contest between job and heart, the job always comes first. The army is a tough profession and you don't survive seventeen years of service without growing a few calluses on your heart, and a forgetful conscience. I had absolutely no problem bullying and manipulating Lydia to get at the overdue truth.

Lydia was now kneading her fingers and doing something funny with her lips. Like everything with this girl, even her nervous ticks were weird.

I let a full two minutes pass before I broke the silence. "I visited your parents yesterday. They asked me to send their love."

In fact, they had not—but they should have.

She made no reply to this.

"I also told them you're pregnant."

After a moment, Lydia replied in a peevish, childish voice, "I wuz gonna tell 'em . . . I swear I wuz . . ."

"I thought I would save you the trouble, Lydia." I further informed her, "I also met your old high school principal, Mr. Henry Livingston."

She stared back, but I had the sense I had just broached a topic—i.e., her past—that made her uneasy.

Before she could recover, I continued, in a soothing tone, "I must inform you, Lydia, that we had a long talk about you and about your troubles in school. He told me about all the boys you played doctor with in grade school, and about the three teachers you seduced in high school. He also told me that he strongly suspected you were sexually abused in your home, and that abuse compromised your ability to act appropriately in sexual matters."

"Well . . . he's a big, fat liar." That petulant expression popped onto her face. She broke eye contact. "He ain't got no idea what he's talkin' about."

I leaned across the table and, in a harsher tone, I told her, "But that's not true, Lydia. We both know you're the one who has been lying. For instance, why did you lie about Willy Packer?"

"I got no idea what yer talkin' about."

"Then let me refresh your memory. It wasn't a divorce, but a funeral, after Willy drove off a mountain road."

I studied Lydia's face; it was hard to tell what was going through her brain, or even if there *was* a brain inside her head. I recalled Henry Livingston's admonition that Lydia would not recognize the truth if it kicked her in the ass. As with any experienced defense lawyer, I am used to clients who lie. They lie for one reason or another—usually to cover something up, like guilt, or to protect others, or to shield the reputation of their unit or their institution, or in a few cases, to hide an extenuating embarrassment.

I recalled one memorable client, a good-looking, married young captain who was sleeping with the general's wife when his own wife was murdered in his home. He had the perfect alibi, but regarded it as a matter of personal honor to submit to a life sentence to protect his mistress's reputation, without recognizing that he and she had already left their reputations stained on the sheets of the general's bed. Sean Drummond, however, has a far more jaundiced view of honor. Once the general's enlisted house aide hinted at the relationship to me, I dragged the general's wife up onto the stand and browbeat her into confessing the truth. She got a divorce, the captain got convicted on the lesser charge of adultery, the wives at the officers' club got something interesting to talk about, and the

MPs pulled their heads out of their asses and found the real killer, who happened to be his wife's lover.

People lie for an infinite number of reasons, sometimes even when it's detrimental to their own welfare, and sometimes the lies are noble, even admirable—but they all *know* they are lying.

But Lydia Eddelston was different. I suspected that if I hooked her up to a lie detector and asked her to repeat the many lies, mistruths, and distortions she had told Katherine and me, she would pass with flying colors. She wasn't born, she was trapped; fate, birth, and DNA, had formed an unholy alliance against her. Bred in a broken-down trailer with parents who neglected and perhaps abused her, she had neither the smarts nor the good looks to alter or escape the tragic circumstances of her life. Yet, escape was what she desperately needed and, when reality failed to provide it, she chose fantasy instead.

The truth was right there in front of me, if I had only cared to look—it was in what she chose to read. Those Hollywood publicity rags that extolled a life of beauty and glamour and wealth that was as make-believe as it was seductive to such an unformed young mind. Or the romance novels filled with women who were saved from their wretched circumstances by a lusty, brawny Adonis who promises to love and adore them forever. It is called escapist literature for a reason, and for most, that is all it is—a brief, imaginary interlude that dissipates the instant your fat, unshaven lout of a husband bellows for dinner, or your whiny child howls for you to change his poop-filled diaper. But for Lydia, I thought, it had become something more than that; it had become the sustaining lie of her universe.

In her mind, and in her heart, Danny Elton was that barrel-chested, rock-jawed stud that permeates the modern romance novel—handsome, muscular, a man's man—a woman's savior if you're willing to let your imagination play with the pixels a bit.

After all, he was good-looking enough in a coarse way, and manly in that way that some rednecks exude a certain stupid virility. But, I suppose, when you're drowning, a frayed life vest can be every bit as tempting as a luxury liner.

And when Lydia danced and pranced, naked, in front of Danny, in her head, she was Madonna gyrating her loins to seduce the gaping multitude, or Catherine Zeta-Jones taunting Richard Gere in *Chicago*. And that, it struck me, is what I had observed in those elusive expressions on Lydia's face in the photographs. It was all a dream, make-believe—but it was real enough for her. She was no longer plain, squatty Lydia Eddelston from Justin transported to a steamy shithole in Iraq; she was in a faraway place where Danny Elton was Robert Redford, and Lydia was the smoking hot enchantress, the answer to his dreams.

Unfortunately, those dreams had turned into a nightmare for her, for the four other accused, for the army, and for the entire nation. It was time to separate the truth from the fantasy, and I knew how to do it.

I looked at Lydia and continued, "I don't know if you're repressing your memories, or trying to hide your past out of shame and remorse. But it no longer needs to stay hidden, Lydia. Talk to me. I'm not judgmental, and anyway, you were a victim, a young girl who could not protect herself from a larger predator. There's no shame in it, Lydia. Talk to me."

She sat silently, her face perfectly still, her eyes frozen on the tabletop. She appeared either unwilling, or unable to address this charge.

Time to twist the knife a little deeper. "I know what you did at Al Basari. I know you were trying to keep Danny Elton as a lover, and I know he chose June over you, and I understand how much that frustrated and infuriated you. You tormented and humiliated the prisoners the same way Danny was humiliating you."

Tears were running down her cheeks now. She actually started to sniffle.

I knew what she wanted to hear, and I told her, "Danny Elton is a bad man, Lydia. He's a bully, a louse, a liar. He used you and he abused you. He abused you sexually, and even worse, he abused you emotionally. You gave him everything a man could want, did everything he asked you to do. That he couldn't see your beauty, and your love for him . . . Well, he never deserved you in the first place."

She was nodding now. "He's an asshole!" she told me. "I did! I gave 'im ever'thing. I only wanted to please 'im . . . make 'im happy . . ." She reached up and wiped a sleeve across her runny nose. "He treated me like shit."

"Yes, and those you thought were friends, like June Johnston, they were even worse, weren't they?"

"She's a mean bitch!" Lydia yelled. "I trusted her, y'know?"

"Yes, and she stole Danny and rubbed it in your face in front of everyone."

She was furious now: her fists were clenched and her face was red. "She knew how I felt 'bout Danny. I tole her. She always talked like she understood that."

I nodded my head. "And all the while, she was plotting to take him away from you."

"She couldn't wait to flash her tits'n ass in Danny's face. And that dumb fool, Danny, he was too stupid to see what a big phony she wuz. She don't care nuthin' about him." The tears had stopped now, replaced by raging anger. "She ain't nuthin' but a lyin' *whore*."

"And now, just like you, she's carrying his baby."

Lydia looked at me. "If I had a gun, I'd blow her stupid head off."

"I can certainly understand why you feel that way," I told her. "And to make matters worse, now the two of them are blaming everything that happened at Al Basari on you. They're claiming it was all *your* idea, Lydia. They're both going to testify that you pushed things much farther than they wanted to go. It's not the truth, but that doesn't matter. It's two against one. It's what the court will believe."

"You think?"

"Danny and June have already told me as much." I awarded her a look of resignation. "It's sad. You'll end up in prison, and they'll probably run off and get married."

Her response was to look across the table at me with an expression of shock. "Married? You think they're . . . uh . . . uh . . . ?" She took a number of deep breaths. I could see she was starting to lose it.

Before she had a total meltdown, I leaned back and said, "But you don't have to let it go down that way, Lydia. You shouldn't let them win. You need to come clean. I can't protect you if you withhold the truth from me."

"It wasn't my fault," she wailed.

"I know that, and I know what happened, Lydia. I know they pushed *you* to do those things. I know they taunted you, and I know they shamed you into it. I know they gave *you* no choice."

As I had observed on the tape, this wasn't strictly the truth. But Lydia Eddelston, as Katherine had inferred, was brittle, and I didn't want her cascading into an emotional collapse; that meant composing an alternate moral reality to replace the one I was deconstructing, one she could feel, if not content to inhabit, at least not totally uncomfortable in.

"That's the plain truth," she told me. "Sometimes I'd tell Danny I didn't like to do that stuff . . . and he, uh . . . he'd jus' tell me, 'Hey, baby, it's jus' a thang.' Said he loved me."

I quickly asked, "Did Danny kill General Palchaci?"

She stared at me for one of those interminably long pauses, then said, "Uh-huh . . . yeah, he did."

"You're sure?"

"Yep . . . I know he did it."

"How? When?"

"It was near the end. He . . . y'know, Danny . . . he never could get that old guy to break. He tried, and he tried . . . it pissed him off somethin' awful."

"Why did it piss him off so much? Surely General Palchaci couldn't have been the only prisoner who refused to talk."

"Cuz that Captain, he kept tellin' Danny that that general was the most important guy to git talkin'. Said we wuz wasting our time on all them other prisoners. Said that general knew more'n all 'em. He kept pressurin' Danny to git that guy to open up."

"Captain Willborn told him that?"

"Sure did. So Danny, he finally got all fired up, and he gave the old guy a special session. He—"

"Special session?" I interrupted. "Is that different than a special treatment?"

"Yep. That wuz when Danny or the interrogators gave somebody the treatment on their own. Y'know, without us."

"Us?" I asked, "I presume you're referring to yourself, June, and Andrea. Right?"

"Yeah," she replied. "That night, it was jus' him'n Mike and the prisoner. Danny said he'n Mike were goin' to the dining facility for a snack . . . but that ain't what they did. They had this empty cell down near the backside. Sort of off there . . . all by itself."

"Were you present?"

She nodded. "It was real late, though. After June and Andrea had left."

Brian Haig

"So you were the only one present to witness the murder?"

Again, she nodded. "I could hear what was happenin' down there, though. Danny, he always used to carry this steel baseball bat . . . like that badass sheriff in that old movie . . . uh . . ."

"*Walking Tall?*" I suggested.

"I guess. Danny even slept with that bat. Anyways, he'n Mike, they wuz takin' turns whackin' away at that old man."

"How long did this last?"

"I wuz makin' coffee in the lounge cell, and I wuzn't checkin' my watch or nuthin'. It . . . it wuzn't like half an hour, though. More likely five minutes, or thereabouts."

"And you could hear what they were doing?"

"Well . . . not ever'thing."

"Did you see anything?"

"Nope. Like I tole you, Danny and Mike said they wuz goin' to the mess to git some food, so I stayed in the lounge."

"Tell me what you could hear, Lydia."

She seemed to think about this. "A guy's voice sayin' stuff to that old man. And the noise of the beatin' . . . y'know, these loud whacks, only more squishy-soundin' . . . sorta like when you throw watermelons on the ground. I didn't like it none. Even stuffed my fingers in my ears."

"Did you ever witness with your own eyes what they were doing?"

She shook her head. "I tole you, I wuz fixin' coffee."

"And are you sure the voice you heard was Danny?"

"Sounded like Danny."

"How far away were you?"

"I dunno. That empty cell was on the far side of the cellblock. Probably like thirty cells away."

"Could you hear what they were saying?"

354

"I jus' remember that Danny sounded real angry. Like I said, after I heard a few of them whacks, I tried not to listen. I plugged my ears shut."

"Did Danny ever mention what happened that night to you? Ever discuss what he and Mike had done?"

"Nope, never." She looked away for a moment. "Never really asked him about it, neither. Don't guess I really wanted to know 'bout that night. That guy, he died, right?"

Right. I changed topics and instructed Lydia, "This next question is going to be as difficult for you as it will be uncomfortable for me. But it's important to know the truth. Were you sexually abused as a child, and by who?"

She looked back at me, and, while she did not physically recoil, mentally she certainly took a big step back. She was willing to open up about a brutal murder, but she didn't want to touch the topic of incest.

I allowed her a moment to overcome her inhibitions and, when she didn't, I said, "I'm sure your parents ordered you never to talk about this. Maybe your father, or your mother, or both, threatened you to protect the family secret."

By the way she began biting her lip I could see that Lenore and Silas had done exactly that, and Lydia was struggling to get past an injunction she had obeyed for God knew how long. Of all the crimes in the world, incest brings forth the most conflicted feelings for the victim because, after all, the victim is torn by loyalty to the very loved one who raped her, by the eternal shame of having submitted to acts that both nature and society find grotesquely abhorrent, and because a young child, in order to survive and not go entirely mad, has to banish the memory of what was endured into some dark corner of the mind, to repress it, very often to make it disappear.

Often the father who abuses his daughter is, by day, a perfect parent, adoring, caring, even doting, the guy on the sideline at the kid's soccer match who cheers her on and takes her to the ice cream parlor afterward. It is only at night, after the lights go out, that he becomes a monster. Thus, just as the victim's fate is separated by day and night, by lightness and darkness, it becomes more and more difficult to illuminate what truly happened.

I continued in a more forceful tone, "But that no longer matters, does it, Lydia? You're twenty years old. You're all grown up. You're a soldier, and you've gone to war. You're on your own, a woman, an adult in the eyes of the law, and certainly in my eyes. You don't have to be afraid any longer."

She leaned back in her chair, and I allowed her the time she needed to get past her reluctance. She eventually took the first tentative step. "I never liked it much."

"Of course you didn't," I reassured her.

"I tried to git him to stop, but he . . . he jus' wouldn't."

"Who wouldn't stop, Lydia?"

"You got to promise you won't hurt him, okay? I know what he did wuz wrong, but you cain't tell nobody."

"I can't make that promise, Lydia." I asked, "Who was it that abused you? Your father? An uncle? Who?"

"Wuzn't my pa, no." She added, after a moment, "Wuzn't Uncle Clete, neither."

"You're sure, Lydia? You can and should tell me the truth."

"Pa beat me sometimes, but he never did any of that other stuff."

"All right. Who did do that . . . that other stuff?" I asked, adopting her neutral euphemism for being repeatedly raped.

"Jimmy . . . my big brother. When I wuz real little, he'd touch me . . . you know, he'd feel my privates. Wuzn't till I wuz nine or ten, 'fore he started goin' all the way."

"How long did this last?"

"How long?"

"Yes. How old were you when it stopped?"

"It ain't never stopped."

"Oh . . ."

"Jimmy's real big. He don't really take no for an answer."

"And your parents were aware this was going on?"

She nodded. "They tole him he better cut it out. Pa even beat him a few times after he caught him. Jimmy's the real stubborn type, though. So Ma and Pa just made sure I got good birth control."

I thought back to the expressions of shock and horror on Silas's and Lenore's face when I informed them that Lydia was pregnant. So that's what they were thinking—they were scared shitless that their stupid son had impregnated their daughter. Talk about parental nightmares.

I asked Lydia, "Was that your primary reason for enlisting in the National Guard? To escape from Jimmy?"

"I guess. But Jimmy, like I said, he's awful willful. He up and joined the Guard, too. Ended up in my same unit."

"I see." I took a shot in the dark and asked Lydia, "And what about the night you first approached Danny Elton in the bar back in Ohio, back before the deployment to Iraq. Was Jimmy present that night?"

"Sure was." She nodded. "Figured if I hooked up with Danny, maybe he'd lay off me. Jimmy can git real ornery toward guys I flirt with . . . but Danny . . . well, he don't take no guff off nobody."

"And how did your brother react?"

"Oh . . . he looked real pissed, but he jus' sat there and stewed." She smiled at this small victory.

But this revelation opened a fresh possibility regarding the mystery that was most personal to me—who was killing the lawyers—so

I asked Lydia, "Was Jimmy with your unit in Iraq? Was he at Al Basari?"

"He was gonna be, but . . ."

"But . . . ?"

"He got bumped 'fore we left. Turned out he had rickets on account of he don't eat too good."

"Yes, that can happen." I asked, "When was the last time you saw Jimmy?"

"'Fore we left. Ain't heard from him since." She shrugged. "Jimmy never was much of one for letters."

I had one other question. "I know you were mad at Danny and the others. Was it you who electronically forwarded the file of photos to a reporter?"

She appeared upset that I would ask this. "Wasn't me, no . . ." she insisted, confirming what I suspected. "I never even saw them pictures . . . leastwise, not till the newspapers started puttin' 'em in everybody's faces. They wuz all stored in Ashad's trailer. That's God's honest truth."

I thanked Lydia and explained that her insights would be very helpful in building her defense. That wasn't exactly true, but she didn't need to know that.

She smiled and asked me one, and only one question. "You really think Danny's gonna run off and git hitched to that lyin' bitch, June?"

Are you kidding me? I drew a deep breath, then told her, "My advice, Lydia, is to forget about Danny."

I got up, turned around, and walked out the door.

I stepped out of the interrogation room and while I walked back to my car, I pulled out my cellphone and called Chief Terry O'Reilly, chief of my security detail. The moment I identified myself, he said, "I'm not in the habit of being disrespectful to my superior officers, but you know what? You're an asshole."

"That's nothing. You should hear what my friends call me."

"Don't bug out without telling me again. You got a death wish, or something?"

"I was fine," I told him. "Hey, I checked the backseat every time I got in the car. I even carried my amulet in the shower."

"The range is only five miles."

"Oh . . ."

"Next time it's me whose gonna cut your throat."

I gave him a second to cool off, then said, "I need you to do me a favor."

"Really? My balls are swinging from the colonel's keychain on account of your skipping on me and now you want a favor."

"I want to make amends, Chief. Come on, it'll be good for your career."

I then told him to notify his CID and FBI buddies and have them run an all-points check with local police to see if a James or Jimmy Eddelston was staying anywhere within a thirty-mile radius of West Point. Check the hotels, boarding houses, short-term rentals and, since Eddelston was a country boy, don't overlook the local campsites. Also have his CID superiors check with the National Guard to see if they have a thread on him.

"Hey, thanks for telling me how to do my job," he said, dismissively. He then asked, "He's some kinda relation to the pee-chick, right?"

"Her brother."

"Shit, you mean there's two of them?"

"If he's in the vicinity, he should be regarded as dangerous."

"This got anything to do with the killings, or are you just trying to find out if peeing in faces runs in the family?"

"Maybe both. He may have had a motive to kill the lawyers."

"Want to tell me about that motive?"

"Have a nice day, Chief." I hung up, left the MP station, and got in my Prius.

Sometimes, you can smell when the endgame is coming. I checked my watch. I had only eighteen hours left to solve a murder dozens of investigators had failed to crack after two months of investigations. I was okay with that.

But I had the sense that I now had a big bull's-eye painted on my back. Something told me that I had become the next target.

Chapter Thirty-One

The weather had turned chillier, and light snow was falling, when, at 4:30, an innocuous blue sedan glided to the curb, and I climbed into the backseat. I had spent an hour dodging through buildings, running out back entrances, and doubling back to shake Chief O'Reilly's watchdogs.

An equally inconspicuous young man in a de rigueur gray suit sat behind the wheel. He punched the gas and the sedan shot forward.

I introduced myself and asked his name.

I saw his eyes observe mine in the rearview mirror. He chose not to make any reply.

I said, "Are you kidding me?" and thought I had heard a chuckle. "Where are you taking me?"

"Don't worry about it."

With the CIA it's always smoke and mirrors silliness, even when it doesn't have to be. After another ten minutes of driving through back streets, without conversation, I asked him, "Hey, have you ever heard the story about the KGB officer and the CIA officer who met at the end of the Cold War to compare notes?" When there was no response I continued, "So the KGB guy says, 'How secretive were we? I'll tell you, comrade, I've been with the KGB twenty years. My wife has been with the KGB this whole time. Her office is right across the hall from mine. All these years, and she still doesn't know what I was doing for the KGB.' So the CIA guy looks unimpressed and answers, 'Yeah, well I've been with the CIA thirty years, and even *I* don't have a fucking clue what I'm doing.'"

The driver grunted, then replied, "That's very funny."

He then wheeled into the double garage of a private home, then got out of the car and pulled the garage door closed. Another car was parked in the spot to the right. He told me, "Get into the backseat of the other car."

Did James Bond have to put up with this shit? But there was no use arguing. It was a Blue Ford SUV, with Margaret Martin behind the wheel, and now, me seated in the back.

Margaret welcomed me warmly by saying, "Get your head down low."

The other agent pushed open the garage door, then Margaret backed out, turned around on the street, and wheeled off back the same way we came.

She said to me, "A pair of our chase cars tailed you the whole way. We don't think you were followed."

I was going tell her my stupid KGB-CIA joke but even I didn't want to hear it again. I settled for, "This is bullshit, Margaret. Ashad and I could meet in front of a press conference, and nobody would have a clue who either of us is."

She glanced at me in her rearview. "Is Army CID providing security for you?"

"I gave them the shake."

"Yes, you did—we just confirmed it. Look, this is your fault. Ever since you stumbled onto Amal, everyone is being hyper-cautious."

I was tempted to tell her that I didn't "stumble onto" Ashad, I merely followed the trail of breadcrumbs they had stupidly left in his wake; but I suppose that merely reinforced her point.

I asked Margaret, "Where are we going?"

"Relax. We'll be there in another minute."

Perhaps I was being paranoid, but it suddenly occurred to me that the CIA might renege on this deal, and she was taking me to a barren bank of the Hudson River, where a crew of swarthy assassins were sharpening their knives—especially when we pulled into the parking lot of the Econo Lodge on the far end of Highland Falls, and I saw the last person I had expected, or wanted, to see walking toward the SUV.

"What's he doing here?" I asked Margaret.

"I think he's about to tell you."

Mark Helner opened my door and stuck out his hand. "Surprised to see me?"

"Nearly speechless." I then suggested, "Why don't you follow my lead?"

"Look, my superiors told me to come up here to . . . to, well, to apologize. So . . . I . . . Look, I'm sorry I took your security clearance and your badge." He put out his other hand; my CIA pass was in it.

I almost laughed in his face, but Herr Helner looked like a man who had left half his ass on some assistant director's shelf back at Langley and I didn't want to push it too far. But I couldn't resist saying, "Keep it, a souvenir to always remind you of the special moment we shared together."

He did not appear to appreciate the generosity of this offer and reverted back to form. "Don't let it go to your head, Drummond. You may have won this round, but there'll be a next time." He took a step back. "The real reason they sent me is to minimize the number of people read on to Ashad's status."

That sounded like a closer version of the truth.

Margaret was already walking briskly in the direction of the ground floor rooms of the two-floored building. I looked around, and saw two or three more men, also in gray or blue suits, loitering, and trying to act inconspicuous—but such formal attire in the largely blue-collar village of Highland Falls was like wearing a sign that says, "Guess who works for a federal agency?" What this agency needed was a big budget cut.

Margaret looked over her shoulder at me. "Come along, Sean. Your guest is waiting for you."

At 5:00, almost on the dot, Margaret used her passkey to open the door to room 133 and I stepped inside. She reminded me, before shutting the door behind me, "One hour. I'll be back."

I looked around. It was an anodyne motel-hotel room furnished blandly and inexpensively in the same cookie cutter fashion they all use, so you could travel from Boston to San Francisco and wake up the next morning and wonder what the hell you were still doing in Boston. I did not see Amal Ashad until the bathroom door opened and he stepped out, aggressively wiping his hands on a face towel. He looked at me. "Sorry. I had to piss the whole way up on the helicopter."

I made no reply to this inauspicious introduction, nor did I proffer my hand to shake, which he observed as if he didn't care.

"So how do you want to conduct this . . . this . . . ?" He rolled his eyes and asked, "Exactly what are we to call this, Colonel Drummond? A blame session, a meeting of the minds, or an interrogation?"

I was here to get his answers to my questions, not answer his. I ignored him as I pulled the office chair over from the desk and placed it about four feet directly across from the lounge chair in the corner of the room.

He watched me with what I assumed was professional detachment. He suggested, "I assume the chair in the corner is mine."

"Take whichever chair you wish."

He chose to sit in the office chair, which was about three inches higher than the lounge chair, and you sat upright; thus it was the natural seat of superiority and ergo, authority—the interrogator's perch.

I sat in the lounge chair, which had the only important distinction I cared about—it was the more comfortable piece of furniture. He smiled.

I asked, "Have I done something to amuse you?"

"Not really." He shrugged. "You just made a mistake only an amateur would make."

I leaned forward in my chair until my face was ten inches from his. "I'm not here to play Interrogation 101 games with you, Ashad. I don't care who has the bigger chair, the bigger ego, or the bigger prick. You're going to tell me what I want to know, or after tomorrow, you and your lovely wife will spend the rest of your lives running from the press and international prosecutors." I added, "Also those cute little children of yours will know what a truly sick prick their father is."

"So it's going to be that way." He relaxed back into his chair. "Do you mind if I call you Sean? It just seems so asinine to stand on formality while you toss around your stupid threats and insults."

As I had anticipated he would be, Ashad was a tough customer and a cool one. Face to face, he appeared to me, physically, at least, pretty much as his photos suggested, and as my imagination had pictured him—broad shouldered, slim-waisted, a narrow, intelligent face that was clearly Arabic by extraction. But like a lot of Americanized Arabs, it was a more animated face than you find in the homegrown variety. Something about America's casual, carefree culture makes its citizens more openly emotional and visually expressive than most of the world's citizens. With Ashad, however, I suspected it only ran skin-deep.

Also he had anthracite black eyes that, in contrast to his more lively expressions looked frigid and icy-cold.

In response to his question, I replied, "Call me Sean, or Colonel, or asshole, or as you wish. We are not friends, Ashad. We are never going to be friends."

He shook his head, dismissively. "Okay, Sean. So . . . why don't we get the big question out of the way, the one I know you're dying to ask?"

"There are many big questions I'm interested in."

"Here's some advice, Sean. You have only sixty minutes of my time. Don't waste a minute of it." Satisfied that he had established the pecking order for this meeting, he leaned forward until his face was almost in mine. "Did I kill General Yazid Palchaci? Did I take a bat, or a crowbar, and pulverize him so badly that that little niece he raped wouldn't recognize him?"

"What makes you think I suspect you?"

"Because I've seen the pictures of Palchaci's corpse. Because we both know none of the girls were capable of that, don't we? The damage was so . . . so . . . unfeminine. Because, in any regard, it's just not how they roll. So I think this leaves Mike Tiller or Danny Elton, or both . . . or me, as suspects." He paused for a moment. "But in the event you don't know him well enough, Mike's definitely not your man."

"Why not? Nobody is above suspicion until I decide who the real killer was."

"He's a weakling. Oh, I'm not referring to his physique, which is certainly impressive. But he's an almost neurotic follower. Timid, not very bright, so anxious to please, he bleeds subservience. Why do you think Danny chose him as his sidekick?" He then answered his own question. "Mike reaffirmed Danny's view of himself. Mike did whatever Danny asked of him. Mike is a vocational lapdog."

"All right, that explains Elton's attraction to Mike. So why did Mike go along? What did he see in Elton?"

"It's not complicated. For the most understandable of motives— free pussy, as much as a man could indulge." He smiled at me. "That was a rare and invaluable commodity in Iraq. The girls liked him, too. He has big hands, if you understand that expression."

"So, that leaves Danny, right?"

"Danny . . . yes." He stroked his chin a moment, as though contemplating that possibility, but the result looked Mephistophelean. "He's certainly my number one suspect." He dropped the-hand-on-the-chin pose. "I'll bet he was yours also, at one time."

"Go on."

"Very good, Sean. Straight from the manual. Keep the target talking."

"So keep talking."

"The question you should ask, is why I picked Danny to handle my cases? I assure you, he wasn't the only guard at Al Basari with a cruel streak. The prison was such a mess, a lot of those guys were on power trips."

"Why don't you tell me, Ashad? What made Elton so special?"

"It came down to one factor. He was easily the most corruptible."

"That's an impressive epithet."

"I'm sure you studied his record, as did I, prior to selecting him. Such a long unbroken chain of failures; failures to get promoted; failures to keep a job; failures to maintain his marriages . . . Danny is one of those men who just naturally fucks up everything he touches, so . . ."

"So . . . ?"

"I entered his cellblock one night to check one of my charges. I heard all this yelling and cursing. I found a dark corner where I could observe Danny and Mike without their knowledge. I watched them yank a prisoner out of a cell, and work him over for nearly twenty minutes. The man hadn't done anything particular, in fact, he didn't even grasp why they were beating the shit out him . . . it was just Danny having his fun. Then, these two girls showed up. I learned later, Lydia and Andrea were making a social call. Danny tossed the man back in his cell and, within minutes, the four of them had entered an empty cell and engaged in something I could never have imagined in a military prison in a war zone. All four of them, on the floor, naked, having an orgy, Mike on Andrea, Danny on Lydia."

"And you watched this?"

"I couldn't tear my eyes from it. Over the next month, I sneaked back again and again to observe them. From a psychological point of view, the group dynamics were so absorbing. Danny is such a unique and powerful personality. Like a prehistoric predator, he naturally senses the weakness in others, and he exploits them. He created his own little world in there."

"A warped world," I commented.

"Yes . . . one exquisitely shaped by the peculiarities and eccentricities of his very monstrous personality. I tell you, it was like something out of a Joseph Conrad novel if only Conrad had had a pornographic bent."

"Why didn't you step in? Why didn't you stop it?"

"*Stop* it?" he asked in an incredulous tone.

"You're a case officer of the CIA, for God's sake. Presumably you were trained on the Geneva Convention and your ethical duty to adhere to it."

"Stop it?" he repeated, rolling that phrase across his tongue as though he had never heard it before. "To the contrary, I began reassigning all my cases to his cellblock. To avoid attention, it took the better part of a month. But Danny's sick little world, that's exactly where I wanted them. They *deserved* to be there."

Ashad stared at me, apparently blind to the fact that the world he was describing was, in fact, not Danny Elton's world; it was *his* world. For sure, it would not have existed without Danny, or somebody like him. But it needed two special ingredients—victims, the men Ashad wanted tortured and broken; and the sanction of a superior officer, somebody who not only allowed it to exist, he encouraged it, and perhaps he even protected it.

"Did you tell Elton what you wanted him to do? Did you instruct him and describe how to break down the prisoners?"

Again, it seemed I had amused him. "Danny?" he answered. "The man is a force of nature. He needed neither motivation nor instruction from me. Well, an occasional challenge came up . . . a certain prisoner responding irrationally, and always, since none of the five soldiers spoke a hint of Arabic, there were communications issues. In those special cases, yes, we put our heads together. But, Danny was at his best when left alone to run his little chamber of horrors."

"So you're saying this was all Elton's fault?"

"Nobody's talking fault."

"I am."

"Fault? What do you know about the men I put in that cellblock, the type of animal I was dealing with?"

"What I know is that the man who put them in that cellblock lost any claim to moral superiority."

"If you're arguing moral equivalency, wake up, Sean. These animals wrapped little children in bombs, filled their pockets with candy, then sent them into police stations to be blown to pieces. They cleansed neighborhoods by castrating and beheading human beings, then dumped their corpses in the streets for their neighbors to gawk at. When they occasionally captured American soldiers, they raped them, tortured them for days, then blew their brains out, making a video for the soldier's family to see how pleasantly their final days passed. They are inhuman degenerates, completely amoral scum."

"I do not believe the Geneva Convention makes that distinction. If they walk upright on two legs and comb their own hair, they are human beings, protected and covered by the dictates of international law."

"None of those men ever gave a shit about the Geneva Convention. They aren't even signatories. None of these animals ever cared about the law or showed any inkling of decency when they were out on the streets committing crimes that are too foul for a civilized mind to grasp. Oh, sure, once they are caught, then they care. And you know what? I enjoyed telling them I was playing by their own rules."

Clearly, Ashad had persuaded himself that what he had done was righteous, moral, and just, that he was the hand of God. And, in a way, I could almost side with him. Almost. Certainly, I could see how a man shaped by his unique background, uprooted from his country by religious persecution, watching from afar as members of his family were butchered, and now, having to face the same men who had done that butchering, men who were, even now, doing far worse, could give himself a moral laxative and decide to make them atone for their sins. Perspective determines morality.

And further, I thought, had Ashad pursued this vendetta on his own, had he not suborned the efforts of five American soldiers, I might even be shaking his hand and thanking him for his service.

Well, maybe not.

Clearly, though, I was engaging in an exercise of mental masturbation trying to make him feel remorseful or even minutely guilty, so I changed topics and asked him, "Then, is it your belief that Danny Elton murdered Palchaci?"

"You know," he answered, "I believe he did."

"You must have a reason, or reasons, for that belief."

He actually laughed. "In fact, Sean, for the very same reasons I imagine you once thought he did it."

"Maybe I'm a little slow. Remind me what I used to think."

"Because Danny Elton has a few loose bolts in his head. Because a man always trying to prove his masculinity, to be the king of the hill, would see it as the supreme validation of his manhood. Because, after doing all he'd done up to that point, he needed something fresh, something . . . shall we say, something more invigorating to get his kicks. Because Danny has absolutely no moral qualms, because he's the type who could bash in a man's head just to see how it feels."

"That's all you have to persuade me he's a murderer?"

"If you're asking me for evidence, or to say I witnessed Danny clubbing Palchaci to death, I have none, and the answer is no, I did not observe it." He then asked, facetiously, "Do you have a better suspect in mind?"

"In fact, as you know, Ashad, that leaves you."

"How utterly disappointing," he replied, using an expression he must have picked up at some Ivy League soirée. He smiled, condescendingly. "Everybody has been telling me how clever and resourceful you are. Sean, I really expected more out of you."

This insult was meant to piss me off, but I knew what he was doing, and I knew why. I'm good at judging people and this guy scared me. After spending more than a decade crawling inside people's heads and mind-fucking them, it had become who he was. The man was certainly clever; or, on reflection, cunning was the better fit. I would not want to be on the other side of the interrogation table from him—though actually, I already was on the other side.

But this wasn't my first rodeo either, so to piss him off, I smiled back.

He crossed his hands behind his head and leaned back, a faux posture of boredom, as if to say I still wasn't measuring up to his mind-fucking standards. He observed, again in a sardonic, condescending tone, "I thought deductive logic was one of the tools you lawyers use." He looked at me closely. "I make absolutely no sense as a suspect. Think about it."

So I thought about it. "You're too modest, Ashad."

"Well," he replied, in a rare moment of candor, "that's the first time I've ever been accused of that."

"You know the first line of defense employed by every murderer?" I paused then answered my own question. "They all try to pin it on somebody else."

"Do they really?" He shrugged. "You need to be careful of circuitous logic, Sean. They tell you somebody else did it, so you assume they are lying; but what if somebody else actually did do it?"

"This is where the process of elimination comes into play. If it wasn't the girls, as you say, and it wasn't Mike Tiller, as you also say, and it wasn't Danny Elton, as I say . . . that leaves you."

"What about motive? What possible reason would I have to kill Palchaci?"

"Well . . . let's see. He was Sunni, he was one of Saddam's bloodiest henchmen, he slaughtered and buried at least three Shiite villages, and he wouldn't squeal, so you looked bad to your bosses. On a more personal level, he was a more obnoxious asshole than you, and you didn't enjoy the competition. Have I overlooked anything?"

"Nothing I can think of . . ." he said, as though these were all valid points. "Well, except . . ."

"Except . . . ?"

"Yazid Palchaci wasn't one of my cases. I wasn't responsible for his interrogation. He didn't make me look like a failure because he wasn't on my docket."

"I find that hard to believe. You were deliberately picking prisoners tied to the Sunni insurgency. Every report I've seen says Palchaci was a big honcho, an organizer, a recruiter. He checked every block of your profile."

"Except one."

I looked at him.

"I deliberately arranged for him *not* to be assigned to me. Captain Willborn can corroborate that if you care to ask him."

"Then why did Elton tell me that on several occasions you talked about taking a baseball bat and bashing Palchaci's brains out?"

"Is that what he said?" he replied. "I don't recall using those specific words."

"The quote may not be exact, but he definitely told me you dreamed of killing Palchaci."

He smiled. "Now that does sound like something I said."

"The legal term for this is intent, Ashad. I have at least one witness who heard you express the manifest desire to murder a man in the fashion in which he died."

"I believe that brings us around to modus operandi. Isn't that another element from your criminal procedure manuals?"

"What's your point?"

"Not only did I *not* kill anybody, no actual physical damage was inflicted on any of my other cases. Sexual humiliation and abuse were my weapons . . . at worst, their pride, their manhood, their egos were mangled. But my orders to Elton were quite limiting and specific. Violence was banned. No beatings. Nobody was to be permanently damaged, and nobody was."

"So you're a great guy after all."

He shrugged. "I even did my best to keep a close eye on the night crew."

"Obviously not a close enough eye, Ashad. Palchaci was murdered and you're telling me Danny Elton is your top suspect. He was the head of your night crew, was he not?"

"I cannot be held accountable for the actions of one stupid man. All those insipid photos . . . now you know why I had them record their activities. I even found a hiding place where I removed the lighting, so I could occasionally slip in without being noticed. One night, I even gave them a video camera."

"And to think I thought you were just a garden-variety peeping Tom."

This insult did piss him off, and he shot back, "You also viewed that video, did you not? Margaret told me she showed it to you." He leered at me. "Did you enjoy it? Was it a turn-on?"

"I found it sickening. You can infer from that something about my feelings toward the man who wanted it filmed."

He seemed to realize that I had gotten under his skin and he drew a deep breath and brought his emotions under control. "Yes, well, after I watched it, I counseled Danny about Lydia and that ridiculous riding crop." He added, "You know, she scared the shit out of me. Near the end there, especially. She was spinning out of control."

"Hell hath no fury like a woman scorned."

"A defense attorney with a guilty client is no piece of cake either."

He smiled at his own witticism. I did not smile back, though I did find it funny.

He then said, "I could easily have arranged for Palchaci to be my case . . . but you know what? I *would* have killed him. Does this sound strange to you?"

"No stranger than arranging for five soldiers to sexually molest your cases."

"Maybe, except I would never have used a bat. I would've found it so much more gratifying to snap his neck with my own hands."

We sat and looked at each for a moment, he with his stone-cold eyes, and me, with a skeptical expression. I finally asked him, "Who do you think forwarded the file of photographs to Melvin Cramer and brought your house crashing down?"

"To be honest, I've thought about that quite a lot."

"You should be happy to know that, in this instance, at least, I do not consider you a suspect."

"Well . . . that's reassuring." He paused then informed me, "I haven't got a clue."

"I'm not asking for clues, I'm asking for your best guess."

"Fair enough. It's my belief that your client, Lydia, did it. I think her fury at Danny became so consuming that she didn't care how much trouble it caused, or who it hurt, including herself. She wanted to hurt him, and she wanted revenge on June as well. Making sure those photos went public was the best way to accomplish both goals, was it not?"

I nodded at this logic. "How was your relationship with Captain Willborn?"

"Fine. Why do you ask?"

"Well . . . just that Willborn has expressed some negative feelings toward you."

"Really? What did Nate say about me?"

"He called you an arrogant asshole with an inflated sense of his own intelligence and self-worth. He said you kissed your Cornell ring every night before you went to bed, and that everybody in that prison thought you were a buffoon, a putz who was trying to hide his own well-founded insecurities and inadequacies, when all the American-born officers knew you were just a raghead who caught a lucky break." Willborn hadn't actually said that last part, of course, but a little artistic license wouldn't hurt anything. I added, more accurately, "He also said you were a selfish, stingy prick who stole all the credit for his work."

This barrage of negative comments appeared to surprise him.

I continued, "I think it's fair to say he hated your guts. He believes you are dead and though, ordinarily, people speak only fondly of the dead, his only fond memory of you is that you are dead."

He stared at me and stated, "He always was jealous of me and my success."

"Why didn't he share in that success? Weren't you a team?" "No, that was just a necessary facade. Naturally he was well aware of the success I was enjoying with the night crew and he begged me to include him. I said no. Why should I say yes? He brought nothing to the party. No language skills, which I did not need, in any regard. Nor did I find him particularly adept as an interrogator. He was too clumsy, not psychologically astute, too impatient . . . frankly he was not tough enough . . . certainly, not for the type of men I was handling."

I took a shot in the dark and asked Ashad, "Is that why you arranged for Palchaci to be assigned to him? To make amends by giving Willborn a shot at the big time?"

"You figured that out, did you?"

Not until now. But I nodded anyway.

"Yes," Ashad informed me. "That was very much in my mind. The bigwigs in the Green Zone were desperate to know what Palchaci knew. The man went back nearly thirty years with Saddam. There were a lot of blanks he could fill in. Also we knew he helped organize the Sunni insurgency, particularly the recruitment of former military members who were angry at being disbanded. I did Willborn a big favor. I gave him a chance to shine. He could make a big name for himself."

Ashad had now given me answers to everything I wanted to know, and I said to him, "I'm through with you."

He looked at his watch. "But there's still thirty minutes left."

"I said I'm through with you."

He actually looked crestfallen and a little annoyed that he wasn't important enough to merit a full hour of my time. But then he smiled. "You dog. You're more skillful than I thought. You really put one over on me."

"Is that right?"

"You never suspected me of killing Palchaci, did you? Misdirection, right? It was a red herring to get what you really wanted out of me."

"I have no idea what you're talking about."

He did not believe this, nor should he believe it, and he looked a little put-off that I had put one over on him, and now wouldn't admit it. He took a deep breath, then said to me, "Tell me something. I'm dying to know and I have a sense you have it figured out. Who did kill Palchaci, and who leaked the pictures?"

I stood up. "Fuck off, Ashad."

I then walked toward the door and left, closing it gently behind me.

Waiting about thirty yards away, sipping from a thermos of coffee, and standing beside Mark Helner, Margaret watched me come out. She appeared surprised that I had finished early and approached me. With an expression of concern, she asked, "Was everything okay? We told Amal to be open and to answer all your questions to his fullest ability."

"I got everything I wanted out of him, Margaret. But I'm not happy that you didn't tell me the truth."

"Which truth would that be?" she answered, unaware how telling that response was.

"You and your people already put him through the lie detector wringer. You didn't care if I interrogated him because you were already confident that he didn't kill Palchaci."

"So what if we did? What does that change?"

"Army CID just wasted two months trying to find a killer without the benefit of a key witness. You deliberately impeded the conduct of a criminal investigation and, as a result, five soldiers are being prosecuted for an act they did not commit."

Margaret shifted her feet and tried her best to look unaffected by this charge. "He has no idea who killed Palchaci. You're right. We interrogated him for weeks. He nearly got strap-burn from being hooked up to the lie detector so many times. And, yes, naturally we delved deeply into that line of query, and you know what? He didn't know anything."

"And what if he did know who killed Palchaci? Would you have shared that knowledge with Army CID?"

"I won't waste my time answering rhetorical questions that have no bearing on reality,"—in other words, no—"but we're confident that he doesn't know who killed Palchaci, so . . . no harm, no foul."

I looked back at her.

"What?" She raised an eyebrow. "Did we miss something?"

"The problem, Margaret, is that you people don't think like criminal investigators. Ashad does not know he knows, but yes, he does know."

It took her a second to unravel that verbal puzzle and, when she did, she asked, "Then who did it?"

"Fuck off."

Chapter Thirty-Two

The same hostess was on duty at the Thayer Hotel dining room and she appeared to recognize me. "Congratulations. You remembered to book a reservation. Your guest has already arrived."

She led me to the table where Captain Nate Willborn was already seated. I stuck out my hand and we shook.

I told him, "I'm glad you decided to join me."

"Did I have a choice? That confusing note you sent up with my dinner last night got my interest, Sean." He looked at me and repeated the words on that message. "*I know you're the one.* What the hell is that supposed to mean? The *one* what?"

I fell into the chair, and leaned toward him. "It's no longer Sean, Captain."

"Oh . . ."

"Tonight is official, not personal."

He had already ordered a drink and I noted that he either liked lemon in his Scotch, or iced tea was his beverage of choice tonight. He obviously knew he had made a big mistake the night before and he wasn't in the mood to repeat it.

He told me, "That sounds scary." He then asked, "Should I get my lawyer?"

"That is certainly your right, Captain Willborn. But in that case I'll assume you have something to hide and we'll reconvene this meeting in the MP station after I read you your rights, have you charged, and slapped in cuffs." I looked at him. "An innocent man has nothing to fear from a simple conversation. We can have this talk relaxing over a good meal, or we can have it with you chained to a table in the MP station. You pick."

"You wouldn't."

I stared back without replying.

"I think you're bluffing."

"A lot of people have thought that before and now regret it."

"I didn't do anything wrong."

"Nonsense, Nate. Everybody has done something wrong. The army has enough regulations that even Mother Teresa was guilty of something. The only question at issue is how wrong."

"You don't have enough to charge me with anything."

"That may or may not be the case. But as an officer of the court, I am legally obliged to inform you at this point that you are not yet a suspect, but neither are you entirely above suspicion. This means you have to talk to me."

He edged back into his seat and appeared to ponder the meaning of this legal doubletalk. In truth, you either *are not* a suspect, in which case there is no need or obligation to talk, or, you *are* a suspect, in which case the stupidest thing you can do is talk without a lawyer by your side. But most army field officers, who, in fact, are charged with enforcing the Uniform Code of Military Justice, are not really all that knowledgeable about the nuances and subtleties of the legal code. That's why the army has lawyers—and that's why I really did not want Willborn to have his lawyer present.

Despite his background as an interrogator, curiosity got the better of him, and he could not resist asking, "What is it you *think* I did? I didn't kill anybody."

"Did I say you did anything, Nate? And I'll ask you not to put words in my mouth or thoughts into my mind."

The waitress appeared. I ordered a burger and a beer for me and, without asking his preference, pork chops for Willborn. I never believed in giving a condemned man the choice of his final meal. A drink, however, is a different matter, so I did ask him, "Would you care for a beer or maybe a gin and tonic?"

"No . . . I don't think I should."

The waitress left and I asked Willborn, "Have you ever met Melvin Cramer?"

"Who?"

"The reporter who published the pictures and broke the scandal."

"Oh . . . I thought that name sounded vaguely familiar. No, I haven't. Why?"

"I had a chance meeting with him the other day."

"You did?"

"In fact, I asked him who sent the pictures."

He tried his best to appear nonchalant about this revelation and asked, with an attempt at phony indifference, "And what did he say?"

I changed subjects and informed him, "I also read your officer efficiency reports from the time you served at Al Basari."

"Those evaluations are confidential," he snapped. "You had no right to see them."

"To the contrary, Captain, a member of the bar in pursuit of the defense of a client is allowed to see documents that otherwise might be considered private." I shook my head. "I think your career is in big trouble, Nate. Your bosses did not appear to have high regard for your performance over there."

He shot back, "Those evaluations were unfair."

"Really? They looked straightforward enough to me. Your performance as an interrogator sucked."

"They were holding me to an unreasonable standard. I cannot be expected to get men to talk who have no intention in hell of revealing what they know. As I told you before, I was getting the toughest cases in the system."

"But that was your *job* as an interrogator, Nate. Other soldiers were out in the streets fighting the insurgents, getting blown up, being shot at. The only thing asked of you was to get the prisoners to squeal." I noted, "Ashad did not seem to have any difficulty getting his cases to tell what they knew."

"Don't try that shit on me. He tortured them."

"Still, he was effective. You weren't."

"I had some successes."

"Not according to the record I read or the people I spoke with." I lied and told him, "One officer familiar with your performance suggested that you couldn't get a canary to sing, that if you turned on a radio no sound came out."

"Then you're talking to the wrong people."

I changed topics on him again. "You once mentioned that, had you known what the members of the night crew were doing, you would have reported their activities to higher authorities, that this was your duty as a commissioned officer, and that it was one you would gladly have performed. Do you stand by that statement?"

"Yes, I recall saying that. I meant it when I said it, and I haven't changed my mind."

"I have other witnesses who say you were well aware of the nature of their activities, that you repeatedly asked Ashad to include you in his interrogations, and that you were furious when he said no. You even begged him to let you share in the credit for his successes."

"That's a bald-faced lie. But with Ashad dead, I'll never be able to prove it, will I?"

I placed my elbows on the table and leaned toward him. Interrogatories with a suspect are a mind game, and there generally are two schools of thought about how to proceed. In one, you pick a single incident or strand of testimony and bear down on it, picking at detail after detail, looking for inconsistencies or incongruities, then you flay them with their own mistruths, lies, and exaggerations, until you get to the truths. In the second, you throw charge after charge at them, a continuous broadside, disorganizing their mental defenses, keeping them off-balance, and keeping your eye open for an exposed flank.

Or to put it in the tactical vernacular of the army, it is a choice between concentrating everything at a single point of attack or dispersing your forces to assault on multiple avenues at once, preventing your opponent from amassing his forces in defense; eventually the line begins to crack in one place, and you rush in and exploit it.

I think Willborn knew what I was doing, attacking him on multiple fronts, some of which were nothing more than feints. And he had to know, also, that eventually, I would find that crack.

In that vein, I told Willborn, "Here's something else I find interesting. I reviewed the files compiled by my predecessor on this case, Captain Bradley Howser." I asked, "Did you know or ever meet with Captain Howser?"

"I can't say I had the pleasure."

I waited a beat, then asked, "Are you sure that's a truthful statement, Nate?"

"Not that I recall . . . no . . . no, I'm sure I never met him," he insisted.

"Well . . . that's odd."

"What's odd?"

"Captain Howser was a very exacting attorney. His files were remarkably meticulous and accurate. Reading through them this morning, I found a notation that he met with you. Two days before he was murdered, in fact."

Willborn stared at me a moment, then forced himself to ask, "Murdered? I . . . but I heard it was a car accident. Was I misinformed?"

"Due to new evidence, army CID has reclassified it from an accident to a homicide. The investigation has been reopened and they're now throwing everything they have at the pursuit of his killer."

"Is that so?" He stopped staring at me and looked down at his fork. Because it was the only appropriate thing to say, he murmured, "Well, I certainly hope they get him."

"They're just getting it off the ground, beginning, as all murder investigations do, with the issue of motive. This process could take a while, as you never know the motive until you know it. He may have had enemies, either professional or private, or he may have welshed on a gambling debt to the wrong people. There are so many avenues you have to run down, it just takes time."

He continued to stare at his fork and avoid my eyes.

So I continued, "Of course, the good news, or the bad news, is that whoever killed Captain Howser in all likelihood also murdered Major Martin Weinstein. This should greatly simplify the task of determining a motive. Do you see where that makes sense, Nate?"

"I wouldn't know, but . . . I don't think it necessarily follows. Maybe Weinstein was having an affair with another man's wife, and maybe Howser was the victim of road rage. You should avoid sloppy reasoning that leads to bad correlations."

"Yes, you certainly must be careful of that," I replied with all the insincerity his admonition deserved. "As I said, Nate, I don't regard you as a suspect, at least not at this time, but . . . well, this is a crazy idea . . . but, I've been constructing a sort of scenario in my mind . . . nothing firm, yet . . . in fact, I haven't even shared it with anyone, but . . ."

"But what?"

"Well . . . I just wondered if you would humor me, if you wouldn't mind if I ran a few of these ideas past you. As I said, some of them are really out there, but you were at Al Basari, after all, and I hoped you might give my ideas a sanity check."

He continued to sit and watch me as the waitress arrived with my beer and burger and his pork chops. But he had to know at this point that I was on to him, and further, he had to know that it was foolish to sit here and continue to talk to me without his lawyer present. But if I could read his mind, I think he was convincing himself that he had to know what I knew at this point, and the only way to do that was by remaining a sitting duck.

Then again, maybe he was just hungry.

I have been in this position countless times before, but in truth, you never really know what's running through the suspect's mind at the moment when you are closing in. They are like a wolf with his leg caught in the hunter's steel trap; should he tug and struggle and try to break free; should he cut his losses, gnaw off his own leg, and flee; or, should he stick around and try to eat the hunter when he shows up?

I thought his confidence as an interrogator should argue for the former. Just as a professional quarterback knows he can throw a better spiral than the man on the street, Nate Willborn regarded himself as unequalled in the art of interrogation, at least when compared against a common layman, such as myself.

But an experienced courtroom litigator is not a layman, and a legal interrogatory is not same thing as an interrogation conducted for intelligence purposes. Willborn's training and expertise was in how to get men to reveal battlefield secrets, men who already are demoralized and dispirited after being caught. But the fact of their guilt is already settled: the only challenge left is to get them to betray their country or their conscience.

I, on the other hand, make my living getting liars to reveal the truth, to see both that it is in their best interest and, in fact, that there is no other recourse than to admit the truth: to wit, their guilt. A small distinction but, under our present circumstances, an important one.

As I thought he might, Nate made the decision not to gnaw off his own leg and flee. He would stick around and tug and struggle to get out of the trap. They nearly all do, but you can never be sure.

The moment the waitress departed, he told me, "If you want my opinion as to what happened, I already told you I don't have a fucking clue. But if you want to play this game . . . okay . . . sure, I'll play along."

"But that's not exactly accurate, Nate. You were there. You knew all the main suspects, and you have already expressed to me your opinions about who did the crimes. Remember?"

"Yes, I recall that meeting. But those were just, as you said, my opinions."

I took a bite out of my burger and he lifted his fork and knife and began cutting into his pork chops. His hand was a little shaky, and he was making an effort to control it by cutting his meat—the result looked like a man trying to saw through his plate.

Still chewing, I suggested to him, "Why don't we start with the mystery of who released the photographic files to Melvin Cramer?"

He lifted his fork and bit into his first piece of pork chop.

I continued, "We know from the testimonies that Danny and/ or Mike took all the pictures. As did everyone else, I made the initial assumption that the night crew had their own computer and they downloaded their pictures into it, then, via e-mail, they forwarded the electronic files to Ashad. Not so, according to their testimonies. There was no computer in the cellblock. Anyway, Danny Elton is that rare American creature who does not know how to use a computer. Do you see where I'm going with this, Nate?"

"No. Explain it."

"Rather than forward the files to Ashad on the mornings following the special treatments, Sergeant Elton actually gave the cameras he used the night before directly to Ashad. The only computer at Al Basari with those files loaded on its hard drive was the one located in the office trailer shared by you and Ashad. It was located, as you know, in a quarantined area, locked, and under constant guard. I haven't checked yet, but I imagine that access to your trailer was strictly controlled. Correct?"

"You had to have a pass issued by the counterintelligence officer at the battalion headquarters," he confirmed. "Maybe Ashad sent the files before he died. Did you ever consider that?"

"Yes, that's certainly possible. But it would be professional suicide for Ashad to blow the whistle on himself, not to mention causing the dismantlement of a program that he, himself, had constructed. That doesn't entirely disprove it. But the doubt factor does go way up."

He looked down and, using his utensils, he toyed with the food on his plate a moment. When he looked up he suggested, "You're assuming that Ashad was entirely rational. He wasn't. The night crew . . . that was his operation, his brainchild. What kind of a mind conceives of such a thing?"

"I'm afraid that's just not persuasive, Nate. The night crew and its activities, perverse as they were, benefited Ashad. He was, in your own words, selfish and self-interested." I shook my head. "No, I just don't see it."

He then had another thought, and tried it out. "Another thing I never mentioned before, because I didn't want to impugn the reputation of a man who died for his country, but near the end there I thought Ashad was going mad."

"Mad?" I asked. "Are you saying mad as a generalized term, or as a clinical expression of nuttiness?"

"Insane, nuts, unglued . . . that's exactly what I'm getting at. He wasn't acting rationally. He became . . . forgetful, experienced nightmares, frequently complained to me about trouble sleeping. It was becoming more and more difficult to have a lucid, coherent conversation with him."

"And do you have an opinion about the cause of this mental derangement?"

"I'm certainly not a trained psychiatrist, but, yes . . . I suppose I have formed an opinion. Guilt. He was consumed with it. As I said, at that time I had no idea about the existence of the night crew, or of their activities, or of Ashad's role in those activities. But in retrospect, knowing what I now know, what all of us now believe . . . I think Ashad's conscience was eating him alive."

This did not sound at all like the Amal Ashad I had met only an hour earlier. That man was too arrogant and full of himself to experience an iota of guilt or remorse. I asked Willborn, "So you don't believe it was . . . say, someone who might've been jealous of Ashad's success, who disliked Ashad, both personally and professionally, and who wanted to destroy him?"

"No." He stuffed another bite of pork chop in his mouth. "To be honest, I find that theory entirely irrational and silly. Don't you?"

"I'm just throwing ideas at the wall to see what sticks, Nate. But this session is already proving both beneficial and illuminating." I paused a moment to let him worry about the meaning of that. I then said, "I have a few more off-the-wall ideas. Would you care to hear them?"

It took a moment for him to reply. "If you think I can be helpful."

"Very good. The next one deals with General Yazid Palchaci and his death. According to the coroner he was murdered sometime late during the night of 20 December. Further, he was beaten to death with a blunt, heavy object, most likely a baseball bat, which were fairly common objects at Al Basari, both for the recreational activities of the troops, and also, for use by the guards as deterrent symbols with the inmates."

He nodded, indicating he was following my logic.

"Now, unknown to the killer, there actually was a witness to Palchaci's murder."

"There was?" He took a deep breath. "I was under the distinct impression that nobody knew anything about that night."

"Yes, that had been the case, Nate. But as so often happens with criminal conspiracies," I explained, "one of the accused has experienced a change of heart, which attended a change in their testimony. This witness informed me that he or she overheard the murder, and the murderer."

"Is that right?"

"The witness confirmed that the killer did use a baseball bat. My witness was in another cell, making a pot of coffee, and overheard every hit and blow. If you're interested, Palchaci's killer was definitely alone, and definitely a male."

Though he did an admirable job of controlling his facial muscles you could see in his eyes that he never expected to hear that there was a living witness to Palchaci's murder. All these months thinking he was free and clear, and suddenly, a witness changes her mind, and suddenly, he's got one foot on the gallows. He couldn't resist asking, "Does your witness know the name of the killer?"

I thought about lying to Willborn but that wouldn't serve my purpose. "No," I answered, choosing a different lie and shaking my head. "Only that the killer was definitely not Mike Tiller or Danny Elton. The witness is quite certain of this."

"So it was a near miss." He relaxed back into his seat. "There were . . . what? Nearly nine to ten thousand males in the prison that night."

"Nearly all of whom were either locked in their cells, or in the chained-in compound outside the prison walls."

"All right, I stand corrected," he replied. "So maybe five or six hundred American males are left, any one of whom could've murdered Palchaci."

"Essentially, yes." He leaned even further back in his chair, and his muscles visibly relaxed with the relief of knowing he'd caught a lucky break. This was not how I wanted him, so to tighten the screws a bit, I posited, "Of course, a more thorough investigation should quickly narrow that number down to a workable pool of suspects."

"And how will that work?"

"It's actually not all that hard, Nate. For one thing, it had to be somebody who had free and unrestricted entry to the prison. Two, the killer knew when Elton and Tiller left the cellblock to drop by the dining facility for a late night snack. As it happens, June and Andrea also had left minutes earlier to go back to their tents, which might be how the killer knew the coast was clear. He might have had the whole night crew under observation, waiting for the moment to strike. Do you see the conclusion this leads to, Nate?"

"No . . . maybe you should explain it."

"The killer had to be someone who knew all about the existence, the activities, and the habits of the night crew. He knew, for example, that Sergeant Elton often carried a bat, so, by using a bat to kill Palchaci, he probably reasoned that Elton inevitably would become the prime suspect. And he believed that once Danny and Mike left the cellblock he could be alone with Palchaci."

"That sounds like a lot of unproven assumptions. I really hope this isn't a preview of how you normally solve crimes and defend your clients."

"It all depends, Nate. Sometimes it's a straight road, other times you're stumbling through a foggy maze. Very often, the killer, out of either remorse, or the inevitability of detection, steps forward and offers a confession. It saves everybody a lot of time and trouble, makes us all look good, so to reward this forthright behavior we might shave a few years off their sentence."

He looked at me and said nothing. But this description, vaguely suggested as it was, must have sounded to him like an invitation to confess, which it also was. If he decided to take a pass on my offer, it made it harder on everybody. But in an ironic way, if he took my offer, he made it harder still.

To reinforce my offer, I said, "When that doesn't happen, Nate, we throw around ideas until one of them looks good, we get the bad guy, and we throw away the key. In this particular case, however, with the whole world watching, and where our suspect may have committed multiple premeditated murders, a ride on the hot seat is a real possibility." I looked him in the eye and emphasized, "A voluntary confession might be the only way to avoid that outcome."

He glanced down at his plate, and I could see he was wrestling with himself.

When he looked up, he said, "It's just not very . . . reassuring that you would consider such crazy ideas."

"Yes, but that is how it works, Nate. We start with the loopy stuff, and sooner or later, some of it starts to look frighteningly sane. Now, here's an even stranger one. Do you want to hear it?"

"Uh . . ."

I took that for a yes. "Say you had a promising young inter-rogator, he's ambitious, he has hopes and dreams of a long military career, but he's under unbearable pressure from his bosses, and is getting terrible performance evaluations, because none of his cases are talking. So to afford him an opportunity to correct this impres-sion, his so-called partner gives him Palchaci as his case. The Gen-eral is one of the highest profile targets in the entire system. Senior officials in the Green Zone keep asking why this man isn't talking. So this young interrogator spends months trying to get Palchaci to crack. When the normal methods fail, he goes to Danny, and he begs and pressures Elton to do whatever it takes—it worked for Ashad after all—so they beat him, and eventually, they put the old man through the night crew's special wringer. Unfortunately, none of it works. Palchaci continues to lecture our young interrogator on the stupidity of the war, and he even has the temerity to complain that the special treatments aren't decadent enough for his tastes."

I paused for a moment. Willborn appeared to be transfixed, hearing me describe something he thought only he knew.

I said, "Just imagine, if you will, how satisfying it would be for this young officer to take a baseball bat and beat that man to death. Every blow would feel so well-deserved. Palchaci was, after all, a bad man, an evil man, a man who had done so much harm, and killed so many people. And now, adding to his crimes and misdeeds, he was derailing the career of an ambitious young officer."

Nate Willborn had stopped eating now. His plate was pushed to the side, but he was still holding the knife and the fork in his hands, as though he didn't know what to do with them, or with himself.

Eventually, he insisted, "Except Palchaci wasn't my case. He was Ashad's."

"Is that so? You'll have to forgive me because, as you're aware, Major Mary Ingle has blocked me from viewing the interrogator's assignments. And the daily logs kept by you and Ashad are, of course, missing."

"I'm telling you he was Ashad's case. So I think, according to your scenario, Amal Ashad should be your most promising suspect. Everything you have described applies as easily to him, as . . . say . . . to me."

"I certainly recognize that, Nate. In fact, this is why I haven't yet brought this analysis or the suspicions that emerge from it to the attention of Army CID. I don't want to impugn the character and reputation of a promising young officer who may have done nothing worse than have the bad luck to be in the proximity of a lot of reprehensible behavior."

He was now watching me very closely, like a man who just fed his last dollar into a slot machine, knowing a jackpot is a million-to-one shot, but still unable to tear his eyes from the spinning symbols.

I told him, "In a case like this, what I normally do is dig deeper. Once you understand the motive, it becomes fairly easy to understand who did the killing. The why takes you straight to the who."

"Is that right?"

"There are a lot of people I can talk to, and plenty of promising leads I intend to follow up on. For instance, given the new witness testimony and these new revelations, I am now confident I can persuade a judge to overturn Major Ingle's injunction and release the interrogation assignment logs to me, or at least to Army CID, to confirm who was responsible for Palchaci's interrogation. Further," I continued, "I can confidently rule out Amal Ashad as the killer of Major Weinstein and Captain Howser. Dead men tell no tales, and neither do they commit murder, right?"

"I suppose that's sound reasoning."

"But is there a causal link between the killing of Yazid Palchaci, the exposure of the night crew's activities to a well-known reporter, and the murder of the two army lawyers? I don't know. But had both Weinstein and Howser begun to suspect the same man as Palchaci's murderer, or had they both met with the actual killer and created the fear in his mind that he was at risk of exposure, that could certainly tie all the murders together."

Clearly he knew now that the case against him was very strong, and I had described enough loose ends to hang him. When he finally looked up from his plate, he said, "This is a very complicated case for you, is it not?"

"Homicide cases always start off complicated, Nate. You have a victim and you have a killer, but between the apprehension and the conviction, you have motive, modus operandi, unpredictable witnesses, evidentiary issues, a judge, an opposing attorney, and a jury. You build one block at a time and eventually, you have seven members of the court martial board nodding at every word you say." To reinforce that point, I noted, "For instance, I have yet to check Major Weinstein's files and records, but when I do, I may find that he also met with the killer shortly prior to his death."

"I never met him," he said without any attempt at conviction, as though, at this point, he was merely reading off a script long after the audience had left. "Nor did I have any reason to kill him."

"Yes, well, the FBI can check and see which suspect may have traveled to Colorado and Northern Virginia on the days Howser and Weinstein were murdered. Once they have a name and a photo, it's amazing what they can dig up. If you drive through a toll stop, say on 95 going south, and they have your license plate number, very often, there is a picture of you behind the wheel. If you stop at a highway rest stop or stay in a hotel, nearly all of them have cameras these days, and there you are, in living color. Charge cards leave records. Once shown a photo, waitresses and hotel attendants remember a face. If you took a flight, there's a record. I must tell you, Nate, it's really hard to kill people in this day and age, and not leave a trace. There's always something."

"Yes, sir," he answered. "I encourage you to do exactly that. I'm innocent and the deeper you probe, I'm confident that I'll be vindicated."

"That may well prove to be the case, Nate."

"But from this discussion I have the sense that you have a lot of circumstantial evidence that you think points at me."

We exchanged stares for a moment. "Yes, it definitely does look that way, Nate."

He now had become that wolf with his foot caught in the steel trap, and none of his tugging or struggling so far had dislodged it. But he had to attempt one last jerk and said, "Still, everything you've said so far sounds circumstantial. You cannot convict a man on circumstantial evidence. No court martial board will render a guilty verdict on something so flimsy and conditional."

"But that's not exactly correct, Nate. In fact, I have sent many men to prison on nothing but circumstantial evidence. The Supreme Court recognizes its legal validity. It's not nearly as difficult as you might think. Given all that I have unearthed so far, and all these promising leads we just discussed, I am confident I can name the killer and provide CID with an incontrovertible case. By tomorrow or the next day, at the latest, I expect to have enough evidence to refer this case to the proper authorities, and to request an arrest."

I dropped a fifty-dollar bill on the table and informed Nate, "Now I really must be going. It's late and I have to walk back to my apartment in Highland Falls."

"I can give you a ride, sir. My car is in the parking lot."

"Thank you, Captain, but I need the fresh air." I added, "Partner Lane is a short walk. Out the front gate, hang the first right, then up the big hill to the house at the top."

I stood and looked down at Nate Willborn.

We locked eyes for a moment, and I saw exactly what I expected to see—the tugging had not dislodged his foot and the time to gnaw off his own limb and escape, had passed.

There was only one option left. The time had come to eat the hunter.

Instead of bidding him adieu or farewell, I told him, "See you later."

Chapter Thirty-Three

I departed the hotel through the front entrance, and then plodded slowly down the hill, directly to the road that led to the front gate, all my senses on high alert. As the crow flies, the distance from the Thayer Hotel to the rented house on Partner Lane was probably a quarter of a mile; on foot, however, it was more like half to three-quarters of a mile. Said otherwise, Nate Willborn had, at best, fifteen minutes to kill me.

Modus operandi. Man is a creature of habit, as much in how he chooses to kill another man as in the way he puts on his pants in the morning. Nate Willborn had killed one man with a baseball bat, one with a car, and one with a knife. All three weapons were different, just as there were differences in time, place, and the choice of his victims. But the essential method was remarkably similar in one regard. Misdirection. Willborn designed his murders to mislead the investigators, diverting suspicion to another man in one case, hiding behind the randomness of an unobserved death in another, and, in the last, leaving clues at the crime scene that were intended to make it appear that someone driven by Islamic madness was seeking retribution.

But in all three cases, he timed and designed his killings to avoid witnesses.

In a court of law, modus operandi is one of several variables you use in trying to prove or disprove a criminal charge, depending on whether you are prosecuting an accused, or defending a client. In this case, I was considering Nate's past methods as a blueprint of how he intended to kill me.

The note I had sent up to his room with last night's doggy bag was a taunt, a warning, but more than that, it was an invitation for him to consider killing me.

For, if you considered the pattern he had employed in all three murders, it was clear that Nate Willborn was what a criminal specialist would classify as an organized killer. He planned in advance, so I had given him time to mentally organize his assault. He applied misdirection to conceal his crimes. And he employed the principle of surprise: certainly, that had been his method against Howser and Weinstein—though it would not be with me.

I thought it was a good bet that Willborn would not try to murder me until I was outside the grounds of West Point, as the sidewalk on post was both well lit and under the direct observation of the guard at the front gate.

As I walked through that gate, the MP saluted and said to me, "Good evening, sir."

I saluted back, and returned his ritual greeting. "Good evening."

I continued walking, still at the slow pace I had been using. I walked the short block to the street sign that said "Partner Lane" and hung a right onto the road that would be his killing ground. In my left hand was the amulet Terry O'Reilly had issued me; my right hand was stuffed inside my pocket.

I paused when, to my rear, I heard the MP at the gate call out to another pedestrian passing by his post, "Have a good night, sir."

I looked straight ahead, up the long steep hill to the house at the top where Katherine and Imelda were probably having dinner, or going over the case. As this was a side street in a sleepy village, there was no traffic. The overhead lighting was sparse and spotty, with long swaths of the road hidden in shadows. Small, old homes lined both sides of the street with narrow distances between them. It struck me, however, that Willborn's avenue of attack would be from the right; he would not want to risk detection by trying to cross over to the other side of the street.

So I kept my eyes to the right as I continued my ascent.

I was nearly at the top when it occurred to me that I might be wrong. Willborn might've changed his mind. He might've left the hotel dining room, checked out, jumped in his car, and tried to make a run for it. That would be the smart thing to do, and Willborn was certainly smart enough.

I almost began to relax when a figure came sprinting out of a dark space between two houses. I spun to the right and threw up my left arm just in time to catch the brunt of a metal baseball bat swung with full force. I felt the force of the blow and a stab of intense pain, but adrenalin kicked in. My right hand came out of my pocket and in it was my .45 caliber pistol, fully loaded, with a round already chambered, and the safety off.

Just as Willborn was raising the bat over his head, and before he could bring it down again, I raised the .45 and there was a moment, less than a second, in which we stared at each other. I watched his eyes go wide as the realization dawned on him that rather than me, he was about to die, then I fired one round into his face, and six more fast rounds into his chest.

The .45 caliber was designed for the US Army in the early years of the twentieth century in response to the war in the Philippines and the threat of doped-up Moro warriors who absorbed bullets from smaller-caliber weapons, and kept attacking with their bolo knives and machetes. The weapon is not particularly accurate. Because they are large, the bullets it discharges are low velocity. But at a short distance it is an ideal weapon for killing people. The force of the first bullet struck Nate Willborn in the face. The six I pumped into his chest put him down on the tarmac.

I bent down and felt for a pulse. Not even a dying flicker. I then stood up, pressed the amulet in my left hand, and waited for Chief O'Reilly and his crew to come running.

Chapter Thirty-Four

Terry O'Reilly was joined by several members of the village police, and an array of military police officers from the academy, all of whom were loitering around the crime scene without any good reason to be there. Killings are always like cop conventions.

The first responders from the village tried to impose their authority, but, as both the killer and the corpse were dressed in army uniforms, it was hopeless, and they were quickly muscled aside by the military investigators. The Military Academy, being the main reason for the village to exist, not to mention its largest single employer, was a bit like the Vatican in Rome; its power and influence may officially end at the border, but God and the federal government set their own rules.

I was seated on the rear of the ambulance that had arrived, as per standard procedure, because a man had been shot. But the EMTs, after one glance at Captain Nate Willborn's body, recognized that he wasn't in need of a doctor, but a mortician, so they diverted all their attention to my left arm.

The head EMT had just informed me, "Absent an X-ray I cannot confirm this, but your radius is clearly fractured and I would guess your ulna may have trauma as well."

Without a medical journal I had no idea what he was saying, but judging by the pain pulsing from my left arm, I think he was saying it was broken. The EMT gently placed my arm in a sling and advised me to keep it immobilized and to see a doctor, ASAP.

Now that he knew I had not experienced a life-threatening injury, O'Reilly and another man in a bad suit moved in to initiate their interrogation.

O'Reilly gave a good demonstration of cool professionalism by starting off, "Jesus H. Christ . . . I mean, Jesus H. Christ. You blew that guy's fucking head off. Then you pumped six more rounds into his fucking heart. Holy shit . . . Jesus H. Christ."

This sounded like a fairly accurate rendition of what I had just done, though Jesus was definitely not a coconspirator. I nodded.

He said to me, "Haven't you ever heard of the fucking expression, excessive force? You were less than three feet from the guy. One bullet from that cannon you used was more than enough to stop him. Jesus H. Christ. Why did you keep shooting?"

I was tempted to tell him that he was asking the wrong question. Why had I stopped firing before my magazine was empty—that was the question he should be asking. The .45 automatic carries seven rounds in the magazine and one in the chamber. I had deliberately left one bullet in reserve in the event the others didn't do the trick. The French call it a coup de grace, an elegant way to describe the inelegant butchering of a man who survived an execution. Thankfully, my bullets hit the mark, so I did not have to discover if I was really that cold-blooded.

"He wasn't worried about excessive force, so neither was I, Chief." I added, "It's a dark night. I had no idea whether my bullets hit him."

"Bullshit . . . that's bullshit. From that distance, you couldn't miss. This looks like something personal."

"I barely knew the man."

403

"Bullshit."

I stared straight ahead.

"What was your relationship with the victim?"

"He was one of the witnesses in the trial. I met with him once or twice to clarify certain elements of his testimony."

"More bullshit."

I made no response.

"Was he testifying for, or against, your client?"

"If you're suggesting that I would assassinate witnesses to influence the outcome of the trial, there are enough prosecution witnesses in this case to fill five morgues. You insult your own intelligence with that suggestion, Chief."

"When was the last time you met with him?"

"Less than an hour ago. We shared dinner. At the Thayer Hotel. I was walking back to our house when he attacked me."

"Yeah? So what got said at that dinner to make him decide to kill you?"

"It was a nice, quiet meal. I enjoyed his company. Ask the restaurant staff."

"Are you saying you have no idea why he was trying to kill you?"

"I can't read his fucking mind, Chief."

"Neither can I. You blew it out of his head."

I suggested, "If I had to take a guess, he didn't like lawyers."

O'Reilly replied, with real conviction, "I can understand that."

"Under the circumstances, I think he should be regarded as a suspect in the murders of Captain Howser and Major Weinstein." I then made the helpful recommendation, "You and the FBI should try to establish if Willborn was in Colorado the day Howser died, and the DC area the day Weinstein was killed.

"No shit. I think I figured that out on my own." He bent toward me, and warned, "Here's a little good advice, counselor.

While, circumstantially, this looks like self-defense, it's definitely something more than that."

"I'm not following your logic, Chief."

"Then let me make it clearer for you. You gave us the slip a few hours ago, getting rid of your protection, which might also be construed as eliminating any possible witnesses." He asked, "Why did you give the shake to my boys?"

"Weren't they behind me?"

"Don't try that shit on me, Colonel. You know you did. You took them on a chase through post, then all those little shops in town you dodged in and out of."

"Chief, I will not be held responsible for the incompetence demonstrated by your agents." I shook my head. "I believed they had my back. I had no way of knowing otherwise."

He fell back on his favorite conclusion and said, "Bullshit."

"You said yourself that they are good boys, able to follow me without me even knowing it."

He recognized his own words, and clearly did not enjoy having them thrown back in his face. His jaw became tight and his hands balled into fists. "I'm tempted to put you in cuffs and haul your ass down to the MP station on post where we can continue this discussion in a more conducive environment."

"Ordinarily that would be an option, Chief. Except the killing occurred off-post, here, in Highland Falls, meaning neither you nor the army has the jurisdictional authority to investigate, or to produce charges against me. And if you take one step in my direction in an attempt to apprehend me, I'll have you charged with assaulting and kidnapping a superior officer."

He did not acknowledge this, as it was not in his interest to do so. But it was a reminder to him that he was dealing with every cop's worst nightmare—a lawyer as a suspect.

But like the good cop he was, he had to get one last lick. "This isn't over, Colonel. Army CID will offer the village police everything at our disposal."

"Are you through?" I asked. "My arm requires immediate treatment in a hospital."

O'Reilly was a good guy and I got no joy from treating him this way. Despite not being on the criminal end of things, so far his instincts and insights about what really happened were mostly spot on.

Poor Nate Willborn had gotten himself into something much bigger than he understood, maybe too big for anybody to understand, both back in Iraq, where he had killed a man and ignited a scandal, and then, here, at home, where he murdered two army lawyers to cover up what he'd done over there.

Along the way he had placed himself in a position where the fate of an entire war rested on whether he was discovered or not. Some three thousand men and women had already given their lives to the cause; tens of thousands more had lost limbs, other body parts, and in some cases, their minds. It did not seem fair or just— at least, not to me—that after everything they had fought and sacrificed so much for, the one chance for it to become a success should be thrown away because one army captain became upset with his lousy performance reviews and decided to take out his frustration on one stubborn Iraqi prisoner.

I did, however, feel some sympathy for Nate Willborn. He had voluntarily left the cool, leafy suburbs of Boston only to end up in the worst shithole on the planet, a madhouse in a country he did not understand, as part of a war he also did not fully understand. Around him Amal Ashad and Danny Elton and the rest of the night crew were going mad. It should surprise nobody that Nate Willborn caught a little whiff of that madness.

But once I decided that Nate Willborn murdered Palchaci and two army lawyers, it occurred to me that there really was no way to place him under arrest and on trial, at least not without exposing the continued existence of Amal Ashad and the cover-up of what really happened at Al Basari—throwing away the one good chance to win the war.

The truth was, I convicted Nate Willborn in my mind, and I then maneuvered him into a position where he saw no choice but to kill me. The discussion he and I had shared over dinner was a preview of how any competent prosecutor would present the case against him at a trial in front of a board of his peers; I was confronting him with the criminal narrative and the evidence that would be used against him. In turn, Willborn was revealing to me the alibis and lies he would employ to conceal his guilt. His defense was weak. It was full of holes large enough to drive a guilty verdict through, and I think he recognized this.

I'm a good lawyer: I certainly did my best to make him recognize it.

Of course, I gave him the time-honored chance, as any good lawyer or cop would do, to turn himself in, and try to work a deal.

But if I was honest with myself, it was an offer I knew he would never take. I knew he had killed two men in cold blood to conceal his crimes, I knew he had sat back and watched five American soldiers be pilloried and tried for a crime he committed, I knew he deserved to die, and I knew it would be better for everybody concerned if I pulled the trigger and blew the brains out of his head.

And, too, O'Reilly was right about another thing. I could have easily aimed my .45 to maim or disarm Nate Willborn.

Where he was wrong was in suggesting that was ever an option in my mind.

Chapter Thirty-Five

The cops from Highland Falls took my statement, though having no understanding of the Al Basari court martials, they released me with the usual admonition to remain in contact until the case was closed.

I needed to see a doctor about medical treatment for my arm, but I needed treatment for my head first, so I wandered back down to Main Street and walked into the first establishment I could find with a liquor license, which happened to be called South Gate Tavern.

It was located only yards from the academy's Thayer gate, and the décor was an interesting muddle of Irish paraphernalia and military accessories, and I even recognized most of the unit patches pinned to the wall behind the bar.

All around me, pictures were hanging on the walls, photographs of soldiers and officers currently serving at war, in Iraq or Afghanistan—though from some of the shots it was hard to distinguish which. Everybody deserves a hometown, but for soldiers whose lives are as transient as tumbleweed, I suppose a bar has to do.

A few of the faces were old enough to have lines and creases; most, however, looked young, eager, and unblemished by age, disillusion, heartbreak, or crushing disappointment. I don't recall ever looking that young, idealistic, or free-spirited, and certainly the face I see in the mirror these days tells a different story; it looks a little worse for wear, shorn of the naiveté and innocence I wore the day I first swore the oath to protect the Constitution of the United States and to defeat all enemies, foreign and domestic.

I occupied a booth in the darkest corner of the bar where I sipped from my Scotch and brooded, occasionally glancing up to the faces on the walls.

To my left, I observed an enlarged photograph of a smiling, attractive young female soldier in battle dress who bore a strong resemblance to June Johnston. She was blonde, fit, fresh-faced, and pretty—a poster girl for the modern army recruiter, the prom queen transformed into a cold-blooded killer. A second lieutenant's butter bar was pinned to the center of her battle dress, so probably she was a recent graduate of the officer factory less than a few hundred yards away. That accomplishment aside, I wondered what made her any different from June, Lydia, or Andrea.

Boys and girls. Apart, they are fine, but together in close quarters, you have the equivalent of dynamite and C4 with an unstable fuse. For the army, despite all its regulations and authoritarian leaders, sex is like kryptonite. You can order men and women to ignore the color of skin or even sexual orientation, and you can usually make it stick. But try ordering boys and girls not to screw and you have the equivalent of ordering salmon not to swim upstream.

Fate and circumstance had deposited five soldiers at Al Basari, five unique individuals who came into the army already shaped and twisted by their own life experiences, each guided by their own neuroses, pathologies, and psychological scars. And ultimately, they found one another and went on a journey together, a journey into madness.

This was not supposed to happen, not in an army that prided itself on discipline, order, and impermeable notions of brotherhood and sisterhood. But happen it did, and I found myself wondering what could've been done to keep their demons caged up, or at least to give the better angels of their nature a fighting chance against the darkness in their souls.

The truth is an army is no better or no worse than the society from which its members are drawn. Ours is a great nation, as is the society that forms its bedrock, which produces a great army. But occasionally, an odd duck slips through, and we all end up with mud on our faces. War does not change us, but it seeps through the weaknesses in our armor, it finds the faults and fractures of the human psyche that are already there. Amal Ashad, Nate Willborn, and the night crew were not predestined to do what they did, but those who were supposed to prevent such behavior never really stood a chance.

After my fifth Scotch, I pulled out my cellphone and the business card with Thomas Bernhardt's private phone number scribbled in his pinched writing on the back.

He identified himself when he answered. I gave him my identity back.

He came right to the point and asked, "Have you solved the killing?"

"I have."

"Good. Then who killed General Palchaci?"

"You. The United States government. Everybody who could've prevented this but did not."

"What the hell are you talking about, Colonel? Have you been drinking?"

"Yes, but not nearly enough. You sent an army to win a war, Mr. Bernhardt, without the men and material required to do that job properly and to succeed. That prison was a nightmare, a disaster.

It was so scandalously short of manpower that the officers and sergeants running the place never had a chance. It was chaos with each man and woman trying to do the work of ten. This scandal did not have to happen but you made sure it was inevitable."

There was silence on the other end. When he did speak, Bernhardt snarled, "I do not have to listen to a drunken rant from you, Drummond."

"Tomorrow that certainly may be true, but tonight, you'll listen to whatever I have to say or tomorrow will be the end of the presidency. Is this clear enough for you?"

He thought about it a moment, then said, in a more enlightened tone, "Look, I understand what you're saying, but this war is very unpopular with the American people. Congress is severely divided as to its wisdom. The federal budget is already under unbearable strain . . ." and he went on a long diatribe about all the pressures he and his boss had to endure not to do the right thing. I let him go on awhile because he's a lawyer; that's what a lawyer does.

But the first time he paused to catch his breath, I told him, "Fuck the politics. A soldier in a foxhole is not there to protect your president's ass or ensure his reelection. He risks his life and limb, and his only expectation is that you give him everything he needs to win. Because you and your president failed to do that, one more American soldier died tonight."

He responded to this news somewhat coldly, asking, "Is that so? Who is he?"

"Captain Nate Willborn. An intelligence officer. An interrogator at the prison."

"Why did he die?"

"Because he murdered Palchaci, because he forwarded the photos to a reporter, and because, to keep them from exposing these crimes, he killed two good army lawyers."

"Ah . . . I see." There was a pause before he asked, "Well, how did he die?"

"I killed him."

"Oh . . ."

"But if you're inquiring about the technical determination of death, it may have been the bullet that blew most of his head off, though it's certainly possible that the six rounds I pumped into his heart caused it to stop functioning. A coroner will figure it out. I'll let you know."

"Well . . . are you in any trouble? Are there, uh, any complications from his death?"

Instead of addressing his pressing concern for avoiding further scandal, I asked him, "Are you ready to hear the deal?"

"Uh . . . let's hear it."

"First, call General Fister, chief of the army JAG corps. Tell him to approve my request for resignation from this case, effective immediately."

"I thought you said you would resign only if you couldn't clear your client of involvement in Palchaci's murder. Are you sure about this?"

"Despite every professional ethic I already violated, Mr. Bernhardt, I cannot keep secrets that might exonerate or mitigate my client's guilt while I defend her."

"I see. If that's the way you feel . . ." He paused, probably confused by this reference to legal ethics. "Just be sure to word it damned carefully. Avoid any mention of Ashad, or how that led to your involvement in Willborn's death."

"I neither asked for, nor do I need, your advice on this matter, Mr. Bernhardt. I believe I've already demonstrated tonight that I know how to cover your president's ass."

He made no reply to this, but he couldn't miss, or dismiss, the real meaning in what I was telling him. I had killed a man to protect the secret of what really happened at Al Basari. With the burial of Willborn, the truth would be buried with him.

"All right . . . well . . ." He cleared his throat. "Are there any other conditions?"

"You will offer each of the defendants, except Sergeant Elton, a one-year sentence, and a less than honorable discharge in lieu of the bad conduct discharge hanging over their heads. I really don't care what Elton gets. It won't be enough."

"Jesus . . . Is this a joke?"

"The punchline will be my morning press conference. Be sure you and your boss have your TVs on."

"For God's sake, be realistic, Sean. One year? The President will be scorched by the press. The Iraqis will scream murder. *One year* . . . after what those people did. The whole world is watching . . . we can't . . . I mean, that's just . . ."

I interrupted his stammering. "The public will forget all about Lydia and her friends after I tell the press what I know."

There was a moment before he said, "Well . . . I . . . Uh . . . I suppose I can manage this."

"I did not ask you to manage it—I said *do* it."

"Got it." It's not often that you get to boss around the right hand of a president, and a chance like this might never come around again—the chance for an overnight colonel's eagle, the chance for a free sixty-day leave—but you have to know when enough is enough.

"One year," he repeated as though the number stunned him. "Do you think their attorneys will accept that offer?"

As he was an attorney himself I should not have to explain this, but I replied, "Show them the video you showed me."

"Yes . . . I suppose that's sound advice."

There was silence on the line for a minute. But if I could picture his face, I was pretty sure he was smiling so hard he couldn't speak. In the morning he would march into his boss's oval office, assure him the Ashad deal was back on track, and advise him to sign the paper to authorize a victory in the war.

When that silence was broken, it was Bernhardt, saying, "Listen, Sean, I know this is not exactly an auspicious start to our relationship, but you've impressed me on this case. The way you've handled this . . . I'd like to have you on my staff."

I made no reply.

He said, "You know, you'd be a fool not to seriously consider my offer. It's the White House, the chance to make a real difference. It'll be good for your career."

I told him, "I'll think about it," then I punched off.

I walked to the bar where I ordered one more Scotch for the road. I knocked it back, walked to the door, and left to break my own heart.

Chapter Thirty-Six

Katherine was standing in the hallway when I entered the home that had been our office for the past week.

Her arms were crossed. An expression of worry was on her face. She took in the sling on my arm. "Are you okay?"

"Never been better."

"Is that arm broken?"

I replied in my most macho tone, "You should see the other guy."

"O'Reilly's people told us you were in an altercation. They said you killed a man."

"He did try to kill me first."

"How? More importantly, Sean, why did he want to kill you?"

"With a bat," I replied, not exactly answering her question.

She stared at me.

"The same way he killed General Palchaci. He used different methods on Captain Howser and Major Weinstein, but he wanted to kill me for the same reason he killed them."

"And what was that reason?"

"I have no idea," I lied. "Apparently, he went to war and went mad. He became a sociopath. I was walking back here and he came running out of the dark with his bat. He just went nuts."

This was a lot for her to take in; at first, she looked startled, but she always was quick and I could see her wheels starting to turn. With Katherine, as I said, this was always dangerous. She has an uncanny knack for knowing my thoughts.

I took a deep swallow, then said, "I have to inform you, Katherine, that I have tendered my resignation from this case. I'm leaving tonight."

She looked shocked. But more than that, she appeared hurt and confused. "Don't be ridiculous, Sean. I know that I've complicated things, but there is no reason for you to resign. Withdraw it . . . please."

"The decision is final, Katherine."

"Do you want to tell me why? I believe you owe me an explanation."

"You don't need me." I looked away. "I have confidence in you, Katherine."

Tears were now welling in her eyes. Her lips were actually trembling. I was feeling a little unsteady myself, and I knew I had to get this over with quickly, or I might never get over it. She looked as beautiful and sexy as I'd ever seen her.

She took two steps forward and threw her arms around my shoulders. "If this is about Nel, let's talk about it." She squeezed me tighter. "Don't you at least want to stick around to hear who I want?"

She tried to look in my eyes, but I refused to look back. "You should marry Nel. He's a fine man and he loves you. You deserve the life he'll provide."

"I don't care about his damn money, Sean."

"I know that. I'm just not the right man for you."

She took a step back and looked down at the floor.

I told her, a bit more brusquely than I intended, "Ask Imelda to pack my duffel and have it shipped to my apartment in Arlington."

I then bent forward and kissed Katherine on the forehead. She was still looking down at the floor when I closed the door behind me.

Too much Scotch was coursing through my veins to legally or safely drive back to DC, so I decided I would treat myself to a night in the Thayer Hotel, where I had stayed so many years before with my father for his class reunions. I would sleep late and rent a car in the morning. I might even request a Prius. Maybe I would charge it to Nelson. He owed me one.

As I passed through the Thayer Gate onto Academy grounds, I looked up and saw the West Point crest engraved in stone, the same crest my father wore on his West Point ring. Duty, Honor, Country—three simple words that are scalded into the hearts, into the minds, and indeed, into the souls, of every man and woman who graduates from West Point.

It is, in my view, a great motto for the Academy, and for the army, but also, it is a warning, a caveat emptor, for duty is boundless, and the nation and its army demand much of those who would wear its uniform. In return for a lifetime of low pay, shabby housing, frequent moves, authoritarian and often irrational bosses, a life of tremendous hardship, physically and emotionally, all the army asks in return is that you always answer the call of duty, even when the burden of that call entails great personal sacrifice.

But if you think about it, no man or woman, or, at least, no sane one, knows what they will be asked to give until it is actually too late, until you can't get it back.

Maybe Katherine and I could've made a wonderful life together. She is a beautiful woman, a stimulating and enchanting partner, and she always keeps me on my toes, though that last part might have proven troublesome. At least our kids would have stood a good shot at being cute.

I thought I loved her and I believed her when she said she loved me; that's always a good place to start. Still, we were profoundly different people in so many ways, and maybe those differences, no matter how hard we tried, would've led to a trainwreck.

Katherine, being a civilian attorney, has the luxury of always doing things her own way. It was one of the things I love and admire about her. She is not a saint, but she has the saint's capacity to never compromise her beliefs, her ideals, or her principles.

But that, as I said, is a luxury. A soldier who happens to be a lawyer sometimes has to decide which comes first, being a soldier with the ageless imperative to always win our country's wars, or acting every inch the lawyer with the sworn obligation to put your client's interests above all other considerations. To honor one is to betray the other.

There was no way I could continue on this case, or continue with Katherine, not after what I had just done. I had concealed a crime, I had killed a man to bury that secret, and I had just fixed our case.

I knew Katherine would never understand this, and I knew I shouldn't try to make her understand it.

As for Lydia, June, Andrea, and Mike, one year was certainly less than they deserved for all they had done over there. But no matter how flawed their behavior, they were in a war zone, they were there of their own volition, and that has to be taken into account.

But maybe I should have remembered to warn Bernhardt not to send them to the same prison.

I had enjoyed my time with the CIA but I think I had sensed, even before I took this case, that that chapter was coming to a close. It was never a great fit anyway. They live in a world of shadows, and yet, somehow, I kept getting sunburned. Much like the army, they are great people, and great patriots, and the American people should be thankful for all they do to keep us safe. I'm not sure they'll do it better without me, but I know I'll do better without them.

Anyway, the White House might be fun. I could tell Phyllis what to do, for a change. That has a certain appeal.

Acknowledgments

My very deepest thanks to all those who contributed to this book, particularly Alan Turkus, who acquired this manuscript and is such a pleasure to deal with; Kjersti Egerdahl, who had the thankless task of overseeing every aspect of its production and did so with such care and grace; Charlotte Herscher, who so expertly performed the editing miracle of making it readable and, I hope, enjoyable; and Sherri Dietrich, who did the very skillful copyediting. This was my first book with this outstanding crew, and it was such an unmitigated pleasure that I sincerely hope there are many, many more. Also my usual thanks to Luke Janklow and Claire Dippel, my agents, my friends, and my beloved coconspirators.

About the Author

Brian Haig is a West Point graduate and career infantry officer. Before retiring from the US Army he served four years as Special Assistant to the Chairman of the Joint Chiefs of Staff. He has appeared on Fox News as a military analyst, and this is his ninth published novel, including several *New York Times*, *USA Today*, *Washington Post*, and national bestsellers. He currently lives happily in Texas with his wife.